In memory of
Frederick Morgan
(1922–2004)
Founding Editor of The Hudson Review

Contents

Foreword

EDITING A literary magazine is a cumulative venture. It goes from issue to issue, the effort divided between reading and selecting manuscripts, many un-
solicited, and compiling final choices each time into a well-rounded
whole—a painstaking and exhilarating process. Occasionally, simply by
virtue of certain contemporary ideas, a theme will emerge among several
writers that becomes a focus of a single issue. But each time the main concern is to bring to readers what Frederick Morgan, *The Hudson Review*'s
founding editor, referred to in introducing an earlier anthology as "intrinsic
excellence." Momentum gathers over the years as the magazine reflects
rather than predicts the intellectual tenor of the age, always moving forward
rather than trying to repeat past successes, remaining youthful by responding
to new writers. "A literary review," as Morgan wrote, "is a community of
minds in interaction"—that of both writers and readers.

Several years ago, in the magazine's desire to seek out younger readers in
the New York area, the editors initiated a Writers in the Schools program at
two Harlem high schools with the idea that material from *The Hudson Review* could be integrated into the curriculum. A selected text from a current
issue is studied by the class, and then the author is invited to give a reading
and to talk with the students. It soon became clear during these lively and revealing classroom discussions how many of the stories and memoirs from the
Review addressed the students' own experiences and conflicts about coming
of age as they learned the true value of integrating the lessons of literature
into their own lives. Their enthusiasm, and that of their teachers, became the
impetus for this book.

The nucleus of *Writes of Passage* was selected from those stories and
memoirs with which the students most closely identified. We then looked
back twenty-five years or more to discover that while each contribution to

The Hudson Review had been accepted on its own merit, without regard to subject, the magazine had in fact cultivated a coming-of-age genre. This enduring theme, engaged here by both established and emerging writers, is after all a mainstay of the literary imagination. It elicits from readers at different stages of their own lives an empathy for the vulnerability of youth on the threshold of maturity. While each story or memoir reveals a transforming moment, an acknowledged understanding of a morally complex world, the infinite variety of ways in which individual writers come to this realization gives the collection a quality of surprise and even of suspense.

All of these stories and memoirs made their first appearance in *The Hudson Review*, including the previously unpublished story by Tennessee Williams, which was discovered in typescript among the Tennessee Williams Papers at the Harry Ransom Humanities Research Center at the University of Texas by two Williams scholars. According to them, Williams had written in the top right-hand corner this retrospective comment: "Not a bad story. Rather prophetic. T. W. (Written about '36)." The story was printed at last in our magazine in 2003.

Special appreciation is due my colleagues for their invaluable help in selecting and preparing this anthology: Dean Flower, an advisory editor since 1982, also for his insightful Introduction; Ronald Koury, managing editor since 1985; assistant editors Candi Deschamps, Julia Powers, and Joanna L. Siegel; and editorial intern Zoë Slutzky. We are particularly indebted to the donors who generously support the Writers in the Schools program and to the teachers and students of the Young Women's Leadership School and the Heritage School, both in New York City, for their continued enthusiasm and participation. Our warm thanks as well go to the authors and copyright holders of these stories and memoirs for their gracious cooperation. Finally, to our publisher, Ivan Dee, who made this book possible for all to read and enjoy, we express our gratitude for his understanding of our vision.

PAULA DEITZ

New York City
January 2008

Introduction

LIFE-CHANGING EVENTS may occur to us at any age, and for any number of reasons—the death of a loved one, a financial disaster, a fortunate marriage, a nasty divorce, a new job, moving to a new home or country, suffering an accident or a disease, falling in or out of love, being caught up by war or politics or a natural disaster—the list is endless and unpredictable. But there is one change we all experience, which occurs when we discover that somehow our childhood is over and it is time to become an adult. Coming of age, we often call it, or simply growing up. It has obvious physical manifestations that we associate with puberty, adolescence, sex, and hormones. Other life-changing events may be avoided, but nobody escapes this one. Emotionally and physically it is probably the greatest metamorphosis we will ever know. But the interesting part is not really physical, as we know when somebody snaps "Grow up!" to an adult who thinks he already has. Coming of age does not *necessarily* occur between the ages of thirteen and nineteen, though it often does, nor does it ensue automatically from getting a driver's license, losing your virginity, registering to vote, buying alcohol, or leaving home. Coming of age requires a different sort of discovery and knowledge. It takes place as a kind of revolution in the self, when we learn that who we *were*—the child, the innocent, the dependent identity—must be abandoned and that who we *are* or *will be*—our singular, independent adult self—becomes clear. The experience is usually marked by some intuition of uniqueness or moment of prescience. Things will never be the same, we say. And we *know* it's true.

The short story seems particularly well suited to convey experiences like these. While novelists prolong and complicate the coming-of-age experience—think of Charlotte Brontë's Jane Eyre or Charles Dickens's Pip, Zora Neale Hurston's Janie or Faulkner's Caddy Compson, Toni Morrison's

Milkman or J. D. Salinger's Holden Caulfield—the short-story writer selects a moment, a critical turning point, and claims only its lifelong importance. But that moment can be more piercingly final than anything that happens in a novel. Novelists devote hundreds of pages to the long ordeal of innocent kids and confused adolescents seeking their adult identities. The short story winnows it down to its essence, seeking an absolute pivotal truth, and leaves the rest to the imagination. By its very brevity and selectivity, the story says that whatever happened later, indeed all subsequent experience, is irrelevant. Emotion, if not fact, demands that no other experience can rival it.

Kermit Moyer's narrator in "Learning to Smoke" tells it this way: "I'm completely stunned, a confusion of feelings buffeting around inside me. But this much I know for sure: something momentous has happened. From this moment on, nothing will ever be the same." It's a nice summation of how the genre works. Note how skillfully Moyer links "moment" and "momentous." And consider too how much rhetoric is involved—rhetoric meaning the art of persuasion, not deceptive verbosity. Moyer uses the present tense throughout his story, as if it were all happening *now*, but the moment is poignant because we know it's being remembered. He tells us at the start that "It's the summer of 1956, a little over two weeks since my thirteenth birthday," and a seventeen-year-old girl, his cousin, is teaching him how to French inhale. So the present tense dramatizes his feeling of its timelessness: the story is really happening in the present-tense activity of the author's memory—just as vividly, perhaps even more so, than it did in the original event.

A great many coming-of-age stories work this way. They either announce from the outset that the experience is a memory, or they delay that admission until the end, or they imply it by more subtle, indirect means. Liza Kleinman in "What Went Wrong" uses the direct approach: "Childhood, as I remember it, is a tangle of shifting allegiances. It is a series of passionate friendships, each as heavy as the last with the promise of immortality." Paula Whyman in "Driver's Education" delays it until the final paragraph, in effect reframing the experience as a memory. Julie Keith's "Pneumonia" keeps us in her child-narrator's point of view, using a simple past tense; but when the little girl, Susannah, turns on a light by reaching up to punch a button on the wall, or tells us that "no cars were being made anymore because of the war," we know these events were taking place in the 1940s, sixty years before the story was written and published. Think how that increases the impact of Susannah's closing statement:

> Glancing from parent to parent, protected by my lie, I knew too that I must hold the truth of all this and much more inside me forever, the way I would

keep my piece of robin's eggshell hidden forever. The possession made a dark, unholy place somewhere deep inside me, a place where I could keep all that I saw and divined and understood.

Not only did the child Susannah have to lie about her hateful parents, she had to keep the truth hidden for some sixty years in that "dark unholy place" within her, and only now can she reveal it. It's a fascinating shock to discover that the real narrator is not a naive child but a troubled and haunted seventy-year-old woman.

At least twelve of the short stories in this anthology purport to be memoirs. The author writes in the first person, trusts us with the most intimate secrets, and recalls the past in such convincing detail it seems to be documentary history. Fred Licht's "Shelter the Pilgrim," about his Jewish family's dangerous move to Berlin in 1937, sounds utterly autobiographical. You would swear that Robert Love Taylor must have taken those accordion lessons described in "Lady of Spain" and that Peter Makuck as a teenager surely had a souped-up car exactly like the one in "My '49 Ford." And who can read about James Wallenstein's basketball dreams at summer camp ("Summer's Lease") or Randolph Thomas's spending a summer with his youthful aunt ("May Prescott") and not believe that the author has only thinly disguised his own experience?

The truth of the matter, however, is a little more complicated. Fiction that sounds like autobiography may well be that, or a form of that. Many writers draw directly, even shamelessly, on their own lives for their material—think of Hemingway, Thomas Wolfe, Evelyn Waugh, Philip Roth. But that doesn't mean they are telling the literal truth. They are all expert liars. If Peter Makuck persuades you that his '49 Ford actually existed and was his own—not just something invented for a story—his craft and art have succeeded. That is exactly what he meant to do. Perhaps the artistic accomplishment is greater if the story has no factual basis at all in the author's life. Some writers thrive on that and tell us nothing about themselves. What matters is that the story be believable, that it *seem* authentic, that it offer a convincing *illusion* of truth.

And where exactly does this aura of truth come from in fiction? Is it all merely clever tricks and lying? William Trevor suggests a useful, and very eloquent, answer in his memoir "In Co. Cork":

The pleasure and the pain experienced by any storyteller's characters, the euphoria of happiness, the ache of grief, must of course be the storyteller's own. It cannot be otherwise and in that sense all fiction has its autobiographical

roots, spreading through—in my case—a provincial world, limited and claustrophobic.

If Trevor is right and all fiction must "of course"—he means "of
necessity"—be autobiographical, it's an easy step to the recognition that
memoirs are a form of fiction too. We may grant memoirs a certain validity
by reason of the label itself, which says in effect, "This story is *not* fiction, it
actually happened to me." But good memoirs rely on all the same crafty
strategies that fiction does. They use convincing narrative voices, complex
points of view, artful selection of details (too much is deadly, too little is un-
persuasive), a sense of drama and discovery, expressive figurative as well as literal language, sharp conflicts, and satisfying resolutions—or at least
clarifications—by the end. Memoir writers want above all to make their experience into a convincing story—leaving many things out, if need be, to
gain their effects.

Consider how artfully Jocelyn Bartkevicius designs her memoir "Hat
Check Noir," beginning at the end when her family's nightclub, the Emerald Room, was demolished in 1996, then going back to 1962 and telling how
she came of age there, bringing us full circle at the end to that destruction
again. Factual as the story may be, what makes it succeed is how artfully
Bartkevicius conveys the tawdry, magical place and the way she once felt
about it.

Or consider Nicole Graev's memoir "Tight Jeans," which is a kind of essay on the power of the male gaze to define and control women. But Graev
makes it into a richly personal story with a clear narrative sequence, focusing
on a single central image—those "low-riding, ass-hugging, dark blue
jeans"—which defined her new self at the tender age of six, and which remains a symbolic space she still feels squeezed and wedged into. "Tight
Jeans" may be an essay-like memoir, but it has all the juice of fiction.

Whether identified as story or memoir, coming-of-age narratives may
sometimes strike us as classic—instantly recognizable, easily categorized,
mythic perhaps, or even generic, as if the experience were a *rite de passage*
that everyone goes through in one form or another. But the stories in this anthology do not support that idea. Jan Ellison's "The Color of Wheat in Winter," for instance, might be seen as a typical story of a teenage girl, confused
about who she wants to be—a daughter responsive to her mother's needy
emotions, a cool teenager who smokes pot and lets her date use
her sexually, a child again to her seldom-seen father, a sexy *chica* to her Mexican co-worker (married, with children). But none of the conventional
rituals—dating, learning to drive, venturing into sex, donning her first party

dress—helps her at all. If anything, rites of passage *hinder* her coming of age, and she has to defy them completely in order to glimpse her new self emerging, as it does at the end, in risky new territory. There is nothing retrospective about this story either; you can only hope the new Frances will survive. Another story that may seem a classic for males' coming of age is Robert Schultz's "Hardball." For what is baseball, as Schultz learns it from his father, if not the perfect rite of passage, which requires discipline, responsibility, and acceptance of "time-honored conventions"? What's more, the deeper lesson seems to be that a mature man must learn to play hardball in life: rules are rules, and if someone gets hurt, that's too bad. But again the real coming of age depends on *rejecting* the ritual's lesson. When at the critical moment Schultz refuses what his father has taught him, he finds "a small coal of pride began to glow" because he "had hit upon a value of my own, subversive and true." He doesn't name the value, but it is clearly compassion, and it trumps anything baseball has to offer.

Perhaps the title of this collection is a misnomer. More often than not, coming-of-age stories hinge on the rejection of rites of passage rather than on their observance. In fact, Schultz speaks for many others here in celebrating the subversive value of what he discovers. In some stories the subversive verges on the aberrant. Catherine Harnett's "Her Gorgeous Grief" describes the truly strange obsession of a girl's mother with the deaths and disasters of strangers. She drives for hours to attend murder trials and funerals, pretending to be a friend or acquaintance of the victims, dressing carefully for each occasion, studying the newspapers for information she can use in the deceit. Yet these shameless invasions of privacy and vicarious grievings—followed by embarrassed and hasty retreats—have their transforming effect at last, when the daughter steps into her mother's fantasy and discovers whose grief it really is that she must share. Again, violation of ritual releases the deeper understanding. James Wallenstein's narrator in "Summer's Lease" discovers how meaningless the rituals of basketball and summer camp are when his father dies, but he comes of age only when he takes action and violates their boundaries—taking his own risky path, climbing that wobbly tower, and bearing the cold alone.

Crossing boundaries might be another, equally useful way to define this generic trait. Finding oneself in foreign territory—figuratively and literally—is clearly a function at least if not a cause of many comings of age. Elise Juska's narrator in "Northeast Philly Girls" hungers to cross over into that foreign social territory of Philadelphia where the girls are all brazen, painted, and redolent of cigarettes, hairspray, and bubblegum. Peter Makuck's narrator in "My '49 Ford" only begins to realize what fateful boundary he has crossed when, at his new college near the Quebec border, everyone speaks French. Jacqueline W. Brown in "Willie" leaves the boundaries of Harlem when her aunt dies but finds herself, on the long train journey south, gathered into a larger racial community—her true country. It's her mother who has become the complete stranger. And the most dramatic boundary crossings of all occur in Barbara Wasserman's "Spain, 1948," where an impulsive trip of two rather giddy American girls from Paris down into Spain and back—for noble causes, risking arrest in the aid of complete strangers—leads to the emergence of two women at the end, who soberly recognize the moral ambiguities of their hasty good intentions. That they do not speak the language speaks volumes about them—and about too many not-so-innocent Americans abroad.

The classic boundary crossing, in Western Christian literary tradition at least, must be Adam and Eve's expulsion from the Garden of Eden. It's no accident that Charles Dickens's most unforgettable coming-of-age story, *Great Expectations*, marks its pivotal moment with an echo of Milton's *Paradise Lost*. When Pip leaves home, ready to launch his ambitions, he sees that "the mists had all solemnly risen now, and the world lay spread before me." For Milton's Adam and Eve, of course, the moment is sorrowful and choiceless. "The world was all before them," but they leave Paradise reluctantly, "with wand'ring steps and slow."

Modern coming-of-age stories often retell this fable, that when the mists of childhood illusion dissipate, the adult world turns out to be painful and difficult, a shabby and depressing antithesis of Eden, befouled by human greed and corruption, sex and death. Regretting the natural loss of innocence, we look back to childhood and adolescence *as if* they were paradise. So William Trevor's memoir "In Co. Cork" comments on the way his youthful imagination once colored everything in the rural Ireland where he grew up. Seeing a married doctor and a lady in disgrace, who are having a tawdry affair, he thinks, "They are breathtaking in their sinning, and all their conversation is beautiful; they are the world's most exciting people." Steven Millhauser's symbolic fable "In the Penny Arcade" follows a similar paradigm. Expecting magic and revelation, "something mysterious and elusive," again and again he is disappointed on closer approach, finding nothing but falsity, dusty and decrepit mechanisms. He is too old now for innocent belief. Wisdom, he decides, must be to resist the "conspiracy of dullness" that adults impose on the world by failing to believe in magic and imagination. So for Millhauser the "only penny arcade, the true penny arcade," is a kind of Paradise Regained by conscious acts of will.

Jocelyn Bartkevicius makes something similar of the once-magical Emerald Room in "Hat Check Noir," and so does Carl Wooton, telling of those wondrous bicycle-spinning days in "Ramblers and Spinners." In Wooton's case, paradise lost consists not just in the family's financial disaster and the loss of those expensive bicycles but in the moment when he realizes Bradshaw Morgan's superiority: "He had challenged us with something much more than just the number of spins we thought were possible. He had shown us a grace and ease that we did not know how to measure and, thus, did not know how to achieve." Similarly affecting is the recognition in Mairi MacInnes's memoir "Porrock." Not that much of her youth was paradisal, with its disillusioning move to a strange city near London, her cruelly repressive mother, and discouraging voices on every side. But her wonderful dog Porrock—who learned to sneak aboard trams and go into town (and back!) by himself, and who drops in for meals at the houses of strangers—was a paragon of sociability, freedom, and unself-conscious joy. When MacInnes goes away to school, escaping home at last, Porrock changes too, and so paradise is lost—as it must be, of necessity—for both of them.

In one form or another, Adam and Eve and the sexual serpent are in all these lost paradise stories, none more transparently than in Tennessee Williams's "In Spain There Was Revolution." Its Edenic fable could not be clearer:

"I learned about women from you."
"I'm just the first lesson, am I?"
"First and last."
"Get out, you liar!"

Equally portentous is the idyllic setting in the Ozarks, at the end of summer: what looks like "flawless beauty" is really desiccation and impending death. Williams describes a landscape that seems unwilling to admit "without any bright evasion the solemn fact of things dying." Bright evasion is exactly what the two lovers engage in, she saddened and he annoyed that their sexual pleasures must soon come to an end. Both vigorously deny—in their oblivious innocence—that the revolution in Spain has anything to do with them. Of course neither of them comes of age: that was Williams's point, when he wrote this fable in 1936, that America itself needed to come of age.

Putting aside these centuries-old and potentially coercive formulas, one might still ask about gender in the modern coming-of-age story. Is there any distinctively *female* version of it? Or any prevailingly *male* form? My impression from the array of stories collected here is that women's coming-of-age narratives frequently involve the question of how they, often quite literally, see themselves—a question that is unanswerable until they see how others see them. That almost never happens in the stories about males. Clothing and physical appearance matter more to women perhaps, but the deeper

issue for them lies in discovering how to see and understand the *self*. And
that discovery, for many women, seems to require negotiation with the eyes
of others. Nicole Graev's "Tight Jeans" explores this dynamic at length, but
for me the best and most archetypal instance of it comes in Jocelyn Bartkevicius's "Hat Check Noir" when she meets one of the nightclub's exotic
dancers in the ladies' room:

> She wore a sheer blouse over her costume, her stomach puffed a bit like my
> cousins'. We were the same height, but I was girl skinny and I kept my head
> down. She told me she was not always like that, that she was watery before
> her time of the month, that mine was the kind of body to be proud of, that
> mine was the kind of body she could have. She looked at me with desire and
> regret as I had looked only at possessions (like the rabbit stole of a friend's Bar-
> bie). And she looked at me, at my waist and thighs, until I left, walked back
> out into the darkened dining room, into the music, the smoke, the night.

Comparable moments of exchanged gazes occur in Dena Seidel's "Good
Times," Paula Whyman's "Driver's Education," Liza Kleinman's "What
Went Wrong," Jan Ellison's "The Color of Wheat in Winter," and Jacqueline
Brown's "Willie," though in some cases it will take careful searching to find
them. But none of the other renditions has quite the spellbinding power — or
poignancy — that Bartkevicius achieves.

The maleness of men's coming-of-age stories in recent years is even
riskier to pin down. There are strong temptations to mention sports (baseball,
basketball, golf, and show-off bicycling all figure here), sexual initiation with
an older woman (which males tend to rhapsodize about, nostalgically and
dishonestly), father-son rituals (which often leave out women entirely). My
impression is that vocation — literally, males finding themselves in and
through work — may be a defining, if not unique, component. John Van
Kirk's "Newark Job," an apparent homage to Hemingway, is not so much an
initiation into the father's work (he's a slumlord's plumber) as it is the boy's
discovery of his father's compassion — that his father's love is more than fa-
milial and cuts through differences of race and class. That's a very different
lesson from the one taught by the doctor father in Hemingway's "Indian
Camp." Leaving home and working the carnival circuit is John McCormick's
initiation into adulthood in his memoir "In the Mean Time." Down those
mean streets he must go, but his real coming of age occurs when he tries to
hop a fast-moving freight car. He stumbles and falls, and survives only because the man behind him helps. "You saved me," the boy says, feeling "foolish and ashamed." That admission, that he cannot save himself, may be
crushing to his tender male ego, but it's pivotal to his growing up. He now

can find his real self, "trembling, sweating, and relieved beyond the telling to be alive and moving, my friends with me." Many of these male stories hinge on similar discoveries: that a man's vocation—i.e., his deeper calling— is learning to surrender egotism, self-love, fantasies of heroism, the theory of being tough, playing hardball, and going it alone. For the adolescent American male, at least, these lessons seem critical to achieving real manhood— and the hardest to learn.

Despite all the ready-made formulas we may have, coming of age can still occur in surprisingly different ways and at unexpected moments in life. Elizabeth Spencer's "Sightings" concerns a fairly ordinary coming of age, that of a teenage girl whose divorced parents burden her, each in a different way. What's fresh about it is that we experience it entirely from her father's sympathetic but dimly comprehending point of view. Who says that a coming-of-age story *must* be told by the one experiencing it? Hayden Carruth's coming-of-age story "Intelligence, Anyone?" is another oddity. It occurs when he takes an IQ test at the age of eight and is discovered to be "well up in the classification of genius." That proves to be the watershed moment of his life, a "disaster" that shapes all the rest. Even in his sixties, after going "through all kinds of hell," including alcoholism, electroshock therapy, and endless narcotic medication, he takes an IQ test again and finds his brain is still undamaged, and *still* shaping his life as it always has. It's a comic but rueful discovery. Wendell Berry's "The Hurt Man" goes even further: the coming of age occurs to a five-year-old boy. Yet it is all entirely credible and moving. The innocent boy, Mat Feltner, watches a mystery unfold before him when a stranger, severely injured and bleeding to death, comes to the Feltner porch. Amazingly unperturbed, his mother responds "as though she knew him without ever having known him before." As she steps into the emergency, Mat has this revelation:

> What he saw in her face would remain with him forever. It was pity, but it was more than that. It was a hurt love that seemed to include entirely the hurt man and disregarded everything else. . . . To him, then, it was as though she leaned in the black of her mourning over the whole hurt world itself, touching its wounds with her tenderness, in her sorrow.

No child could write this, of course, but the words represent what he understood that day when he was five. The moment is piercingly final and timeless. "He learned it all his life," Berry tells us, and "from that day, whatever happened, there was a knowledge in Mat that was unsurprised and at last comforted until he was old, until he was gone."

There is something ceremonious about that conclusion, and it occurs in other coming-of-age stories as well. No matter when or how the events actually occurred (memoir) or supposedly occurred (story), the *real* experience of it comes only when the words are written. The pivotal moment of Mat Feltner's life is shaped afterward, discovered in retrospect, its meaning designed and composed long after its origin. The same is true of Hayden Carruth's memoir, written when he was in his sixties, looking back and seeing the whole shape of his life. Tight jeans? A '49 Ford? A dog named Porrock? All the stories in this book are constructed in belated understanding, in the aftermaths of jolting, painful, magical experiences. That doesn't make them false, but it is a reminder of our need for order and control in an often tumultuous world. The very act of writing itself is essential to the ceremony these stories perform. They are indeed not just rites but "writes" of passage, and the title is not a misnomer after all.

DEAN FLOWER

THREE CHILDREN LOOKING OVER THE EDGE OF THE WORLD

They came to the end of the road
and there was a wall across it
of cut stone—not very high.

Two of them boosted the third up
between them, he scrambled to the top
and found it wide enough to sit on easily.
Then he leaned back and gave the others a hand.

One two three in a row they sat there
staring: there was no bottom.
Below them a cliff went down and down for ever

and across from them, facing them, was nothing—
an emptiness that had no other side
and turned their vision back upon itself.

So there wasn't much to do or look at, after all.
One of them told a rhyme, the others chimed in,
and after a little while they swung around
and let themselves back down.

But when their feet touched solid road again
they saw at once they had dropped from the top of the sky
through sun and air and clouds and trees
and that the world was the wall.

> —Frederick Morgan
> From *Death Mother and Other Poems*, 1979

Writes of Passage

WILLIAM TREVOR

In Co. Cork

—ᗰᗰ—

ALL MEMORY is grist to the fiction writer's mill. The pleasure and the pain experienced by any storyteller's characters, the euphoria of happiness, the ache of grief, must of course be the storyteller's own. It cannot be otherwise, and in that sense all fiction has its autobiographical roots, spreading through—in my case—a provincial world, limited and claustrophobic.

I grew up in what John Betjeman called "the small towns of Ireland"— in my case, Mitchelstown, cut down to size by the towering Galtee Mountains and the Knockmealdowns, Youghal by the sea, Skibbereen lost somewhere in the back of beyond.

There were others besides, but to these three in Co. Cork I go back often and look them over. Mitchelstown is still famous for its martyrs and its processed cheese, a squat little town, looking as though someone has sat on it. A good little business town, my father used to say, knowing about such matters.

Youghal, smartly elegant in my memory, is tatty on a wet afternoon. A carful of German tourists crawls along the seafront, the misty beach is empty. Once, people pointed here, and remarked; I listened and my eavesdroppings told of an afternoon love affair conducted on that brief promenade, he a married doctor, she a lady in disgrace. I see them now as I made them in my fascination: she is thin, and dressed in red, laughing, with pale long hair; he is Ronald Coleman with a greyer moustache. They smile at one another; defiantly he touches her hand. They are breathtaking in their sinning, and all their conversation is beautiful; they are the world's most exciting people.

I walk away from their romance, not wanting to tell myself that they were not like that. On the sands where old seaside artists sprinkled garish colors, the rain is chilly. Pierrots performed here, and the man and woman who rode the Wall of Death sunned themselves at midday. From the Loreto Convent we trooped down here to run the end-of-term races, Sister Thérèse in charge. The sands haven't changed, nor have the concrete façades of the holiday boardinghouses, nor the Protestant church with its holes for lepers to peer through. But Horgan's Picture House is not at all as it was. It has two screens now and a different name, and there are sexual fantasies instead of Jack Hulbert in *Round the Washtub*.

In Youghal there was a man who shot himself in a henhouse. Life had been hell for this man, the voices whispered, and the henhouse, quite near the back of our garden, developed an eeriness that the chatter of birds made even more sinister. The henhouse isn't there anymore, but even so as I stand where it was I shudder, and remember other deaths.

Youghal itself died in a way, for yellow furniture vans—Nat Ross of Cork—carted our possessions off, through Cork itself, westward through the town that people call Clonakilty God Help Us, to Skibbereen, at the back of beyond.

Memory focuses here, the images are clearer. Horses and carts in the narrow streets, with milk churns for the creamery. On fair-days farmers with sticks standing by their animals, their shirts clean for the occasion, without collar or tie. A smell of whiskey, and sawdust and stout and dung. Pots of geraniums among chops and ribs in the small windows of butchers' shops. A sunburnt poster advertising the arrival of Duffy's Circus a year ago.

It was a mile and a half, the journey to school through the town, past Driscoll's sweetshop and Murphy's Medical Hall and Power's drapery, where you could buy oilcloth as well as dresses. In Shannon's grocery there was a man who bred smooth-haired fox terriers. He gave us one once, a strange animal, infatuated by our cat.

In the town's approximate center, where four streets meet, a grey woman still stands, a statue of the Maid of Erin. E. O'Donovan, undertaker, still sells ice cream and chocolate. The brass plate of Redmond O'Regan, solicitor, once awkwardly high, is now below eye level. In the grocers' shops the big-jawed West Cork women buy bread and sausages and tins of plums, but no longer wear the heavy black cloaks that made them seem like figures from another century. They still speak in the same West Cork lisp, a lingering careful voice, never in a hurry. I ask one if she could tell me the way to a house I half remember. "Ah, I could tell you grand," she replies. "It's dead and buried, sir."

The door beside the Methodist church, once green, is purple. The church, small and red-brick, stands behind high iron railings and gates, with gravel in front of it. Beyond the door that used to be green is the dank passage that leads to Miss Willoughby's schoolroom, where first I learnt that the world is not an easygoing place. Miss Willoughby was stern and young, in love with the cashier from the Provincial Bank.

On the gravel in front of the red-brick church I vividly recall Miss Willoughby. Terribly, she appears. Severe and beautiful, she pedals against the wind on her huge black bicycle. "Someone laughed during prayers," she accuses, and you feel at once that it was you, although you know it wasn't. *V. poor* she writes in your headline book when you've done your best to reproduce, four times, perfectly, *Pride goeth before destruction.*

As I stand on the gravel, her evangelical eyes seem again to dart over me without pleasure. Once I took the valves out of the tyres of her bicycle. Once I looked in her answer book.

I am late, I am stupid. I cannot write twenty sentences on A Day in the Life of an Old Shoe. I cannot do simple arithmetic or geography. I am always fighting with Jasper Swanton. I move swiftly on the gravel, out onto the street and into the bar of the Eldon Hotel: in spectral form or otherwise, Miss Willoughby will not be there.

Illusions fall fast in the narrow streets of Skibbereen, as elsewhere they have fallen. Yet for me, once, there was something more enduring, nicest thing of all. Going to Cork it was called, fifty-two miles in the old Renault, thirty miles an hour because my mother wouldn't permit speed. On St. Stephen's Day to the pantomime in the Opera House, and on some other occasion to see the *White Horse Inn*, which my father had heard was good. In Cork my appendix was removed because Cork's surgical skill was second to none. In Cork my tongue was cut to rid me of my incoherent manner of speaking. To Cork, every day of my childhood, I planned to run away.

Twice a year perhaps, on Saturday afternoons, there was going to Cork to the pictures. Clark Gable and Myrna Loy in *Too Hot to Handle. Mr. Deeds Goes to Town.* No experience in my whole childhood, and no memory, has remained as deeply etched as these escapes to the paradise that was Cork. Nothing was more lovely or more wondrous than Cork itself, with its magnificent array of cinemas, the Pavilion, the Savoy, the Palace, the Ritz, the Lee, and Hadji Bey's Turkish Delight factory. Tea in the Pavilion or the Savoy, the waitresses with silver-plated teapots and buttered bread and cakes, and other people eating fried eggs with rashers and chipped potatoes at half-past four in the afternoon. The sheer sophistication of the Pavilion or the Savoy could never be adequately conveyed to a friend in Skibbereen who had not had the good fortune to experience it. The gentlemen's lavatory in the Victoria Hotel had to be seen to be believed, the Munster Arcade left you gasping. Forever and forever you could sit in the middle stalls of the Pavilion watching Claudette Colbert, or Spencer Tracy as a priest, and the earthquake in San Francisco. And forever afterwards you could sit while a green-clad waitress carried the silver-plated teapot to you, with cakes and buttered bread. All around you was the clatter of life and of the city, and men of the world conversing, and girls' laughter tinkling. Happiness was everywhere.

ELISE JUSKA

Northeast Philly Girls

—ᒧᒧᒧ—

NORTHEAST PHILLY girls lived close. Their houses were close, clothes were tight, families crammed together on long city streets. On the corners they stood in clumps, girls with big hair and tight jeans and fringed leather pocketbooks. They held lipstick-wet cigarettes between two fingers and exchanged bubblegum, lighters, compact mirrors, all with smooth, pink sleight of hand. These girls had names I wanted—Colleen, Eileen, Christine—the long "e" insisting on femininity. Their boyfriends were cool and wiry, dropping kisses on their cheeks or loose arms around their necks. At night, so I heard, the boys took them to the St. Lucy's parking lot where they pressed up close in the warm backseats, and later the girls emerged older, more knowing, having acquired fresh gossip and kissing bruises they would display like badges of honor on the corner the next day.

At age twelve, I suspected that in the Northeast, like at summer camps I'd heard about, girls grew up more quickly because they lived so close. They got to see things. They got to hear things. They couldn't avoid it; there was no place else to go. Becoming a grown-up in Northeast Philly seemed as easy as catching a cold.

Riding in the front seat, heading to Aunt Jean's house, I watched the city out the window. Neighborhoods in Northeast Philly all looked like this one: blocks of row houses built shoulder-to-shoulder, cramped with stop signs and parked cars and corner delis and kids who walked so close to your car their knuckles nearly skimmed the hood. To me, the thought of having other people living on the other side of my wall was terrifying; if they started a fire in their house, mine would definitely go down with it. In our town, eight miles outside the city, houses were discrete, separate. Around here, neighbors yelled to each other from their front stoops.

It was grey December, the Saturday of the annual St. Lucy's Christmas fair. For the holidays, the row houses were decorated to the hilt with multi-colored lights, life-sized mangers, plastic reindeer hitched on roofs. Like every year, Mom and her sister, Aunt Jean, would sell homemade ornaments at the fair while I spent the afternoon with Terri. I dug my nails into the arm-rest as anxiety started its slow creep up my spine. It was a feeling I'd grown accustomed to around my cousin—having nowhere to hide.

I sunk low in my seat as Mom turned onto Hartel Street. The usual gang of boys was playing hockey in the street. Even though it was getting cold out, Northeast boys never seemed to go indoors. Their goalie nets sat ragged by the curb, their St. Lucy's jackets heaped on the sidewalk. The boys were a sweaty hub of crewcuts, baseball caps, Flyers jerseys, and gold earrings around which the neighborhood ebbed and flowed to its own kind of time.

The boys took a step back to let our car pass. I stared at the floor. Mom stopped and maneuvered our SUV into an empty spot in front of Aunt Jean's. Mom was good at parallel parking, from having grown up on a street like this. When she turned the car off we sat there a minute, listening to it tick and sigh under the hood. Mom's long maroon coat was belted at her waist, scarf wrapped snug around her neck. Maybe being in the cramped streets of the Northeast made her feel self-protective, too.

"Ready, kiddo?"

Not really. I would have preferred to have stayed right where I was. But I nodded, not wanting to admit how much I dreaded spending time with Terri.

Mom grabbed one bag of ornaments and I picked up the other. When I opened my door, it got stuck in a grey snowbank. Behind us, the boys sounded loud and too close. Across the street, a mother yelled: "Danny, put your jacket on!" As I pried my door loose, I could see the edge of a neighbor's curtain pulled back, and it was just these kinds of details that made the Northeast seem like a place that knew too much.

Aunt Jean was stirring a cup of coffee with the unused end of a knife. The top end was greasy with butter and toast crumbs. She had the portable phone in her hand and wore a bathrobe with sweatpants underneath. The kitchen table was covered with ornaments: Baby Jesuses in walnut shells, clothespin soldiers, wax-paper stars.

"Ed called," Aunt Jean said.

Uncle Ed—though I wasn't sure if I was supposed to call him "Uncle" anymore—had been caught with another woman in September. Aunt Jean and Terri were in the Clover parking lot, carrying shopping bags full of school supplies, when they saw Ed's head in the backseat of a green Volvo.

He was with a woman. Girl, actually. She was twenty-two, a cashier at Clover, and her name was Janine.

"What did they catch him doing?" I'd asked my mom. "Kissing?"

Her tense face paused for a minute, as if she was about to say something. Then she firmed up again, thinking better of it. "Yes. Kissing."

But Terri had a different story. "I saw the whole thing," she told me. "Her shirt was halfway open. And Dad's hand was on her butt." She could have been describing one of her soaps.

Lingering in the kitchen doorway, I watched Aunt Jean sip her coffee, running one hand through her reddish hair. You could tell she and Mom were sisters, if you studied their faces only. They looked like older versions of their St. Lucy's graduation photos, both with blue-grey eyes and thin-lipped smiles. Back then, they wore their hair full and flipped at the ends. Now, Aunt Jean's hair color changed every month. Mom's was a steady grey.

Aunt Jean banged her cup on the table, as if her wrist were too rubbery to hold it. Mom grabbed a paper towel and sopped up the spilled coffee leaking toward the Baby Jesuses. Then she took the phone and hung it on the wall. She whipped a plastic bag from beneath the sink and started packing ornaments, briskly, like baggers at the Acme. "Jean, if you want to tell me about it, tell it quick. We're going to be late."

I knew how Mom would pull her out of it. First she would listen to her describe the call, shaking her head back and forth, slow and steady. Then she would tell Aunt Jean to tell Ed to stop calling. Period. Maybe if I stayed quiet she'd forget I was there.

"Eunice, go upstairs and tell Terri we're ready," Mom said, which was exactly what I didn't want to do.

My cousin Terri and I were the same age (actually, I was three months older), but somehow she always made me feel much younger than she was. Terri had a talent for experiencing every adolescent rite of passage before I got to it. By age eight, she was using deodorant. By ten, she wore lipstick on special occasions. She'd had her ears pierced when she was six months old. Every time I saw her, she'd acquired some new piece of knowledge (what a blowjob was, how a tampon worked) to bestow upon me. For years I'd absorbed this information, wishing I had something to offer in return. But by age twelve, I'd resigned myself to the fact that city girls just grew up faster, and there was nothing I would ever know that Terri didn't know already.

I dragged my feet upstairs, dawdling in front of Terri's framed school picture. She wore a plaid uniform because she went to Catholic school. Nothing appealed to me about Catholic school, except that you could go home at lunch, which was convenient if you forgot your homework. My friend Molly said it was the uniform that made the Catholic kids "rebels." I rolled the word on my tongue: *rebels*. It sounded like *marbles* and seemed like them too, smooth and bright, a coveted flash in the palm.

I found Terri sitting on her bed, leaning over a pink notepad. Her bedroom walls were freshly plastered with soap stars. Her bed was unmade and her rug lumped with clothes. Her hair was in a ponytail, sticky with gel and spray. She wore a denim vest over a pink turtleneck, black stretch pants, and dull white Keds with pink laces. My cousin was slightly overweight, but the fact that she wore such tight clothes anyway made her intimidating.

"Hi," I said. Terri didn't look up. "My mom told me to get you."

She scribbled for a moment longer, as if unaware of me standing there, then snapped the cap on her pen. "Want to see something?"

This was the way visits went with Terri. They didn't begin at the beginning. She sucked you right into her life at that moment, as if you'd never left.

Terri stood up and stepped toward me, then yanked down the collar of her turtleneck. On her neck was a swollen spot, the size and color of a prune. "Hickey."

I wanted to look closer but didn't dare. I had a fleeting fear that I might catch it.

"I got it from Glenn," she said, letting go of the shirt. The neck snapped back in place, hugging the hickey inside like a secret. "He's my boyfriend."

"Oh." No one in my sixth-grade class had boyfriends. Definitely, no one had hickeys. Maybe, living so close together, people in the Northeast simply got to touching other people faster, their hands in their hands, mouths on their necks, hands on their butts. I had a flash of Uncle Ed smushed against twenty-two-year-old Janine, their lives rushing at each other like bumper cars to collide helplessly in the backseat of that green Volvo.

Terri picked up the notepad and put it on her dresser. The dresser, while seemingly innocent—a jewelry box, a statue of Mary—was actually full of secrets. Tubes of lipstick. Letters to soap stars. Even a lacy pink bra tucked away in her sock drawer. On her dresser top was a half-used bottle of perfume called "Surrender" that she sprayed on her wrist like bug repellent.

"Give me yours," she commanded, and I offered her my arms. Standing so close to the dresser, I could see the notepad. *My Friends*, it said in bubble letters. Below were three columns: *Yes*, *No*, and *Maybe*. My name was under *Maybe*.

Terri ran a lipstick around her mouth. It was the same way she used to fill in coloring books: quickly, messily, veering out of the lines. She blotted her lips on a tissue, like I'd seen Aunt Jean do, then hooked my arm in hers. "Let's go," she said. From the pink trash can, the lip print smirked at us, bright and wet.

On first glance, St. Lucy's gym/auditorium was like Terri's dresser: all inno-cence. The room was packed with long folding tables, cupcakes, arts and crafts. Stiff basketball hoops hung on either end and a giant, crepe-papered box of raffle tickets hunkered by the door. Every hour, one of the priests or nuns plucked a ticket from it, setting off a wave of commotion until the win-ner stepped up to claim his or her Christmas ham.

On the stage, Santa Claus presided at the end of a long line of mothers and babies. The mothers chatted while they waited, rocking their strollers with one foot and shaking their heads back and forth. They looked like Mom did listening to Aunt Jean, which got me wondering how many husbands in Northeast Philly had been found in the backseats of cars with twenty-two-year-olds.

When we arrived, Terri surveyed the crowded gym with her hands on her hips and her eyes cut narrow. Looking for Glenn, I guessed.

"Maybe I'll go hang out with my mom," I said. It was worth a shot.

Terri rolled her eyes. "Don't be a dork. I want you to meet Glenn." She picked up my hand and began threading through the crowds, unfazed by strangers' chests and elbows. Though I was almost positive I didn't want to go where we were going, I couldn't help feeling a certain cool pride, being in public and attached to Terri's hand.

As we approached the stage, Terri slowed her pace. In front of us was a door marked "Backstage Only." Terri scanned the room once more and, not spotting Glenn, pulled upon the door to reveal a narrow staircase.

"Come on," she said, giving me a poke between the shoulder blades. When the door closed, the noise of the gym clipped off and I heard a differ-ent kind of music: muffled talk, running water, the laughter of teenage girls.

"Come *on*," Terri said again, though she wasn't moving any faster than I was. I started up the staircase, lined on either side with framed pictures from old school musicals: kids frozen singing with rounded mouths or grinning with hands thrust high in the air. They seemed unreal, out of place. When I reached the top step, I could see a door marked GIRLS. It was propped open, revealing a slice of tiled floor and fluorescent light.

The room was packed with Northeast Philly girls. Brazen, painted, smelling like aerosol and bubblegum. They were older than us, freshmen at least. They wore pink combs in their back pockets and tight jeans with cop-per-colored rivets. Their hair was in big waves, crimped and curled after what I imagined was the collective effort of painful rollers, hot irons, and all-night slumber parties. The image of one girl curling another girl's hair seemed to me the most profound and intimate gesture of friendship.

One tall girl held her face an inch from the mirror; she was dressed like one of Santa's elves but looked more like a "Price Is Right" model. A big-haired blonde girl had one leg propped up on a sink like a ballerina. She was shaving around the cuffs of her jeans and saying, "I don't want Mike seeing my ankles all hairy."

The elf said, "You think all Mike's going to see is your ankles?"

"Shut up."

"You shut up!"

A stall door slammed open and a short, bowlegged redhead popped out. "Why don't you both shut up?" She squeezed into a spot in front of the mirror. "Better shave the whole leg, just in case." Laughter filled the room.

"Pig," said the ballerina.

"Hey, it's not my fault Mike's getting lucky tonight. I'm just telling it like it is!" The redhead circled her mouth with lipstick as the room laughed again.

I didn't get their jokes. But I understood their tone: a raw, secret language. It was as if, alone together, the girls' street-corner femininity was tossed off and their true selves laid bare. I longingly imagined the downstairs bathroom: an old woman cranking the handle of the paper-towel dispenser, a mother changing her baby on a duck-print palette on the floor.

The girls were drowned for a moment by the hand dryer. This was Terri's opening. She grabbed my hand, lifted her chin, and sashayed us though the door.

No one noticed. We waited by the wall as the dryer slowed to a moan.

"Hey," Terri said.

The elf glanced over. "Hey there."

I felt Terri's finger between my shoulders again, forcing me forward. "This is my cousin, Eunice," Terri said. "She's from the suburbs."

A few looked over that time, surveying me up and down: a girl from the suburbs? I felt vulnerable, transparent under their pink-lidded eyes, as if with the word "suburbs" these girls could see through to my very core: never had a boyfriend, never been kissed, never had a hickey or a bra or lipstick in her sock drawer. Any inner life I'd possessed walking in there was snuffed out by the closeness of their scrutiny and the closeness of our bodies.

Then somebody yelled: "Hey, who has a cigarette?"

"Hang on," said the redhead. The ballerina resumed work on her ankles. I felt the interest in us soften and disperse, like a dandelion head blown off.

Terri looked at me and frowned, as if I hadn't done my part. "So anyway," she said, loudly, as a toilet flushed. "Anybody know where Glenn is?"

"Glenn Teti?" the ballerina murmured, inspecting her ankles.

"Glenn's in the changing room," yelled a voice inside a stall. "Somebody out there give me a tampon."

I could feel Terri inhale. "What's the changing room?"

The redhead glanced at us, smiled, but said nothing.

The voice yelled, "You know, where all the play geeks go to change clothes before shows. Guys, I'm not kidding. I'm leaking."

The room laughed again, as I felt Terri tug my arm. "Come on," she hissed, then said, "Bye guys," and pulled me out the door.

We hurried a few steps down the hall, then stopped, our eyes adjusting to the dimness. Terri squinted in the direction of the stage. At the end of the hall was a velvety curtain, beyond which was the incongruous image of Santa Claus holding kids on his knees and asking them what they wanted for Christmas.

"Let's go back," I said.

Terri shook her head. "I want to see Glenn." Our voices were thick and whispery, like criminals.

"You don't know where he is."

"You heard her. The changing room."

"But you said you didn't know—"

"I remember now. I can hear voices from there already."

I listened, but there was no way to distinguish between the muffled sounds of the stage and the girls laughing, toilets flushing, hand dryer droning, faucets running. The bathroom door opened. Some girls left, some entered. From the gym, a cry went up. Someone must have won him- or herself a ham.

"I'm going back," I said, and turned to walk away.

Terri caught my arm. I knew she would try to convince me to go with her, but this time I wasn't going for it. I didn't care what she said. She could call me a dork. A nerd. A baby from the suburbs. I wasn't going.

But when I turned and saw her face, her features looked soft, her eyes wide. Sweat had appeared on her upper lip, above her bright red lipstick line. "Eunice?" She sounded like she might cry. "You have to come. Please. I can't walk in there by myself."

It was the most vulnerable I had ever seen her. She pursed her mouth, lipstick blearing like a squashed berry. Tears wobbled in her eyes. I felt embarrassed for her, for having to admit her helplessness. Yet at the same time, I felt a sense of pride. Terri needed me. She was depending on me. For the first time, I had something my cousin wanted. It was the only argument I couldn't have refused.

Walking down the dark hall, groping the walls, was Northeast Philly in all its unabashed intimacy. I could smell my cousin's perfume mingled with sweat and hear her labored breaths.

"I think it's back here," Terri said. On the floor was a thin stripe of light from a crack in the curtain. My heart pounded as she fumbled in its thick folds, and when she pawed her way through I found myself in what had to be the changing room: raw, splintery wood floors, long dressing mirrors, sporadic folding chairs and a dozen teenagers sprawled in them. The smell of cigarettes hung sour in the air.

This time we didn't have to vie for attention. The room fell silent. It wasn't as crowded as the bathroom, but somehow the space made it more impenetrable. I recognized the ballerina, sitting a few feet away. She looked different—smaller, blonder, softer—not the kind of girl who talked about tampons and getting lucky. The boy next to her (Mike, I assumed) wore a scummy baseball cap turned backwards. The other kids sat clumped in the far corners, smoking and watching us.

Suddenly Terri exhaled: "Glenn! Hi!"

It shouldn't have surprised me, but it did. Somewhere in the course of our dark, nerve-wracked journey, this person "Glenn" had begun to take on mythic proportions, and by that point, I think I'd stopped believing he was real.

Sure enough, a skinny blond boy rose from the back and walked toward us. His body reminded me of a strip of bacon, thin and lean and rubbery. His face was almost totally covered in sandy freckles, and a shock of blond hair fell over one eye.

"Hi there," he said. "What are you doing here, kid?"

Terri tried to affect a sultry shrug, but her denim vest bunched up around her ears. "I don't know."

Behind Glenn, someone let out a wolf whistle. He threw a glance over his shoulder, then smiled down at Terri. I waited for her to introduce me, but she was gazing up at his face, barely able to contain her smile.

"Who's your friend?" he asked, lifting a chin in my direction. For a moment I fell in love with him too, just for asking.

"She's not my friend." Terri flipped her ponytail over her shoulder. "She's my cousin." She took a step toward Glenn, and with a sinking feeling, I realized she was abandoning me. I had been a device, a second body to get her through the door. Now that she was in, I was going to be on my own.

Glenn pushed the blond hair out of his eyes. Like a silent invitation, he turned and started walking to his chair. Terri followed. I felt myself begin to panic. Should I go and leave her here? Should I follow too?

I noticed Mike, the boy who was getting lucky, was looking at me. He had a spiky crewcut, gold earring, and a football shirt full of tiny holes. It reminded me of the punctured lids we used on bug jars in science. "So, what grade are you in?" he said, leaning back so his chair legs rose off the floor.

I looked at the ballerina, hoping she might recognize me. But she was trying to light a cigarette, frowning at the tip.

"I don't go to St. Lucy's." My voice sounded small. "I live in the suburbs."

"The suburbs, huh?"

"Leave her alone, Mike," said the girl, sounding bored. She exhaled smoke as I searched her face for something, anything, a hint of female empathy. But she just wanted Mike's attention back. She pushed down on his knee, so his chair legs clattered forward.

Then, from the other end of the room, I heard a cough. I looked over and saw Terri perched on Glenn's knee. She was holding a cigarette between her messy red lips, her pinky finger thrust to one side. In that moment, my cousin's image began to unravel all at once, like an unclenched ball of yarn. I saw her as the others must have seen her: a lumpy twelve-year-old, with gawking eyes and breasts like two raisins poking through her turtleneck. When she coughed again, Glenn and his friends started laughing. Terri smiled, pleased by the attention. She was their joke and didn't know it.

Angry as I felt, I had to get her out of there. I gathered my nerve and said: "Terri. Let's go."

I tried to sound firm, like my mom, but Terri pretended not to hear me. I waited as I had before, for her to look up and reel me in, but I knew it wouldn't happen. She wasn't the same girl who had moved so confidently around her bedroom, flashing me her hidden hickey. This girl looked young, and silly, legs dangling off Glenn's lap and feet not touching the ground.

Like everything else about Northeast Philly, Christmas Eve Mass at St. Lucy's was close, tight, warm. Hands touched hands, breath found necks, knees banged knees. Usually I felt claustrophobic there, stuffed in a warm church with so many strangers. But this year the closeness felt different. I felt removed from it. I had something private, a secret that I guarded warm under my tongue like a Communion wafer.

My parents sat on either side of Aunt Jean, who wore a tight red dress and a small, fake smile. Next to her was Dad, then me and Terri. Terri's was the same dress she wore last year, red with white pompoms dangling off the hem. Her neck was uncovered, but I could see only a faint yellow stain of the hickey.

It was the first time we'd seen each other since the day I walked out of the changing room. We didn't say a word as the cheerful neighbors crowded the walls and aisles. When the usher asked our pew to make room, we all squeezed down until Dad's elbow was crunched against my arm and my leg was pressed against Terri's.

Once touching, Terri couldn't help but speak. She turned to me with an eager smile and blurted: "So, do you want to see something?"

I knew what she was doing. She was trying to make amends for making me look foolish, for ditching me at the fair. She was tossing me bait, like she had for years, but this time I didn't want it. This time I knew something my cousin didn't: that I wasn't the only one who'd looked like a fool.

I was saved from responding by the organ, swelling with the first few bars of "Joy to the World." As the stuffed church began rising to its feet, Terri clutched my arm. With her free hand, she pinched her fleshy thigh, brown silk rising like a second skin. "Nylons," she mouthed, with a satisfied smile.

When the Mass was over, we went back to Aunt Jean's house. Usually my family went home after church to hang stockings and leave out carrots for the reindeer. But Mom wanted to be there for Aunt Jean. "It's a difficult year for her," Mom murmured, as Dad inched the car out of the St. Lucy's parking lot.

Aunt Jean's living room was dressed in tinsel and fake holly. On the coffee table sat a plate of crackers with a limp fan of cheese. By the TV hung two glitter-lettered stockings—one "Mom," the other "Terri"—which struck me as so sad and so lonely that I kept my eyes averted from them, like I did from people who tripped on the street.

We pretended to have fun, nibbling and drinking and listening to Elvis's "Blue Christmas." Neighbors filtered in and out, bearing cards and cookies. Mom told the story about the Christmas Dad threw his back out trying to assemble my ten-speed, and I laughed hard to help her out. Dad cracked a few dumb jokes (Aunt Jean laughed hardest at those) and drank a beer, juggling nuts in his hand like loose change. Aunt Jean drank grasshoppers from a skinny glass, occasionally singing a few bars with Elvis. Terri snuck cheese and crackers into her mouth from the stack hidden in her hand.

By eleven the neighbors were gone, the crackers were gone, and Aunt Jean was about to go for her fifth refill when we heard a knock. Mom sat up straight, like a soldier on guard. Dad's beer stopped halfway to his mouth. Aunt Jean stood, brushing crumbs off her lap, and teetered toward the door. I could hear the screen door yawning open and the sound of a sloppy kiss. Twice.

When Uncle Ed walked in, you could tell he was surprised to see us. "Merry Christmas, folks," he mumbled. He'd dressed up for the occasion, in pressed jeans and a red sweater. He wasn't wearing a shirt underneath, and the red knit was tight against his stubbly pink neck.

Dad nodded and said: "Ed." I smiled at my knees. Uncle Ed was carrying a sloppily wrapped present, which he handed to Terri.

"Here you go, honey," he said, pushing his sleeves up and down.

Terri paused for a minute, scanning the room for a cue that she could unwrap it. When Aunt Jean said, "Go ahead, hon," she tore into the present like a dog into meat. She flung the red bow aside, skinned the wrapping from the sides. Aunt Jean watched her with a flushed smile, but I knew it wasn't the present she was excited about. Terri pried apart the stapled box flaps and pulled out a life-sized, blond Barbie doll head. Just a head. It had hair you could style and cut yourself, then pump to make more grow.

"Thank you, Daddy!" Terri said. It sounded strange to me. Since September, my uncle had been so completely reduced to blunt, bad "Ed"—a man whose entire history would forever consist of only a Volvo, a hand, a butt, and a twenty-two-year-old—that I'd almost forgotten he still *was* Terri's daddy.

"Ed, that's sweet," Aunt Jean said. She flicked a glance at Mom, then dared: "You want a beer or something?"

Uncle Ed's eyes skittered from Mom to Dad to the two limp Christmas stockings, then settled on the carpet, which was littered with crumbs and shreds of wrapping paper. "Nah," he muttered. "They don't want me here."

He turned and headed for the door. Aunt Jean hurried after him, half-running. From behind me, I heard low murmurs and the sound of the screen door slapping shut. Then my aunt was rushing past us, leaving a trail of chilly air in her wake.

Mom went after her. Soon I could hear raised voices from the kitchen and the sounds of Aunt Jean crying. Without a word, Dad picked up the remote control and turned the TV on. Loud. In those crowded quarters, it was a valiant attempt on his part to respect the women's privacy and, more importantly, preserve his own.

Terri just sat there, gazing at the doll head in her lap. She placed a hand on it, like priests did when they blessed new babies, and let the blond hair slide under her palm. She looked so sad and so alone, I couldn't be angry at her anymore. I wanted to make her feel better, but didn't know how.

"Hey, Terri, want to see something?"

Her head snapped up, maybe embarrassed I'd been watching her. "What?"

"I can make a French braid. For the doll." I tried to sound nonchalant. "Want me to show you how?"

She shrugged. "I guess."

Terri put the doll on the floor. We knelt down beside it. For a moment, it felt like we were little kids again. I showed her how to start with the hair at the top, separating and twining the thicker strands, then working my way down the back. I twisted the hair as carefully as I could, creating perfect braids, then weaving all the individual pieces into one final twist.

When I was finished, Terri said, "Let me try." She raked her fingers through the doll's hair and started over.

She was too eager, as I knew she would be, her chubby fingers plying the hair too fast. All of her strands were too thick or too thin, too short or too long, but I didn't say a word. As Terri worked, her breaths were measured and serious. When she finished, I said her braid looked good.

As Terri unbraided the doll again, Mom appeared. In one arm she was carrying our coats; the other was around Aunt Jean's shoulders. My aunt was smiling thinly, but it looked better than the fake smile she'd worn before.

"Ready to go?" Mom smiled. "It's almost Christmas."

It didn't feel like almost Christmas. Any other year I would have been in bed by then, willing myself to drift into sleep, but I felt too old for that now. Too aware of other things. As we zippered our coats and said our goodbyes, every gesture felt extra weighty. Mom hugged Terri tightly. Aunt Jean ran a hand over my hair. Even Dad gave Aunt Jean a peck on the cheek.

I faced Terri by the door, wondering if I should hug her too, but decided that would be going too far. Instead I said, "Maybe sometime I'll show you a French twist?"

"Okay," she shrugged.

Outside it had started to snow. Hartel Street blinked and blazed and glowed. A red-lit WELCOME SANTA sprawled across a neighbor's roof. In the dark, the boys' hockey nets were crouched on front lawns, waiting for the next game. By the time Dad had brushed the snow off the windows, it was nearly midnight. Our tires whispered through the cramped streets that would widen as we neared the city line. I watched the row houses slip past my window, rooftop after rooftop, wondering if the Northeast Philly girls were inside them, tucked in their beds, falling asleep.

But when our car stopped at a red light, there they were: a furtive clump on the corner, in long fuzzy scarfs and fur-trimmed leather jackets. They stood close to keep warm, stamping their feet in their sharp-heeled boots. Their heads were lowered around the orange glow of a single cigarette. The flame trembled and caught as I watched, one cigarette and then the next and the next, lighting their faces, spreading from tip to tip.

KERMIT MOYER

Learning to Smoke

MY COUSIN Frenchie is teaching me how to French inhale—a neat trick that involves jutting out your jaw just far enough to draw the smoke up from between your lips directly into your flaring nostrils. I'm sure that the dizziness I'm feeling is caused less by the carbonized tobacco hitting my still-pristine lungs than by the taste of Frenchie's cherry-red lipstick on the Parliament's famously recessed filter tip. It's the summer of 1956, a little over two weeks since my thirteenth birthday, and we're sitting beside a vacant trail on the trunk of a fallen pine tree that is as ramrod straight and devoid of branches as a telephone pole. The morning was grey and overcast, but now the sun has come out of hiding and is scattering its golden light like so many glittering coins through the woods around us. We're baby-sitting the baby daughter of an actor at the park's summer theater. But at the moment Zoe is sound asleep, her rosy little cheeks so pudgy that I have to keep restraining myself from reaching out and poking them with my finger. What impresses me is the fleshy miniaturization of Zoe, the surprising ways that she is and is not yet a person.

Pleased with myself, I exhale from my mouth a cloud of smoke I've successfully drawn up into my nostrils. I can't get over the implicit sensuality of smoking—the sexiness of the gesture itself, the caressing conjunction of fingers and lips, the cigarette's long cylindrical shape combined with the suggestive ways it can be handled, and most of all the snaky swirl of your suddenly visible breath languorously rising upwards. It's like a sexual advertisement. No wonder the naked women in my fantasies are always holding cigarettes between their long fingers while they gaze back at me through dissolving webs of bluish-white smoke that drift up from lips parted as though in response to some secret rapture.

"Why's it called 'French inhaling'?" I ask Frenchie. She's seventeen, four years older than I am and a veritable fund of sophisticated lore.

"Beats the hell out of me," she says in the tough-guy voice she affects sometimes, as if she thinks she's a gun moll in a gangster movie. I like the way her overbite makes her front teeth protrude slightly under the arch of her upper lip, which in the bright sunlight is furred with a light layer of down, otherwise nearly invisible. "But it's an interesting question, isn't it?" she says, shifting into her intellectual bookworm mode. The sun glints off the lenses of her glasses, and she shifts her head toward me a little to move out of the light. "I mean, why's it called 'French kissing'?" she says.

I smile back knowingly but in fact I have no idea what she's talking about.

"I guess the French must've invented it," she says. "Maybe they've got some kind of weird oral fixation going on over there." She bends forward toward my lap, where I'm holding the cigarette, lifts my hand up, and takes a drag while I'm still holding it. Then she leans back. "I can tell you one thing, though," she says, smoke drifting from her mouth as she talks, "having Frenchie for a nickname isn't exactly—well, let's just say—" She turns her head to one side and exhales the rest of the smoke. "It wasn't so bad when I was little—'Frenchie'—it was sort of cute—but since about the seventh grade—"

"I know what you mean," I say. "Being named Chester's no picnic either—"

Frenchie chuckles. "Remember how mad you used to get whenever anybody'd call you Chester Drawers? You'd get so furious—" When she laughs, she extends her upper lip downward to cover her teeth in a way that makes her seem more self-conscious and shyer than she really is. "The only nickname worse than Frenchie," she says, "is this girl at school. Her nickname is actually—are you ready for this? 'Pussy'! Pussy Pasquale! Can you believe that?"

We both shake with laughter—my own laughter no doubt a little high-pitched, excited as I am not only by what Frenchie is saying but also by how much she seems to assume I know. The urge to ask her how French kissing works is nearly irresistible, but I'm not sure how to go about it without spoiling the impression of precocity I'm trying so hard to convey. So I just tap a little caterpillar of ash off the end of the cigarette and pass it back.

After looking at her red lip-prints on the filter for a second, Frenchie glances at me with a little smirk and says, "Watch. Want to see how you French kiss a cigarette?" She brings the Parliament to her mouth, sticks the pointed tip of her tongue into the tiny gap made by the recessed filter, and twists the cigarette back and forth as though she's boring a hole. "*Voilà!*" she says with a laugh.

I'm still not sure what she means, but excited by the possibility of a more practical demonstration, I say, "We're 'kissin' cousins,' right?"

"Uh-huh," she says. "I guess so." She gives me a sidelong glance from behind the white frames of her glasses. "Why? What's on your mind?" She takes another drag, then touches the excess ash against the tree bark and rolls what's left of the cigarette back and forth between her middle finger and thumb. When she exhales, a breeze blows the smoke into my eyes and makes them fill with tears.

"I don't know," I say, wiping the water from one eye with my finger. "I just thought since we're kissin' cousins, maybe you could give me some lessons—"

"Kissing lessons?" she says. And then, with mock sympathy, wiping the moisture from under my other eye, "Poor Chessie . . . Won't anyone kiss you? . . . Here, because you've been such a good boy . . ." And she puckers her lips over her teeth, leans close, and gives me a smack on the corner of my mouth. "There—kissin' cousins—now it's official—"

"Okay," I say, "but what if we were cousins in France? Then we'd be French-kissin' cousins—"

Frenchie's laugh seems to take her by surprise, coming out in little staccato bursts that make me feel a rush of pleasure at my own power.

"I'll say one thing for you," she says, "you're persistent. And I like the way your mind works—that's two things." She stubs the cigarette out against the tree trunk and flicks the butt into the bramble, then leans back and gives me an openly speculative look, her eyes narrowed behind the lenses of her glasses and her head tilted to one side so a blade of dark-blonde hair falls away from her neck. "All right," she says. She takes off her glasses, folds them, and tucks them into a pocket at the side of Zoe's stroller. Zoe is still sleeping, her mouth moving as though she's chewing something. "We'll play pretend . . . But you have to close your eyes first . . ."

As I shut them, I'm already beginning to feel a constriction in my chest, like my skin is getting too tight for easy breathing.

"I'll be your French cousin . . . Just think of me by my real name . . . Your beautiful cousin Francesca . . . Now, open your mouth . . ."

I open wide, as though I'm awaiting a tongue depressor.

"No, silly, not like that . . . Just open a little . . . That's right . . . Okay . . . Now, just relax . . ."

I feel her take my chin between her finger and thumb and gently tip my head back, and then there's the soft pressure of her lips on mine, oddly cool and dry, until her mouth slowly opens, releasing the musky odor of lipstick and spearmint and nicotine, and suddenly I feel the wet warmth of her tongue on my tongue, so surprisingly intimate and alive that at first it's like some moist sea creature emerging from inside the petals of a flower, and I involuntarily catch my breath and shudder. But instead of pulling away, Frenchie presses her tongue in even further, working her mouth like a guppy's to loosen my jaw while she explores the soft inside of my mouth, her mollusk-like tongue curling around mine with a slight sucking sensation. Her other hand is at the back of my head now, her jaw working as if my mouth is a pulpy piece of fruit she's eating. She gives a last little spasmodic lunge and then pulls away and takes a deep breath.

When I open my eyes, she's brushing her hand across her forehead, covering her eyes so I can't see them. But I can see her chest rising and falling, and I can hear how ragged her breathing is.

"Whew-ew . . . ," she says. "Lordy, lordy . . ."

The taste of her is still with me and I can still feel her tongue filling my mouth. I'm not quite sure how to come back from the sensation, as if ordinary conversation is now ruled out, or as if we'll have to speak another language now, you might say another tongue, one I don't yet know but am eager to discover.

"Makes you a little breathless, doesn't it?" she says.

"Yeah . . . That was really . . ." But I can't find the right word. Instead, I take hold of her hand and place her open palm against my chest. "Feel," I say, imagining that the way my heart is pounding will tell her everything she needs to know.

But Frenchie just giggles. "This is a switch, isn't it?" she says. She gives my chest a little tweak. "I mean usually it's the guy who feels the girl up"— talking as if nothing important has happened, or as if what we're doing is just some kind of joke.

"But couldn't you feel how fast my heart was beating?"

"Don't worry—I think you'll live." She casually tucks a strand of hair behind her ear with a stroke of her finger. "Anyway, now you know how to French inhale *and* French kiss. The next thing you know, you'll be speaking the language—"

"But we aren't finished yet," I say, stung by how offhand she sounds. "You said the guy's supposed to feel the girl up—"

"You do and I'll slap you silly—" And she raises her arms to shield her chest as if she actually expects me to give it a try.

So I do. I grab her wrists and pull her arms apart to clear the way to her chest, where the words PENN STATE undulate across the front of the loose white sweatshirt she's wearing.

"Chessie! Stop!" she squeals. "We'll wake up Zoe!"

But doing the teasing instead of getting teased feels too good to stop, so I struggle with her for a second, both of us laughing now, me trying to pull her arms apart and her trying to hold them together, until I realize that whenever she succeeds in pulling her arms closed I can actually feel her breasts, loose and apparently naked inside her sweatshirt, freely slipping and sliding beneath the backs of my hands where I'm holding her wrists.

She seems to realize what's happening at the same instant I do, because we both freeze, staring hard into each other's eyes and panting, not laughing anymore. I'm still gripping her wrists, which she's got mashed up against her chest. We might be practicing a wrestling hold or demonstrating some new dance position. I'm paralyzed, without a clue where to go from here and feeling panicked at the possible consequences of what I've accidentally done, when to my amazement, instead of getting angry or bursting into tears as I'm half expecting, Frenchie starts slowly moving her arms back and forth against herself, purposely dragging my knuckles across the springy little nubs of her nipples. She's looking right at me, our eyes are locked together, her face somehow naked without her glasses, and as she strokes her breasts with the backs of my hands, which are still gripping her wrists, her eyebrows give a quizzical little lift, and I instinctively nod back, without knowing exactly what she's asking but feeling the blood suffusing my face and pumping into my loins, where I'm already hard as a rock. And Frenchie smiles at me, yes, as if we've just crossed some line or arrived at some agreement that pleases her.

"Wait," she says. We've been sitting hip to hip on the log, half-turned to face each other, but now Frenchie smoothly swings her far leg over me, pivoting on her near foot so that suddenly she's straddling my lap. "Like this," she says. It's as if she's showing me some new form of Indian wrestling, and I'm actually thinking maybe that's what this is, when she leans down and finds my mouth again, eagerly this time, her own mouth already open so our front teeth click together, her tongue grappling with mine, alternately plunging in and pulling away in an urgent kind of back-and-forth pursuit. To keep from going over backwards, I shift around on the tree trunk so that I'm lying lengthwise now with Frenchie sitting on top of me, straddling my hips. Even through my jeans and her shorts, I can feel the soft, ridged slipperiness of her crotch grinding against me. Without even having to think about it, I reach up under her sweatshirt and cup my hand around one of her breasts, hefting the strange mercurial weight of it and strumming the stiff nipple with my thumb. Frenchie groans way back in her throat, arching her back and sort of vibrating herself hard against me down there, her mouth parted and a corner of her upper lip lifted in a kind of Elvis Presley sneer. Her eyelids are half-closed and fluttering like she's hypnotized, and I can feel the unstoppable current starting to rise up the stem of me, rising up and up, until it's suddenly here, a sweet obliterating convulsion that seems to turn the very core of me to liquid, making me hunch my back and jerk my pelvis up into her like I'm trying to buck her off me. With a deep groan, as if she may have seriously ruptured something, Frenchie drops down onto my chest, where she shudders and groans again, her hips moving spasmodically. She gives a shivery sigh and buries her chin in the crook of my neck, and for a second I'm afraid she may have lost consciousness altogether.

I'm completely stunned, a confusion of feelings buffeting around inside of me. But this much I know for sure: something momentous has happened. From this moment on, nothing will ever be the same.

Frenchie's body is trembling silently against me now, as if she might be crying. I can taste the beginning of my own tears, too, hot and salty at the back of my throat, surprising but somehow appropriate, and I'm wordlessly patting Frenchie's shoulder, praying that she's not hurt, when suddenly she lifts her head and says, "Zoe's awake, the little monkey! She must've watched the whole show!" And I realize that Frenchie isn't crying after all. She's laughing.

When we get back to The Mount Bethel Inn, which is where all the actors at the summer theater stay, it's going on four o'clock and the whole wide porch is vacant. The brown cane-backed rocking chairs, clustered in groups of three and four, are motionless and empty, and the jukebox is squatting silently in the corner like some great carbuncular toad, its green-and-yellow lights bubbling away so it looks like something alive and waiting, which only heightens the odd sense I have of everything hanging in suspension, as if I'm one of those cartoon characters who hasn't yet realized that he's just walked off the edge of a cliff.

Frenchie says, "I'll take Zoe up," like I didn't know the routine by now, and then unnecessarily adds, "You stay down here." She lifts Zoe's legs out of the stroller seat, settles her against one hip, and pushes the stroller forward with her other hand. "Get the door for me—will you, please?" I hardly know what I'm doing, but Frenchie is not only okay, she's serenely efficient, seemingly untouched by what's happened to us. Back in the woods, when she noticed the wet spot on my jeans, she just wrinkled her nose and said I'd better wear my shirt untucked for a little while.

I hold the guest-room door open and brush the palm of my hand over Zoe's curly head as Frenchie carries her past me into the dimly lit foyer. "Bye, Zoe," I say. "See ya." I wave bye-bye and Zoe raises her little fist and opens and closes her fingers at me, as if she's grabbing a handful of air.

After Frenchie and Zoe disappear up the staircase, I go over to the jukebox and study the list of song titles, finally settling on Elvis singing "Love Me" in hopes that if Frenchie hears it maybe she'll get the message. But then, just as I'm fishing a dime out of my pants pocket, I hear someone shout, "Hey, Chestnut!" I immediately freeze and turn around, my face flushing with heat, feeling like I've just been caught red-handed, although caught at what I'm not sure.

Out in the road, a bunch of my cousins are coming back from the pool. They're wearing swimming suits and picking their way gingerly down the macadam in their bare feet. The twins, Donna and Debbie, are holding striped beach towels wrapped around their shoulders, Gary is carrying a rolled-up green army blanket, and B.J. and Joey are passing a football back and forth. They're bathed in such a soft golden light that from where I'm standing in the shadow of the porch they seem to inhabit another world entirely.

"Hey," I call back, trying my best to sound normal. "How was the pool?"

"You really missed it," Gary says—he's a couple of years older than the rest, almost old enough to drive, the natural leader of our group. "Joey went off the high dive."

Joey's only a year younger than I am, but he seems even younger than that because of being so shy. "Yeah," he says, uncharacteristically pleased with himself. "At first it was sort of scary, but then I just closed my eyes and did it—"

"Way to go, Joey," I say. "That's great! I was up there forever the first time I went off—"

"We thought you and Frenchie were going to come," Gary says. "What happened?"

"Nothing," I say, being careful to keep from looking Gary in the eye. "Zoe fell asleep and we didn't want to wake her up."

"Where did you guys go anyway?" Donna asks. She and Debbie are the same age as my little sister Janet, right at the point where they've stopped being tomboys and have started acting prissy.

"Nowhere," I shrug. "You know—the hiking trails behind the pool, back toward the fire station—nowhere in particular."

"So where's Frenchie?" B.J. asks, working his shoulder muscles in tight little circles the way he always does, like he's a boxer who's just stepped into the ring. B.J. is Joey's older brother, but they're as different as night and day.

"She just took Zoe upstairs—she'll be down in a minute—"

"Yeah?" Gary says. "You'd better go check." He smirks and gives me a wink. "I think she's got the hots for the little baby's daddy. Ever hear the way she talks about him? The actor? You know what they say. Where there's smoke, there's fire—"

Gary's famous for his dirty mind, but the pang of jealousy I feel when he says this is actually physical, like a stitch in my side. "That's crazy," I manage to croak, but I've known all along that Frenchie has a crush on Zoe's father. Although I have to admit that he's good looking, he also happens to be way too old for Frenchie. He's got a thatch of floppy brown hair that gives him a certain boyish look, but he's grey at the temples, and there are little fans of wrinkles at the corners of his eyes. "Anyway, Zoe's with them," I say, but of course this is a fact that now convinces me of nothing.

"All I'm saying," Gary says, tossing the army blanket to B.J. and motioning for Joey to throw him the football, "is if you go upstairs to check, you'd better take a fire extinguisher just in case—that's all I'm saying."

"Very funny."

Gary catches the ball, then cocks it back to his shoulder and waves at Joey to go out for a pass. Donna and Debbie have continued on down the road, and the football sails over their heads, making an arc that intersects perfectly with the arc of Joey's path. All Joey has to do is snag the ball out of the air, but somehow he flubs it. The ball ricochets off his chest and then keeps hopping and leaping down the road like it's purposely avoiding Joey every time he tries to grab it.

"Butterfingers!" B.J. shouts. He's got his towel wrapped around his waist and tucked in like a sarong.

"You gotta keep your eye on the ball, Joey!" Gary calls.

"I couldn't see it!" Joey calls over his shoulder. "The sun got in my eyes!"

Gary turns back to me. "You coming? You might as well, unless you want to hang around here forever—"

"Naw, that's okay—Frenchie'll be looking for me—"

"Okay, stay if you want to," Gary says. "But remember what I told you—where there's smoke—"

"Yeah, I know," I say. And at that very moment I have such a vivid image of Frenchie kissing Zoe's silver-haired actor father, kissing him the same way she kissed me, that I have to reach out and hold onto the log railing to keep my balance. The railing is so covered with hieroglyphics it looks vaguely archaeological. Somewhere along here are my own initials, cut two years earlier, when I was just a kid, a completely different person from who I am now. I look down, for some reason expecting to see that I've miraculously found them, that the carved letters under my fingertips are in fact my own initials, but what I see instead, carved so long ago that the letters are barely discernible—like the ridges of some ancient scar—is the word LOVES. Just that single word: Nothing else is legible. Somebody loves somebody, but you can no longer tell who.

ROBERT LOVE TAYLOR

Lady of Spain

—*m*—

WHEN THE Lady of Spain revealed herself to me, I was fourteen years old, the owner of an Allstate motor scooter and a large and shining Polina accordion. The accordion lessons had begun several years earlier with a tiny rented instrument and were held in the Sunday school room of the Britton Baptist Church. My teacher, a red-cheeked, dark-haired woman named Lorena Harris, wore little makeup and pinned her soft dark hair atop her head in a circle capped by a delicate net. I thought her the member of a strict religious sect, perhaps a Nazarene. The Nazarenes, my father once told me, had founded the town of Bethany, then a few miles away from Oklahoma City instead of surrounded by it, and to this day Bethany permitted neither the sale of tobacco nor the showing of movies. I also had the notion that the Nazarenes had no musical instruments in their church—that they only sang their hymns, and therefore would surely scorn Miss Harris's beautiful accordion, so lavishly trimmed in chrome and pearl. I entertained the idea that she might keep it a secret from them, lead two lives or more, like the spies on television who, throughout that innocent decade, kept track of communists, and this was a pleasant notion that bore much embellishment. Late at night, when I grew bored with the radio broadcasts of the latest humiliation of the Oklahoma City Indians, I saw her take her accordion from its plush velvet case, strap it effortlessly to her chest, and begin to play, somewhere in smokeless, movieless Bethany, secret melodies, intricate versions of "Lady of Spain," "Dark Eyes," "La Golondrina." I always imagined her alone, by herself in a room, a version of myself, doomed to solitude but redeemed by strong feeling.

Closed up in my room with bunk beds, an old desk of my father's, and plastic model airplanes dangling above me from the ceiling, I played my accordion for Lorena Harris and for my mother. For Miss Harris I played "Blue Moon," "Sentimental Journey," "Are You Lonesome Tonight"; for my mother, "Whispering Hope," "Nearer My God to Thee," "Sweet Hour of Prayer." The accordion was costly, paid for in large part by money that my mother had managed to put aside from her grocery allowance. It had ten shifts on the treble, so that a single note might be made to sound at one moment rich and deep like an organ and in the next shrill and high like a piccolo. Three shifts lined the bass, and a marvelous black-and-white zigzag design decorated the front of the bellows. Its weight alone bespoke a vast and intricate interior, a secret realm of lever and wheel. What made the sound? A system of trembling reeds, Miss Harris told me. In my mind the word *reed* was highly significant. It was biblical. I remembered that among the reeds of the Nile the baby Moses had been hidden from the Pharaoh.

My father had to travel days at a time from one end of Oklahoma to the other, selling class rings and diplomas and band uniforms to reluctant school districts. I had heard stories of his tribulations. It was all politics, he said. His competitors were expert at politicking a superintendent. They did not permit their products to stand on merit. They sold their souls and robbed him of his rightful customers. I imagined smooth-talking, pallid men, plump in pin-striped suits and black-and-white wing-tipped oxfords. They drove big somber Buicks and their daughters were cheerleaders, their sons quarterbacks.

Such children I had nothing to do with. Anyway, they did not seek me out. My best friend Steve, who had only recently given up his accordion lessons in order to devote more time to baseball, was a quiet, nice churchgoing boy like myself. I knew he had betrayed something important when he quit his accordion lessons. His mother, I remember, attended all his lessons and had a small beginners' accordion of her own that she practiced on, using Steve's music. I heard her play on several occasions, late afternoons when, out of a need for companionship, I played catch with Steve. The songs floated forth from her bedroom as if from a phonograph record, distant and dreamy. Even the bright polkas sounded plaintive and sweet. Several years older than my mother, Steve's mother wore dresses rich with eyelets and lace. Her husband scowled a lot, though he was cheerful enough when spoken to. He was a U.S. marshal. Once I saw his picture in the *Daily Oklahoman*. He was handcuffed to the notorious murderer of entire families, Billy Cook, and although considerably shorter than the killer he looked like he meant business.

My father was surely cut out for better things than measuring the breadth of the fingers of high school juniors for their class rings, the length of their legs for band uniforms. I knew that given the opportunity he would do nothing at all, or else be an artist. A high school teacher of his had urged him to pursue a career in commercial art, but he had graduated from high school in 1932 and had to take what he could get. Selling, he once told me, was the backbone of the country. But there was no conviction in his voice.

During this time his was a quiet presence in the house. He enjoyed a cigar with his evening paper. Then he went out to the office that he had built a few summers ago adjoining our garage, where he worked evenings and sometimes well into the night on his designs for class rings. I liked going out there and was always pleased when asked to deliver a telephone message from a customer, usually some superintendent or principal canceling an appointment. After relaying the message, I sat on a small sofa just behind the desk, lingering amidst an amazing clutter of papers—what could they have been?—orders, bills, magazines, unfinished designs. I remember liking to find copies of the newsletter put out by the company that he worked for, Star Engraving Company of Houston, Texas, a mimeographed pamphlet really, printed on a dozen or so pastel sheets stapled together, its chief function to report on the volume of business done by the sales force, ranking the top salesmen in various categories (rings, caps and gowns, diplomas, invitations, and the like). Finding my father's name most often near the top of each list, I was proud. Sometimes there were notes written by the sales manager or even the president of the company congratulating selected men, the week's leaders.

My father worked diligently at his broad desk, a cigar gone out in the ashtray, a crooked-neck fluorescent lamp glowing and humming softly above his head. Frequently he used a magnifying glass, holding it steady a few inches from the sketch, which might have been a representation of a lion's head or the entranceway to a high school, an Indian's profile or a crouching tiger, or a coiled rattler. Once he had drawn (not for a ring design, of course) a picture of my mother, a pencil sketch of her head in profile, a good likeness and life-size, her long hair upswept in front and cascading into tiny curls on the side and in the back. It was done, I had been told by her, when she was pregnant with me. She looked stern, even a little angry, but a certain serenity also came through. The picture hung in a white frame above their bed, and I thought it a very romantic thing to have drawn and wished that I had such a gift.

What do you think of this? he said, pausing to show me what he worked on. Pretty good, eh? There's nothing in McDowell's line to compete with this.

I believed him an excellent artist, but except for these moments of pride in a new design he spoke disparagingly of his talent. It had been compromised, he said, spoiled before it could be properly developed.

The Allstate motor scooter was the cheapest offered by Sears, its engine only slightly larger than the one on my father's power mower. It had a foot brake and tires the diameter of hubcaps. On it I was nonetheless enabled to crisscross Oklahoma City, circle it, ride out Western Avenue until on either side of me the plains stretched endless, the trees disappeared, and the strong wind in my face smelled of hay and occasionally of cattle or horses. Back in town, I paid visits to girls and took them for rides. They had to ride behind me on the tractor-style seat, their legs straddling my hips, their arms wrapped tightly around my chest. Often I could feel their hair brush against the back of my neck, and I shivered and wished, as we crept up a slight rise, the throttle wide open, for more speed, more power.

That summer I worked as a carhop at the Orange Julius stand on May Avenue, near the Lakewood and Lakeside shopping centers. Sometimes carloads of teenaged girls came in. These girls, mightily rouged and perfumed, their dark mascaraed eyes flashing, hinted in no uncertain terms of the wonderful pleasures one might have in the back seat of their father's Pontiac or Olds 88. I flirted mercilessly and cultivated a swagger, a nonchalant wink, a rakish grin. They told me I was cute, oh so much cuter than the boys their own age, and I began to fancy that I would always have a taste for older women. It did not surprise me that the girls seldom left a tip. Wasn't the feeling we had so briefly shared beyond the realm of appetite and commerce?

Steve, who also worked at the Orange Julius stand, said that if he ever had the chance, he would be in that back seat in a jiffy. I feared for his soul but suspected that he wasn't as likely as I was to be put to the test. My attraction, I believed, was somehow connected to playing the accordion, and Steve had left his accordion-playing to his mother.

What would you do, I asked him, if you were in the back seat of one of those cars with girls in them.

We were picking up trash on the lot during a lull in customers, stabbing at paper cups and wadded napkins with our spears, as we called the broomsticks with nails in the end.

I would know, Steve said. I'd know what to do all right.

What.

It all depends.

If they let you kiss them then, what would you do?

It still all depends.

On what.

It was not the ethics of the situation that concerned me. I was after reliable information, and suspected that Steve might have known something I didn't. I knew precious little, it seemed to me. My two sisters were younger than I was and no help. My curiosity was not just academic. Having kissed a girl before, I was keen on repeating the experience. Was it as pleasant for the girl though? That's what I couldn't imagine. A memory that I cherished was of a party given by my cousin and a few of her girlfriends at which kissing was the object of several games. These girls were a year older than I was, dazzling in their promise, with such smooth red lips and soft warm cheeks, the air surrounding them thick with the scent of a variety of perfumes. A boy was mysteriously chosen and led into a darkened room where one of the girls awaited him, kissed him before he could properly see her, and then he was sent back out to the lighted room, to be greeted by giggles and jeers. I wanted to stay in that darkened room. Let them laugh—in there I wouldn't hear a thing.

That night on the lot of the Orange Julius stand, Steve seemed annoyed by my question, but at last said that what you did after a girl let you kiss her depended on whether she let you kiss her on the cheek or on the mouth.

On the mouth, I said.

Then you just keep kissing her until she says quit it.

What if she doesn't say quit.

They always say quit.

A car came in then—my customer. The girl in this car sat very close to her date, and her hand rested on his thigh. I was the one she looked at—there was no mistaking it—and in that look I suddenly seemed to see all I needed to know. I vowed to memorize her eyes, and also the shape of that hand resting securely on her date's thigh. It was a small hand, the fingernails long and red. Her scent, I told myself, was like fresh almonds, her voice like a love song. She said, I could drink a pint. And her date said, Two pints, thick, no straws. When I picked up their tray after they were finished, she winked at me. Her boyfriend, a big guy in a letter jacket, left no tip. He sprayed gravel getting out of the lot and laid down rubber on May Avenue. Wherever he was taking her, he was in a big hurry. Too big a hurry, I concluded. I knew now that I would treat her different. I'd take my time.

This was the summer that my accordion teacher got married. I saw the man briefly one day as I was leaving my lesson. Leaning against the fender of her car, he smoked a cigarette and seemed on the verge of sleep. Tall and lanky, long-necked and tightly jeaned, he had a head shaped like the grill of an Edsel, with hair congealing into dark ribbonlike strands that curved over his head and curled at the upper reaches of his neck. I could not imagine him with a regular job, or even with one such as my father had. He would stand around like that all day, smoking, contemplating the trees, leaning on some fender. The money from my lessons—I saw it in a flash—would make possible his squalid languor.

Have a good lesson? my mother asked.

It was okay, I said, keeping my eye on the new husband as Mother pulled the car onto Britton Road.

I hope you did, she said. I certainly hope you had a good lesson. It means a lot to have a good lesson.

That was Mr. Cox back there, wasn't it?

Mr. Cox?

Miss Harris's husband.

I didn't see anyone.

He was right there. Leaning against her car.

I must not have noticed.

I'm sure it was him.

Well, maybe it was.

It was him all right.

Maybe it was. I wouldn't know the man if I saw him. I've got other things on my mind.

What could she see in a man like that?

I said I didn't see him.

Where are we going.

Home.

We don't usually go this way.

We had passed Western Avenue and now were in Britton, which was like a small town, though really part of Oklahoma City, on the very edge of it. There was a Main Street with a T.G.&Y. store, a C. R. Anthony Department Store, a Western Auto, and a drugstore that had a good soda fountain. Western Avenue connected it to the city, to supermarkets and shopping centers and subdivisions such as Nichols Hills, where we lived. I rode here often on my motor scooter and liked to imagine that I had come to a town far away from Oklahoma City, perhaps in Texas or New Mexico. In the drugstore I purchased cherry Cokes and then examined the rack of paperback books near the cash register to see if there were any new titles among the westerns and detective thrillers and to read the covers avidly. I picked up a copy of *Playboy*, then a bold new magazine, and discreetly flipped to the centerfold photograph, careful not to linger too long on it before putting it down and then feigning interest in *Field and Stream* or, even duller, *Sports Illustrated*.

At the drugstore my mother pulled into a parking space.

You drive, she said.

Since I had never driven a car before—aside from backing and pulling forward on the driveway—this command came as a surprise.

You've got to learn sometime, she said. She took a deep breath and opened the door. I realized that I was to trade places with her, and I managed to do as she did, get out and cross to the other side, the driver's side.

Have I said that my mother was a beautiful woman? She was. I found this somewhat of an embarrassment, another instance of how my family was not right. Mothers were supposed to be plump and grey, slightly younger versions of grandmothers, but mine was trim and dark, with auburn hair and hazel eyes that flashed brilliantly. Around the house during the summer she wore shorts and high-heeled wedge sandals, usually with a halter top. When she picked me up at my accordion lesson she was on her way home from the volunteer work that she did every Thursday at the big Veterans' Hospital on N.E. 13th Street, and so she always wore what she called her grey-lady uniform, in fact a grey dress rather like a nurse's uniform except for the grey color. But on this Thursday she wore a scoop-necked blouse, white with bright red and green trim around the neckline, and a flowing full skirt, also white, trimmed with the same bright colors as the blouse. So preoccupied with scorn of my music teacher's husband, I had not even noticed this bold departure from her usual Thursday style of dress until, seated at the wheel of her DeSoto, I watched her get in beside me, the engine running smoothly, air conditioner humming.

Push the lever to R, she said. You know how to back up. Just watch where you're going.

Where are we going?

I don't know. For God's sake, I don't know. Nowhere. Anywhere. Will you just go, please.

But I had been struck by two unnerving realizations: first, that I was scared to death to back into the traffic that was steadily coursing through Britton, and, second, that my mother was upset. Tears were in her eyes, and she began to rummage through her purse, at last pulling forth a crumpled tissue. It did not seem the right time for a driving lesson. The car loomed large and lethal, but at the same time was dangerously vulnerable. I kicked at the brake pedal and pretended to have trouble finding R on the gear-shift column.

I don't know, I said. Maybe there's too much traffic.

You just have to watch where you're going, she said, wiping at her eyes with the tattered, lipstick-stained tissue. It will be all right. Just go.

And so I backed the big DeSoto out onto Britton Road ever so slowly, looking from one side to the other. Sure enough, a car had to stop in order to allow me onto the street. Mortified, I pressed the accelerator. The immediate surge forward took my breath away. I gripped the wheel firmly and vowed to remain calm. One only had to concentrate, watch the road ahead, glance now and then into the rearview mirror. Would I have to stop? No, I had traveled this route often on my motor scooter and knew that there was no stoplight or sign between us and the open highway. Once outside Britton—a matter of only several blocks—traffic would fall off, the wide flat prairie land on either side of us, the highway stretching straight ahead as far as the eye could see. The knowledge of this ahead was comforting, and as we crept past the last of the storefronts, and then at last the frame houses on their small treeless lawns gave way to the full breadth of the sky and the land leveled out into immensity, I was certain that I could drive this DeSoto to the end of the continent if need be.

My mother began to sob, softly at first, so that I could easily enough pretend not to notice, and in fact I succeeded quite well in not noticing, such fun it was to see the highway ahead, to feel the power of the big engine, a hundred times greater than that of my motor scooter, that strange sense of limitlessness, as if this were my life itself opening up before me, a straight line to eternity.

I glanced at the speedometer. We were going sixty-five miles per hour yet scarcely seemed to move, so vast was the land that we moved across. The sobbing had grown louder, and, in the quickest of glances, I saw that she covered her face in her hands. The crumpled tissue had fallen to her lap.

It's no good, she said. Everything's all wrong. Every time you think things are getting better, they only get worse.

I didn't know what to say. Really she didn't seem to be addressing me but rather talking to herself. Perhaps she didn't mean for me to have heard. The road was smooth. Soon we would come to the Edmond turnoff. A few distant trees bent to the strong wind, and now and then a red swirl of dust whipped across the highway. The sky was pale blue, cloudless. I was absolutely confident.

Keep going, my mother said. I can't go back yet. I don't care if we end up in Tulsa. I'll tell you when to stop.

I drove and drove. We skirted the city, staying always on the edge of it, away from the traffic, making an almost complete circle by the end. It is one of the most dreamlike memories that I have, those dizzying plains all around, the red soil badly eroded, the tufts of sharply pointed weeds bordering the highway, now and then the skyline of the city appearing, those twin bank buildings rising like grand grey monuments tall and eternal from the sealike vastness, now to the west, now to the north, at last again to the south, and then windmills in the middle of nowhere or oil derricks thumping steadily into the depths of a land that looked as dry as the dust ever blowing across it. The car rolled along, heavy and smooth and quiet. My mother's tears subsided. She told me about the sorrow of her life, and her voice might have been the very sound of the landscape. I cannot imagine that place, that straight highway, those gullies and the red flat land without hearing again her voice as it came to me across the car, the grief in it as pure as any I have ever known.

The reason for my mother's not wearing her grey-lady uniform on that particular afternoon was that there had been a special party on the ward. The veterans had seemed to languish of late, and the women who gave their own time to cheer up the men had agreed that something extraordinary had to be done. Thus the party. It was to be, my mother said, a *real* party. Everyone was to dress up for the occasion in his best clothes. There was to be music, dancing, entertainment, refreshments, the ward decorated with bright-colored streamers and balloons. The balloons would contain messages, and the veterans were to be encouraged to puncture those balloons and find the messages, which would be cheerful, optimistic phrases from *The Prophet* and *The Power of Positive Thinking*. My mother did not care for this last idea. It was treating them like children, she argued, when what they needed was to be treated as responsible adults. How else were they to regain their pride and dignity. She was overruled. The men of the ward were *not* like other men. In many ways they were like little boys—boys who had been asked to assume the responsibilities of manhood before they were ready. They needed to find their lost childhoods. My mother saw that there was no arguing with the other women. At least they had accepted her suggestion that uniforms be put aside in favor of nicer clothes, even though one of them said quite vehemently that to do so was to invite trouble. Wasn't that silly, my mother said to me, and of course I agreed, having no idea what such trouble would mean.

I was never to find out exactly what did happen at that Thursday's party to make her so unhappy, though she talked to me often of her work with the veterans, of how much that work meant to her and at last of the one veteran that she took a very special interest in. Sometimes we went for long drives similar to that first one, drives that she spoke of to my sisters and my father as instruction, but increasingly that instruction occurred late at night in my room, when I lay in the top bunk of my bed only half awake. Sometimes she actually slept in the bottom bunk—other times she returned to her own bed before dawn. I confess that sometimes, tired from a particularly busy night carhopping at the Orange Julius stand, I fell asleep as she talked. Nonetheless, I remember with absolute clarity the underlying sorrow, the sense of lamentation and attendant relief, the strange feeling of shared grief, the notion that I had become for her a confidant, as much sister as son.

I constructed in my own mind a version of the Thursday party, seemed at last to see it as though I had been there. I put this version together as I rode out the highways that crossed wheat fields and prairies, rutted soil and pasture, the same territory we covered in the DeSoto for my instruction. The special veteran would have been waiting for her. He was a lot like me, she had told me, not in looks, of course, but in temperament. *Sensitive* was the word she used. Shy. Kept to himself and thought a lot. Liked to read, and read everything he could get his hands on. She brought him books, paperbacks that she purchased at Rector's downtown, and he received them eagerly, gratefully.

He never had a chance, she said. His father mistreated him, and then he was drafted and sent to Korea. Something bad happened to him over there. Maybe something bad happens to them all, but some can't forget it. Some are haunted by what they had to go through. Can you imagine? It's hard for us to imagine.

I could imagine.

She would have had a book for him on that Thursday, a mystery novel with a lurid cover, carried in her large straw handbag. He would stand to one side of a group of talkative men, somewhat taller than most of them, his face in shadow. Music comes from a portable record player, one similar to my sisters', the size of one of my father's suitcases, with the speaker across the front. It is lively music, music to jitterbug to, to rhumba or samba to. Xavier Cugat, Tommy Dorsey, Bob Crosby. Occasionally a ballad sung by Jo Stafford or Margaret Whiting, a love song, not too sad. Records the women would have brought from home, records such as my parents had, in booklike albums, six big 78s per album, each in its own slot within. Some of the men bat at the balloons. Others dance—this part was harder to imagine. I was no dancer myself, and I concluded that neither would her veteran be. But the others— I had little to go on, junior high school formals, to which the girls wore stiff gauzy dresses.

She would encourage him to dance, for she was a good dancer herself. I had heard my father say so, and even remember seeing him dance with her in our living room. They reminded me of Fred Astaire and Ginger Rogers, whose movies my sisters loved to watch on television, my father spinning her and twirling her, drawing her close, dancing cheek-to-cheek, twirling again so that her full skirt fanned outward and she began to laugh, saying, That's enough now. You'll knock something over. This room is too small, the way you dance! Oh, my father said, you always spoil the fun. Just like your mother! Come on. Let's show the kids what real dancing is like.

But she had had enough, and so the best I could do was picture something like that, incomplete but lovely while it lasted. For the others though, not for my mother and the veteran whom she wished to help. Off to the side the two of them stand. She looks pretty in her white dress, so pretty that the other women are envious.

You should dance, she says. Dancing is good for you.

No, he says, I don't feel like dancing.

Well, would you like a cup of punch then?

No, thanks.

I've brought you a book.

I'm tired of reading.

And with that he turns and leaves her, making his way across the crowded dance floor, through the crepe-paper streamers and the floating balloons and at last down a long narrow hallway and into the tiny room where she would not be permitted to follow him. The room would have bunk beds — made of black metal though, not varnished maple like mine — and a single curtainless window with bars on the outside. He would throw himself upon the bottom bunk and glower at the mattress springs above him, his jaw clenched tightly. Then his terrible memories overcome him and he closes his eyes, sinks into the nightmare of war, bombs flashing and exploding all around him, friends shrieking and dying everywhere.

My mother makes her apologies to the other women.

I have to take my son to his music lesson, she says. He can't carry that heavy accordion on his motor scooter.

She sought understanding from me. While I pretended to understand, much in fact escaped me. I believe I learned to become a good listener, and perhaps, after all, that is a kind of understanding. Coming home late from the Orange Julius stand, my lungs filled with the sweet night air, I sat on the living room floor of the silent house and counted my earnings, then went to bed and awaited my mother's arrival in the bunk beneath me. Sometimes I heard a sound from my parents' bedroom first, the raised voice of my father, and then their door opening, shutting, and her soft footsteps in the hall. I imagine her pausing to look into my sisters' bedroom, seeing them deep in their own dreams, motionless in their twin beds. Why had she not chosen one of them to confide in? One was too young surely, only seven at this time, but the other was just a year younger than I was. This one, however, Carolyn, the elder of the two, was considerably more spirited than I, even scrappy, and often argued long and hard with her mother over issues that I would have let pass as trivial. She seemed to me in fact to go out of her way to pick a fight, and both girls got along better with their daddy, though even he could become the focus of their tempers. There is something with mothers and daughters, finally and significantly, that does not exist with mothers and sons: fundamental antagonism, no doubt a rivalry. Whatever, I was chosen and not one of my sisters.

She came to my doorway and I heard her breathing, even now hear it, and smell again the scent of her perfume, a smell in memory more carnal than floral. Are you asleep? she asks. I know that an answer is not required. She enters my room, and I hear her pull back the bedspread, the sheets, and then feel the bedframe move slightly as she eases herself into the bunk beneath mine. Are you awake? she asks. This time I say yes.

Once she said this: I knew nothing about men, not the first thing about love. My mother told me nothing. I was married to another man before your father. I was too young, and though I cared deeply for him and he loved me, that marriage failed. I thought I would never marry again.

All my life, she said another time, has been a sacrifice for others. I didn't finish high school because my father needed me to bring in an extra paycheck to help support the family. I was the oldest, and happy to help. I know that he was grateful. I worked in Baker's Shoe Store downtown, selling hosiery, and then at the jewelry counter of John A. Brown's. That's where I met your father, and when we were married another long sacrifice began. I learned what it meant to be a mother as well as a wife, to be responsible for a home. Please understand. I don't resent what I've been given. I love my children, all of you. But I have to ask—do you understand this?—when my own time will come, when I can begin to live for myself. Is that so much to ask for, a life of my own?

I said no, that it certainly was not, but I really had no idea what it would mean for her to lead a life of her own. I responded on an abstract level, guided only by a sense of fairness. Life was short, she said, and was one's own. You could kill the life within you if you neglected it. The life within—that's what mattered, that's what must not be allowed to die. It had to be kept alive.

From their hidden homes in the big elm outside my window, the crickets whirred, and above the branches that I loved so much to climb upon in the daytime, the stars no doubt held their own in the broad night sky. Everywhere an eloquence that would not—no matter how much it insisted—be comprehended.

I did not practice my accordion often in the summer, but some mornings before the heat grew deadly I strapped the heavy instrument to my chest and labored mightily to perfect "Clair de Lune" or "Santa Lucia" or "The Washington Post March." My own favorite was something called "Sweet Sugar," a fox-trot in the key, if I remember correctly, of B-flat. Dutifully, to please Lorena Harris (now Mrs. Cox), I worked on chromatic scales, on arpeggios, on bass runs. In the afternoons I rode my motor scooter or had my instruction in the DeSoto.

Before I knew it, August came. In that month heat was general, day and night. My father purchased a small air conditioner, still somewhat of a novelty in those days, and had it installed in a living room window. This room, shut off from the others in order to keep the chilled air effective, became a cool refuge. When the air conditioner was turned on in mid-morning, we all sat around it, watching "Queen for a Day" or reruns of "My Little Margie" or the old movie musicals that my sisters were so fond of. Summer was my father's off-season, since the high schools that he called on were not in session, and so he often sat there in his big green chair, sometimes with a *Daily Oklahoman*, the cigar smoke puffing out from behind it. Mother kept busy in the kitchen or in the back of the house, claiming that the heat did not bother her, though frequently joining us by mid-afternoon—the heat of the day, as she called this time. On milder mornings she might be found stretched out on a towel in the backyard, tanning her legs.

In our talks she came to speak less of her youth—of her overly stern mother and sweetly indulgent father—and more of her dissatisfaction with my father. They argued fiercely all during those years. This had become simply a fact of our family life. Why don't they get divorced? Carolyn wondered. How can two people live together and fight all the time? It made no sense to me either, but mine was not an inquiring mind in those days—if it *ever* has been! Maybe they still love each other, I said to Carolyn. In my heart I knew that this could not be true. Hadn't I heard her say as much?

She began to urge me to visit the ward with her.

I've told the men about you, she said. It would mean so much if you came to visit them.

She wanted me to play my accordion for them. "Lady of Spain," she kept saying. Wouldn't I play "Lady of Spain" for the men on the ward?

It was the last thing I would have chosen to do to end the summer, but there was no resisting her. She wanted "Lady of Spain." She would have it. I thought she might have wanted "Whispering Hope" or perhaps my last recital piece, a complicated arrangement of "The Stars and Stripes Forever" that she had praised fervently, even though I'd made several mistakes and left out an entire section. But it made no difference to me. I'd played "Lady of Spain" almost from the start of my lessons—in increasingly difficult arrangements— and was fond enough of its quick pace and rollicking rhythm. In the sixth grade I'd played it for my girlfriend, who did a dance to it with castanets, on a program for the entire school. Perhaps it was that triumph that my mother remembered. Or perhaps the melody was a favorite of one of the men. Whatever, she had got it into her head that I would play "Lady of Spain."

All right, I said. When?

Thursday, she said.

This gave me five days to prepare myself. Once I had agreed, and the date was set, I began to feel intensely nervous, the way I always felt before those yearly recitals in the Baptist churches that Lorena Harris found for her students to perform in. The more recitals I played in, the more nervous I became beforehand. What got me through was the thought that it would soon be over.

The dynamics of "Lady of Spain" were crucial. So Lorena Harris had taught me, and as I took out the accordion and slid my shoulders into its cushioned straps I seemed to see her clearly before me. She wore a sky-blue blouse of thin gauzy material and a tiered skirt that made a soft swish when she crossed her legs. A strand of her dark hair had come loose from her hairnet, and the top button of her blouse was undone. Soft here, she says, raising a finger to her lips. Now *crescendo*!

Sometimes the student who had his lesson after me did not come, and my lesson continued overtime. We were surrounded by tiny folding chairs, and back of us hung a large bulletin board filled with color pictures of Jesus at the important stages of his life, from manger to cross. On a desk to one side of Lorena Harris, the Sunday school lesson books were stacked in three even ranks. A banner across one wall displayed in large black letters John 3:16, For God so loved the world that he gave his only begotten son . . .

My mother would be waiting in the car, of course, but so would the new husband of Lorena Harris. It was pleasant to think that he was kept waiting. I imagined it while unsnapping the bellows of the accordion, saw him as I listened to the air flow through the mysterious corridors of that strange instrument. He wore pink-soled suede shoes and leaned on the fender of her little Plymouth, his palms pressed against the clean and shining metal. He would have to wait. "Lady of Spain," I played. *Lady of Spain I adore you.* And when I was finished, I played it again.

I practiced hard for the men. As I have said, I was scared to death. There was an edge to this fright that made it worse by far than the usual recital nervousness. Who, after all, were these men that were so eager to hear me play? What did a veteran look like? They have feelings, my mother had told me, just the same as you and me, only they've never been given a chance. But what would they look like?

At the Orange Julius stand the lights that encircled the lot bobbed back and forth in the strong wind, and I fancied them eyes, the eyes of the veterans. With the girls who drove up in their fathers' big cars, I flirted as usual, but my heart was not in it.

I asked my father if sometime in the fall I might go along with him on one of his sales trips. I must have been feeling guilty for having agreed to play on the ward. Unlike those veterans, he had never been to war. When the

Japanese bombed Pearl Harbor, he had gone down to enlist but was turned away because he had recently become a father—I was the child, of course.

Yes, he would take me along with him sometime. He did not look up from the book he was reading—I think it must have been Sandburg's *Young Abe Lincoln*—and did not remove the cigar from his mouth. The floor lamp shone brightly on his head, through his thinning hair and onto his pink scalp. When my mother and I left for the Veterans' Hospital, he was not home. I thought it just as well. He prided himself on her not having to work outside the home and did not even approve of her volunteer work. Perhaps also he was suspicious, a little jealous. He had good reason to be. Years later, when my mother at last went through with her divorce, she told him she planned to marry one of these veterans. And she did. I could not have foretold such an event, but I sensed the reason in my father's fear of her work.

I hope you know how much this means to me, she said to me in the car.

I assured her I did.

It did not matter how well I played, she said. It was the gesture itself that counted.

I told her I understood.

I did not. Otherwise why would I be shaking so? When at last it came time to strap on the instrument, I felt faint. The great black thing was impossibly heavy.

The men milled about, tall and short, young and old. Some wore blue pajamas with white trim at the sleeve and pants cuff. Others dressed as if for a formal ball, white shirts and bow ties, gleaming black shoes. Still others wore T-shirts and blue jeans. I thought there were hundreds of them, but surely there could not have been more than thirty. The room itself was small. Couches and chairs had been pushed back against the walls, and some of the older men, their mouths hanging open and eyelids half shut, slumped in the big cushions, clutched the arms of the chairs as if they expected sudden movement. Through the high oblong windows above the seated men, the glass so thick it was almost opaque, I saw the bars that I had imagined.

Grey ladies circulated among the men, carrying trays of paper cups and paper napkins. One of the women I had met before—she had come to our house on several occasions—but the others, perhaps there were six of them altogether, I had never seen. Yet they looked familiar. The grey dresses, of course, were identical, the same stiff uniform my mother wore. They smiled pleasantly, handing out the punch with ease. They might have been, I realized, the mothers of my friends.

My mother led me from group to group. *This is my son.* I shook innumerable hands, gripping firmly as my father had taught me. No, they invariably said, you couldn't have a son this big! They were all well mannered, soft-spoken, polite. One man kissed my mother's hand.

I must have been brought there to meet the man my mother would later marry, though I remember no such meeting. The man I've come to know as my stepfather must have been one of the inconspicuous ones. He would have preferred watching me from a distance. My mother has explained to me that he cannot work because he refuses to be bossed around. They live on a government pension in an apartment complex near Will Rogers Field. Fearing robbery, they seldom go out. It is not an unfounded fear. Apartments all around them have been hit. He recently screwed shut their windows and during my last visit sat up all one night, his recliner turned to face the window, watching to be sure that no mischief was done to my poor, shabby car.

My father remarried—twice, but the first marriage was brief. She was a schoolteacher, a widow, and must have known right away that she had made a mistake. By then he had become a little wild, spending a lot of time in singles bars and not keeping track of where the money went. He lost his job—also more than once. He took to representing several companies, no longer handling profitable class rings and diplomas but textbooks, which he lugged around to the adopting school districts all over Oklahoma and the Texas panhandle. He no longer worked on his designs for class rings, of course. The house where he'd had his office was sold when he went into bankruptcy, not long after I started college. In the end he achieved a degree of stability. His last marriage lasted four years, until his death by heart failure quite suddenly last year. He was sixty-nine. He had begun to draw and paint again and was tolerably solvent.

That afternoon in the ward I played "Lady of Spain," and as I played, my fear passed away. In its place came a strange elation. The men listened, and their listening was of a different order from what I felt at recitals. They too might have played the tune, the sentimental quality of it giving way to a passion that went into the depths of all music and included my mother in it, drew her into it. *Lady of Spain!* When I saw her, that grey lady, that dark-eyed Nazarene atremble in the shadows of shades of men, it was as if I saw all the women I would love. This was music, this was the life within, this was the love I would sell my soul to possess. The air that set the reeds to quaver, God help me, might have been my own breath.

JOCELYN BARTKEVICIUS

Hat Check Noir

Who told thee that thou wast naked?
—Genesis 3:11

THE EMERALD ROOM has been smashed to pieces, carted away by trucks. Mounds of dirt and broken concrete spill out into the parking lot. The Emerald Room was once a fortress, a huge stucco building set on an island of concrete extending across the sand and into Long Island Sound. The place, so vast in my childhood and memory, looks small in its emptiness. I climb over a mound and find the high concrete pool deck intact. The waves below beat against it. The in-ground pool remains, still aquamarine and white. At the bottom, in a few feet of murky water, is a broken dining room chair, emerald green vinyl, torn. I stand on a mound and see, half buried, the filter system's round wooden cover. There, underground, my stepfather's brother died in his arms one summer day. My foot just misses the bleached skeleton of a cat, sharp eyeteeth exposed, more fierce in death than in life. It is 1996, and The Emerald Room, like Forty-second Street New York, has been disassembled. Gone are the last traces of seediness, the final remnants of desire.

My mother must have gazed for years across East Broadway. From the little tar-shingled house we shared with her mother and brothers, she could see The Emerald Room's neon sign, the cars pulling in, and hear, on a still summer night, a snatch of jazz from the band. Summer afternoons we walked together on the beach or on the sidewalk along East Broadway, and I learned that the road was wide—a boulevard—so that men had room to pull up and yell things about her legs in those shorts, her breasts in that blouse.

At night she'd look out the front window at the club framed by the beach, Long Island Sound, and East Broadway, and I'd look out the back door at the small amusement park. I listened to the drumbeat of the merry-go-round, felt it boom in my chest. Nearly back-to-back, our dreams pulled us in different directions. I hoped for the quick pleasure of an evening: pink cotton candy dissolving on the back of my tongue, a fast ride in a circle, the rise and fall of a carousel horse, arm held out for the unreachable silver ring, the drumbeat taking over my heart. My mother, too, longed for glitter and excitement: sequined blouses, satin high heels, live big-band music, vodka Collinses burning their way down her throat. But she also dreamed of something more substantial: of rescue, being transported out of the shack, her mother's house—house without a father—into the arms of the man in the dark suit and flashy car, into the story line she'd watched so often in *To Have and Have Not* and *Casablanca*, her favorites.

In 1962, when I was six, she married again, and The Emerald Room was ours.

In the darkened room, the hydraulic stage rose above our heads. Couples sat at vast tables or cozy booths, bottles and glasses before them. I sat with my stepfather, Kirdy, and my mother. They were shapes, presences, shadows blocking the stage lights. They were whiffs of cologne, a vague warmth. Kirdy disappeared, returned, the music changed. He disappeared and appeared again. The band started "Tequila" with a quick Latin beat. The exotic dancer, in sequined G-string and pasties, pranced round the stage. In front of me, on a crisp white tablecloth lit by candles, was a plate of food I'd picked over: a few French fries, a glob of ketchup, half a steak sandwich, crust of bread. In front of me was the stripper holding out her arms, rocking her torso hula-hoop fashion, twirling the tassels on her pasties. You looked straight ahead, your vision as unwavering as the channel lights above.

The Emerald Room was a film noir set, Kirdy the hero. He moved quickly through darkened rooms in a black suit, smoking cigarettes, downing Scotches. He was Rick in Casablanca. Saturday night was the rise of the stage, the blare of the horns, the beat of the drum, cigarette smoke, a woman disrobing, an M.C. telling jokes, couples dancing, the clink of glasses, the family table in the dining room, moon over Long Island Sound as we drove off for breakfast at the Duchess Diner. The Emerald Room was a prominence, a concrete block constructed by Kirdy and his brother, set out from surrounding buildings (cottages, Malafronte's meat market, Anne's Newfield Bakery, the tiny branch of the A&P). It stretched from land to beach to sea.

Waves splashed against concrete, against rusting support rods that jutted out into the crests and above, signaling that the brothers weren't yet done, that they would pour more concrete, extend The Emerald Room farther out against the tides. Summer days meant sitting by the saltwater pool looking out over sparkling water or down at people lying in the sand, at Kirdy and his brother who dug for clams below. Home was an old two-story grey clapboard just a mile from the club, but away from the beach, a place where the poor and bums didn't live. My mother and Kirdy built a barroom—a little replica of The Emerald Room—a vast rectangular addition with red geometric rugs and a black-and-gold padded vinyl bar. They made a baby, a colicky girl who cried all night. Home was the new room filled with smoke, men at the bar, women along the walls on couches and chairs. Downstairs the party, upstairs the children. Home was the new baby screaming in the dark, until I climbed into her crib to calm her down.

Sunday was a somnambulistic blur, a visit with my father and then *bam*—Monday morning, and the fluorescent lights of school, the smell of children's puke made of sour milk and spaghetti sauce. At the reading table we got our first word, "Look," in giant letters under a picture of Sally. Little blonde Sally looked at Spot the dog. "Look," we all said. We turned the page and Spot was running. "See Spot run," we said. We were learning baby talk, baby read. We were reading about how someone thought we lived, like Dick and Jane, all pudgy-cheeked and smiling, tucked safe away on a tree-lined street. Father lived with them and smiled and wore baggy suits so you didn't think about what was underneath. He waved goodbye to Mother who stayed home, protected in her apron, cotton shield. She baked all day, invented ways to make children smile, keep them chubby and small, especially the girls, while Dick ran wild through the neighborhood with Spot. Dick and Dad out in the wild world and all us girls inside.

But I knew the secret place adults went to at night, the last moment of the show, "Tequila," what it all built up to, what everyone was waiting for.

Other than Barbie's, the exotic dancers' were the first grown-up bodies I saw exposed, or almost, since by law they stopped at G-string and pasties. My mother and grandmother always covered themselves carefully, sleeping in long flannel nightgowns or pajamas, emerging from the bathroom fully dressed each morning. Barbie, you would think, with her sculpted curves, that idealized woman's body for little girls to play with, to hold in idle hands, would intersect with Saturday nights. But our play was tame, scripted by Mattel. She shopped for new clothes, went to parties, set up her big cardboard Dream House.

Barbie didn't have a body and she wasn't a woman. I held her in my hand. I saw molded pink plastic. The strippers had bodies, soft bouncy flesh, curves and fat under lightly tanned skin. Barbie was hard and unforgiving, immovable in those days before the snapping, bendable knees. Her foot was perpetually arched like my mother's, jutting from open-toed high heels. Strippers had arched feet too, but glided across the stage, smooth and graceful, raising a leg high into the air to remove a silk stocking. Barbie was a mannequin, a clothes hanger. The idea was to dress her, and we even got directions with the clothes: Dress Barbie feet first, the way a real model dresses. Her legs grew dark from the sweat of my hands. Her body remained immovable as her beehive hair, unkissable plastic lips pursed forever in petulant disfavor, blue eyes staring, perpetually fishlike. The exotic dancers moved and danced, blew kisses, peeled off clothes like onion skin.

Those first three years in the club, before I was tall enough to work the hatcheck room, I shadowed my mother like an understudy, a tiny replica quiet at her side. By day we sat near the pool, laughing and drinking—Tom Collinses for her, pitchers of Coke for me. Now and then Kirdy and his brother swam the length of the pool underwater, emerged laughing loud, telling jokes. Aside from that the brothers painted, built, and repaired as if The Emerald Room rested on their shoulders.

By night we sat at the family table looking calm and pretty while Kirdy jumped up to cook steaks and lobsters, work the lights, talk to his brother, greet customers, or grab a quick shot in the bar with the men. It was the perfect table, just inside the French doors from the lobby, set diagonal to the stage. It allowed clear access to the lobby, light panel, and hydraulic lever that worked the stage. Kirdy could survey the whole dining room: the entertainers, the customers, his wife and stepdaughter, the waiters in their tuxedos carrying drink trays in the air or holding out arms lined with plates of lobster and steak. Three lines of drinks fanned out on our table—Send one to the Stellas, the regulars said. Shotglasses of amber fanned out in front of Kirdy, tall frosted glasses ringed with citrus near my mother, and Seven-Ups with maraschino cherries by me. Their drinks disappeared as steadily as they arrived while I rarely got through my second, and my mother and Kirdy lost me, perhaps, in the blur.

The show began with a roar as the hydraulic car lift—converted and concealed beneath the stage by Kirdy and his brother—raised the stage above the tables, transforming the wooden dance floor into a platform for entertainers. The band, in a permanently raised shell behind the stage, played something from Benny Goodman as the master of ceremonies burst through the kitchen's swinging double doors, jogged across the room between tables, up the three steps, and stood mid-stage, mike in hand, legs wide as if balancing on a moving ship. He told the kind of jokes I wasn't supposed to get: men turning up in the ladies' room, babies conceived in back seats of cars, and a few I really couldn't figure out, though I tried to memorize them for later, when I'd gain knowledge or experience, maturity or sophistication—whatever you got with the passage of time.

Near the end of his act, the comic introduced the singer. She walked out of the kitchen, sultry in a red satin evening gown with stiletto heels to match. She sang slow jazz and popular tunes, "Moon Over Miami" or "Misty," which the women called out for. Her hair glowed under the bright lights until the comic came back, initiated applause, and helped her down the stairs. He told one more joke, then introduced what they'd been waiting for, a woman with a name as exotic as her dance, something foreign, like Monique, Jade, or Tanya. (Less often she had a hooker name, like Candy Kane, after whose act Kirdy berated his agent in a long long-distance call.) Sophisticated as the singer, the dancer paused at the swinging kitchen doors, then walked out slowly—back straight, hips rolling—to the stairs where the comic offered his hand. He served her up like a lady. He saved his special voice for her introduction, low, almost hushed, and he looked at her with reverence. She could really dance, this Monique, Jade, or Tanya (unlike Candy Kane, who bounced and wiggled), and she changed her dance for each song, for each layer of clothing she removed—one or two pieces per song—from "Satin Doll" to "Take the A Train" to "Tequila." At the transitions, Kirdy rose up from our table to work the lights, turning off one or two of the channel lights as the dancer undressed, illuminating her body with soft pastels.

Within three years our world split open. Beneath the concrete pool deck where we drank and laughed, Kirdy's brother was electrocuted while tending the filter system, falling back into Kirdy's arms. Before: sun on the water, brothers clamming at low tide, brothers and wives drinking by the sparkling pool, freshly painted buildings, Kirdy's laugh. After: the hushed women by the pool and Kirdy perpetually working, still life in overalls with scraper and paintbrush. And still he kept up those Saturday nights.

On Saturday mornings we prepared for the night. Kirdy's work began at dawn. I'd creep downstairs and find him leaning over a row of cards and sipping coffee, an eyebrow rising and falling, planning his work, reading his life. If he saw me in the doorway he waved me away or collected the cards, then jumped into his old station wagon—the back filled with tools, boxes, planks that hung out the back window—to go buy the food (live lobsters, headless shrimp, a side of beef). He carved and cooked what could be prepared ahead of time. One cracked and callused hand gripped the side of beef while the other sliced through it quickly, carving steaks on the butcher-block table in the nightclub's kitchen. His white apron was bloodstained by the time he turned the lobsters over on their backs, one by one, and gutted them while their claws writhed. He cooked the stuffing, stuffed the lobsters, slid them into the oven. He cut potatoes into French fries. He oversaw the setup, the stock, the staff. My mother's youngest brother, Norman, who had followed across East Broadway in our wake, helped out in the kitchen, cleaning the broilers and throwing salads together.

With the TV on, my mother lounged on the couch in her orange bathrobe, saving up for the night, encouraging me to join her. My sister, now a toddler, napped at her side or sat on the kitchen floor peeling labels from cans of Campbell's chicken noodle soup and Shop Rite peas. Come rest, my mother said, conserve your energy, and so I went outside with a superball or hid out in my room with Barbie. Rest, my mother believed, was all that stood between her and pasty skin and dark circles under the eyes. She worked to maintain a presence fit for the owner's wife, to look—until we closed the club at 2:00 A.M.—like the prized younger woman she was. As my mother got ready those long afternoons, a movie flickered in the background. Lauren Bacall won Bogart's cold heart in some nightclub in Martinique, or Sam Spade solved a crime and broke a heart.

Kirdy would race in, head to his small bathroom in the old part of the house to ditch the flannel shirt or white T-shirt, his dirty painter's pants. Don't forget your balloon pants, my mother teased. She'd shown him the new men's suits in *Life*, the slimmer pants, but he resisted. You could parachute from a plane in those baggy, pleated things, she said when he emerged in a dark suit.

The bathroom steamy from her shower, her hair in curlers, my mother stood in a nightgown applying makeup to her pretty face. In the door frame hung the night's possible outfits: a pink sequined blouse and black skirt, a little black dress, a red Jackie Kennedy suit she never chose. She believed a woman's instep must be prominently arched, must thrust itself out of black or silver spike-heeled shoes, and she lined the shoes up beside the closet door. If she caught a glimpse of me flying past the door with my tomboy walk, she stepped out of the bathroom, called me back, and made me walk up and down the room, practicing the stride her shoes produced, preparing me for womanhood. Stay on the floor, she said. Put the energy into your hips, not your legs. And she'd demonstrate. "Wrong" was walking up on toes, bobbing vertically. "Right" was sliding hips from side to side, head drawing one continuous line parallel to the floor.

Slender, buxom, clear-complected, and pretty (you're Irish and you're beautiful, a stranger said to her one night), with nothing to hide, my mother used clothes and makeup to accentuate. She wore high heels to extend long legs and firm calves, outlined eyes in black, filled in and carefully arched slender brows, reddened and blotted lips. Lift the toilet seat on a Saturday afternoon and you'd find a perfect square of tissue imprinted with my mother's red lips, floating like a lily pad.

The year I turned ten my mother became the maitre d' and I became the hatcheck girl. I made the transition from sitting at the family table to being an entrepreneur. One Friday afternoon Kirdy walked me into the bar, led me behind the counter, and opened the old silver-toned cash register. Like an abbreviated slot machine, it rang up two black zeros with a two-syllable ring. Kirdy, who had been working on the hydraulic system beneath the stage, looked incongruous behind the bar in his grease-stained pants and faded flannel shirt from Bradlees.

Here, he said, counting out twenties, a loan against the first few months' take. He gave me a small stack of twenties, more than I'd ever held in my hands. Next we went into the kitchen. This is for your tips, he said, and pulled down a roll basket from the shelves. He sent me off with my mother to Alexander's department store where I invested in my concession. We looked at the special hangers, thick varnished wood, pine and cedar, suitable for heavy fur coats, suitable for displaying to customers in expensive suits. I was not used to such extravagance: Barbie clothes cost ninety-nine cents, or the better ones a couple of dollars. A new shirt for me might cost a few dollars more. And so it frightened me to spend nearly a hundred dollars that day on enough hangers to fill two large shopping bags. All that money, all that heft to carry out of the store, and nothing to play with or wear.

That evening I went with Kirdy to fix up my concession. He brought a vacuum cleaner, Windex, and a roll of paper towels. Any change from the hangers? he asked. I must have looked pained when I gave him the few coins left from shopping. It's a business, he said, an investment. He put a five in my tip basket and walked away.

A hatcheck girl was the movies, woman in black, red lipstick against flickering shadows, a nightclub in New York, the 1940s. A hatcheck girl was me, ten and skinny and just tall enough to reach the hangers and shelf above. I lined fedoras in a row, green plastic numbers leaning against them. Far back in the narrow wedge of the room I tended, I rubbed my face in a rabbit coat, leaned back into the minks, disappearing into animal skins, into darkness.

At home I played with Barbie, blonde and bubble-headed, dressing her up in satin and velvet. On Saturday night she stayed home and I dressed myself in black and fake sequins to work at the club. I dressed Barbie, I dressed me, and what was the difference? Her body was curvy but plastic, mine soft but flat. It was the end result that counted, the clothes, not us.

Outside it was 1966 and the good girls still wore Peter Pan collars, crisp white blouses, pleated skirts, and knee socks. The radio played the Beatles and Rolling Stones until my mother switched to "The William B. Williams Show," which had Frank Sinatra instead. Shadows on the evening news: people shouting, fists up; people on fire; soldiers running, diving onto the ground. People were saying things like, *maybe it's time to drop the big one over there*, a slogan they picked up on TV. But inside The Emerald Room it was still 1945, the big war just over, Kirdy and his customers swaggering in the hubris of their monumental victory. They thought back to their tour of duty over there (or for the women, to the letters they wrote our boys over there). They danced to the same music, threw the American dollar around, left me wool hats and fur coats, dropped a fin in my tip basket, and ordered up bottles of Scotch as they watched the burlesque show imported directly from Forty-second Street, New York, New York.

I worked a long narrow wedge of a room off the lobby. If I leaned on my counter I could see the lush red lobby stretching out before me, the telephone booth, the carpeted staircase to hotel rooms (for summer tourists and weekend revelers), and the cigarette machine with Fred the policeman leaning against it. To my right, French doors opened onto the dining room, where a woman disrobed slowly to "Satin Doll." To my left was the bar, cool green and dark, teeming with men holding cigarettes and shots of Scotch. On the counter my breadbasket overflowed with bills. Just outside the lobby, a valet met cars under the marquee, opened doors, mumbled obsequious pleasantries, took keys. The marquee was white, art deco, a wedge. On top of the marquee, "The Emerald Room" in huge green letters against a block of white light faced up East Broadway, the avenue that followed east along Long Island Sound. On the tinted front window of the bar, "The Emerald Room" glowed in green neon. From inside the coatroom I imagined those signs, how they called people into our world.

Downstairs in the foyer beyond my left wall was the grand entrance, invisible from where I stood. When customers entered, the Venetian blinds banged as the lobby door shut. I felt a blast of cold. I'd hear them scuff their shoes on the stairs, wipe their feet on the rubber mat. And then (some just ahead of the men who held the door or saw to the car keys) the women emerged into my field of vision. Next to my counter, a sign leaned against the wall: *Hats and Coats Checked, 25 Cents*. But unless I spoke, the customers, mesmerized by the music, the laughter, the colored lights of the dining room, were likely to walk by.

Would you like to check your coats? I'd ask newcomers. They would turn abruptly, startled perhaps at seeing a child. The regulars faced me immediately upon entering the lobby, the women waiting impatiently for the gentlemen to help with their coats. The couple we called Fred and Ginger (for their elaborate dance routines between shows) stood that way, barely speaking, the woman looking somewhere off beyond me with distrust, as if she expected me to smear a Hershey bar on her rabbit coat. The men held their wives' coats like beloved animals, in two hands, lifted them over my counter, exchanging fur for plastic tags. They'd slip the tag into a pocket as I hung the coat on a thick wooden hanger with a twin tag over the hook.

Though newcomers were surprised, they were sometimes less disdainful, and those new men stopped to flirt with me on their way from dining room to bar. The men's bathroom—with its "Gents" sign hand-painted by Kirdy— was strategically located in the bar, virtually men only on Saturday nights. On trips to the bathroom, before their wives missed them, the men could stop for a shot, catch a score from the TV, and flirt with a little blonde hat-check girl whose slightly made-up face and faux sequined shirt belied her age. The women's bathroom—with a preprinted plastic panel labeled "Ladies"— was in the dining room, a short walk from even the least desirable tables, just down from the swinging door to the kitchen, far from the exit to the lobby.

On summer days I walked with Kirdy out into the water in front of The Emerald Room or a half-mile away at the point (where the Housatonic River empties into Long Island Sound) and searched for clams. Kirdy tied the mesh bag around his waist, and I tossed clams over as I found them. His green-plaid boxer bathing suit ballooned out, rose and fell with the waves. He bought me a bright red clamming fork with enamel paint that stayed intact and bright in spite of being immersed in corrosive saltwater and being scraped against sand, stones, and clams. Together we raked the ocean floor. We walked carefully, feeling the sandbar beneath the water, feet like hands tracing the ripples left by the undertow, searching for clams. Like clamming forks, feet recognize the difference between clam and rock, the angle of protuberance, the texture, the ridges. With a wave of his hand, Kirdy dismissed the new poison signs that stretched out along the shore.

Look at this, he said, something moved in here. He held out a conch shell half the size of my fist. I walked toward him, my legs heavy against the water. He held the shell sideways, opening facing me. A hermit crab stuck out its claw. I took the shell to observe more closely, the claw retreating and jutting out, grabbing at the air. There he goes, I said, letting the crab sink slowly into the murky depths. Kirdy lifted his rake and put another fat cherrystone clam into the mesh bag. You know your mother won't eat these, he said. He nodded toward the poison signs. She'll listen to that, he added. I know it, I said. He shrugged. Well, he said, she doesn't know what she's missing. It's just gonna be you and me, kid.

I reveled in the rare moment of culinary fellowship; usually I was the butt of such remarks, abstaining while he and my mother gobbled down squid, frog legs, pungent fried fish, or escarole and chicory thick with olive oil and bitter herbs. We turned back to our work, silent in the rhythm of our raking and the waves. After an hour we walked back out of the water, clamming forks and burlap bag full of clams becoming heavier as the water subsided. I trotted over the hot sand while Kirdy walked slowly, oblivious to pain. We took home a bushel bag full of fat clams, their grey shells etched with white grooves. I made cocktail sauce out of ketchup, horseradish, Tabasco, and lemon, while Kirdy opened a dozen clams with a flick of his flat, dull knife. Whatever poisons the signs warned against were imperceptible to eye, nose, and tongue and we ate the clams raw just as we had for years.

At home, Norman baby-sat some evenings. He was my mother's baby brother, only twelve years older than I, and in the days when we lived together in my grandmother's house, I had pretended he was my big brother. One night he came in and as usual turned on the TV and opened a beer. I got out my patent leather Barbie case, designed to suggest a woman's carry-on makeup case. Play Barbie, I said. Get outta here, he said. Please? I opened the cardboard Dream House, took Barbie and her clothes out of the case. Forget it, Norman said. Come on, I said, whining slightly.

Finally he agreed, a long shot come true. I grabbed the Ken doll from the closet upstairs.

Barbie can fix up the house while Ken goes to work, Norman said. He grabbed the doll and took off into the kitchen. Ken went to work shoeless, dressed in tight brown pants and a striped sweater. I set up furniture in the three-sided house: sturdy cardboard couch and chair in a deep red plaid, a pullout bed. I found a tiny plastic hanger for each Barbie outfit and hung everything neatly in the open closet. Kneeling, I brought out my favorite Barbie dress: red velvet strapless top with white satin flowing knee-length skirt. I dressed her from the feet up (like a real fashion model), struggling to pull the fitted top over her breasts. When she was ready I hunted for the missing white high heel, and found it just as Ken came home from work.

Ken came home from work via Norman sliding across the floor on his knees. He held Ken by the torso, and began knocking furniture around with the stiff plastic legs. Ahhh, he said, feigning a scream, Ken comes home drunk! Stop it, I said. He kicked the furniture out of the house, ripped the clothes from the closet. Quit it, I yelled. Ken comes home drunk, he said, and beats up Barbie. Ken kicked Barbie, harder and harder, sometimes striking her stomach or legs, sometimes getting my hand instead, until he knocked her out of my grip.

In the concrete edifice, an ocean away from Long Island, a boulevard away from my grandmother's house, far from home and dressed in a mock-adult costume, I took a break from the hatcheck room to sit at the family table. The dancer's long strides took her round and round the stage. Couples at tables nearly touching the stage looked up at her, up long legs at her G-string, up a softly rounded belly to the underside of her breasts. Farther back, I sat with my mother and Kirdy. The dancer unfastened her top, and suddenly a hand was on my arm. Kirdy leaned over, shook my arm. The silver top sparkled in the dancer's hand. His hand gripped my arm tighter, his face moved close to mine. You see that? he said into my ear. He shook my arm again. That's a pig, he said. Around and around she danced, shaking, strutting. All faces were raised to her. I don't ever want to see you up there, he said. He moved his face away and let go of my arm. The smell of Scotch and Old Spice lingered about me. My face felt warm, I wanted to tell him that in all my girlish imaginings, of which there had been a few—an embrace from one of the Beatles, becoming the TV detective called Honey who flirted and kept an ocelot for a pet—never once had I imagined stepping onto a stage and undressing before a roomful of people. But I said nothing. I looked straight ahead, my vision a steady beam like the channel lights he got up just then to tend. The dancer sat on the edge of an emerald green chair, removed one spike-heeled shoe, pulled her stocking down slowly. Kirdy dimmed the lights.

Fifth grade was recitation: *four threes are twelve, four fours are sixteen, four score and seven years ago*. It was the German shepherd in the yard alongside our classroom howling with the twelve-o'clock whistle. Mr. K.—the most popular teacher, and the first man we'd had in grade school—said, I had to leave my car at home, it's a stationary wagon. He said, take a good look at that grammar book, store it at the back of your desks, and you'll never see it again. Not once that year did we study his abhorred grammar. Girls whose parents worked real jobs wore pleated skirts, white blouses, knee socks, Band-Aids on knees. We brought our Barbies and cases to school, showed them off secretly in the coatroom, then concealed them beneath our coats. Fifth grade was history, geography, hangman on the blackboard, murals at the back of the room. At lunchtime we played Red Rover and fence tag, boys and girls at war, capturing and imprisoning each other against the chain-link fence at the top of the hill.

School was a grade divided in half and choosing your half: the artsy wimp section (usually girls) that stayed in with Miss H. to draw, or the gutsy athletic one (usually boys) that played touch football out in the sun. It was huddling and then racing up and down the narrow side field, a former airstrip said to be haunted by ghosts from a plane crash. It was Mr. K. as quarterback on the girls' team. It was running out as wide receiver, watching the ball spiral out from Mr. K.'s fingertips into my arms. Outside, we ran with the boys— our legs fast, our skirts flying up. But back inside (quietly, one hand beneath the reading table, a big foot dragging your leg toward him, a fingertip lifting a hem), Mr. K. reminded us that we were girls.

An intermezzo of memory: I walked through the dining room, comic on stage to my right, waiters at the kitchen doors to my left. In the dim ladies' room I walked past the dancer who was fixing her makeup at the mirror, went into the middle stall, and when I emerged she was still there, standing by the black vinyl seat of an old dining booth, her body round and smooth as a scaled-down Botticelli nude. She was soft, silent, her black hair long and shining. She was staring at me. I washed then dried my hands, and the electric dryer drowned out the music and voices from beyond the door. I kept my head down, intent on my hands, dry beyond dryness, warm air spreading over them. Finally I had to turn and she was standing there still. She wore a sheer blouse over her costume, her stomach puffed a bit like my cousins'. We were the same height, but I was girl skinny and I kept my head down. She told me she was not always like that, that she was watery before her time of the month, that mine was the kind of body to be proud of, that mine was the kind of body she could have. She looked at me with desire and regret as I had looked only at possessions (like the rabbit stole of a friend's Barbie). And she looked at me, at my waist and thighs, until I left, walked back out into the darkened dining room, into the music, the smoke, the night.

School followed Saturday night, Saturday night followed school. I didn't know our work was suspect until Cindy, my best friend from school, couldn't come to the club to swim in the pool or build castles on the beach, not even on a hot Indian summer day with no show, entertainers back in New York City, waiters and band members in their day jobs. That year I went to church from time to time with Cindy's family and sat surrounded by stained glass and booming arpeggios in an unfamiliar church. Before my mother's remarriage, when we'd lived with her mother, I'd follow Grandma up the hill to the small church on Maplewood Avenue and sit quietly beside her as she played the organ in the choir loft.

But Myrtle Beach Church had been torn down as the neighborhood began to crumble. Church that year with Cindy's parents was a drive to Milford Center, older girls from the rich side of town who shot looks at us and said, girls from the beach, *those beachies in our church*. It was the minister reading from Genesis.

It was finding out that until the snake came to entice them, the first woman and the first man did not realize what it meant to be naked, how bodies must be concealed. They sinned, and then the Lord came down to walk upon the earth and said: *Who told thee that thou wast naked?* And because they'd found out, the snake had to slide on his belly, the man had to work hard planting seeds in dust, and the woman had to suffer pain in childbirth. But she also had to feel desire. Only to the woman did the Lord assign two consequences, only to her did he speak of desire. And her desire brought more trouble: *Thy desire shall be to thy husband, and he shall rule over thee.*

"Tequila": breasts bouncing, silver-tasseled pasties spinning to the quick beat, dancer circling the stage, spinning, spinning, mesmerizing the men with that siren song. Tanya held two long boa constrictors and then they held her, crawling over the surface of her body, wrapping themselves slowly around her arms, and then her torso. One extended down her thigh. Her hips gyrated. The snakes clung to her flesh.

At the end of her act, she pranced—clothed in pasties, G-string, and snakes—down the steps, across the dining room, through the swinging doors, and into the kitchen. When I went in to order French fries from Uncle Norman, she was still there, standing under the fluorescent lights, the two snakes stretched out across the butcher-block table. Norman tended a broiler, then turned to look at the snakes. Their scales were iridescent in the fluorescent light. *Here,* Tanya said, *touch them.* I ran my hand lightly over one snake's midsection. It was not scaly, not slimy. Cool and dry, the snake lay quietly before me.

On New Year's Eve 1966, I stood alone in the coatroom. Outside, the teenagers I admired were having parties in basements or vans parked along the beach, wearing torn jeans, keeping warm by dreaming up the Summer of Love. My parents were somewhere in the dark, inside the vast dining room or taking refuge out back, on the pool deck over Long Island Sound. The band played "Sing Sing Sing" and the customers, more than a hundred of them, formed a line, a long snaking line of people, hands on the hips of the person in front. The line bounced and gyrated among the tables and booths, around the stairs, up into the elevated tier of the back dining room. They wore cardboard hats—pointy gold and silver hats, fake fezzes with scalloped bands, glitter-covered tiaras. They wore leis of red, silver, and green, and clutched plastic horns or spinners, which they blew and spun like mechanical mating calls. They were crazed, circling the room like a wagon train. They danced and bumped to the heavy drumbeat, then burst through the double doors to the kitchen, invading even the off-limits enclave of the club.

A lone man stepped up to my window. He staggered a bit, then leaned his elbows on my counter. Happy New Year, sweetheart, he said. His eyes were half closed, his lips puckered for a kiss. I stepped backward slowly, back into the row of coats. C'mere, he said, Come on. He opened his eyes. I stared at him, but didn't move.

Oh, he said, your tag. He fished in his pockets, pants then jacket, inside and out, then the chest pocket of his shirt. He slapped his chest and sides. Come bring me my hat, he said, it's New Year's Eve. He took out a ten-dollar bill. The band stopped. A pause between songs. The undulating line must have remained in the kitchen; there was an eerie silence in the dining room. The man waved his money at me. And then I heard them, the crowd laughing and blowing horns, strange moose calls, as they moved from the kitchen to the bar and then headed for the lobby, passed my coatroom, gathered up the drunk man with them, and danced back into the dining room, full circle, as the band leader started the countdown, ten, nine, eight, seven . . . The crowd shouted numbers along with him. When they reached one, he yelled Happy New Year. Horns blew, churners churned, bells rang. The band started up "Auld Lang Syne." Couples kissed, then ran to the pay phone to call the people they loved.

Just like that it was 1967. I stood in the hatcheck room alone.

The snake crawls, the man labors, the woman aches and desires. My stepfather's garden was a film noir set, an island of concrete reaching out over the beach, into Long Island Sound.

These were the bodies: the dancers' barely clothed bodies up on the stage gazed upon by anyone who could afford a nice suit, a full bottle of good Scotch, and a date in fur and sequins; the fifth grader's fully clothed body surreptitiously touched under the reading table by a popular teacher; the child's bare arm grabbed in the night by a stepfather intent on moral lessons; the

first man's and first woman's bodies concealed from each other and even
from their maker; the customers' bodies covered in suits and fur; the girl's
body pressing back into the depths of the hatcheck room, away from the prof-
fered kiss of a drunken man; and even a Barbie doll's molded plastic form
beaten by her drunken boyfriend. Bodies to be exposed or concealed, bodies
to be caressed or molested, women's bodies steeped in desire or calling it
forth from the men. I asked Kirdy about the club, some amorphously phrased
moral question. It's the customers, he said, I only give them what they want.

The money came from the men's pockets, a thick fold of bills held together with a clip. The women stood high up on the stage, making everyone
look. At the end of the night Kirdy gave them some of those dollar bills. Did
they undress to make the men look, or did the men and their money make
them undress? Did Barbie draw Ken's wrath—and I Uncle Norman's—or did
Uncle Norman as Ken produce it on his own? Did something in our bodies
make Mr. K. run his fingers along our legs, or did he decide to do it on his
own? Perhaps there was a simple answer, someone standing behind the curtain like the Wizard of Oz, a powerful booming voice fooling everyone until
the curtain drew back and we looked behind the curtain. I tried for a moment to look behind the curtain. But I was only ten.

I tried to imagine Barbie at the club. But at The Emerald Room, the fine
nuances of clothing (a color, a texture, a cut) and the fine nuances of the
body (a curve, a walk, a glance) seemed to take on subtle meanings. You
could risk getting it wrong. Or you could stand back, keep quiet, watch. I
crossed East Broadway as if it were a wide and dangerous moat, entered the
great stucco club set up on its concrete island. There, with her idealized
woman's body, Barbie's directions seemed all wrong: Dressing her from the
feet up like a real model was somehow moving in the wrong direction; her
velvet and satin dress seemed destined for more than a quiet evening with
Ken. It called for touching, for swift removal. And so Barbie stayed home in
her Dream House, in my lavender room, world of my childhood. I took my
place behind the counter at The Emerald Room, in the shadowed recesses
of the hatcheck room among the furs, beyond the touch of the men. At
school I tried to sit at the far end of the reading table. And soon I put Barbie
away for good.

By 1970, urban renewal swept closer and the neighborhood began collapsing
around us. Tourist strips like ours—designed on a small scale after Coney
Island or Atlantic City—turned into homes for the dregs. Street people with
vaguely biblical names—The Cat Lady, Jimmy the Fisherman, Junkyard
Ruthie—walked the streets and slept in alleys, abandoned buildings, on the

sand, or in corners of garages for a few dollars' rent. Gone were my grand-mother's house, the amusement park out back, the church, the neighbor-hood. The great old expanse of East Broadway was obliterated with sand, dirt, and rocks. The neighborhood gone, the rides and boardwalk and hot-dog stands torn down, summer people stopped coming to the beach. The Emer-ald Room remained just outside the wrecking ball's arc, tucked away behind a row of old apartments and St. Gabriel's Roman Catholic Church.

The years passed in a blur of drinks, stage lights perpetually dimming. Rivers from upper New England carried layers of waste; chemical sediments lined the shores and decimated shellfish beds. Waves eroded the beach. Disco—not burlesque—drew crowds, and as the regulars grew older, died, or moved away, no young people replaced them. Old soldiers faded away, and 1945 became a distant memory culled from the movies.

Day by day our world disintegrated. Kirdy hired Charlie Pride for a con-cert and advertised on a local country radio station, but admission fees didn't add up. Kirdy asked my cousins and me how to decorate for teenagers, how to attract them, and in spite of our shrugs tried "splash parties"—rock bands out by the pool. But like the country music crowd, teenagers spent little money. And both crowds lacked the glamour of burlesque. Drinks fanned out on Kirdy's table. Thick tongued, he descended into reminiscence: the night Don Rickles imitated the way he and his brother walked, head down, pacing round and round the stage, yelling out, I'm looking for money, look-ing for money. The night Christine Jorgensen undressed behind her scrim, reading poetry while slowly shedding her clothes.

By the time I turned twenty, the men at the bar trembled before taking the morning's first drink. Old enough to serve liquor, I worked the bar on sum-mer days. In the dark smoky room, cut off from the salt air, the waves, the town, I walked among the tables setting down shots. Send one to Kirdy, the regulars said, and I placed before him a shot of J&B and a short glass of Schlitz. White paint peeled from stucco. The rooms upstairs—where enter-tainers once changed and slept, where summer people rented all season—stood empty. Even dear old Miss Spooner at last stopped coming. No more Miss Spooner from somewhere up north arriving for her summer therapeu-tic holiday to hobble down the back stairs, black orthopedic shoes left at the landing as she swam the length of the pool or walked with her stark white, overly arched feet in the warm sands. The rooms became a refuge for people just a step away from a night on the sand or the shelter of an abandoned car. The carpets tore. They smelled of mold and ammonia. In the cool green bar, smoke residue settled on the mirrors and tinted windows. "Gents" faded from the men's room door. Vinyl ripped from the chairs. I'd sit in the bar waiting for customers, looking out the tinted glass front door into the empty parking lot.

In 1979, Kirdy ran his last burlesque show for a small, aging audience. Hatcheck girls were no longer useful: customers draped shabby cloth coats over empty chairs, men no longer wore hats. I raced among the tables, balancing the plates of steaks and lobster tails that lined my arms or holding a tray of drinks above my head. Soon, gale-force winds lifted waves above the sea wall, up over the pool, across the deck to batter the glass doors of the dining room. Water seeped in beneath the doors, warping the linoleum, breaking the stage. Instead of shopping for lobsters and beef each Saturday morning, Kirdy went to auctions and flea markets on Sundays, departing before 6:00 A.M. He pushed aside the dining room tables and chairs and piled up bargains until the dining room looked like his own private flea market: glass tables, floor lamps, jars and bowls, bright kitschy paintings, wrought-iron lawn furniture, a stool with goat's feet, a little demon stool.

Nearly a decade later, in the beginning stages of lung cancer, Kirdy finally relinquished his share of the business—what was left of it—to his brother's son. Vandals shattered windows, entered the building, tore down mirrors and doors. Kirdy suffered through a long illness and died. He began to haunt my dreams.

I'd hear his disembodied voice calling my name or see him over my shoulder, in my peripheral vision, or sitting in a chair at the far edge of a room. The men upstairs grew older, seedier. Cats lived among the wreckage in the dining room. Norman, still clinging to what was left of The Emerald Room, rented a small apartment at the edge of the parking lot, watched the building, fed a black-and-white cat named Sylvester. Schylveschter, he'd call in falsetto, forcing a lateral lisp.

In 1995, I walked through the old club with Norman, looking for a memento. Everything of value was gone. The nephew had taken old neon signs and painted out Kirdy's name. White porcelain dishes, ringed in green, lay in shards. My wooden hangers were gone. Up high in a corner I saw a stylized letter "E" for Emerald Room, a speaker cover Kirdy and his brother had made by hand. Norman, overweight and limping, wearing a frayed cotton shirt and old cut-off chinos, climbed a shaky ladder to cut down the speaker. For nearly an hour he labored with wire cutters and pliers until the speaker came down in a shower of plaster and Sheetrock, nearly knocking him from the ladder.

For a few more months, The Emerald Room stood alone. And then the backhoes came. My mother sent me the local newspaper which had printed the story: last of the shore blight to be removed. Thank God, people told reporters. You'd think God drove the backhoes, I told friends. The same year Forty-second Street in New York was renovated—turned from a strip of sex shows to a boulevard of canned family entertainment—on a cold foggy morning in early spring, The Emerald Room was knocked to the ground and the pieces carted off.

My mother, who still lived in the renovated house about a mile away, saw the cranes rise up from the fog as she took a daily walk along the beach. She walked closer and saw the metal ball swinging to and fro, smashing the walls. The Emerald Room fell in upon itself. The hotel on the top floor landed in the dining room, crushing the emerald chairs, the hydraulic stage, the little goat-legged stool.

What was it like, I asked her, when she called to give me the news. Oh, it was nothing, she said, I remember it like it used to be, not what it had become. Then she paused. After a long silence she added that it was decimated as a corpse, and with all its sadness, she could accept its passing as a relief.

The summer of 1996, I return to stand on the wreckage of The Emerald Room. I walk across the parking lot from Norman's broken-down apartment. Don't go, he says. I step over mounds of dirt and concrete, walk back to the pool, look down at the waves, at the rusted rods protruding from the concrete island that Kirdy and his brother never finished extending. I look down at the old filter cover, the dead cat, the remains. A few days later, in a dream, Kirdy arrives for a picnic. Seven years after his death, it is the last time he appears in my dreams. We drive to the rubble with my half-sister in the old blue LTD Kirdy bought her when she turned sixteen. She parks the car at the side of a mound, two wheels raised up on the dirt. The car tips over, but Kirdy, stronger in death than in life, lifts it up, moves it to a flat spot across the lot, and sets it on its tires. My sister and I spread out a crisp white tablecloth for the picnic. Where was the dining room? I ask. I don't know, he says, I can't remember.

Willie

WILLIE COOPER was my aunt. I didn't call her aunt as I did my mother's other sisters. I called her Willie. She was the crucial person in my life.

When I was three I longed for long hair like Willie's. I wanted everything about me to be like Willie.

But Willie said I wouldn't be hunchbacked like her. When I was a grown woman, she said, I would look like all the other women, not like her. Disappointed, I cried. Consoling me, she said, "You'll look like your Mama, Virture. And like our sisters Naomi and Alma, and like the women I sew dresses and evening gowns for. You'll look beautiful."

"I don't want to look like them. I want to look like you, Willie."

Apartment 32
The living room of our apartment at 50 West 112th Street was also Willie's sewing room. When her sewing machine wasn't in use, it stayed in its place, closed and covered by a pea-green damask drapery with faded yellow fringes. Two glass animal figurines, an elephant and a giraffe, and a sapphire blue tin box sat on top of it. When the sewing machine opened up, the living room was transformed into a sewing room. The floor was carpeted with fabrics pinned to tissue-paper patterns. Spools of thread, ribbons, and crinolines were on hand. Yard goods as sheer and crisp as organdy and as heavy and soft as corduroy and plush wool waited to be pressed on the ironing board held up horizontally by one end of the sewing machine and one arm of the sofa. Other materials were draped and strewn with buttons of different sizes and shapes. Willie smoothed her hand and the buttons over the cloth before choosing combinations. She said she wanted to feel whether they'd be comfortable with each other.

I played with the buttons that were coarse and grainy like I imagined the stones were at the bottom of the ocean. I submerged them in the aquamarine waves of cloth I folded under the sewing machine. Shaking the material to cause turbulence, I pretended the stony buttons drifted toward lands where people spoke strange languages I invented from mixing English, a little Chinese, and a hint of West Indian accent I heard in the neighborhood.

Willie's ring-binder notebook was open to the pages with her customers' addresses and appointments for their fittings. Her dressmaking was well known among young women in the Harlem nightclub scene. They were hatcheck and cigarette girls, dancers in chorus lines, singers with small bands and combos, and glamorous frequenters of night spots. When they came for fittings, they unburdened themselves of thoughts and clothing while they assessed their lives and loves. After they left, Willie reminded me that I should not repeat what I had heard.

Willie and I slept in the living room. She unrolled her quilt and blanket onto the sofa. She rolled my cot from the closet and opened it in the middle of the room, leaving just enough space for us to walk sideways between the sofa and the cot in case we had to go to the bathroom. After I was in bed, I watched Willie sew by hand. She sat next to the lamp that lit up the sequins and satin she worked on. Her long, twisted braids looked like swollen streams meandering down her mountainous chest until they settled along the edge of the pool of blue satin lying across her lap. Her fingers flexed like the arms and legs of a ballet dancer, fingernails glossy pink, although never polished or buffed. The thimble on her right middle finger sparked and clicked as it darted over and under, in and out, like fireflies I followed in the dark from the front porch down South. The crooked bones that jutted out of her back were like sharp peaks reflected against a shaded sun on the wall behind her. I wanted to keep looking at Willie, so I tried to force my eyelids to stay up. But they were too heavy, and I had to give in to sleep.

50 West 112th Street was a transient hotel. Six of us lived in Apartment 32 on the third floor: Willie and me, my mother and father, my father's brother Uncle Ted and his wife Alice. Residents of the building rented furnished and unfurnished rooms by the day and by the week, and unfurnished apartments by the week or by the month. We rented by the week, even though we lived there permanently, from the time I was two until I was thirteen. Except for P.S. 170, the fortresslike elementary school in the middle of the block, 50 was the only building on 112th Street that wasn't a five-story walk-up tenement. 50 had seven floors, which meant it had an elevator. It had a wide stoop, in contrast to the narrow ones of the boxy, grey houses along the block. And, most

distinctive, it had a sign that hung outside reading "Rooms and Apartments for Rent, Transient and Permanent."

50 was a busy place, as people were frequently checking in and out through the window in the manager's office in the lobby. Saturday evening brought the largest number of couples registering for a room, though I had no idea at the time what they were up to. Some were exuberant and impatient as they paced and pressed the button for the elevator that would lift them to the floor with the room number scribbled on the slip of paper from the manager's pad. Others looked cautiously suspicious, glancing furtively around the lobby and into the brassy elevator as it rattled and jerked on its chains, bumped down to the lobby level, and the expressionless operator swung open the gold-colored accordion door. Sunday mornings when Willie and I were leaving the building to go to church, couples quietly formed a line to check out. Some had their eyes closed, half asleep, leaning against the wall.

Faces familiar one week weren't around the next.

Weekday afternoons were almost as busy as Saturday evenings. Neighborhood people passed through the dimly lit lobby en route to making the necessary contacts to play the numbers. Their faces were intense. They muttered and mumbled numbers under their breath, heads nodding to the count, as they walked with determination and a sense of urgency. Time was crucial, as the numbers for the day had to be prepared and played on time.

Willie avoided arranging fittings after four in the afternoon. Meanwhile, inside our apartment, Miss Millicent and Angie joined me and Willie around the kitchen table to write their numbers. Miss Millicent was a delicately built woman whom I envisioned being blown away by a strong gust of wind. She had salt-and-pepper hair and spoke in such a soft voice she seemed to be whispering most of the time. She announced that she had reached her third score. At first I didn't understand how she could have made three scores, since I knew Miss Millicent didn't play baseball, therefore couldn't run across home plate. Then she explained to me that a score was twenty years and how to multiply three times twenty. I thought about what a long time it would take for sixty Christmases to come and go. Miss Millicent lived in a single furnished room on one of the upper floors. I overheard talk that about ten years ago a man she had lived with for many years had left her. Since then Miss Millicent wasn't seen with anybody except Willie and the numbers group. Like my family, Miss Millicent rented her room by the week. When I asked her about her arrangement (hoping I'd find out why we paid rent by the week instead of by the month), Miss Millicent said:

"Child, it might save me a few dollars, which God knows I could use, but to tell the truth, you got to put aside a lot o' money to pay your rent at the end o' the month. I can't save up that much. Maybe if I hit big some day I can do that. The way it is now I'd have to work four more hours a day for six whole days straight to get together enough for a month's rent. And besides, I can't count on nothin' beyond a few days. That's why I play the numbers by the day. Some people put 'em in for the whole week. But me, I'll see what happens today, then maybe I'll see what happens tomorrow, if I'm still here. That's the way it is when you're poor."

That must mean, I thought to myself, that we didn't have enough money to pay for a month's rent. But how could that be? We had money. We didn't get relief or stand in a long line for soup and bread like I saw other people doing. I had everything. Willie made me beautiful dresses, even if she used leftover pieces and remnants.

Miss Millicent mentioned certain family members, saying she received a letter from so-and-so, that a cousin would be coming to visit her on such-and-such a day, but she was never seen with anyone. When she came to write her numbers she put on a starched print housedress and brushed her hair until it was slick and shiny. She came alive when she joined us.

"I come here to be with you ladies more religiously than I go to church," Miss Millicent said. "It's nothin' to do with believin' in God or nothin' like that. I just feel like I belong here with you all. Those women in the first two pews look at me like I'm not good enough to be there. But I'm okay here."

Angie, the other regular visitor, had two teenage daughters about whom she worried a lot. She tried to think of ways to keep them from going outside on the street. She fussed about their clothes, nagging them that their dresses were too short or too tight-fitting. Willie was often caught in the middle between Angie's instructions and the girls' preferences. Angie had cause to worry about her older daughter. Willie and I had seen the girl coming out of a bar on 118th Street when Angie thought she was in school. We didn't tell Angie we had seen her daughter, but the following day Willie spoke to the girl about it. But even when she wasn't fretting about something, Angie was fidgeting with her hands, rubbing them on her lap as if she were ironing out wrinkles, squirming in her chair, pacing, and talking nonstop. She chopped off parts of her words, making it a puzzle to complete what she was saying.

Spread out on the kitchen table were a 3 × 5 notepad, the racing results page from the newspaper, a dog-eared paperback entitled *Your Fortune from Your Dreams,* and coin purses half opened, poised to surrender their contents. Conversation concerned others' hits and how winnings would be spent. Pennies, nickels, dimes, and quarters were carefully counted. The pennies were heaped in a mound at one end of the table. The nickels and dimes were stacked high in front of each woman. The quarters were laid out in straight lines like railroad tracks along the sides of the table.

On a particular spring afternoon in 1936, Miss Millicent was complaining about her poor plight. "I showed up on time, no, early, for fifteen years
to clean somebody else's house on Park Avenue. Now I got nothin' to show
for it. They told me I can't get no pension 'cause I didn't pay in. If I could've
paid in I could've saved for myself in the first place. Anyway, a good hit will
make up for it. I'll take that 10:30 shiny silver train to Chicago. I'm not waitin'
no longer for those no-good relatives o' mine to come here. Sometime I think
they never had no intention o' ever comin'."

Restless and bursting to tell her dream, Angie put an end to Miss Millicent's stream of complaints. "Look here, ladies, let's get to it. We're here to
tell our dreams and write our numbers."

Words overlapping, creating new words as she went along, Angie spewed
out her dreams like a pressure cooker letting out steam. She recalled detail
after detail, determined that no part of her nighttime world get lost in the
light of day. Her face lit up with a newly found reason for living. Her hopes
were high, soaring ever higher as a promise of a number drew near. One after another dreams burst forth, as colorful as firecrackers on the Fourth of
July. The dream Angie saved for the last was the one "nibbling away at her
insides" because she didn't understand it.

"The night before last I dreamed my mother's younges' sista, she's my
aunt, but I never think of her as my aunt, well, she was sittin' in my livin'
room, you know, in the chair next to the winda, sippin' a tall glass o' ice tea
with a slice o' lemon floatin' on top. It was in August. I know 'cause it was a
very hot day and she was talkin' about how she and her husband was goin' on
vacation and the pinafo' dresses she was takin' with her. You know she love to
brag and show off. After that she was sayin' she got bad attack o' gas. I mean
ingestion in her stomach. Then right in the middle o' all that she stopped and
looked at me straight in the eye, straight as a arrow, very serious, and told me
I should quit my job, you know, the one I just got a few weeks ago. I remember sayin' to her in my dream 'You must be crazy, girl, as hard as jobs are to
get today,' but the way she look at me I could tell she meant business. I got
nervous, in the dream, you know, so I was tryin' to explain to her that I didn't
want to quit the job, that it suit me fine. I do my housework early while everybody is out the way, then I go to work at the lunch counter late in the afternoon. When I get home at night, they're all asleep. See, at the lunch counter
evenin' is the busiest, and they need me the most then. So naturally, I was anxious to ask her why she was tellin' me to quit. But then I woke up, as mad as
could be 'cause I'll neva know what she woulda said. Now I'm thinkin' and
thinkin' about what the hell is waitin' for me on this damn job."

"Well, Angie, if you did quit this job, you'd be home evenings with the
girls, and that's not such a bad idea," Willie ventured to say.

"And maybe with your husband too, if you can find him," Miss Millicent whispered, almost to herself.

Agitated, Angie raised the window to the fire escape, leaned out, closed it, came back to the table, circled it, and concluded, "I'm not here for advice. Now, darling" (addressing me), "tell me what number I should play."

It was time for me to delve into the dream book. I narrowed down the subjects of Angie's dream and looked up the numbers corresponding to them in *Your Fortune from Your Dreams*. First I located the number for "aunt," then the number for "tea," then "job," after which followed several minutes of disagreement over whether to use "summer," "vacation," and "indigestion," also parts of the dream. Decisions were reached. Once the numbers were identified, it was Willie's turn to use her method of taking percentages of each number, combining the decimal fractions, and coming up with a final composite three-digit number to play. The most tedious figuring completed, the racing results were checked. I didn't understand what part the step played, but it was important enough for Willie to bring out her large magnifying glass to study the seemingly endless columns of minute numbers.

At five years of age I wanted to add, subtract, divide, figure percentages and decimals as fast as Willie did. Instead, I counted the dimes, quarters, nickels, and pennies each person needed to play for the day and I wrote the totals on a separate slip of paper. And I didn't understand what dreams really were. If our eyes were closed and we were sleeping, how could we see so clearly? How could we feel hot, cold, afraid, happy?

The dream that flashed before me at the kitchen table was the recurring one in which I was coming down a slide on a sandy beach. The slide glistened from the sun and was very hot against my legs. I was thrilled to be speeding downhill. As I neared the bottom I noticed the water was dark and slimy in contrast to the white sand. I became panicky the closer I got to the bottom of the slide and to the edge of the water. I wanted to stop sliding, but I couldn't. The speed and the water frightened me. Then I noticed that my mother was standing at the bottom of the slide, at the edge of the muddy water. I stretched out my arms, shouted to her to catch me before I plunged into the murky deep. "Mama, Mama," I called, but she wasn't listening. She was absorbed in something far away. I realized there was no hope of my being rescued. I closed my eyes so everything would be dark like the water I'd soon be sinking into.

I didn't tell anybody about the dream. Not even Willie. And I definitely didn't want to turn my dream into numbers. I wanted my mother to see me before I plunged into the muddy water.

Miss Millicent was still involved in Angie's dream. "Angie honey, I wish my aunt or my cousin or just about anybody was in my living room, even if it was only in a dream. All my dreams are about money, how to stretch it out, what bills to pay first. Ain't that terrible? Come to think of it, I ought to play the number for 'money' every time. Look that up right now, darling."

The women discussed whether to play their numbers "straight" (in exact order) or "in combination" (they would hit if the number came out with the three digits in any order). The latter cost more pennies, nickels, dimes, and quarters. It led to more counting and figuring.

"If I combinate 563, will twenty cents be enough for me to play it 'til Friday?" Angie asked.

Willie set to adding and multiplying again.

Finally, the list of numbers was written on 3 × 5 slips of paper, neatly folded, wrapped in leftover scraps of fabric from Willie's box of remnants, tied with grosgrain ribbons, and placed in Willie's sewing bag, which contained sewing already in progress. She carried the flax-colored linen bag, embroidered with pink and green silky thread, to the store around the corner. Willie's arms were too long for her body, and her right arm hung higher off the ground than her left arm. That was why she carried her sewing bag in her right hand. Willie and I had concluded the reason her right arm was higher was because the huge bone that stuck out on the right side of her back pulled the right arm up and made the left shoulder slump. I knew I couldn't fix it, but I liked knowing the reason for it.

In the store Willie bought the meat that the butcher reported was the leanest he had that day. My mother always wanted pork chops. Accepting the neatly trimmed meat wrapped in thick pink paper, Willie passed the numbers neatly wrapped in prints and solid colored fabric to the runner, who never left home base.

Changes

By December of 1941 Willie was no longer using her sewing machine. She sewed by hand. On the evening of December 7th she cried. President Roosevelt's voice on the radio announcing that Pearl Harbor had been attacked and the country was at war sounded as though he was crying too. I imagined he was removing his eyeglasses and wiping them at the same time Willie was.

A tenant on the floor above us banged on the radiator and yelled for heat. "You cheap bastards down there in the office, you don't have no trouble beatin' down the door to get your rent, but you can't send up no damn heat. You're murderers, just like the Japs and the Nazis."

"They're worse than the Japs and the Nazis," another voice shouted through the pipes. "At least the Japs just started killin' us with bombs. They dump 'em and sneak away. These bastards freeze us to death little by little.

We stupid dopes are payin' them for nothin'. We stayin' here in 50 and let-tin' them suck us dry."

More joined in, up and down the line, banging and yelling. I unbraided Willie's hair and spread it out around her shoulders and down her back. Her hair was like a shawl with curly black fringe at the bottom.

Two months later, on February 12th at three o'clock, a woman with high heels and crimson lipstick waited in the schoolyard of P.S. 170. She wore a swing style coat that blew open in the wind, revealing a low-cut purple dress. I hadn't seen her in the schoolyard before. When I drew closer to her, I re-alized she was my mother. Handing me my gloves and glancing fleetingly in my general direction, she said:

"Willie died. Put your gloves on."

Obediently, I struggled to fit my fingers into the too tight gloves. The at-tempt was a failure, but I was grateful that it gave me something to touch and feel. I am alive, I assured myself, even though I felt like I had left my body behind, there in the schoolyard on 112th Street, and gone somewhere far away. Clearly, I didn't belong to the body standing in the schoolyard. These weren't the fingers that used to fit easily into these gloves. Impatiently, my mother said:

"Hurry up. Time is passing. There are too many things to do. The un-dertaker has to hire a carpenter to make over a casket to fit her short size and then build up the sides and the lid deep enough to cover her chest. That's going to cost more money."

My mother's bobbed hair blew into her face, and she tossed her head to make it fly back in place. Her open-toe and -heel sandals clicked on the side-walk as she pranced down 112th Street. I tried to keep up the pace behind her, but I was forced to stop every fourth or fifth step to pull up my stockings. The garters Willie had made me from leftover elastic used for her customer's puffed sleeves that had fit me snugly were suddenly too loose. And when I bent over to pull up my stockings, my arms seemed longer than they had been when I came to school that morning. Willie's arms were too long for the rest of her body, I thought. I wondered whether the undertaker would cross her arms over her chest like those I'd seen of a dead man lying in a cof-fin pictured in the newspaper. If so, no wonder the undertaker needed to have the sides of the coffin built higher. But there was no time to think about such things. Looking back at me, my mother remembered something else.

"You'll have to go with Willie's body on the train South, to Leesville. We're burying her down there. As soon as we get upstairs, show me the patch in her quilt where she keeps her money. I've gone over every single square in that thing, and for the life of me I can't find the one she left open, or just basted, or however she did it. I can't feel anything inside any of those patches, and they're all sewed up as far as I can see. We'll have to use that money, whatever it comes to, for your train ticket to Leesville and back. Maybe you can go for half fare."

Maybe I won't need a round-trip ticket, I thought. Maybe I'll die, and then I can stay in Leesville. I can be buried right there with Willie. We'll still be together. Now all I have to do is make sure I stay alive until we get there, I reminded myself. I have to take Willie back home. She wanted to go home after coming north.

The Train Ride

Penn Station bustled with people the morning of February 15, 1942. They raced across the marble floor, slippery from a layer of grey slush. Sunlight streamed in through the steel arches of the domed ceiling. Faces looked up at one huge face with black hands hovering over them, as if their destinies depended on it. The excited conversations of the crowd sounded hushed to a low rumble, like the ruffling of drums before building to a climax. For the time being the rumble, though restless, was controlled by the overpowering space. One voice prevailed over the muted ones. It came from the loud-speaker announcing times and track numbers for arriving and departing trains. On one wall crisp white letters against a black field stood up and sat down, like obedient soldiers. Some boasted "On Time."

Servicemen in army, navy, and Marine uniforms crowded into Penn Station that morning, along with travelers in civilian winter clothes. I recognized a few of the red, yellow, and blue insignias on the olive green overcoats of the soldiers. Uncle Ted and I had drawn and colored army symbols while he explained the functions of the units to me. However, I wasn't as familiar with the navy and the Marines. Even though we sang "Anchors aweigh, my boys" and "From the halls of Montezuma to the shores of Tripoli" in school, I knew of no friends or relatives in those branches of service. Signs with painted fingers pointing to Air Raid Shelter Areas hung around the station. Over a table hung a sign saying "U.S.O. Welcomes Our Servicemen," and a young woman with her hair neatly rolled in a high pompadour offered coffee and powdered doughnuts to servicemen passing by. A ticket window sign read "Travelers' Aid."

I was eleven. Headed for Leesville, South Carolina, I was taking Willie's body to be buried in her hometown. I watched two railroad workers load the grey wooden box with the casket onto the train. By its size, the box appeared to contain a child's casket. My mother had said the casket had to be altered to accommodate Willie's short length and protruding chest and hunchback. Willie and I had made this trip together several times before, but on February 15, 1942, Willie was in the baggage car and I was in a passenger car. The seat next to me was empty. An image of my middy blouse hanging alone on the clotheslines outside our kitchen window, buffeted by the wind, came to mind.

As the train left Penn Station and rolled through the black tunnel, I felt a warmth circling my shoulders. I first thought it was a back draft, but the flow came from a different direction and was of a different temperature. It grazed my skin like the wispy voile of a blouse Willie had made for herself two summers before. The light at the end of the tunnel began as a pinpoint, brightened and expanded until it burst wide open into the glare of the over-cast day. Out of the darkness and in the light, the train tested out its new life by gaining speed and setting out officially on its journey.

The train wound its way through freight yards among mazes of tracks that fanned out in curved angles. The brakes and locks screeched. We passed dingy factories with cloudy windows and smokestacks spewing gloomy grey-ness. In the distance, bare branches sketched a thin pencil outline against the charcoal grey sky. But the smooth, steady rhythm of the train was in sync with the beat of my heart. As the wheels speeded up, so did my heart rate. The train and I were one.

In Washington, D.C., I changed trains. Here the signs reading "Colored" and "Whites Only" were more conspicuous than those designating air raid shelters. Along with the other colored passengers, I waited on the platform to board the "colored car" on the Southern Railroad. We hadn't spoken to each other earlier in the trip, but as we gathered in Washington's station, segre-gated from the white passengers, we shared our destinations, talked about the towns further south and the reasons for our trips. When the other colored passengers heard the reason for my trip to Leesville and the fact that I was traveling alone, they joined in the mission. We all watched as Willie's wooden box was transferred to the Southern train. Embraces and "God bless you, child" and "Put your trust in the Lord" were bestowed on me under the "Colored" sign. On that day I was very glad that I was colored and that I be-longed in the colored car.

Portions of the decorative gold painting on the side of the colored car had been erased by time and the elements, but some of the swirls defied aging. The brass handrails that led us up the steps and into the car, as well as the legs of the seats inside, were elegant if not shiny. The original color of the velvet seat covers had faded to an indescribable hue, and the softness of the fabric had worn away and flattened to a thin cottony mesh.

But what the colored car lacked in decor it made up for in friendliness. The colored passengers who boarded for the first time in Washington brought baskets and brown bags of potato salad, biscuits, fried chicken, corn bread, collard greens, and baked macaroni and cheese still warm from the oven. Settled in their seats, they told me what a brave girl I was for bringing my "teeny weeny dead aunt" back home. They spoke about the cold weather, about the atrocities of the war, racial discrimination, and the food we'd share during the trip south. Then, like the hero dashing onto center stage, our colored conductor appeared, assigned exclusively to us in the colored car. On that day it was our privilege to have Mr. Hammon (so his nametag read) at our service. He was a huge man with a huge bass voice. He huffed and puffed as he tore tickets in half, lifted and took down luggage, positioned pillows behind our backs, fetched paper cups for drinks poured from thermoses, complimented ladies on their dresses, their hairstyles, and of course, their cooking, for which he was generously rewarded. He received double portions of every dish and more to take along to the end of his route. But Mr. Hammon deserved every bit and more. He catered to us with politeness and dignity. I was aware he was keeping an eye on me as he went about his activities. As we rode south, I felt the warm feelings from him and the others, but the part of me that wanted to show back my feelings wasn't working. I moved forward with the train, stiff and cold. When he passed by and saw me staring out the window, Mr. Hammon said:

"You go right ahead and cry if you want to."

"I don't feel like crying," I said.

"Well, that's fine. But when you do feel like crying, don't stop yourself. Let those tears come on out," he said.

It struck me that I hadn't cried since Willie died, at least not out loud. I wondered if everybody could tell that.

We rode through farm country where fields stretched as far as I could see, but barren of the crops Willie and I used to see when we came south during the summertime. Cold, hungry, and stripped of their trappings, I imagined the skeleton trees tipping their threadbare hats as we sped by. A few wooden plows, tired from their labor, had slumped to the ground in the middle of their workplace, and were left there to sleep. Wake-up time was still several weeks away, so their stiff limbs didn't stir an inch, even with the shrill of our train whistle.

I thought I recognized a particular field that had been covered with an abundant crop of cotton the summer before. I had told Willie I imagined the puffy little buds of cotton had once belonged to a family of clouds. The cotton buds had behaved like brats, had disobeyed the rules of the clouds, and had pulled away from their family in the sky. After floating down to earth, the cotton buds finally found the right pod to nestle in. "And that's how the cotton buds broke away from the clouds in the sky and came to grow in the cotton fields," I ended my story. Willie had said, "Cotton feels nice and soft, but picking it tears your hands up. All of 'em, my brothers and sisters, used to come home in the evening with their hands cut and bleeding. I didn't go through that, though," she said, "because I was crippled and Papa said I couldn't work in the fields like the others. But I did everything else. I cleaned, washed clothes, ironed, and sewed for all twenty of us. The others were up and out by 6:00 or 6:30 in the morning so they could pick as much cotton as they could before sundown. I was up at 5:00 or 5:30 going out to the smokehouse for ham, cooking hominy grits, and making biscuits. You know, everything we ate and drank came right from our own farm. At noontime and at 6:00 I carried lunch and dinner to all of them out in the fields."

The farther south we got, the more frequently the train stopped. Mr. Hammon said we were wabashing. Just before gathering full steam, the train came to a screeching halt. Then, no sooner had the long, shrill screech ended when the wheels began to work up to a lazy walk, dragging along the tracks. Then it went into a trot, only to slow down again for the next stop. But it kept going forward. I was going forward, with Willie.

Occasionally a little town had its name painted on a weather-beaten shingle nailed to a wooden shed at the side of the road. But more often there was no shed or sign to designate the train stop. Some stops had benches in the dirt road next to the tracks, one bench with "Colored" written on a slat, the other with the words "Whites Only." But regardless of what the signs said about the places, it was Mr. Hammon's lyrical announcements that brought them to life. He called out some destinations in high notes (considering his deep voice), like a rooster crowing in the backyard early in the morning. Others he rang out in rich bass tones that reminded me of big tobacco leaves.

"G O O Olsboro, where the squash and the yams look like gold and taste like honey. They may be hard when you dig 'em out of the ground, but after you cook 'em up they're soft like the butter you churned and melted on top of 'em."

Dark old men with deep lines carved into their faces stood tall and waved as we rode by. They seemed to grow out of the soil. Mr. Hammon whispered to me to wave back. I didn't know why he wanted me to, but I waved. I thought they nodded silently. I wanted to acknowledge their nod, but my body wouldn't respond. It felt stopped up, like my nose when I had a bad cold. I wondered if the dark old men, who looked wise, understood that I was stopped up and couldn't let out what I was feeling.

As the train rolled slowly along, Mr. Hammon stood at the open door to speak to the people standing on the roadside. "Good day, Mr. Taylor, and how are you doing today? You all had quite a bit of rain yesterday. I can tell. They had a little snow up north. Yep, we're on time today."

When he walked up and down the aisle, Mr. Hammon paused sometimes to sit with me. Talking half to himself and half to me, he said, "I like to see the same faces. They come out at the same time every day to see the train pass by. They get their watches out and check the time. Like you see, we stop the train off and on so we can talk. We tell each other what's happening. I told them about you bringing your little aunt back home to be buried. They know you're from New York City. They may not say much, but their prayers are with you."

As we slithered along the tracks into South Carolina, the sky was almost dark. The names of the towns Mr. Hammon called out were familiar to me. People got off and on at places that weren't even clearings in the road. Once, Mr. Hammon stepped off to speak to a woman apparently waiting for him there. After a couple of minutes, he got back on the train and explained to us:

"Sorry for the delay, folks, but I needed to give Miz Sadie news from her sister-in-law in Raleigh. Her brother's overseas. Anyway, thank God, he's all right, according to Miz Sadie's sister-in-law."

When we pulled out of the station in Columbia, I knew we'd soon be in Leesville. Columbia, the state capital, was thirty-two miles from Leesville, Willie had said.

Mr. Hammon took my suitcase down from the rusty overhead rack and held my coat for me. We walked to the open door at the rear of the colored car and stood there in silence, our heads bowed, almost in prayer. The countryside glided past. We wiped droplets of rain from our faces. The train started to slow down from its already lazy lope. I spotted Aunt Mattie and Uncle Mirt among a gathering of people standing in the road. I recognized almost everybody there. They were distant relatives, uncles and aunts by marriage, cousins-in-law, and more cousins second and third removed. I remembered how my head used to spin when Willie explained kin connections to me. People said the towns of Leesville and Batesburg were inhabited by the Coopers, the Humphreys, and the Williamses.

Mr. Hammon sang out, "L E E Esville, the home of Jackie's little aunt. This is the end of her journey."

Some of the passengers in the colored car hugged me goodbye, but I barely felt their arms around me. It was as if a coat of armor prevented their embraces from reaching me. Why can't I feel things? I wondered.

The brakes screeched. It was cold and raining when I stepped off the train. Willie's box, with her inside, was placed on the wet ground next to the train tracks in Leesville.

Leaving Willie's World

Back at 50 I looked for traces of Willie, but they weren't there. Her dresses that had hung behind the living room door were gone. Her quilt roll was gone. So was her hem marker. The trays that had held buttons, bobbins, and snaps were nowhere to be seen. Her baseball notebooks, crammed with facts and figures, were gone. A feeling of panic overwhelmed me. What will I do to find out when the Newark Eagles played the Cuban Stars the last time at the Polo Grounds? What on earth was Satchel Paige's ERA last year?

The box of remnants was gone. The sewing machine was gone.

The suspicion that I had only imagined my life with Willie crept into my thoughts. I went about looking for proof that what I remembered was real. First, I detected tiny holes in the upholstered arm of the chair made by the straight pins Willie had stuck there. Next, I smelled Evening in Paris toilet water when I pressed my face against the back of the door where her dresses used to hang. Once, when we had been at the toiletries counter in Grant's, I had been fascinated by the midnight-blue bottle of Evening in Paris. I had unscrewed the top and doused the toilet water on Willie's dress. She didn't like the scent, but the saleslady said we had to buy it. Willie shook her head and said, "As strong as that toilet water is, we'll be smelling that night in Paris for many years to come." The Evening in Paris–drenched dress was gone, but the musky fragrance on the back of the door lingered, holding its own among the wood and its coating of paint.

Willie was real.

The Remember People

The pastrami sandwiches on rye with mustard and coleslaw that Daddy brought home from his job didn't delight me like they used to. He said it was because they weren't freshly made behind the counter and bitten into right away. He said the rye needed to be warm and moist from the hot pastrami and the plate it was served on needed to be hot, stacked near the oven, and smelling of the seasonings the meat was roasted in. We both knew my decreased delight was more complex than the pastrami sandwiches, though. Even Angie's gumbo with tomatoes and okra was tasteless of the flavors I knew were there. Just as my tears were blocked, so were my taste buds. Still, we went to Daddy's favorite deli, in the Bronx near Yankee Stadium. There we could eat hot pastrami sandwiches on hot plates. And Daddy and I could talk.

"Why did she do it, Daddy? Why did Mama throw away Willie's quilt? Her remnants? Her sewing machine?" I blurted out.

I asked Daddy whatever pressured and perplexed me, without really expecting him to have answers. His explanations seemed too simple, leaving

me more perplexed. Still, I liked trying to trace his route of thought to figure
out how he got from the confusing to the simple.

"Now listen careful," Daddy said, sipping his beer. I ordered celery soda.
"I'm gonna tell you something you don't know. You see, there are two kinds
of people in this world, the people that remember and the people that forget.
They're either one or the other. Now, your Mama, she don't like to remember. See, people who like to forget think if they get rid of stuff that reminds
them of the thing they want to forget, then they'll forget about it. Do you see
what I'm saying? They think if they don't see, they won't think. And if they
don't think, they won't remember. Now, I believe your Mama don't want to
be reminded of Willie. For some people, it's too much for them to remember. What I'm saying is, if you remember, then you may remember some
things you don't want to remember. So some people say, 'No, no, I ain't
gonna remember.' But you and me, we go on and put ourselves through it.
Some time when I'm coming home from work on the subway I start remembering things from times before I was born, things that make me cry."

"How can you remember something that happened before you were
even alive, Daddy?"

"I remember what I heard, what somebody told me, and I think about
how it musta been. See, I'm not saying it's always good to remember everything. You'll feel bad, bad sometimes. Yes sir, you and me, we must be suck-
ers or something, huh?"

"But how could Mama not want to remember Willie? Are you going to
forget Willie?"

"Never."

"Me either, Daddy. I'll always remember her. Even her remnants. She
used the big pieces of material for my slips and the teeny pieces for hair ribbons, button covers, belts, and handkerchiefs. She hemmed the edges for
your white handkerchiefs. Remember, Daddy?"

"Of course I remember. I'm gonna use them for years to come."

"Remember the fuzzy collar on my winter coat when I was in second
grade? That was left over from an outfit Willie made for a chorus line girl.
And remember that dress she made me with the blue and white striped collar and cuffs? She sewed that from a lot of scraps."

"Yeah, I remember. You wore that dress on the train when you and Willie
went south the summer of '36. Yep, you and me, we belong to the Remember People."

"Do you remember that time you and John Quincy were talking till late
one night and you were so sleepy you wanted him to leave? You dozed off,
then woke up and he was still talking and you said, 'Oh, you're leaving now.'

John Quincy said, 'I didn't say anything about leaving,' and you said, 'I must've heard you say it in the short little dream I had. It's a shame things don't happen for real the way they happen in your dreams.'"

"Yeah, I remember that. Man oh man, he kept talkin' about some ol' Model T Ford and all I wanted was to hit the sack. Anyway, after I said what I did, he finally did get up and say, 'Well, Dub, I believe it's time for me to go,' and he didn't get no argument from me."

Daddy and I laughed. "Yes siree, you and me, we're Remember People, all right," he said.

"Maybe Mama wants to forget the hard life they had growing up down south. She was so glad when she and Willie went to Atlantic City. They all say their father worked them too hard."

"Yeah, well, everybody around those parts said he was like a slave driver. I'll tell you one thing, I didn't mess with Mack Cooper. Them hard steel blue eyes shot through you like bullets from his shotgun. But the man had to be hard. He had to be strict. He had to run a farm to earn a living and raise nineteen children by himself. You see, there wasn't much to look forward to down there, except workin' on a farm, 'specially for colored people. Your Mama wasn't the only one who wanted to leave. We felt we could do something beside farming. And even if jobs was hard to get, at least we could see what white people was doin'. At least we could see what was possible, maybe for us, someday. Yeah, your Mama wanted more. She'll always want more. And that's good. She don't want to remember the way it was. She wants to think about better things."

"But once I heard her tell Willie that she wished she could remember their mother, like Willie could. And, Daddy, sometimes she can't remember what just happened, like where she was and what she did. At first I thought she wasn't telling the truth, because she swears it didn't happen, but I realized she really couldn't remember."

"I know, I know. You see, when you can't remember, you want to forget you can't remember."

"Maybe she wants to remember more. You think she'd remember with me the way she remembered with Willie sometimes?"

"Maybe she might."

"Will you remember me, Daddy? You think maybe you'll forget me?" I said.

"Forget you? Forget you? What's going on? Are you crazy or something? How could I forget you? What the hell is wrong with you?" Daddy was yelling and customers in the deli were looking at us.

"Nothing's wrong with me, Daddy. I'm just asking if you'll forget me, that's all."

"What makes you ask such a question? I can't believe you would even dream it's possible for me to forget you." Daddy wiped his eyes, and I realized I had hurt him. "Of course I won't forget you. I can't forget you. It's impossible. That's just the way it is."

I cried. It was the first time since being without Willie. Daddy cried too, but he said it was because he was happy I was crying.

JAMES WALLENSTEIN

Summer's Lease

—ᴍ—

FOR THREE SEASONS of the year I was a wary, abstracted kid who made a point of trying not to care much about what kind of kid he was, who knew, or thought he knew, that no matter what people told him no one was really looking anyway. It was my father who'd taught me this. I'm sure that he meant it to be liberating, but it wasn't. The posture of casual indifference that this knowledge seemed to require one to assume was beyond me. I wasn't the least bit indifferent to my own effect, the very one I supposedly knew that I wasn't having. Even if no one else was looking, I was, pretend as I might not to be. It was a difficult attitude to sustain, and by the time the fourth season rolled around, I was happy to be relieved of the strain. Not consciously—but as it approached, I might catch myself now and again smiling at nothing, or running from nothing in a release of buoyancy.

Considering where I was going, I might have been more unsettled, not less. Pequonset, the boys' camp in the Adirondacks where I spent my early teenage summers, was hospitable only to the handful of serious jocks who'd been recruited and given "scholarships" to play basketball, the sport that counted there. The sense of its importance came to us from the man who taught it, Coach Bax. Whether Bax was his first or last name it didn't occur to us to wonder. In the world of Pequonset he had only one name, like a god. Supervision of the other sports was left to regular counselors, college students on summer break who bunked in our cabins, ate in our mess, and were content to get through their assignments without having to break up too many fights. But Bax was different: he was a grown man, a high school basketball coach who'd been coming to Pequonset to impart the fundamentals of his beloved game since before we'd been born, and there was no threat of disorder in his bailiwick. It was said that he had worked as an assistant in a Division One program, but I never heard him talk about it. I hardly heard him talk about himself at all. His style showed an instinct for the preservation of his own mystique. Living near the edge of the camp grounds with his wife and children in the Winnebago he'd driven from some unheard-of mid-Atlantic town, he was to be seen only on the court where his mastery was absolute.

Our ability to put the skills learned in his drills to use was regularly tested in games with other camps in the area. All competition at Pequonset was serious, but intercamp competition was dire. The fact that we had only half or even a third as many campers as at some other local camps—including our archrival, the richer and better-equipped Camp Tehipitee—served to heighten our siege mentality. We might on occasion be less gifted than our opponents, but we were never less intense. In light of our smaller talent pool, such little-league concessions as "giving everyone a chance to participate" were viewed as unaffordable. The camp's pride was on the line in every contest. Backups were kept on the bench, out of harm's way.

It wouldn't have occurred to us benchwarmers to question our idleness. Pequonset's preoccupation with competition made perfect sense. Winning was the purpose of sports. If we weren't playing to win, why were we playing at all? For a coach to keep his best team on the court was only natural.

Any kid who thought otherwise wasn't going to be very happy at Pequonset. There were always a few such unhappy campers, rookies interested in horseback riding or ham-radio operation or riflery who had somehow washed up among us and who, even if they lasted through one summer, didn't come back. It wasn't so much that they were ostracized as that their interests were ignored. The two nags in the stable were barely fit to trot, a tree root had knocked the floor of the rifle range off its foundation, bats had taken over the ham-radio shack. These kids had come to the wrong camp. For that matter, *anyone* who wasn't at least potentially good enough to help us beat Tehipitee in basketball had come to the wrong camp. And that might have included me.

Except that I liked Pequonset, liked it in my complicated way for its uncomplicatedness, liked it well enough to return there for four summers, and might well have returned for more had things not changed. At Pequonset I knew for once just what I wanted, and the knowledge that I lacked the ability to get it did nothing to make me want it less or differently. In a place where there were no girls and little politics and not much to gain from being cool or clever, where there was no other means of distinguishing oneself, bas-

ketball glory was the only thing to want. And to want it, to embrace its inevitability, was satisfying. It made me feel that I was being realistic, that my
aims were concrete, even while I had no better chance of achieving them
than of realizing any of a hundred other desires that I might otherwise con-
ceive. It was in fact the existence of so many alternative plans during the rest
of the year—of plans to be formed, refined, reassessed, and, once I'd understood that they were *childish*, abandoned—that endowed my single summer
dream with its fascination.

And like every compelling dream, mine carried a trace of reality. The
trace in this case was gustatory—a taste of lemon. Excelling on the court was
only a requirement for glory, not glory itself; a kid might score thirty points
or block a shot in the final seconds to seal the victory without winning any
laurels. His crowning might come later: if, in the course of his heroics, he
hadn't taken over a game schoolyard style but had played disciplined, team-
oriented ball, then Bax might invite him home for a Dixie cup of Mrs. Bax's
lemonade. It was the quietest of triumphs, and so remained faithful to the
coach's idea of a truly worthy basketball performance.

Although Bax extended his invitation discreetly, possibly with a request
not to mention it to the rest of us, stealth was difficult in so small a group,
and it was never long before someone would notice that the hero had slipped
away. We'd cross the fields to a stand of trees from which we could see a dot
who must have been the honored guest seated in front of the Winnebago
with other dots who must have been Coach Bax and his wife. The crinkling
of the paper cups in their hands, the creaking of their fold-up lawn chairs between the chrysanthemum beds Mrs. Bax tended every summer, the pucker-
ing of their cheeks as they sipped the lemonade, the furrows visible on Bax's
brow now that he'd washed off his war-paint-thick zinc oxide sun block—
these details had to be imagined because we dared not get any closer. But we
were more than close enough to fuel our envy.

To taste that lemonade was the ambition of every spy in that stand of
trees. But how many had devised a plan for fulfilling it? And not just any
plan, but a subtle strategy, which transcended banal heroic fantasy and
took into account the strategist's athletic limitations? I had: while other
kids measured their success in practice by points scored, I would make an
impression by contributing in all other ways, by blocking out, setting
picks, moving without the ball, taking charges, threading bounce passes
through the lane—by being, in short, the ultimate team player. My every
move was calculated to appeal to the discerning eye of the expert who
knew that the real action took place away from the ball. Bax would be
forced to recognize my value, to see that my play elevated my teammates',

that though I hardly touched the ball, it was no coincidence that my side always won in scrimmages. He would notice how hard I worked on defense and the beating my body took as I selflessly threw it in the way of bigger bodies. And sooner or later, at the end of a game in which I might never have appeared, he would stroll down to my end of the bench and quietly invite me back to the Winnebago. "The starting five could never play the way they do without practicing against him," he'd say to his wife as she poured my cup of lemonade. "This is the one kid out there who really understands the game."

I might as well have planned to grow a foot by drinking gallons of milk. The thinking-man's game I thought I was playing amounted to my running around the court like a chicken that has retained its neuroses even though its head has been cut off. On offense, I set picks that no one used, wound continuously through the lane to no purpose, and, on the rare occasion when someone happened to pass me the ball, refused on my teamplayer principle to shoot it no matter how open I was, making it clear to the other team that they needn't bother guarding me. On defense I pointlessly hounded the man I was guarding even when he was nowhere near the basket, exasperating him but exhausting me. My forays under the basket for rebounds that I'd never come near to getting generally resulted in an elbow to the back of the head, mine or someone else's and sometimes both. My supposedly hyperfundamental game was merely hyperactive, and if I succeeded in attracting Bax's notice it was for him to ask me what the heck I thought I was doing.

But this wasn't how I saw it then. Bax's acknowledgment of my critical role in our basketball success was only a matter of time, I thought. Once it had come, my friends were sure to ask what the coach was like in private. He isn't like anything, I'd say, he's just a regular guy. They'd know that I was holding out on them, but what did they expect?

In the days leading to parents' visiting weekend, Pequonset became a little Potemkin village so that our parents might be pleased with what they saw for themselves and heard from us. Cabins were spruced up, outhouses scrubbed down, fields mowed and chalked, equipment renewed; the counselors turned courteous, the nurses attentive, the cook ambitious; an evening "social" with a nearby girls' camp was held. In my last summer it was decided that our parents would be pleased to see our basketball skills on display.

This exhibition was as different as possible from our normal scrimmages. There was Coke on ice along the sidelines, festoon suspended from the backboard stanchions, music during warmups. Instead of coaching, Bax refereed, charming the parents with his singsong foul calls and broad gestures while the camp director delivered facetious game commentary through a tinny public-address system. Playing loose in keeping with the spirit of the occasion, the jocks smiled whether their hot-dog shots went in or not—the score was an afterthought. Sometimes they even passed the ball to us, the bench-warmers, who for this one game weren't consigned to warm the bench at all. The biggest anomaly of the event was that everyone got to play.

It was one thing for the jocks to take the game lightly. Their reputations were already made. It was another thing for me. The extended playing time was my one chance to show what I could do—not to my father, who had come by himself (my mother would make a separate visit on the following weekend) and was not to be impressed by such things, but to Bax, who from his unfamiliar referee's perspective was sure, I thought, to be struck by the heady, hustling maturity of my every move.

He wasn't. My sense of this exhibition game as a make-or-break opportunity made me even more hyper than usual. With my hail of irrelevant backside screens, denials of imaginary passing lanes, and solo full-court presses, I was a dynamo of useless activity. Had I played in the second half, I'd surely have gotten Bax's attention, in sarcastic form.

As it happened, I was spared this embarrassment. "Whad'yasay we skip out on the rest of this to go sailing?" my father asked at halftime, while some of the other fathers started a pickup game. My father loved to sail and took every opportunity to try to pass his appreciation on to me. These attempts had failed. Sailing bored me. I couldn't see the point of it, hadn't learned the first thing about it.

"Are you kidding? I think I've got four assists already," I said. "I'm going for ten. And you know that kid I was guarding? He's only got two points, and it was a lucky shot. I'm gonna shut him down." I wasn't about to let him make me pass up my big chance, especially not to go sailing.

He took out his pocket comb and ran it through his thinning hair. "That's all very impressive, but I didn't just sit in the car for hours to come here and sit some more. I want to do something too."

"But sailing's not doing anything. You sit there just like you're doing now."

"It's only you who just sits. I sail the boat."

"I'm on the team," I said, nodding at our empty bench. "I can't leave now. It's against the rules."

It was the wrong thing to say. The moment the words were out of my mouth, my father was on his way to speak to the director, who had a word with Bax, who in turn came over to me. "Time alone with the old man. Nothing could be more important," Bax told me, laying his hand on my shoulder. "Go sailing with your pop."

He must have seen my expression fall. "I don't know how much you'd have played in the next half anyway," he added. "We've got to give everyone a chance, you know."

"We'll aim for that point out there, if that's all right with you," my father asked, in an attempt to draw me out. I'd hardly said a word since we'd left the court. It would have been hard to let go of my resentment at being taken away from the game even if I'd wanted to. But my father did nothing to make me want to try, belittling my complaints about a mussel cut I'd gotten wading out and barking boat-rigging instructions at me, referring to jibs and sheets and spars and halyards as though his meaning were self-evident, then doing himself what he'd asked me to do when I didn't understand. By the time we were underway, I half hoped he'd drown.

"That all right with you?" he asked again. I didn't answer. A breeze carried the sound of the basketball bouncing against the asphalt out to us over the water, and I was trying somehow to follow the game from what I heard.

"I'm talking to you."

"Just sail the stupid boat wherever you want," I said. But since I had my back to him and the wind carried my voice away as soon as I'd spoken, I knew that he hadn't heard me.

"You'll have to turn around. Otherwise I'll never catch a word you say out here."

I stayed put, sitting against the mast running my finger along the cut on my foot and looking vacantly at the green-brown wavelets parting before us, the boulders and cedars along the shore and cloud menagerie overhead. My mind was still on the court, even though, as if we had driven over a mountain and lost our car-radio reception in the middle of a broadcast, we were now too far away to hear anything from there. Instead I replayed the first half in my memory. I thought of the loose balls I might have gotten to if I'd been quicker, and vowed to spend more time skipping rope.

After a while my father said, "You're not going to sulk all afternoon, are you? Really, you'd think you were the second coming of Jumpin' Joe Fulks. What does it matter that you missed a little? You certainly didn't seem to enjoy it."

"Did Joe Fulks—whoever the hell *he* is—seem to enjoy himself?" I turned around to make myself heard. "Do you expect me to smile when I play?"

"No, but I don't expect you to look like a maniac either. You seemed crazed out there. You kept running into people—and away from the ball. In fact, the way you play it wouldn't make any difference if there were a ball on the court or not. It might all have been a pantomime." As he said this he began to laugh. He had the kind of laugh that, having started, goes on for a while and plays itself out in snorts and sighs. He never chuckled. When it came to laughter, it was all or nothing with him, calm or uproar.

I started to tell him that he didn't know the first thing about the game, but the wind stuffed most of my words back in my mouth and combined with his laughter to overpower me. I had to shut up till he did. While I waited I realized that I hadn't taken a good look at him since—having driven exactly nine-tenths of a mile past a condemned barn and fire tower onto a pine-lined dirt road leading through a Land-o'-Lakes-style log portal to the center of the camp grounds—he got out of his Buick and ran his big hand roughly through my hair by way of a greeting.

For most of my life I had heard him described as big. The word seemed to refer less to his girth, which was in rough proportion to his height and width, than to his bearing, the size of his presence. But that was before he'd gotten sick, a kidney infection and a bout of pneumonia that seemed to have aged him twenty years. No one described him as big for a while after that. There was supposed to be some compensation in the weight he had lost in the ordeal. Except that now, as I watched him half sitting and half crouching beside the tiller, getting as much use as he could out of a bench that would have been too narrow for him even at his lightest, I saw that he had put all of the weight and a little more back on, that it hadn't come back as muscle, which it was before, and that the vitality and color he had lost with it hadn't come back either. The sallowness of his complexion took the luster from his eyes, like lamps kept on in daylight. His limbs looked flabby, his extremities bloated, his gut rose and fell with the labor of his breathing. Her might again be described as big. But this time, big would mean fat.

As his laughter tapered off he saw me glaring at him and pulled a pipe and tobacco pouch from his pocket. In such a stiff breeze, he needed both hands to prepare his smoke and waved me to the back of the boat to steer.

I nodded my refusal. "Will you please give me a hand?" he asked.

"So that you can smoke? You know you shouldn't be doing that."

He waved dismissively. "Oh, I see. I've insulted you, have I? I'm sorry. I didn't realize that that game was so important to you. There's your problem, you know. You care too much about everything. . . . But why *does* this basketball business matter so much to you?"

"It doesn't. I couldn't care less."

I brooded over his question while he struggled with his pipe and pouch, then found myself yelling at him. "What do you mean, 'my problem'? I had four assists, two steals, and *no* turnovers. My team was plus eight while I was playing and minus five while I wasn't. I'm not the one with the problem. *You* are. You're fat—that's your problem. You wouldn't even be able to make it once up and down the court." His lips curled and eyes narrowed. Then he checked himself, froze his mouth in a wry half-smile, and looked past me as if to consider his situation.

We fell silent sailing towards the far end of the lake where a powerboat seemed to be moving too slowly to keep up the skier it pulled. I started to feel a little bad about what I'd said to him, and was thinking that I'd ask him about the mechanics of water-skiing, but before I'd had the chance he made some kind of announcement.

"Huh?"

"'Coming about!' I said," he said while guiding a rope out of a cleat.

"What's . . . ?"

I heard the sail rustle behind me, then a thud as if from within, and then everything went cold. What happened next is a blank.

I had fallen in. When I came to I was back in the boat, shivering in my wet life jacket and coughing up water, a lump forming on my head. My father was also damp, and sat trying to light his pipe again. "Some sailor you are," he exclaimed while lowering the sail.

We said no more about it. As soon as we got back to shore he stopped in at the camp office to see the director about my bill. When he got out he had other things on his mind.

The summer wore on. My mother came to visit and took me to a Mel Brooks movie at which I laughed so hard that I fell out of my seat. Five straight days of hard rain caused the stream that ran through the middle of the camp to overflow its banks, upending several shallow-rooted oaks—one of which collapsed on the roof of the rec hall—and putting the camp's small fleet of red plastic kayaks and canoes in demand; the odor of damp timber wafted to our bunks from the stilts of our cabins for weeks after the water had receded.

A kid named Randy Edlin joined the exclusive Forty-Sixer Club, which meant that in the course of his summers at Pequonset he had reached the summit of all forty-six of the peaks of the Adirondacks. A kid named Ned Fingerhut, who'd managed to keep his torso hidden all summer, was revealed to have three belly buttons. A kid named Stewart Lieber took a drink from a canteen that had been pissed in. A kid named Harvey Sherzer spent an entire night hugging a tree when the counselor who'd ordered the punishment forgot about him and fell asleep. A kid named Tiny Berman was caught smoking pot. A kid we called Smokey beat up a junior camper, so enraging the director that he went to the unprecedented length of flogging Smokey with the strap of his own belt.

A baseball counselor named Dave who'd supposedly been in the Cleveland Indians' farm system displaced Denis—a longhaired Quebecois tennis counselor who wore a string of beads around his neck, smoked Galloises and insisted that call him "De-*knee*"—in the affections of the camp nurse, whom, like Rocky Raccoon's heartthrob, everyone knew as Nancy. A track-and-field counselor named Bill totaled the head counselor's AMC Pacer. A Scottish soccer counselor named Ian returned in his cups late one night and tried to get us all to sing a Highland drinking song. A swim counselor named Gary got fired for making Harvey Sherzer hug a tree all night.

In the intercamp finale, Pequonset's fourteen-and-under basketball team beat Tehipitee by twenty-three points after their biggest and best player got thrown out for taking a swing at one of ours. The rout was so thorough that even I got in the game, and scored four points.

There were now only two weeks left before we'd be sent home, and expectation was already rising for the outbreak of Color War, when the camp would be split into teams for four days of competition.

Our meetings with Tehipitee were child's play compared to the internecine battles of Color War. The whole summer led up to them. But you had only to count the days to know that we were not there yet, that our regular routine would continue for another ten days or so. Our remaining basketball classes would be looser now that our foe was vanquished, and I hoped that in the relaxed atmosphere certain fundamental skills of mine would come into play and bring me my triumph. In team practices, for instance, I had been unable to show to advantage the left-hand dexterity I'd labored to acquire and vowed to do so now if only I could force myself to play more selfishly. Selfishness, that was the secret, I reminded myself while making my way after breakfast down to the court on one of these mornings. But just then the director intercepted me and suggested that we take a walk.

I hadn't heard of the director taking walks, not with any campers and not in the morning. It was an odd proposal. "But I have Basketball," I objected.

"It can wait." He put his arm around me and began to walk me around an empty softball field between the neglected archery range and the soccer field. "I have some rough news," he continued. "Your dad passed on last night."

Another oddity—the director calling him my "dad." I didn't call him "Dad." Why was he?

"He was just here," I said.

"He went for a run, and collapsed."

"You mean he went jogging?"

"That's right."

I couldn't picture it. I'd never seen my father run, and never seen him fall down. The possibility hadn't occurred to me. My teeth started to tingle.

Very deliberately, like discoursing philosophers, we circuited the diamond. The bases were still in the equipment shed, but as we reached the spot where third would have been I cast a glance at the basketball court. Quite a few heads were turned our way, dumbly, like those of cattle distracted by a passing car from their grazing.

"There's a flight home early this afternoon. I'll have someone drive you to the airport in Schenectady. You'll need to pack a few things for your trip."

As I crossed the footbridge on my way back to the cabin, I ran into a kid named Edmund Pellier who had overslept and was late for the morning's activities. "Forget something?" he asked, not slowing to wait for an answer.

"My father died," I said over my shoulder, and kept walking.

It was a simple explanation. Something had happened, but not to me. The words had been easy to say. Yet it was as though I hadn't said them and they'd come from someone or somewhere else and the statement they formed couldn't be true coming from me, and the subject "my father" was incompatible with the predicate "died." But if the words were a lie, why were my feet now carrying me up the path and through the cabin door and my hands opening my canvas duffel and throwing in the clothes they'd pulled from the shelf? I had no answer for that, none that I could begin to believe.

When I returned to Pequonset a week later, everyone looked surprised to see me, as if I'd been the one to die. Even I was a little surprised to be back. But the solitary mumbling that the members of my family may have heard through the door of my bedroom must have persuaded them that they'd do well to get me out of the house, and I was made to use the second half of that roundtrip ticket.

The camp's surprise quickly changed to deference. In exchange for my loss, I received an unwitting promotion in the social hierarchy. My old group now exempted me from our endless regimen of tests, taunts, put-downs, and dares, while a new group made up of the basketball team's starting five embraced me as a symbol of their commitment to the team concept. The worst thing for their new best friend, they thought, was for him to be alone in his dark hour, and they made sure that I almost never was. Though it might have been guessed from my keeping such company that I was good for fifteen points a game, this worst thing, being alone, was really best. But privacy was an unrecognized need, one that, lacking the self-confidence to insist on, I had to steal to satisfy.

At night, after the others in my cabin were asleep or pretending to be, I'd go outside, clamber to a seat atop a nearby boulder and, gazing through overhanging pine branches, try to preserve my memory of my father. It was in the middle of one of these vigils that I heard a screen door creak, footsteps approach, and, directly below, the splashing of piss against the boulder. When he looked up and said, "Who's that?" I recognized the precociously deep voice of Patrick Smithers, whose early puberty had brought on both the growth spurt that enabled him to become our leading rebounder and a nasty case of acne against which he wielded his special pimple-popping tool, a cross between a corkscrew and an X-acto knife, at the washroom sink. "Who's there?" he asked again.

I didn't say anything, just sat still and hoped he'd go away. But once his stream had run its course, he climbed up himself to find out.

"How're you doin', Patrick?" I asked in as even a tone as I could manage.

"Oh, it's you. How're *you* doin'?"

"I'm fine."

"I'll bet you are. You're a tough man, I know that."

He sat down beside me, and after a while, as if for the first time, asked, "How're you doin?"

"I'm fine."

A few minutes later he said, "I know what it's like. It's tough."

There was extensive nodding on both sides.

"I lost *my* father," he added. "He was a bastard, but it was rough anyway. What about yours? Did he know how to treat your mom, was he a good man?"

It wasn't the kind of question I was ready to entertain. Instead I began wondering what would happen to Smithers if I pushed him off the top of the boulder. Would he split his head open in the fall, or merely break a leg?

A counselor passing below stopped and shined his flashlight on us. "What do you jokers think you're doing out here?" he said. "Lights-out was hours ago." It was Steve Pronatowski, known as Pronto because he was the fastest runner in camp.

"Listen, Pronto. I'm talkin' to my buddy here," Smithers answered, putting his arm around me. "He's got a lot on his mind right now."

"And it'll still be there tomorrow. It's bedtime, gentlemen," said Pronto, and ushered us back to our cabin.

What was Pronto doing prowling around in the middle of the night? As I got back into bed it came to me: Color War was about to break. He had been sent around to make sure that none of us discovered the counselors massed on the hill above us. Soon they'd swoop down in carnival masks or Indian war paint and lead us by torchlight through the woods to a clearing where beside a campfire the director would recount the legend of the Pequonset ghost whose appeasement through the winter depended on the outcome of a contest between the Blue and the Grey. The roll of the teams would be called, captains and lieutenants appointed, friendships and enmities cast aside. We would return to our beds in silence, a silence that would hold throughout the war—all speech not related to its conduct, and thus any communication with members of the opposing team was forbidden and subject to penalty. The cause hung in the balance at every moment.

In any other year I'd have been thrilled to know what was coming, would have woken a couple of friends and sneaked back outside with them. But I found now that I wasn't thrilled at all. Color War would be an intrusion—on what I couldn't exactly say. But I knew enough to realize that my heart wouldn't be in it, that it would put my father that much farther out of reach.

I got dressed and put my flashlight, thirteen dollars that I had stowed away, and three brownies remaining from a tinful my mother had made me in my knapsack. Then I tiptoed over to Thomas Bleckman's bunk. Bleckman was just my size and had the best of every kind of equipment, including a pair of feather-light track shoes that made running feel like flying and a diver's watch, its face crowded with navigation dials. I helped myself to these things and went back outside. It was a long way home, I knew, but with his shoes and watch I thought I'd be able to make it at least as far as Schenectady, where I might be able to talk my way onto a bus.

I hadn't gone a quarter-mile before I was wishing I'd also taken Bleckman's flashlight, a top-of-the-line Maglite that felt as hefty as a nightstick; mine was already dim. I had crossed the footbridge and come out in the open. The moon was full and so bright that I worried about being seen on the camp road and decided that I should make my escape across the fields. As I waded through blue shadows, the ground seemed rougher than it had before and the night cooler, the chill in the swales tightening my throat and the dew soaking through Bleckman's shoes' nylon uppers making me sorry I hadn't brought a sweatshirt. I saw a giant flinty-eyed form humped in the distance and started to run. I stopped and saw that it was a soccer goal, its coated plastic net cording glinting in the moonlight. I kept going, past distance markers on an improvised driving range, through a weedy ditch full of golf balls at the end of the camp property, over the guardrail and onto the margin of the state road.

I knew that fugitives traveled *under cover of darkness*. How far would I go? At least twenty or thirty miles before sunrise, I figured. Then I'd sleep through the day, *with only a mound of earth for a pillow*. There were no lights on the road, no houses or stores, nothing except night birds darting from vines to telephone poles and crickets droning louder than the sound of my steps—a spooky scene, I had to admit if I thought about it, and tried not to, tried just to march like a soldier. A boaty sedan barreled past with its chassis floating on its axles and unsettled me. I'd be all right, I told myself. My father was looking out for me. I wondered why I hadn't looked out for him too.

I walked on and on. I supposed I'd covered five miles or more, and had begun to think about treating myself to one of the brownies in my knapsack when I saw a pair of buildings in the distance, a house with a rounded roof and a tower looming behind—the first structures I'd come to, I realized. Could these be the old barn and fire tower that stood exactly nine tenths of a mile from the camp entrance? But I had gone so much farther than that! I had to have passed them. Yet as I approached them I saw what I was afraid to see. A familiar sign in front warning off trespassers confirmed it. After everything, I hadn't even gone a mile.

Discouraged and thinking there might be some hay in the barn that I could take a little rest on, I looked for a way in. Broken down as the place was, the lock still held on the door, and there were no gaps in the boards big enough for me to squeeze through. I had better luck with the tower. The heavy chain that was supposed to secure the gate was fastened too loosely, and I was able to slip in.

I had never been inside, but I had ridden past the tower often enough on my way back to camp to notice that it narrowed as it went up and that its exposed, zigzagging flights of metal stairs led to a lookout station on top, a little house or cab that I hoped might have some planks to lie on, even a table or chair. Moonlight spilled from the tower's crosshatched iron braces and, pooling at the foot of the steps, seemed to invite me up.

I climbed a few steps and stopped. The tower was unstable. The steps quaked under my feet. The girders creaked. I didn't like heights. The top seemed far up, and there was no railing. I went back to the bottom and started towards the road.

It occurred to me that I might be making a mistake. What if I was *meant* to climb up there, what if the lighted stairway were a *sign*? I turned back, slipped through the gate again, and started to climb, forcing myself to ignore the tower's shaking and not daring to look down till I'd reached the top.

It was a good thing for me that I didn't. A change in the moon's position, or mine, meant that I could hardly see a thing. The well of the tower was swallowed in darkness, and the longer I stared into it the nearer it seemed to swallowing me too. My flashlight cast about as much light as a burning cigarette. I dropped it over the side and listened to it smash against the stairs below. By the time it hit the ground, it was already in bits. I climbed the last few steps.

From the lookout platform, the sky was so close and so starry that it reminded me of a snowy meadow—the stars were packed together like snowflakes and were also as crystalline. I looked at them till I was dizzy and clutched the top of the parapet. The wind blew like mad. The tower was swaying in it. If it couldn't topple the whole structure, it seemed to think that tugging me over the edge was the next best thing. It didn't make me any surer of myself to keep stepping on empty beer cans. I wasn't the first kid to hide out up here, for whatever that was worth. Thinking that I might be able to see the light of the campfire in the woods as Color War broke, I looked back towards camp but saw nothing. The heat I'd worked up during my climb was gone. Every gust made me hold on a little harder and shiver a little faster. This sign that I thought I had seen, whatever it was that had lured me there, had better show itself quickly, I thought. I was too cold to wait around.

When I couldn't stand it anymore, I went to the top of the stairs and tried to make myself step down. The darkness below was overwhelming. I searched with my foot for the first step, but once I thought I'd found it I was afraid to commit my weight to it. One false move and I'd be in as many pieces as my flashlight. They'd never know that I hadn't been holding it when I fell. And even if I was right about this stair, I'd have to take a hundred more blind steps. Sooner or later I'd slip. It'd be better to freeze to death. I'd have to stay till dawn.

I really thought I might freeze. With the platform only three steps across and the boards groaning under every step, it was hard to keep moving. But I was too cold to be still. I tried to stack the beer cans into a little shelter, tried to crawl into my knapsack, tried huddling in every corner of the platform. Wherever I hid, some cold current found its way over the wall or through the chinks and into my bones. I shivered so hard that I was afraid I'd throw myself over the edge.

The wind eventually died down (or maybe I had numbed to it), the shivering stopped, and I slipped into a daze in which it seemed to me that I was still awake, that it was just before daybreak with only the morning star left shining and the sky getting ready to open and the light to break through in powdery specks, that another, warmer breeze came up and felt as it blew over me exactly like my father's hand in my hair when he greeted me, and that my father was there before me, half leaning and half sitting on the ledge. He was big and hardy, the way he looked before he'd gotten sick, but the wall was too low for him to be leaning against and I was worried about him falling over and wanted to warn him. But the words wouldn't come, and as I struggled to utter them I awoke.

Everything was as I had dreamt it: the morning star, the daylight beginning to break through in powdery specks, the warm breeze like my father's hand in my hair—everything except the only thing: my father. He didn't look big and hardy, the way he had before he'd gotten sick, and he wasn't leaning against the low wall of the tower so that I felt I had to warn him. He wasn't there at all. The space in which I had so plainly seen him was empty.

But although I had not been granted a vision of the afterlife, I was permitted to see into the future. I saw that I'd spend years waiting for him to come back, that in every stray flash or whispering breeze or distant chiming I'd seek his presence, and that if these were signs, then, like the light on the stairs tonight, what they'd signal was bewilderment. My eyes lingered on the place where my father had stood. A single pink ray cut through a break in the trees on a ridge top.

I passed Bax's Winnebago on my way back to camp. It wasn't even half past six, but Mrs. Bax was already at work on her chrysanthemums.

"Where are you coming from at this hour, Michael?"

"I went for a walk. How come you know my name?"

"Everyone's heard about your loss."

"Oh."

"I'm sorry for you. You must have been up for a while. Would you like some orange juice or lemonade?"

"No thanks. A little water would be good."

It was still before reveille when I got back to my cabin and put Bleckman's things back in their places. I'd been wrong about Color War. It didn't break until later that day. I took part, mostly because it would have been more trouble not to. They'd have had to change the teams and maybe send me home early too. I didn't care enough to make that kind of fuss. From then on, summer was of a piece with the rest of the year.

PAULA WHYMAN

Driver's Education

THE SIMPLE SAFE SOLUTION DRIVING SCHOOL offered classes at numerous satellite locations in order to serve a larger geographic area. Our classroom was at the end of a deserted corridor in the basement of the Mackleby-Warner department store. At first I thought the basement looked like the set of a slasher movie: The grey tub filled with naked mannequins and spare body parts was the place where the killer hid his victims. Empty plastic hangers stacked to the ceiling on tall, metal poles, and straight pins covering the floor were instruments of torture. If you stepped on the pins just right, they could go through the sole of your shoe. The main level of the store was like the part of the house visitors were allowed to see, everything clean and perfect, with no indication of what might be amiss (ominous music swelling in the background) just One. Floor. Below.

On the first night of class I sat next to Kevin Thorpe by accident, and after that I always sat next to Kevin Thorpe because sitting anywhere else would seem like a slight. And whenever I arrived in class first, he sat down next to me, which made me perspire in the armpits. He was my ideal: blond curly hair, blue eyes, golden tan—California surfer-boy, far from home—and a pimply nose just to make him seem real.

There were other girls in the class. I don't remember them, except that one or two were pretty. There were other boys, too, like the boys who sat in the back of the class, slumped in their seats, laughing at secret jokes, coughing out cuss words when the teacher turned his back. I tried not to look at them when I thought they might see. One of them—I think his name was Todd—was tall and broad, bigger than all the other boys, so he filled the doorway when he walked in. He wore a flannel shirt unbuttoned over a tight, white T-shirt, and he carried a pack of Marlboro Reds in his front pocket. He

made Kevin, who had a solid swimmer's build, look like a scarecrow. I wondered if Todd was eighteen or nineteen and hadn't passed the driving test yet.
Maybe he went on to take it two or three times, or maybe he never passed.
Maybe he's in jail now or on a work-release program; maybe he's straightened himself out, and he'll be at my house next week to patch drywall.

Most of the students were fifteen or sixteen, with learner's permits. I was
one of the youngest. We were there because the free driver's ed program
available in high school wouldn't fit into our class schedules which were full
of college-prep courses or, I suspect in the case of Todd and a few others, because the high school program had proved insufficient preparation for the
test. This class consisted of six weeks of lectures, two nights a week. After you
passed a written test, you could move on to the good part—eight on-the-road
lessons in a car with dual controls.

The classroom instructor was Mr. White. He was a lean black man, forty-
ish, who walked with a limp. One leg wouldn't bend all the way at the knee,
so when he paced back and forth in front of the class, the strain of lifting the
bad leg from the floor and launching it to the next position was visible in the
tendons that stood out on his neck. It was September, and the room was hot.
A fan in the front corner oscillated back and forth but didn't cool anything
beyond the chalkboard where Mr. White scribbled complex x-o diagrams, as
if a football coach were trying to illustrate the correct way of backing out of
a driveway into traffic. Every fifteen seconds or so, the fan would send a small
puff of dust from the chalk tray into the air like a smoke signal. It got so I'd
wait for it, watch the particles float up then rain down in slow motion, like
ash on Pompeii. Each time Mr. White's bad leg came up, we could see
where the toe of his boot had dragged through the chalk dust that had been
blown to the floor. Finally, he wised up and shifted the position of the chalkboard so the fan couldn't blow on it. Kevin and I snickered behind our
hands. This was a bonding moment.

In spite of the heat in the room, Mr. White wore a pinstripe shirt, the
sleeves rolled up to mid-forearm, and brown Sansabelt pants. His forehead
popped with little beads of sweat, which made him seem intense, although
his most common facial expression was one of strained tolerance.

Halfway through the second class, he said, "Let's get this outta the way
now, so you don't sit there wondering about it instead of absorbing every
word I say, 'cause when you're driving, you better hear my voice in your head
until your voice has enough experience"—he enunciated each syllable of the
word "experience"—"to take over." I can hear his voice in my head right
now, but he's not talking about three-point turns.

He sat down on a tall metal stool and, with a grunt, thrust his bad leg out toward us. Then he tapped on his thigh, just above the knee, with a closed fist. It made a sound like hard plastic.

"I got clipped by sniper fire in the village of Quo Luk, Vietnam," he said. "If you think you need to know more than that, ask now. Next topic, lane changes."

There was a hush in the classroom. Someone's stomach growled. What did I know about the Vietnam War? My history class was still talking about the cotton gin. What did I know about getting shot and hobbling around on a plastic leg? I'm still trying to figure it out, my vision admittedly skewed, a cliché fed by years of war movies: Mr. White walks alone on a dusty road, enters a thatched hut village. He sits down on a fallen tree trunk, fumbles for his rations or for a cigarette. His shoes are covered with muck from marching through the jungle. The place is deserted, eerily quiet. The village seems abandoned. Where's the rest of his platoon? He lights his cigarette and notices a shoe in the dirt behind one of the huts, a shoe just like his, but empty, laces cut, in the stained dirt, dirt stained the color of—And right when he realizes he's the only one left, right when he reaches for his gun, a shot comes from nowhere, then another, tearing open his knee. He drops to the ground and hides behind the tree. His mouth twists in angry agony. The blood flows out from between his fingers as he presses his hands to the wound.

My imagination always gets it wrong. He would not have been alone, walking into a village. If he had been alone, he would not have survived.

Week two was eventful. During the break, Kevin asked me out. The class was two hours long, and the break always came halfway through, for twenty minutes. Twenty minutes was a long time. We went upstairs to the shopping level. Kevin bought me green Jelly Bellies, and we played volleyball with a balled-up handout about parallel parking at a net that was set up in sporting goods. He told me his parents were divorced, and his mom still lived in California. He wouldn't see her until Thanksgiving. That's so sad, I told him. I thought about how all the cool kids I knew—the ones who were allowed to stay out till midnight, who wore designer blue jeans and had brand new Betamaxes—had divorced parents. But it wasn't their stuff I admired; there was something romantic about their tragic circumstance, the burden borne in solitude, their stoic worldliness. Not that I wanted my parents to divorce, but I tried to picture them living apart, me and my sister going to stay with my dad on weekends. I couldn't. I was better at imagining myself as Jane Eyre, with no family at all.

The store closed at 9:00 P.M., but our class wasn't over until 9:30, so each night we exited through the darkened hosiery department, past rows of mannequin legs that had been severed at the knee and sheathed in various opaque shades of pantyhose. In the dark they stood above the shopping floor like rent-a-cops, oblivious to the lowlifes slipping by in the shadows. I imagined Mr. White's plastic leg standing tall alongside the others, wearing a sheer sandal-toed variety in nude. Gentlemen prefer Hanes.

The first night of week three, the class ran a few minutes late because Mr. White was going on about the importance of keeping the right amount of empty space in front of you on the highway, one car length for every ten miles of speed. Now, I understand that this will never work, because if you ever have six car lengths ahead of you on I-95, four cars will cut in front of you to fill up the space. But while Mr. White was diagramming car lengths for us, there was a smell of sulfur, and then smoke drifted up from somewhere behind me. I turned around, and it was Todd, sucking on a Marlboro. He narrowed his eyes at me, and I almost looked away. Then, he formed an "O" with his mouth and blew a perfect smoke ring in my direction. Mr. White's voice boomed from the front of the room, and I whipped my head around.

"No smoking during class," he said. This was before the invention of indoor air quality.

"Class is over," said Todd.

"I guess you didn't understand me," said Mr. White. "Put it out, boy."

Everyone watched Todd stand up and shove away an empty desk that blocked the aisle in front of him. The metal feet of the chair screeched against the linoleum at a particularly excruciating pitch. He strutted out the door into the dark corridor. I saw the circle of red on the end of his cigarette recede. When I turned back, Kevin was staring at me. I smiled, but he looked away. A moment later, one of Todd's friends let out a belly laugh. We looked behind us, and in the doorway was a naked mannequin. Todd was hiding in the darkness and with one hand held the mannequin up by its ample and nippleless breast. There was some half-suppressed chuckling and snorting.

"Oh, baby," the mannequin moaned. "You can have the right of way with me." A little puff of cigarette smoke wafted into the room from behind the mannequin's head. There was something else: She was missing a leg.

Mr. White's desk creaked. Like in a tennis match, we all turned to the front to see what he'd do. He swung his leg down from the desk, where he'd been half-sitting. Sweat was popping on his forehead like dew, but being the adult, he exercised self-control.

"Class dismissed," he said quietly, though not the acquiescent or sooth-ing kind of quiet, but rather the kind of quiet that carries a foretaste of menace.

Todd was gone before we reached the hallway. The smell of his smoke still hung in the air.

Kevin and his dad picked me up in a white '79 Caprice. Kevin sat in front, so I had the whole expanse of back seat to myself. The leather squeaked every time we stopped at a light, and Kevin would turn around and look at me, but we barely talked until we were alone. Ever try to figure out what you talked about on a date when you were fifteen? Rocket science and Great Books, right? While we ate pizza, I asked him about California. He told me about surfing in Malibu and Santa Monica, about the tiny scar on his chin from a bad wipeout, about seeing Victoria Principal walk down the street.

"Is she pretty in person?" I asked.

"Sure," said Kevin. "But I guess she looks better on TV."

Everything does. I always wanted to go to California because I was sure I'd be instantly transformed into some beautiful, golden creature.

We saw *Raiders of the Lost Ark*. I didn't tell Kevin I'd already seen it, but I suspected he had too. In between the good scenes, he kissed me, perfectly competent, respectful first-date kissing. I thought about Mr. White and his leg. There was no blood in this movie. Did his leg actually get blown off, or was it amputated? Either way I guessed there would be a lot of blood.

At the end of week three, Mr. White showed us slides of drunk-driving acci-dents and talked about the importance of staying sober on the road.

"Drunk driving is no joke," he said. "You drive drunk, best you can do is lose your license. Worst you can do is kill someone, kill yourself."

Todd and his friends coughed behind me, "Bud. J. D. Drink Bud. J. D."

I wondered how Mr. White ended up teaching our class. If he had a teaching certificate, he could have been a real teacher; I knew that much even then. Now, I think he probably was a real teacher, moonlighting for the extra cash. Maybe he went to college on the GI Bill when he got home with his medal and his honorable discharge.

Back then I wondered what he did in the daytime, but I didn't imagine that he went to work. I figured he slept late, ate corn flakes in his jimmies, and drew up new diagrams for our class on paper napkins. Or he hung around his apartment in a sleeveless undershirt and boxer shorts, not hiding the plastic leg because there was no one there to see, anyway. Maybe he didn't even put the leg on when he was at home. Maybe he hobbled around on a crutch and sat on the couch watching *Hollywood Squares*, cursing. Why did Paul Lynde always get the center square? Why not Rosey Grier or Nipsey Russell? Why'd they always try to keep the black man down? Or maybe there was somebody there. He didn't wear a ring, but I think he had a lady friend who made him dinner sometimes, and then he didn't take his pants off except in the dark because he hated for her to see the stump. Maybe she waited for him in the dark in a red satin nightie, but after that third week he came home and said, "Not tonight, baby," because he couldn't get Todd's mocking face out of his head. Maybe he got mad and had to go out for a walk so he wouldn't slap her when she went all sympathetic on him. "Tell me about it, honey," she'd say, her eyes puppying up. He hated it when she felt sorry for him because of the leg. And she'd pretend she didn't, insist she didn't, but she really did, really. And she hated when he didn't take it off before they made love because he was in a hurry or he wanted it for traction. She hated the way the plastic felt rubbing against her thigh, all cold, when the other side was warm, warm, warm.

Week four, during a break, Kevin kissed me inside the tent camper that was on display in sporting goods. When we came out, he had his arm around me, and Todd was there, lying on a weight bench and pumping iron, clenching an unlit cigarette between his teeth. A vein bulged in the middle of his forehead, and his face was red with exertion. He'd stripped off the flannel shirt and hung it over the weight stand. I could see the outline of his pectoral muscles and his nipples under the T-shirt. I began to sweat in important places. I wondered if this was how animals felt. I swallowed. Todd's biceps overwhelmed the sleeves of his T-shirt, pushing them back so that when he lifted the weights above his head, I could see the black hair in his armpits. I realized I was an animal. When Todd saw me and Kevin, he curled his lip and snorted. I stood there anyway, staring like an idiot, until Kevin put his hand on my waist and steered me back to the elevator.

    "Grit," Kevin muttered. This was another word for redneck. I wonder if it referred to the breakfast cereal or to the axle grease under their fingernails.

    "Do they have grits in California?" I asked.

    "No. Just freaks. Potheads. Rednecks only live in the South, not the West."

    "This isn't the South," I said. "This is a Mid-Atlantic state."

    "Tell the grits that," said Kevin. We were standing near the hanger smokestack. Kevin started to spin the hangers on their pole. "Why do you think Todd hates Mr. White so much?" he asked, as if he knew the answer. He had a whole stack spinning at once. It made a loud clatter.

    "'Cause White won't let him smoke in the classroom," I said.

"Come on," Kevin leaned into me. "It's 'cause he's black."

"No way. He's just bored with the class. It's a boring class."

"You think it's boring?" Kevin looked annoyed.

"The breaks aren't boring," I said.

"I guess not." And he kissed me again. Come on, baby, surf with me.

Right turn on red. Did I know about that before? I never paid attention when I went places in the car until that class. The meaning of a red light was always unambiguous: You stop. End of story. Now, it seemed, it was okay to go on red as long as you took some reasonable precautions. Mr. White used the word "judgment."

"You must have good judgment," he said. "Someone could be turning left from across the intersection." He scribbled a diagram on the board. "Or someone could be coming straight across from the left. And who has the right-of-way in that situation? Mr. Thorpe?"

"The driver with the green light always has the right-of-way," said Kevin.

"Anybody wanna disagree with Mr. Thorpe?" Mr. White asked.

A girl in front raised her hand. "But at a four-way stop, the driver on the right has the right-of-way. So maybe the person on the left has to let me go?"

"But you aren't at a four-way stop. You're at a red light. You got no right-of-way at all. The burden's on you to make sure the way is clear. Mr. Thorpe is correct. The driver with the green has the right-of-way. Exceptions, anyone?"

No one raised his hand.

"I'm sure y'all thought this was too obvious to mention," said Mr. White. "A pedestrian in the crosswalk always has the right-of-way. And even when they don't, even if they're jaywalking, you let 'em go. Why?"

Kevin raised his hand again. "Because you don't want to hit a pedestrian."

"'Cause when they're dead, are you gonna feel good that you had the right-of-way? See, I'm not taking anything for granted in this class," said Mr. White. "Let's review. Right turn on red: When to go?"

"When the way is clear," someone said.

"And you use your what?"

"Judgment," someone else said.

"Good judgment is innate," said Mr. White.

"Who's Nate?" asked Todd.

It was okay to miss one class without making it up, but you couldn't miss more than one and still graduate to the road lessons. The last night of the fifth week, Kevin missed a class. He had stomach flu. I wondered if I would get it. He'd kissed me just the other day, in a fitting room during the break. I was about to let him prove that he could undo my bra-hook with one hand, but we got caught by the saleslady in Better Ready-to-Wear. She knocked on the door and asked if I needed any help. Twenty minutes must've seemed like a long time to her, too.

Kevin answered in a falsetto, "No thanks, honey."

I smacked him on the arm.

"Everyone's called 'honey' around here," he said afterward.

So the night he was sick, he called me at home to say he couldn't come to class, but I'd already left. I wasn't sure what to do at break time without Kevin. A bunch of people were walking to the Orange Bowl for pizza, but I wasn't hungry. I thought about playing basketball in sporting goods, but they'd removed the hoop and replaced it with a dart board. Instead, I haunted the Estée Lauder counter, testing the lavender eye shadow. When I looked in the big round mirror I could see the reflection of Todd and his friends smoking in the mall, just beyond the store entrance. I sampled some lipstick, "Plum Pretty," and ambled back through sporting goods.

"Hey."

I looked around but didn't see anyone.

"Babe."

I stopped and put my hands on my hips. "All right. Who's there?"

"It's not Ke-vin," the voice sang. It was coming from the general vicinity of the camping display. I walked slowly in that direction. "Boo-hoo!" the voice continued. "Loverboy's left you all alone. What will you ever do?"

"Shut up," I said as I got closer.

A cough came from inside the tent camper. "Tough chick. Don't hurt me. Oh, hurt me, please."

I lifted the flap of the tent, and there in the half-light was Todd. "You," I said. "I knew it." I swatted the flap closed and turned to walk away, but Todd was quicker and grabbed my wrist, pulling me into the tent.

He flicked on his cigarette lighter, so I could see his triumphant smile and the dark stubble on his chin. He did not let go of my wrist. "What's the rush? There's ten more minutes." He wasn't wearing a watch, but he was right.

In English class at school we read *A Streetcar Named Desire*, and there was the part where Stanley says to Blanche, "We've had this date from the beginning." I thought of that when Todd put his other arm around my waist and pulled me against him. I could feel his dick pushing at me from inside his chinos. I giggled. He kissed me short and hard, then backed off. He smelled like cigarettes, but he tasted like Trident. He had chewed gum for me.

"What you laughing at?" he asked. He tossed his head, and his brown forelock swung in front of his eyes.

"I don't think I'm your type, exactly," I said.

"What's my type, exactly?"

"You know. Bleached hair, black eyeliner, French-cut jeans. Names like Serena."

"Takes one to know one," he said. He bowed his head to suck on my collarbone where it was revealed at the open neck of my polo shirt and worked his way up to whisper in my ear. "So, that's why we're here," he said, as his hand slithered under my shirt, "'cause I like slutty chicks, not prissy-ass goody-goods." He licked my ear. "And you like Kevins." He straightened up suddenly and stared down at me. "I'm a dumb redneck to you, right, babe?" Without warning, he reached out with the hand that wasn't around my breast and brushed my hair out of my face, tucking it behind my ear in a way that was at once overly familiar and oddly tender. Now, when men do that to me I want to shrug them away. But when he did it, I couldn't say anything. I was having a rare epiphany. Todd, I realized, was a fraud. And it really was easy to unhook my bra one-handed.

Then he kissed me again, and if Kevin kissed like a fish, a teasing nibble here and there, Todd was a shark, carnivorous, devouring. I would sit in class for the rest of the evening feeling like I was covered with a protective film of Todd, and at the same time feeling like I had him inside me, because when I breathed, it was his breath that came out of my mouth, and when I swallowed, it was his spit that ran down the back of my throat.

When I stepped out of the tent to go to class, I saw Mr. White limping by on his way to the elevator. He nodded to me as he passed. Todd came out behind me, and I thought I saw Mr. White's eyes get narrow. Todd had a Plum Pretty face. Ten minutes could be a long time.

Todd missed the next class. I heard he had stomach flu.

The last night of class, everyone was there. I sat with Kevin like always, but I could feel Todd eyeballing me from behind. What if he said something? I didn't want to hurt Kevin's feelings, and anyway fooling around with Todd didn't mean anything, not really.

Mr. White told us he'd review everything during the first half of class, and after the break we would take the written test. If we passed, we could go on to the road lessons. He was going over the part about emergency handling and accident avoidance.

"That's right. Always turn the wheel in the direction of the skid," he said. "And how do you avoid the most common type of accident?"

"Keep enough space between you and the car in front of you," said Kevin.

"Dork," coughed the boys in back.

"Right on, Mr. Thorpe," said Mr. White. "And what do you do if someone cuts you off?"

"Slow down to maintain your distance," someone said.

"Flip him the bird," said Todd. "Ram his ass."

"Beat his brains out," said one of Todd's friends.

"Blow his legs off," said another.

"Slow down," Mr. White wrote on the board in large letters and circled it. Then he turned quickly, grimacing with the effort of propelling his leg around, and stood glaring at the back of the class. After a moment of silence in which we all had a chance to read the doom imprinted on his furrowed brow, he said, "Get. Out." He didn't shout or lose control. "You. You. You," he pointed. "Outta here. Now."

Todd's friends looked like they hadn't heard right. "What about the test?" asked Todd.

"Now you're worried about the test?" Mr. White shook his head in frustration. "Take it from somebody else. Make an appointment at the central office. I don't care. Get out of my classroom."

We stared at the three of them while they stood up and shoved their chairs over, lit their cigarettes, and headed for the door. They took their time leaving so they could smoke and flick their ashes on the floor. One of them muttered, "Fuckin' nigger," on his way out, loud enough for everyone to hear. The collective gasp of the class in response seemed to suck all the air out of the room. I was sure it wasn't Todd. When they were finally gone, and we could all exhale, Kevin reached over and squeezed my leg to say "I told you so." Mr. White sat down heavily on the desk, resting his bad leg on a chair, and stared into the space between him and all of us. I felt sorry for him, more sorry than I felt about his leg. He didn't say anything. No one did. A few minutes later, he called the break. It was early, but he said we'd had enough reviewing; we were ready for the test.

Kevin and I stood in the corridor with the rest of the class, waiting for the elevator. "Do you wanna study during the break?" Kevin asked.

"I don't think we need to, do you?"

"No," said Kevin. "Wanna go camping?" That was his cute way of saying he wanted to fool around. He put his hand on the back of my neck and left it there. It made me feel a little like a dog on a choke chain. I didn't know what to say. I was half-afraid we'd open the tent flap and find Todd in there. Was Todd right about me? Was I a Todd-kind-of-girl or a Kevin-kind-of-girl?

Why did I feel like I had to choose? Did anyone else have to? While I was figuring it out, the doors opened, and there was Todd standing in the elevator instead, smacking his palm with a brand new baseball bat from sporting goods. He looked at me and then at Kevin. I didn't meet his eyes but watched the muscles move smoothly under the skin of his forearm as he raised and lowered the bat.

"Shit," said Kevin, not moving except to lift his hand off my neck.

"What the hell?" It was Mr. White's voice coming from somewhere behind me, and before I had a chance to tell Kevin that the tent sounded pretty good about now, Mr. White growled, "Outta my way," and we all got out of his way. Kevin took me by the arm and dragged me backwards so fast I almost fell on the floor. We stood with our backs pressed against the mannequin dumpster.

"You want a piece of me, you dumbass? You want a piece of me?" Mr. White had instantly assumed this martial-arts-type stance, his fists gathered up near his collar in a pre-strike position. He stood with his legs apart, not at all clumsy on the fake one. "You think you can take me?" Mr. White hissed. "I'm trained in hand-to-hand combat, you white-fucking-trailer-trash."

Todd's eyes widened, as if he'd temporarily blacked out and come to holding the bat with no idea how he got there. I had a sudden image of his parents at home. There was his dad, the biceps all gone to fat around a tattoo of a fiery cross, nailing AstroTurf to the front stoop with a staple gun, while his mom chucked the broken toaster out on the lawn next to the broken TV set.

"Holy shit," Kevin whispered excitedly. "This is gonna be like Bruce Lee."

"They've had this date from the beginning," I said.

"What?" said Kevin.

Sometimes in movies, the fight scenes happen in slow motion, and that's how it seemed to me when I watched Todd and Mr. White. Even though it was over in a matter of seconds, the whole scene plays back slow and dreamy in my mind's eye.

Todd stepped off the elevator and paused as if he hadn't planned on this course of action at all but felt compelled toward it now like a salmon who suddenly realizes how stupid it is to swim upstream yet can't quite stop itself all the same, and then he swung the bat at Mr. White's head. I'm guessing that Todd had a good five inches and forty pounds on Mr. White. He missed anyway. The two men circled, with Todd taking another swing and Mr. White ducking to avoid the bat, his fake knee bending ever so slightly. Then, White made his move. It was so fast that even though I was watching the whole time, I felt like I didn't see it happen. When Todd swung the bat again, Mr. White grabbed it with both hands. Todd hung on, and White whomped him in the chest with the handle of the bat, knocking the wind out of him. Now, I'm thinking that the only reason Mr. White didn't bat him in the nose when he had the chance was that he was trying not to draw blood. Anyway, Todd was on the ground hyperventilating. Mr. White stood over him until he looked like he was going to catch his breath, and then White was on him, pinning him to the linoleum by pressing the side of the bat against his neck and his good knee in Todd's crotch. I tried not to remember the feeling of that crotch grinding against me on the floor of the tent. Todd grabbed for White's neck, squeezing the veins that stood out there as White pressed down on the bat. He held on briefly, his arms shuddering with the effort, but finally he had to let go. Todd was struggling to breathe, his eyes bulging out, when Mr. White leaned in real close to his face and cleared his throat, as if he was about to hock a big loogie on Todd's cheek. But he didn't.

"You'll be glad to see the cops, won't you?" Mr. White said. "Someone call the police," he ordered.

"Come on," said Kevin, grabbing me by the wrist.

"Wait a minute," I said.

"Come on," he repeated, dragging me past the rest of the students who were standing around gawking, and past Todd, who was making gurgling sounds from underneath the bat. I hated to see him like that. His eyes, wet and startled, flitted to me as I walked by, but I pretended not to notice.

"Can you believe how White took him down? Man, that was awesome," said Kevin.

Upstairs we walked to the makeup counter, and Kevin asked the saleslady to call the police. I put on some misty-blue eye shadow.

"Do you think we still have to take the test?" I asked.

"Maybe they'll pass us all because of emotional trauma," said Kevin.

It ended up we had to take the test by appointment at the Simple Safe Solution offices. I half-expected to see Todd there. I still didn't think he had called Mr. White the Name. I wonder if he ever showed up.

After the class was over, Kevin called me a couple of times and asked me out, but I made up excuses.

About a month ago I stopped into Mackleby-Warner. I hadn't been there in years, since I got married and moved from the neighborhood and divorced. I was driving back from the lawyer's office, George Thorogood howling on the oldies station, when I passed the store and pulled an illegal U-turn into the lot. I saw right away that the whole place had gone downhill. All the fabrics looked too shiny and cheap, the lighting was too bright and yellow, and the carpet was grey and unraveling. On a whim, I went to the cosmetics counter and put on the thickest, blackest eyeliner I could find. I prowled the sporting goods department, not really looking for the tent camper, I told myself, and the place where I thought it had been was stacked with paintball guns and in-line skates. There was a hoop, though, so I shot a few baskets.

I walked out onto the mall past some guys who were hunched over their cigarettes, slouching against the wall. Not much had changed, after all. As I passed, I heard a tar-laden voice say, "Babe," and I half-turned, not even half, just enough to see if he meant me.

JOHN VAN KIRK

Newark Job

—ℳ—

"Where are we going, Dad?"
—Ernest Hemingway, "Indian Camp"

YOUNG HENRY BOWMAN woke instantly at the touch of his father's hand on his shoulder. It was not yet light.

"Still want to go, son?"

"Yeah, Dad, yeah," he answered quietly, careful not to wake his brothers, who slept a few feet away. "What time is it?"

"About six thirty," his father said, "plenty of time."

The boy climbed down silently from his upper bunk and put on the clothes he had set out the night before. In the bathroom he washed his face while the man shaved—the washrag and safety razor alternately passing through the stream of steaming water—and he combed his hair in the lower part of the mirror while the man was wiping away the last traces of shaving cream in the upper. Black whiskers swirled down the drain. The boy carried his hiking boots downstairs to the kitchen where the kettle was already whistling, made instant coffee and toast for his father, and fixed himself some tea and a bowl of cereal. He was lacing up his boots when his father came in. "You know you don't have to go if you don't want to, son," the man said. "We're gonna be gone all day."

"No, Dad, I want to go."

After they ate, they went down into the cellar where the tools and fittings were arranged in black buckets. The man quickly selected what he figured he would need, and the boy started carrying the buckets out to the car. The sun was a low, pale glow in a cold, grey sky. Nobody else was out. Some trucks went by on the street at the top of the hill, but that was all. The man carried out the big bottle of gas, cradling it in his arms like a papoose as he laid it gently on its side in the back of the old Ford station wagon. "Two more buckets and we're on our way," he said. When the loading was finished, the boy had to get into the car on the driver's side because both doors on the other side had been wired up with coat-hanger wire and a broom handle after the locks broke. The man turned on the radio as he started the car. He backed carefully down the steep driveway and headed up the hill.

They got to Sarge's Plumbing Supply at about ten after eight. A black boy about Hank's age was washing the windows of the storefront with a long-handled squeegee. Sarge was sitting on a high stool behind the counter with a stained coffee cup in front of him. He was smoking a fat, soggy cigar; and when he put it into his mouth his lips—normally thin as a British major's—would unfold around it, thick and shiny as the lips of a cartoon Ubangi. Behind him was a color picture of a yellow-haired woman kneeling in the center of an arrangement of chrome-plated plumbing fixtures: faucets and taps, showerheads, traps and drains. . . . Her breasts were clearly visible through her sheer yellow nightgown. The white paper calendar that was stapled to the picture said: October 1965.

The hot water heater wasn't there yet.

"If that slumlord you're workin' for would shell out for a quality product, I'd of had one waitin' for ya," Sarge said to Henry's father. "Hell, I got two Westinghouses out back now and a General Electric on the floor. But this other company . . . you can't hardly depend on 'em, you know? I don't like to deal with 'em."

"I know. I don't like it any more than you do; but work is where you find it. And when you don't have a license. . . ."

"Yeah, I guess so, but . . . You know I never figured you for this kind of work anyway, you shoulda been a doctor or somethin'." Sarge looked over at Hank. "You know your ol' man was the best medic I ever seen, he saved a Jap's life when we were over there after the war. He ever tell you that?"

Hank looked at his father.

His father was silent for a moment, looking at nothing; then he looked back at Sarge. "When you expect it to get here?" he asked flatly.

"They were supposed to have it here first thing this morning," Sarge said, rolling the cigar around in his mouth; "but it's a shine outfit, ain't no tellin' when they'll show up."

They waited. The man had a coffee, and he bought the boy a bottle of Coke from the red machine. The heater arrived about twenty minutes later. The driver and his helper put the long box into the back of the old station wagon. They wedged a hand truck borrowed from Sarge in on top of it. Henry slipped into the car through the right-hand window, which he had left open. The man made a wide U-turn in front of the store and snapped off a farewell salute to Sarge, who was now out on the sidewalk inspecting the windows. A tall, loose-jointed black man wearing a bright pink shirt, brown leather jacket, and wide-brimmed purple hat was crossing the street. "Hey, dark cloud," the man called out to him, gunning the motor and accelerating away.

They stopped to eat in a diner converted from an old railroad car. "I know it's early for lunch," the man said, "but I don't like to knock off once we start, and where we're going there's no place fit to eat nearby." The waitress called the man "Honey" and smiled at him like she knew him. They ordered Taylor Ham and egg sandwiches on hard rolls.

"Did you really save a man's life?" the boy asked while they ate.

"I guess so," his father answered, "but that was a long time ago."

The boy waited for the man to say more, but the man just ate in silence. Finally he spoke: "When we get there I want you to watch where you sit down," he said. "Your mom'll kill us both if you bring home any bugs. If you want anything more, you'd better get it now; we probably won't eat again till dinner." The boy had a piece of apple pie and a coffee light with sugar. He felt like a real workingman and swaggered confidently on the way out.

"What are they like?" the boy asked as they drove.

"Who?"

"These people, where we're going."

"They're good people," the man said. "Mrs. Williams is kind of like a real life Aunt Jemima, big colored woman with a pack of kids. And she'd do anything for 'em, her kids I mean, or whosever's kids they are. I think they're her grandchildren mostly; she has a couple of daughters who are there sometimes; the little ones are probably theirs. Billy's her boy, though. He's a good boy, good-looking too, real light, almost olive, about as good-looking a colored boy as I've ever seen. And his sisters are black as coal."

Hank tried to fit the color olive to a person, but he couldn't.

They entered a bleak neighborhood of vacant lots and boarded-up storefronts; newspapers blew in the cold wind. From the backs of some of the buildings brightly colored laundry flapped between steeply tilting grey wooden porches. In one of the lots some men stood huddled around a burning oil drum, their faces as black as the huge burnt sheets of paper ash that floated up from the barrel on shimmering waves of heat.

It was almost eleven by the time they pulled up in front of the sad-looking brick building where the job was. A few curled flakes of white lead clung to the dry grey wood of the doorway and window frames. The mortar between the bricks was crumbling away, and some of the corner bricks had already fallen out and lay broken in the grey dirt of the yard.

"This Mr. Hallinan's building?" the boy asked.

"Just about all the buildings on this block are Hallinan's," the man answered.

"But they're all so . . . I mean . . . they look like they're ready to fall down."

"Well, son, Hallinan is what you'd call a little tight, and I guess he doesn't want to put any more money into these places than he has to."

"But how can you work for a guy like that?"

"See those shoes you're wearing? You think they grow on trees?"

The man had keys, and he opened the main door and undid a heavy padlock that hung from a rusty hasp on a door off the entryway. This door led to the basement, and when it was opened a smell of dry mold and wet ashes flooded the landing, and the boy heard a rustling sound, like squirrels scrabbling up a tree. "Go get some of those bricks outside and prop open the doors, son, while I get us some light and clear the path for the heater." The boy did as he was told. Then, while the man rigged up a caged utility light with a long extension cord, the boy carried the buckets of tools down into the cellar. He didn't mind the cellar so much, his father there with him; but going out to the car alone—though it was only a short walk across the narrow yard—frightened him a little. He saw no one, yet he felt exposed out there, like a soldier behind enemy lines. His working man's swagger fled him, and he felt small and vulnerable.

The man went out for the big torch, and then the two of them working together loaded the hot water heater onto Sarge's hand truck.

"Atta boy," the man said as they eased the rig down the worn and irregular stairs. "Careful there . . . easy does it . . . oookay, that's got her. . . . Yer gettin' stronger, Henry; I don't think I coulda done that part without you."

The boy swelled a little at this. "No sweat, Dad," he said.

They uncrated the big white heater, jockeyed it into position on a small concrete platform sunk into the dirt floor, and set to work. This was the part that the boy liked most. He set out the valves, the tees, and the elbows on a piece of newspaper; he cleaned up the connecting parts with steel wool until they shined, and he brushed the flux onto them when the man was ready. He had learned this while working with his father in his own house and on other jobs back in the suburbs; he had had to work hard to become good at it and to convince the man to take him on a Saturday job, a Newark job. Now the man even let him measure and cut some of the pieces of copper tubing. He measured them with the folding ruler, marked them with the stroke of a small triangular file, and then cut them with the tubing cutter, tightening it gradually as he rotated it around the tube until the circular blade broke through the pipe and the cut piece broke cleanly off. He then reamed out the newly cut part with the flat steel reamer on the back of the cutting tool until the inside edge was smooth and all the sharp copper slivers were scraped away. While he was doing this, the man lit a cigar and got the torch ready. When everything was neatly laid out, the man lit the torch from the end of the cigar and began to solder the pieces in place. Hank laughed when his father asked him, over the hissing roar of the torch, for a female tee. "The one there with the tits," he had said. Looking around while the man methodically sweated the solder into each joint, the boy could see where his father's work began and left off. Most of the pipes in the ceiling, aside from being old and crusted with rust and flaking paint, went every which way; but amidst all that confusion there were a few that ran straight and level, with square corners. Some had little white tags hanging from them to tell what they led to. That was what the cellar ceiling in Hank's own house looked like. But it was only now that Hank realized that not all plumbers worked this way. It made him feel proud of his father. Then the torch went off with a loud pop and sudden silence.

Now the man turned the faucet to let the heater fill with water while he hooked up the electricity. The boy looked at the wires that hung from the ceiling, their tips covered with red plastic screwcaps, ready to be connected.

"Did you run those wires, Dad?"

"About two weeks ago. We do it all, son." He smiled.

By the time the tank was filled, Hank's father had screwed the wires in, turned on the power at the fuse box on the other end of the basement, and switched on the heater. He then shut the water off that went to the Williamses' apartment.

"Time to go upstairs," he said.

Upstairs was like nowhere the boy had been before. The smell hit him first, not the same musty, pissy smell of the basement but a new hot and smoky thick smell: the smell of burning lard and unaired crowded rooms. It poured out hot and stifling into the shabby landing when the door opened, and the boy swallowed hard and almost gagged on going in. But he got accustomed to it quickly, or forgot it, as the scene before him caught him up. His eyes roamed the place greedily, fascinated, taking it in from the floor to the ceiling, from the nearly vanished pattern of leaves and branches on the cracked and peeling linoleum spread like a carpet in the middle of the floor, to the visibly rotten boards that buckled beneath the feet of the rust-stained radiator hissing and steaming under the lone half-boarded window; from the stains like maps on the cracked grey walls to the splintery slats of lath in the crumbling plaster ceiling. Dark laundry hung from a makeshift clothesline in one corner of the room, near the entry to what must have been the kitchen, and two small children slept on a narrow bed in another. In the center of the room was a hide-a-bed, extended, and a sleeping woman lay sprawled across it in a tattered slip. Her skin was as black as loam, and Hank wanted to look more because she was really almost naked and he had never seen a woman naked before except in pictures; but he felt embarrassed to be staring, and he had to look away. That was when he saw the trophies. One of the walls was covered with them; there must have been fifty or more, from small medallions and engraved plaques to two-foot-high plinths and pedestals with Olympic-looking golden athletes on them.

"Those are mah boy Billy's," a soft voice drawled.

He looked to see who was talking to him. It was Mrs. Williams; it had to be. His father was right, she did look like Aunt Jemima, big and black and round and smiling. But in another way she didn't look like Aunt Jemima at all; that is, she didn't look like a cartoon, or a picture on a syrup bottle. She looked real, and there wasn't anything funny about her; and when he looked into her eyes, so dark they seemed black too, he smiled, liking her right away.

"We sure glad to see you, Mr. Bowman," she was saying to the man, "you know how long since we got hot water? Three weeks now. That Mr. Hallinan, he don't care 'bout us over here."

"I'm sorry, Mrs. Williams, but I work durin' the week at my regular job, and every night this week I had to work on another job where they got no heat."

"Oh, ah know you come soon as you could; ah don' mean to complain. You a nice man, Mr. Bowman; tell the truth, ah don't know how that Mr. Hallinan get you to work for him, but ah'm glad he do." She turned to Hank and then back to the man. "And this your boy?" she said.

"Yes ma'am, that's my son Henry."

"Well, he is a fine boy," she said, "so handsome." Hank felt himself begin to redden. Then she turned to him: "And your fahtha," she said, "he's a fine man; you take aftah him an' you be a fine man too, a gentleman."

"Got the water turned off for a while," the man said. "Anybody needs to use the bathroom is gonna have to go over to a neighbor's."

"Oh, that reminds me; Miz Walker next door axt me to ax you if you come today could you go by her place run that thing you got down her toilet; it's been stopped up three four days now."

"Yeah, sure . . . okay. . . . Son, go on down to the car and get the snake and my black rubber gloves; we'll do that first."

Mrs. Walker's apartment was so different from Mrs. Williams' that it was difficult at first to believe it was in the same building. It didn't seem newer, and there was nothing new in it, but everything was clean and shiny. It smelled of lemons. There were carpets—threadbare and faded, but there—on the floor; and there were a lot of framed photographs on the walls. All the people in the pictures were black, and most of them were dressed in formal clothes. Mrs. Walker looked formal too: she was thin, with grey hair, and she stood straight and stiff like a schoolteacher. "Thank you so much for coming over, Mr. Bowman," she said, with what sounded almost like an English accent.

The snaking job was slow work. While his father cranked the steel spring down the toilet, Hank stared out into the living room. Behind all of the neatly hung pictures were the same cracked and peeling walls as next door; under the carpet were the same buckling floorboards; but the furnishings were arranged as if it were a fine house. There were doilies on the chair backs and arms.

When the steel snake was pulled back up, the foul stench that came with it was so strong it burned Hank's eyes and he realized that his father's cigar was good for more than lighting torches.

Mrs. Walker offered them sodas when they were through.

"Thank you, ma'am," the man said, "we'd be glad for the drinks, but if you don't mind we'd like to take them with us to the job next door."

"Of course," she said, opening the bottles, "and thank you again, Mr. Bowman."

Again the nauseating smell and stifling heat struck Hank as he and his father went back into the other apartment, but after the snaking job it didn't seem nearly so bad as before. They quickly set to work. First they had to connect a new line under the kitchen sink; and as the man opened the cabinet a swarm of brown bugs scurried away. The boy jumped when he saw them. "Just cockroaches, son," the man said. "They won't hurt you, but watch where you set your jacket; we don't want to take any home." Hank folded his jacket carefully and set it on the newspaper with the joints and pieces of pipe; he then sat cross-legged on top of it, ready to hand his father the tools and fittings as he needed them.

A short while later one of the little boys who had been asleep on the bed wandered up behind Hank to see what was going on. The boy had blue eyes and was sucking his thumb. He rocked a little as he watched the man work, and he put his free hand on Hank's shoulder to steady himself. Hank turned to him and asked his name, but the little boy ran away without answering, and jumped up onto the fold-out bed, waking the woman in the slip. She looked sleepily over toward Hank and his father, and hurriedly covered herself with a blanket.

Next a new shower had to be installed. This was Hallinan's solution to the problem of old rusted-out bathtub faucets: cut the lines and run a new piece of pipe up to a cheap showerhead. It took longer than expected to hook up because of problems anchoring it, and Hank could see that his father was unhappy with the ugly metal straps he had to use to fix the pipe to the crumbling wall. The man showed the boy how the fittings were designed to go inside the wall. When it was all connected, the man went down into the basement again to turn the water back on. When he came up again, they tested the new work, and Hank listened to the water rattle up the empty pipes. The connections were good, and the hot water was hot.

Then they noticed that a pool of water was forming under the old tub, which stood on four short iron legs, and it turned out that a piece of the drain pipe had rusted away. Luckily the man had a replacement part in one of his buckets, but that took time too. When they were at last ready to repack the station wagon, it was already growing dark.

"Will the men be coming home soon?" Hank asked his father.

"Huh?"

"The men, they'll be coming home from work pretty soon, won't they?"

"I don't know, son, I've never seen any men here."

"But . . . the kids . . . I don't get it."

"These people have their own ways, son. Seems like the men don't stick around long . . . they just . . . I don't know . . . run off after a while."

"And the kids?"

"Don't worry about them, son, you worry about you."

Hank noticed that many of the streetlights were not working, including the one nearest the car. As he and his father were carrying the last buckets of tools and fittings, an old pink Buick with a continental kit came screeching around the corner and skidded to a stop in front of the building. Two black boys a few years older than Hank jumped out of the car, and Hank saw his father tense. The young men opened up the back door of the Buick and helped another one to climb out. They were practically carrying him. Then the car drove off as noisily as it had arrived.

"It's Billy," Hank's father said suddenly when the boys got to the bright area at the entrance to the building. They were just dragging the limp body along now, and Hank saw a puddle of what looked like motor oil form beneath its feet as they struggled with the door.

"Stay close to me, son," the man said. "That's Mrs. Williams' boy." The man ran over to the door and the boy followed. "Henry, you go up and clear the way, and tell Mrs. Williams we're coming. One of you boys watch over my tools out there."

"Sure, mister," one said, "he gonna be all right?"

"I don't know, son. I hope so."

The man moved quickly, and by the time Hank had cleared the way to the small bed in the corner of the main room, he was already coming through the door with the bleeding boy in his arms, the other boy now behind him. "Get the kids out of here," the man said. "Henry, get those clean diapers we saw in the bathroom. Mrs. Williams, you get a scissors and some clean towels. If you have any tape, get it. No, don't wet them, there isn't time. He's weak from loss of blood, but I can't see where it's all coming from. Get me some light over here; the blood don't show up like on us. Hank, you mop him with the diapers, tell me when you find a cut."

The man was working on the face, which had a deep gash that cut through one eye and laid the cheek open to the teeth below it. The lens of the cut eye looked like frosted glass and the split white was red. The boy couldn't believe that this was happening. He was watching his father tape the face closed with Scotch tape, which was all Mrs. Williams could find; the man was having difficulty making the tape stick to the black boy's clammy skin. Then Hank found a pool of blood that he couldn't seem to get mopped up. It was down by the crotch and he didn't want to touch it and he couldn't find anything but blood.

"Dad," he said, "there's something wrong down here."

"Let me see," the father said, with surprising calm. "Ah, okay, give me the scissors."

Hank could hear the mother crying while he watched his father cut away the trousers. The other boy was telling her that they had been just sittin' around against the car by the school when these guys they didn't know showed up and started something.

"And why you ain't cut, George Johnson, and mah boy all sliced to ribbons?"

"We tol' Billy to let it go, but they kep' callin' him Indian and high yellow and he couldn't take it and he went for 'em. I think he cut one of them too."

"Oh, mah lord," said Mrs. Williams. It was a big hole, Hank could see now, as his father wiped up around it. How did the knife get up there practically to his balls? And his leg was like a piece of carved wood, not olive-colored at all, but chestnut, with muscles like a statue, but like an ax had bitten deep into the upper thigh. The life was pouring out of the boy fast. The man took a diaper and cut it with the scissors, then tore it into a long thin strip. This he twisted and then drew up into the boy's groin; he brought the other end around under the leg and then pulled it tight. He must have caught the pressure point just right because the flow of blood slowed even before he got the thing tied off.

"Mama, get the shower warmed up and bring me some towels or blankets into the bathroom," the man said, as he cut or tore away the remaining clothing. He then picked up the naked youth and carried him to the shower. "I got to wash him up to see where else he's cut; thank god they got hot water now." The black boy groaned and shivered as the man slid him into the tub and directed the shower over him. "You're gonna be all right, son. Don't talk. We're gonna get you all fixed up." The water splattered pink against the wall and swirled in a red whirlpool at the drain as the man, getting soaked himself, mopped the boy roughly with a towel. The dark limp body glistened wetly, the drainswirl fading from rose to runny watercolor red.

"Mama, get them blankets now. Looks like I got all the big cuts closed, but we got to get him to a hospital right away."

The man lifted the black boy, wrapped in blankets, onto his shoulder, fireman style, and carried him downstairs and out into the front seat of the car. He then had to clear some of the buckets out to put the seat up for Mrs. Williams and Hank. "You watch this stuff for me," he said to the other two boys on the sidewalk. Mrs. Williams was struggling helplessly with the back door on the right-hand side. "That door doesn't work, ma'am," Hank told her; and he led her gently around to the other side of the car. The man drove quickly and efficiently to the hospital; he did not squeal his tires, but he did go through two red lights, after stopping first to check for traffic. The hurt boy was silent now; he was not even moaning, and Hank was afraid that he might be dead. The fat old black lady, when she wasn't giving directions, was mumbling something over and over to herself. Hank decided that she was praying. Her face was shiny with tears.

At the hospital things did not go as quickly as the man seemed to think they should. The emergency room was not full, but there were a lot of people in it. The only white people there were Hank and his father and two harried-looking attendants who were busy having everyone fill out the complicated admittance forms.

"Can't you see there's no time for this?" the man said. "This boy is dying."

"Yeah, everybody comes in here is dying," said one of the attendants.

"Is he your boy, sir?" the other one asked.

"Of course he's not my boy, you . . . you can see that, but . . . "

"Then he's not your problem, is he? Now Mrs.? What's your name? You have to fill this . . . "

"Hey," the man shouted, "do you hear me? Just how stupid are you? Do you think I patched this boy up and brought him here and kept him alive this long just so you idiots could let him die? Where's the doctor? I wanna see the doctor. . . . "

"I'm sorry sir, but the doctor . . . "

"Just what the hell is going on out here?" boomed a deep rounded voice. Everybody in the place was suddenly quiet. At the doors that led into the inner part of the hospital stood a distinguished-looking black man with a grey moustache and a white lab coat.

"Are you the doctor?" the man asked.

The black man just looked at him.

"This boy is dying. He's been in a knife fight and I had to put a tourniquet on his leg and I think he's gonna lose an eye, but you got to look at the leg, it's an artery that's cut. . . ." The man pulled back the blankets.

The black boy did not look so chestnutty now as he had in the dim light of the apartment. Or maybe it was the blood that he had lost, because he looked grey now. Hank did not know what dead looked like, but he thought that the boy looked dead. The doctor picked up the boy's arm by the wrist and looked at his watch. Then he dropped the wrist and bent low over the boy's ruined face, laying two fingers aside his neck. "The tourniquet?" the deep voice asked gently. The man uncovered the boy's crotch. The doctor looked closely at the torn strip of towel and at the wound just below it. "How long since you put this on?"

"Twenty minutes, half-hour," the man said.

"Get a gurney out here." The doctor's voice filled the room. "I want this boy in surgery immediately, get him typed and get some blood into him." Then he turned to the man and said softly, "They work very hard, sometimes they do not see what is in front of them." A black nurse appeared from within with the cart and with the help of the attendants lifted the wounded boy onto it and wheeled him away through two swinging doors. "You have probably saved this boy's life, friend," the doctor said to the man. "Now I must try to save his leg. As for the eye . . . " he shook his head sadly, "first the leg." The doctor turned and walked away through the swinging doors.

Then they waited. They made a strange trio, Hank thought, sitting there in the waiting room, the white man and the boy, both spattered with blood, and the big black woman, rocking silently. Mrs. Williams suggested that Hank and his father go on home, but the man said that he would not leave her there. He made a telephone call to Hank's mother to say that they'd be late. Almost two hours passed before the doctor came back out. He addressed himself to the woman. "Your boy's gonna live, Mrs. Williams," he said. He looked tired and somehow older than before.

"Praise the lord," Mrs. Williams said. "Can I see him?"

"Soon. He's gonna be out for a few hours, you can look in on him before you go. Right now I'd like to ask you a couple of questions."

"What, Doctor?"

"Are you in touch with the boy's father?"

Mrs. Williams's head dropped. "No sir, ah am not."

"Is there a man around who can talk to him? Someone he looks up to?"

"No, sir, they ain't no man around, an' we don't need one. Mah Billy is a good boy."

"I'm sure he is, ma'am. He was an athlete, I could see that; built like a quarter horse, it's probably what saved him; but it didn't keep this from happening did it? I get lots of boys in here cut up, but not athletes like your boy. He shouldn't be here. But he is. And he's been badly hurt. He's lost an eye, and it's going to be a long time before he walks without a cane. But that's done. I'm worried about what happens now. He's not going to be running any races for a long while, if ever. What's he going to do? Who's going to stop him from going for revenge?"

"But Doctor? You said he was going to be all right."

"I said he was going to live. He's not going to be like he was. His leg is in bad shape, there could be nerve damage, other complications. He'll need therapy. It's going to take time. And he's lost an eye."

"Can ah see him now?"

"Yes, but just for a minute. The nurse will take you in. Goodbye, Mrs. Williams. I probably won't see you again."

"But who's gonna see to mah boy?"

"The regular doctors here are very good. They are more up-to-date than I am. I just help out in the Emergency on weekends since I retired from my practice. He'll be well taken care of. But you remember what I said about when he gets out. Maybe you can get a teacher to talk to him. Or a coach. This can't be allowed to happen again. These kids butchering each other like cowboys and Indians."

As they went deeper into the hospital, the antiseptic smell grew stronger. Billy was in a pale green room with an old black man. Both of them were asleep. One whole side of Billy's face was covered with bright white bandages; the other side was ash grey; the rest of him was covered by the sheets. He looked smaller than before. Some tubes went from a bottle at the top of a pole into a needle stuck in his left forearm. Mrs. Williams knelt beside the bed, touched her son's arm, and seemed to pray softly to herself. After a few minutes the nurse ushered them out again. "Come and see him in the morning," she said. "You'll be able to talk to him then."

Hank and his father drove Mrs. Williams home. As they pulled up to the building, they could see that the buckets of tools that had been left on the sidewalk were gone. The man said nothing. But going in they saw that all the tools had been brought into the entryway and Billy's two friends were leaning against them. Their flashy clothes were rumpled and bloody, and they looked as if they had been sleeping.

"Is he all right?" they asked, almost in unison.

"He's alive," the man said tiredly.

The black boys didn't say anything more, but after the man took Mrs. Williams up the stairs to her apartment, they helped carry the tools out to the car. The man thanked them and held out two dollar bills.

"Thanks for watching my tools," he said, "they're my . . . thanks."

They wouldn't take the money.

"You helped our friend, mister, you don't owe us nothin'," one said.

"Yeah," said the other, "we owes you."

As his father pulled the car away from the curb, Hank looked back at the building, and for a moment, in the dark, he caught a glimpse of it as something other than what it now was, a glimpse, perhaps, of what it had been years before, when the dirt yard had been a lawn, and the mortar between the bricks was hard and white, and the trim was shiny with fresh paint. He saw men with hats in antique cars coming to call on women in dresses. But then the image fled, and he saw the same grey, crumbling wreck of a tenement. The man tuned the radio to the soft music station. They passed the lot where Hank had seen the burning oil drum in the morning, and it was still there, but now the blaze lit up the night like a bonfire, sending sparks up into the black sky, and casting long dancing shadows of the dark men huddled around it. Not long after that they turned onto a brightly lit avenue, and Hank found himself breathing an almost audible sigh of relief to be out of the darkness. He soon fell asleep.

When he awoke, the car was pulling up the steep driveway. It took him a moment to shake his head clear, and after he slid across the seat and out, he leaned lightly on the side of the car and worked his way around to the back to unload the buckets.

"That's all right, son," the man said. "We'll leave 'em till morning. You go inside and get cleaned up for bed. I'll tell your mother what happened."

Upstairs, Hank stretched out in the tub. A few hours ago he had seen another boy stretched out in a tub. The image burned in his mind. He looked down at himself and thought of the fine athletic frame of the other boy, the legs like carved wood. . . . Would he ever grow into a body like that? And then he thought of the blood, of the cut face, the horrible eye, and the gash . . . they had almost cut his . . . god . . . and he thought of that, which he had seen too—he had never seen a black one before—and he felt small and pink and more like a boy than the young man which he so wanted to be. Then he thought of the wounds again, and the foggy eye, and he scrubbed himself hard to wash off the dried blood and the plumber's dirt and all of it. He opened the drain and stood to dry himself, and as he toweled his body off, he watched the blood and grease and dirt swirl down the drain, and he thought of that other drain with the red blood swirling down it, and he wrapped the towel tight around him.

After the bath he went downstairs to eat. His mother had made him some sandwiches and hot chocolate. He had forgotten that he hadn't eaten since lunch. His mother asked him nothing about the day.

"Daddy saved a boy's life tonight," he offered.

"I know," she said.

He looked at her and she at him.

"It's late," she said, "eat up; you have to be up early tomorrow for church. Your brothers are all asleep."

He realized after a moment that he was grateful to her for not asking him more about it, for now that he thought about it he saw that he didn't want to talk about it after all. He ate the cookies she gave him after the sandwiches and then went up to bed.

His father came to see him in his bedroom. It had been a long time since he had come up to say good night. He went to the other bunk bed first, then to the bed below Hank's, gently adjusting the blankets over each of Hank's brothers. Finally he straightened up and stood with his hand on the headboard of Hank's top bunk bed. "I'm sorry you had to see that, son," he said.

"But I helped you, didn't I?"

"Yes, son, you sure did. I couldn't have asked for a better helper. Now, get some sleep."

"Okay, Dad. G'night."

"G'night, son."

Hank watched his father back slowly out of the room. He looked tired. The part of the floor brightened by the hall light shrunk and then winked out softly as the bedroom door was eased shut. Hank stretched out straight in his bed, worked the back of his head into the pillow, and waited for his eyes to get used to the dark.

JAN ELLISON

The Color of Wheat in Winter

—ɯ—

IT WAS ONE of those dirty brown days L.A. dishes out in August, thick with smog and heat, and Eddie's Place was dead for the sixth day running. Eddie was in back counting money and receipts and the cars that pulled up to the drive-through speaker. Frances was on the fryer, Becky at the register, and Johnny was cooking. They stood around and wiped the counters; they patted their foreheads with white rags that smelled of bleach. At two-thirty, Eddie came up front and told them he was going home, they should stay and close. He said it gruffly, leaning his elbow up against the meat cutter, his rough fat cheek in his hand. It was the first time he'd left before closing since Frances started working there in June, when she turned sixteen, and it made her nervous watching him, the evidence of failure collecting in his loose neck and his short, thick arms. It was the same way she'd felt when the Italian restaurant in town had shut down and moved to Bakersfield where rents were low. Sometimes she would peer in the windows when she passed, at the pink plastic carnations still standing in their vases, unaware it was time to die.

Eddie's car pulled away, and Becky grinned; her work was done for the day. Frances watched as Becky refilled her Coke, her thin red hair pulled tight against her head, the blue of her eyelids popping like a painted-on sky. Becky was careless and lazy, but there was something about her Frances liked—the way she careened through her day without examining it, how she fit so easily into her life. Becky headed out back for a smoke, and Frances and Johnny were alone.

Frances dropped a half basket of fries and the grease flew up, messing her apron. Johnny flipped a patty and slapped the cheese. He was stocky, with a broad back and hearty, weathered skin. His movements were small and fluid so that sometimes it seemed he wasn't moving at all. Frances waited for him to speak. He'd begun to talk to her when they were alone, little nuggets of his life falling from him like loose change. She knew he was thirty-five and married, with two teenaged boys, and that before he'd come to California he'd driven long-hauls across Mexico. He was working at Eddie's waiting for a green card so he could send for his family. He wanted his sons to go to college.

He wrapped and bagged the burger and handed it to Frances. Then he leaned against the counter and watched her salt the fries and scoop them into bags.

"Let's run away together," he said.

"Hah-hah," Frances said. She was not used to the way he talked to her, but she pretended she was. She put the fries in the bag, then the napkins and the salt and ketchup packets, and handed it out the drive-through window.

"I'm serious," he said, when she turned back toward him. His eyes were leveled on her face. Then he laughed and so did she. "Ah, chica," he said.

He gave her a ride home. There was a statue of the Virgin Mary on his dashboard, a rip in the upholstery beneath her bare thighs. He tapped his fingers on the console, and she felt a loosening in her, as if she were suddenly capable of a cheaper, riskier life. She told him about her father. How in June, he'd quit his job, bought a share in a hot-air balloon, and left her mother for another woman—Josephine—a sax player with an inheritance. The reason he'd given for leaving was that Josephine believed in his dreams. She wanted to be part of them.

Frances had met Josephine only once, when her father drove up from Santa Monica to take Frances out to lunch. She'd opened the door for her father and Josephine was there in the driveway, standing beside the car in boots and a white cowboy hat with a black wreck of hair down her back. Frances had known her mother was watching from the kitchen window, peering through the thickness of the lemon tree, and she'd known it was not possible to walk out there and get in that car. She told her father she was sick, she couldn't go, and the way he said *it's all right*, with his eyes on his shoes, made her feel as if she'd slapped him but he'd somehow been waiting for it, expecting it as his due.

Johnny listened to Frances talk and made a sound between his lips—something low and mournful, a kind of hum. When they reached the end of her block, she made him stop, and she got out of the car and walked the rest of the way home alone, past the neighbors' yards, their tiny lawns like oversized carpet squares, until she reached her own—her father's idea—a tangle of green that loomed into the heat of the night. Lawns are for ordinary people, he'd said. Hidden among the rich growth was a secret path to a stone reading bench. Frances loved that bench, the idea of it, its valiant stab at some secret poetry.

Frances found her mother sorting laundry in her bedroom. Her long fingers moved quickly, fiercely, as she turned shirts and pants right-side out, checking pockets for tissues and pennies, hair clips and dollar bills. "Your father called," she said. "He wants to see you. There's a barbecue at Gram's house on Labor Day."

Frances said nothing.

"Don't you want to go?"

"I don't know. I guess."

"Your cousins will all be there, hon. Don't pretend you don't care just to save my feelings. It doesn't help."

Frances remained silent.

"I don't know how you'll get there, though," her mother said.

"Maybe Dad can pick me up."

"The traffic will be awful coming up the 5. I could drive you. We'd have the reverse commute. That would give me a chance to visit. I haven't seen Nana in months."

"Don't you have to be at the hospital?"

"I can switch with one of the other girls. There's always someone who needs the holiday pay."

"Are you sure it's a good idea, though, Mom? To go, I mean?"

Her mother paused to look at her. She tilted her head to the side in inquiry.

"What kind of comment is that, Frances? It's not like I'm not part of that family. For eighteen years I've been part of that family. I think I can go to a barbeque if I want to. I know you're trying to keep me from meeting her and seeing your father, but that's my problem, Frances. That has nothing to do with you." She sat down on the bed and pressed her thumbs into her temples. Her naked shoulders rolled inward toward her chest. Frances went quietly to her room to change, closing the door behind her.

Her mother followed, opening the door without knocking. She was holding Frances's new pants—soft corduroy, the color of pearl. "What are these?" she said.

"They're new. I got them at the mall."

"How much were they?"

"Twenty-two, I think."

"It's a lot to spend, Frances. And they can't even go in the dryer."

"But it was my own money."

"You need to be saving for college. You know that. Although I can't imagine how we'll manage it now. We won't see anything from your father. Not unless he moves home and gets his job back."

Frances couldn't help it; she blew air out of her mouth and let her eyes roll to the ceiling. "Mom. He's not moving home." She let each word form its own sharp sentence.

Her mother let out a little gasp. She clutched the pants to her chest.

"Why are you speaking to me that way, Frances? Don't ever do that, Frances Lynn. Do not ever speak to me like that."

Inside Frances, fear bloomed but also something else — the possibility of her own power. She put her hands in her pockets. She could take this further. She could bust them out of the box they'd been in. But her mother didn't give her a chance. She thrust the pants at Frances. "They're stained," she said bitterly. "You'll have to use the stain remover and wash them in hot water."

Frances took the pants and threw them in the corner and kicked the door shut. She dropped onto the floor. She closed her eyes and imagined herself alone and strong, sweeping books off shelves, racing fast across an open field.

When she woke in the morning, the pants hung on her closet door in a kind of splendor — washed and ironed, with a note pinned to the pocket in her mother's slanted, loopy hand, "I got the stains out!" The o's were made into happy faces. Frances put the note in her bottom drawer. She had already decided, some time in the night, not to wear the pants again and to skip the barbeque altogether.

"Chica," Johnny said at work the next day, "it's good to see you." He put his hands on her shoulders, and she felt the heat and bigness of them like a thick quilt around her. She thought of him, afterward, as she pushed her bike up the hill home. Then he was there, pulling up beside her in his truck. He lifted her bike into the back and offered her the keys. "Do you want to try?"

"My learner's permit's expired," she said. Her driving lessons had been abandoned during the difficult summer.

He shrugged his shoulders and smiled.

She took the keys. She stalled on the hills, slipped back, burned rubber. Johnny laughed and gave her instructions. He worked the stick shift for her. Twice he touched her knee.

When they reached her street, she braked to a stop at the corner and turned off the ignition. They got out, and Johnny lifted her bike out and leaned it against the truck. He stood with his hands in his pockets. She could smell him, the smokiness of him, the charred butter and salt, and for a moment she thought she might let herself fall into the gentle curve of his belly, into the plain white cotton of his T-shirt. Instead she handed him the keys.

"Nice driving, chica."

"Thanks, Johnny." She walked her bike a little way and then got on it to ride the rest of the way home. She was aware of him watching her, and it made her conscious of the motion of her legs pumping the pedals. She tried to construct in her mind a picture of what it was he saw, how all the parts of her added up.

Frances's mother was painting the kitchen yellow. Not yellow—her mother explained—*the color of wheat in winter.* It was a designer color she'd seen in a magazine. Frances thought the paint seemed out of place against the cracked tiles, the faded linoleum. It was too lovely, too fresh and new. Her mother seemed out of place there too, on her knees with a roller in her hand. Her face was flushed, her eyes were bright, there was paint on her wrists and her forehead, a thin stripe of it through her dark hair.

"You know, Frances," her mother said, as if they'd been in the middle of a conversation, "when you were little he had a girlfriend and he came back." Frances said nothing. This was news to her, but she didn't want to hear it. She didn't want hope breaking in. What she wanted was for her mother to clear a path forward so she could follow.

In September, when the girls' school she attended on scholarship was about to begin, Frances told Eddie she couldn't work during the week. She would have too much homework. Eddie put her on Saturdays, and she looked forward to that, because Eddie didn't work weekends and she would be alone with Johnny. The idea of him was with her—a shiny stone in her pocket, a powerful secret—as she started back to school, climbing the stone steps those first mornings with a sense that her position would shift. She would move toward the center of things. She had lost weight over the summer, she had grown taller, but it wasn't clear how these things came together until she saw her friends again. "You look so good," Dawn whispered, leaning in close. "You're, like, totally skinny. Now you can wear my clothes."

After school on Friday, she went to Dawn's house with three other girls. That night they drove in Dawn's car to a club in Hollywood. They did bong hits on the way there and listened to Queen and The Cars and the Go-Go's. In the parking lot they drank Southern Comfort out of a thermos, and later, on the dance floor, Frances got caught up in the crush of hot bodies and the loud, raking music. She didn't want to leave.

The next morning she was sick, her mouth dry, her stomach unsteady. But there was a reason to get up. She was on the lunch shift and Johnny would be there. She imagined standing beside him, brushing against him. But his truck wasn't in the lot, and he wasn't at the grill when she clocked in. Instead Eddie himself was cooking, burning the patties and forgetting to put new ones on. Business was not what it had been, he explained. To save on wages, he was giving Johnny Saturdays off and taking the shift himself.

Frances's father called. He wanted to see her. He wanted her to get to know Josephine. She agreed to have dinner with them on a night she knew her mother would be at the hospital. She left her mother a note in case she arrived home first. "Having dinner with Dad," was all she could think of to write.

Josephine wore a green velvet vest and a paisley skirt that fell to her ankles. She had her hair pinned up, a few long strands loose around her face and a few more falling down her back. She wore bracelets inlaid with stones that jingled when she walked.

They went to the Mexican restaurant in town. Frances's father seemed to be growing his hair out. It was pulled behind him in a stringy ponytail. He slid into the booth next to Frances and put his arm around her. Josephine sat across from them. She wore no makeup and her face was an earthy grey, splotched brown around her ears. She ordered herself a margarita in Spanish, flirting with the dark-eyed waiter. She wanted it frozen, she told him, with extra salt on the rim. When the drinks came, she nibbled the edge of her glass with her thin, unpainted lips and talked about Frances's father—*Your dad this, your dad that*—as if he weren't there at all. They were planning to take the hot air balloon to Bakersfield for its inaugural flight. Hundreds of yellow umbrellas had been planted in the hills there—an exhibit by the Bulgarian-born artist Christo. It was going to be fabulous, Josephine said, and Frances should come along. The three of them would have such fun. It was going to be good publicity, to help her father launch his record label. They planned to have *SkipTown Records* painted on the side of the balloon in red letters.

"Well that was just something we talked about," her father said, embarrassed.

Josephine gave him an indulgent smile and reached across the table to take his freckled hand in hers. Her bracelets raked against the tabletop like handcuffs.

What Frances hated—more than Josephine, more than how beaten down her father seemed, how awkward and unlike himself, more than not being able to sit alone with him and talk and have him listen the way he did, as if she had something important to teach him—was the way she herself was nodding and smiling and accepting sips of Josephine's margarita, the way she was acting as if she were happy to fit right into Josephine's plans.

At home her mother sat on the front porch waiting for her. The sun had dropped below the line of smog over the valley, and the sky was wild with color.

"Sit down with me, sweetie," her mother said quietly.

As her father's car pulled away, Frances sat down, and they watched the sky in silence.

"Did they hold hands?"

"I don't know. I didn't notice."

"What was she wearing?"

"I don't know, Mom."

"What is it about that woman he can't live without? Is it because she's musical? I've never heard of a woman playing the saxophone."

There was another silence. Frances was aware of the concrete, cold and hard beneath her.

"She's barely even pretty," her mother said.

On a Friday in October, Frances rode home with Dawn in the front seat of the convertible, winding through the Hollywood Hills like a celebrity. It had rained that morning, and the city below was washed clean, an immaculate version of itself. Dawn's house was huge and new, a white island bursting into a shock of blue sky. Frances loved that house and its pristine acre of grass, sloping beneath the bright clear pool. It was a place where curfews went un-enforced, where parents were harmless and invisible behind the closed doors of the master suite.

Frances pulled on Dawn's Levi's, worn through in the butt and the knees. They glided over her hips and thighs in clean, spare lines. The party was a dark blur—the music and the beer and the pot taking over and remaking her—and after that night she got a boyfriend, a boy named Fred Blue. Frances thought his name full of mystery and contradiction, the opposite, it turned out, of Fred himself. He was selected for her in a complicated rite, like an Indian marriage. He was tall and thin with pink smears—remnants of acne—on his cheeks. Otherwise his paleness was startling, his hair almost white, his skin translucent and blue-veined. He watched her across the pool table, and she gave him a bold, drunken smile. The following week, word came from Dawn's boyfriend's cousin that he liked her. "He plays the drums in a band," Dawn said, and it was decided. Friday night at the football game they held hands. His was bony and damp—an alien thing—and the fact of it made her long for Johnny's sturdiness, his thick waist and easy words. The next day she called in sick to Eddie's. She couldn't bear to be there all day when Johnny was not.

On Monday, Fred picked Frances up at school in his brother's car and gave her a ride home. They drove around and then parked down the street from her house and stood by the car. He put his hands on her waist, and she craned her neck up toward him—and suddenly his tongue was in her mouth. She tried to extend her own tongue, but his mouth seemed filled up. Finally she pulled away and giggled. "I'd better go. My mom will be wondering." She ran a few steps then turned back to wave and smile, the way a girl in a movie might, a girl glowing for the camera in the copper light and painting on her face the fullness of new love.

Fred claimed her Friday nights, from eight until midnight. Each time he took it a little further, working doggedly toward the next milestone. His ministrations were awkward but precise, as if he'd consulted some thick, well-illustrated manual of adolescent sex. First kissing, with tongue, then tongue in ear, on back of neck, under shirt, around tummy and then upward, toward protrusion, left followed by right. Then hands downward toward button of jeans. Frances prayed for wetness, for something loose in her, something slippery and willing. But she couldn't overcome the mechanics, the awareness of every place he put his hands. Her mind fixated on body parts—his hand, her breast, *his thing*. These parts seemed to her remote, cut off from their source. She would guess at what was required—some moan or wiggle—and deliver it up like a sacrifice. She knew the rest would be coming soon—there were unspoken rules about the timing of these things, the intervals—and she began to dread Fridays.

He called every night. If her mother was at work at the hospital, Frances didn't answer. But on nights her mother was home, she wasn't given a choice. "Hello Fred, I'll just go and get her," her mother would say. She would cover the receiver with her palm and whisper with finality, "You will speak with this poor boy when he calls."

On the phone their timing was off. Silence would overcome them, then they would leap to speak at the same time. The cycle repeated—gap of silence, rush of words—until she couldn't bear it, and some excuse would form and burst forth into the receiver: her mother's purse needed finding! the hall needed vacuuming! the Periodic Table of Elements needed memorizing!

"Okay," he'd say. "I'll call you tomorrow."

The first Saturday in December, Frances woke with a jug-wine hangover and the smell of Fred still on her. She took a shower and went to make herself a piece of toast. Her mother had worked the night shift and was still sleeping. There was a quietness of sunlight in the lemon tree at the kitchen window that brought back a memory of how Saturdays had been when she was younger, when she and her father cooked together while her mother slept in. There would be the smell of dark roast coffee and baked sugar and the kitchen taken over by some delicate, perfect thing—corn crepes with mango mint salsa or French toast with figs and lavender honey. The three of them would eat at the old oak table with the morning sun pouring in through the window. After brunch, her mother would take over the kitchen. She would clean and sing, transforming their simple house into a place of polished sinks and lemon-waxed floors.

That was before her father rented the studio in Santa Monica. Before he started coming home only on weekends. Before he met Josephine and moved out altogether. Now Saturday mornings were erratic. Sometimes her mother slept; sometimes she cried. Once, in the middle of breakfast, she'd left the house without saying goodbye. Frances thought it meant an end would arrive, some drama that would decide everything. But after an hour her mother returned with a small shopping bag hanging from her wrist. In it was a gift for Frances, wrapped in tissues held together with a gold seal. It was a new pair of socks.

She was wearing the socks now as she stood at the kitchen window. As she walked outside without shoes and picked lemons from the tree. As she cut sweet peas from the vines that climbed the rock wall out the back door and put them in a vase for her mother. She got on her bike and rode down the hill to Eddie's for the lunch shift. There was a heaviness in her chest and a dullness in her head that even the wind against her face did not clear away. Then Johnny's car was there in the parking lot, and Johnny himself stood at the grill in his apron, slapping special dressing on the buns lined up on the counter. Business had picked up heading into the holidays, Eddie said. Johnny was back on six days a week.

Frances was nervous and careful with him. She kept track of the distance between them. She monitored his smiles, his low easy words. Eddie barreled around, mumbling about specials. In black marker, in his squat irregular printing, he wrote: Tonights Special, BLT, Frys AND Lg coke—$7.95.

"Uh, sorry chief," Becky said. "That's more than the price of them on their own."

Eddie looked down at the sign as if he were just noticing it. "I know that," he said. "That's the trick of a special." He turned and went back to his office, folding the sign under his arm.

Frances took a rag into the walk-in and began to clean. She felt sorry for Eddie and angry with him too, and with Becky. The walk-in door opened behind her and without looking she knew it was Johnny. From behind her, he put his hand on her hip and his mouth next to her ear.

"Hello, Chica," he said.

She let his hand linger, feeling fluid and powerful under her skin.

He put his other hand around her waist and turned her toward him. Then slowly he smiled, and she could see the gold ridges of his teeth like cheap picture frames. The drive-through bell rang, and she slipped from his hands and went to answer it, letting the walk-in door close heavily behind her.

She took the order, then popped the drive-through window open as the car pulled up. It was Fred, grinning, in his brother's car. For what seemed like the first time, she looked at him—the rough cheeks, the pale, watery eyes, shallow and finite.

"Hi," she said, with a kind of bark like a small dog would make. "How *are* you?"

The memory of the night before seemed to enter the room at large. How he'd messed with the button of her jeans until it popped off. How he'd struggled to push them down over her hips until finally she'd stopped him. She couldn't make the leap to what would come next—his mouth *down there*, hand jobs, blowjobs, condoms—objects that seemed perverse and unwieldy, efforts she did not really believe would be rewarded with arousal or satisfaction.

The drive-through bell rang again. "I'm sorry, I have to get that, I can't talk."

"Oh, okay," he said. "I just wanted to know if you knew about the dance, the Christmas thing. Do you want to go?"

"Yeah, definitely. It's this Friday, right?" For a month she'd been expecting him to ask her.

"Yup. Cool. We're renting a limo," Fred said.

"Great. I'm psyched."

Becky leaned in close to get a look. Frances handed Fred his onion rings and chocolate shake, forgetting the straw, the napkins, the ketchup. "See you soon," she said with a miniature wave, just the tips of her fingers moving.

On Monday, Frances got home late from school. Her mother was in the kitchen, the phone tucked between her ear and her shoulder, taking an apricot cobbler out of the oven. The kitchen was heavy with the smell of fruit. Her mother set the cobbler to cool, slipped off her oven mitts, hung up the phone and smiled. She had news. She'd been promoted. She'd be working for the hospital administrator, developing training programs for the nursing staff. She would get a title, a raise, her own office. While she talked, she cleaned the dough from the counter with her long, white fingers. They were fingers that could make a plain dust rag dance over the top of a picture frame, the black keys of the piano, the tricky spot where the leg of a chair meets the seat. They could press warm and firm against your temples and take the pain away.

"Now," she said, "let's go get you a dress for the dance."

The dress they found was midnight blue silk, fitted at the waist with a full skirt to the floor. Frances felt warm and still as she stood before the mirror in the dressing room. Her mother adjusted the straps and smoothed the fabric at her hips and then stood back, finally, and smiled. "Perfect," she said. They bought the dress, and then they bought a pair of high heels and ordered them dyed to match.

The day of the dance opened under a faint cold sky, and in the afternoon it began to rain, the first of the season, grey and unstopping. After school Frances watched the rain tap her bedroom window while she pinned her hair and put on lipstick and pulled on her pantyhose. She put on her heels and slipped the dress over her head and zipped it up the back. She raised her arms in front of the mirror and twisted her body so that the dress flew out around her calves. She saw how well it hung at her waist, how lithe and light she seemed, how smooth the skin was on her bare shoulders. She opened the door and stepped out. When she reached the kitchen, her mother was slumped against the kitchen counter with her head in her arms.

Hearing Frances, she straightened and faced her. "Did you know?" she said.

"Did I know what?"

"That he was having a baby with that woman."

"What woman?"

"Josephine."

There was a silence. "No, I didn't know."

"The least he could have done was tell me to my face. I have to find out from Nana. In a phone call."

Frances could not think of a single thing to say. She watched her mother clench and unclench her fists—the fingers extending and protracting in their own ugly dance.

"You know this means we've lost him, Frances. It was the one thing we had over her. Now it's over. Now she's got him."

Frances could not reply. A current was running through her legs and arms, making it impossible for her to find a comfortable way to stand.

"I guess for you it could be a plus," her mother said. "You'll be a big sister. That might be something you'd like." These last words were nearly lost as her mother slumped over and began to cry.

Frances could sense a gesture inside her, the offer of a hand or a shoulder or a kind word, but she couldn't bring it forward. It was trapped under so much other emotion—anger and confusion and revulsion as she stared at the back of her mother's head. The dark hair had parted to reveal her mother's scalp, pink and awful, and it was this as much as anything that set Frances against her.

"Well, at least we know now he's not moving back home," Frances said.

Her mother stood up and reached for a tissue. She blew her nose and looked at Frances.

"Is that what matters to you, Frances?" she said quietly. "That you're right and I'm wrong?"

Frances shrugged.

Her mother shook her head slowly and pinched her lips together. She turned and brushed past down the hall to her room. She closed the door behind her.

Frances sat down and listened to the rain and the sound of her own pulse in her throat. Fred would be there in an hour. Fred and the limousine.

Finally she heard her mother come out of her room. She stood up as her mother headed past her toward the front door, turning as she reached it and pausing, regarding Frances as if from a great distance, as if noticing her for the first time. She looked her up and down and said nothing. Not how beautiful she looked. Not what a nice job she'd done with her hair. Not how lovely the dress was, how perfect. Not any of the things Frances had come to rely upon and had so abruptly given away.

"I'm going for a drive," her mother said.

"Okay," Frances said. She sat back down. She watched her mother take her keys from her purse and leave through the front door. She listened to the car backing down the driveway and the silence that followed. She let her shoes drop off her feet—they were pinching her toes—and she stripped off her pantyhose.

Then the crunch of the limousine was there on the gravel drive.

Frances put the heels back on and slipped out the back door into the wet December night. The moon was hidden behind a dark ceiling of cloud and the rain fell on her shoulders like small, cool kisses. She pulled her bike out of the garage and rode out the alleyway so she wouldn't be seen. She headed down the hill, her dress tucked under her, the skirt flapping around at her feet. Speed gathered under her and streets she'd known her whole life seemed laden with new meaning, with drama, as if music accompanied them. She took the curves without braking, her pedal scraping the pavement once and then once more. She turned into the parking lot at Eddie's and stopped. Through the window she could see Becky's face, its bright colors aflame, and Johnny—the broad curve of his back, the thickness of his neck. They were laughing, not rushing through the close but laughing and taking their time, standing closer than Frances had imagined they would. She watched them, the bike between her legs, the rain soaking her chest and her thighs and her knees, molding the dress to her body.

Becky turned, finally, and her eyes opened wide as she saw Frances. She pointed, and Johnny moved toward the window. In the instant he saw Frances his face opened with its easy smile. His teeth glinted gold under the bright yellow lights—which made Frances think of Josephine, the clink of her bracelets against the glass tabletop, the sound of something about to break.

NICOLE GRAEV

Tight Jeans

—⟋⟍⟋—

IN 1982, I begged my mother for a pair of jeans. I was six then, and my baggy corduroy overalls would simply no longer do. I put my foot down. I wanted jeans—real jeans—the kind of jeans the big girls wore who hung around outside the minimart: close-fitting, low-riding, ass-hugging, dark blue jeans.

What sparked this fixation? Up until the summer of that year I had never much cared what clothes were put on my body. Sweat suits, snowsuits—whatever my mother selected, as long as it was comfortable, was fine with me. But now I was obsessed. I would drive with her to the minimart to pick up a gallon of milk or a carton of eggs, and as we pulled out of the lot I would lean over the back seat of the station wagon and ogle the girls in jeans who smoked cigarettes and giggled at remarks made by large-looking boys. I would peer hypnotically through the rear window at the girls in jeans as we drove away down the street. By the time we turned the corner at the intersection, their faces would be nothing but blurry masses; but the jeans, with their rigid form and firm contours, leaning boldly against the stucco wall of the minimart as if they stood on their own, were, in all their dark blue splendor, as clear and magnificent as ever. They were unmistakable. That's what I'd be, I thought to myself, if ever I could squeeze into my very own pair of tight, dark jeans—bold, glorious, unmistakable.

We lived that summer in a neighborhood full of children. For me and my brother Adam, who was nine at the time, it was a perpetual playland. Our backyard was connected on one side to the Corvolos' backyard and to the Goldmans' on the other; the Nelsons lived across the street, and the Clarks were only four houses down. With all the kids and roaming space these families had between them, the playing options seemed endless. Our world was several backyards wide; it was free and varied and sprawling, and every corner

of it was ours to share. At least for the first part of the summer. Then Robby
Corvolo got the idea about the clubhouse. Robby was the oldest of the Corvolo boys, and the staggering ten years he had under his belt, combined with
the fact that he owned a dirt bike, put him in a well-deserved position of authority. The clubhouse he wanted to build was going to be the best clubhouse
ever; it was going to be bigger than any of our bedrooms, with a real door that
had real hinges; it was going to have a roof so it could be used in the rain; it
was going to have three coats of paint finished with shellac. And, best and
most important of all, it was going to be for boys only. No girls allowed.

To my horror and the boys' delight, the thing went up—with the help of
Jerome Clark's uncle who dabbled in carpentry. It was creatively named The
No Girls Clubhouse, and across it blazed a huge sign in red letters that said
exactly that: "The No Girls Clubhouse." That sign hissed and sizzled on me
like a brand; it was red and heavy and hot, and I shriveled as it sneered at me
and jabbed me away. It was the first formal barrier I had encountered, and I,
for a reason that I could not help, was on the wrong side of it. For the first
time that I can remember, I experienced the smallness of being shoved aside,
shut out, disregarded. Time spent with the rest of the ostracized while the
boys were inside their impenetrable shelter brought no relief; no matter how
much fun I may have had with these girls, I could never forget that I was with
them by default—that our strongest bond was our deficiency. In a group
comprised solely of girls, I was invisible; they could see me, I knew, but together we were somehow more of an absence than a presence. In retrospect,
it seems to me that my sudden jeans obsession was born out of the sensation
that clubhouse forced upon me—the feeling of being discounted, sub-
tracted, unseen. When I imagined myself inside the clubhouse—or, more
specifically, when I imagined how the boys would see me once I was inside
the clubhouse—the picture was of me, laughing, chatting, performing a secret handshake, and sporting the perfect pair of tight dark jeans.

It didn't take long for my mother to capitulate. I was merciless in my
pleading, and she finally agreed that I was old enough to decide for myself
what I wanted to wear. It was at Aunt Suzy's Clothes for Kids, the origin of
several items in my wardrobe, that I found them: stiff, boot-leg, skintight,
flawless. They even had an added, unexpected touch—two petal-pink ribbons delicately embroidered onto each back pocket, right where my rear end
went. My mother, after eyeing my selection with disapproval, proposed a different pair—one more befitting an active girl my age. They were denim, but
a cottony, shapeless denim. They were *dungarees*. They wouldn't work. After
much bargaining, I returned home that day with what I knew was more than
just a pair of jeans. I returned home with my ticket in.

And it was—sort of—once I had performed my elaborately planned Daisy Duke *coup de main*. Daisy Duke was a character from "The Dukes of Hazard," the cop and high-speed-car-chase show that Adam and I looked forward to watching together every Friday night. Daisy's role on the show was a bit uncertain. She was in some way related to Bo and Luke Duke, the show's stars who fled from the law in a flashy low-rider, and while she didn't really do much to contribute to their victories, the Duke brothers liked her pretty well and she somehow managed to exude hero status. While Adam admired the clever plans of Luke Duke, I was enamored with Daisy. She wore jeans like mine, except hers were ruggedly cut off an inch below the crotch; whenever she got enthused or animated, a fleshy arc of buttock would show through the meager denim shreds of her jean shorts. This occurred weekly during the show's opening credits, which featured Daisy forcefully kicking in a car door with one long, lean leg crowned by a spiked heel. While I knew that cutting off the legs of my jeans was not an option for me, I felt that the pink ribbons perched snugly on either side of my butt somehow made up for this. After several practice runs in front of my bedroom mirror, I was ready to make my move.

I can't imagine what I must have looked like—a scrawny six-year-old girl kicking in that clubhouse door with all my strength. I do, however, remember what I *imagined* myself to look like—none other than the beautiful, feisty Daisy Duke—and I had no doubt that that was whom I looked like to the boys. My jean-clad leg flew up, the door came down, and while my intrusion was met with fierce resistance at first, the club's members were taken with my performance; after some official deliberation mediated by Robby Corvolo, I was awarded permission to spend the rest of the afternoon inside the clubhouse. From that point on, I maintained the status not of club member but of "honorary boy," a title I was proud to have.

As it turned out, the clubhouse wasn't nearly as much fun as I'd expected. While I'd managed to get inside the house physically, I was still under no circumstances to be privy to club secrets. Rituals were performed, code words buzzed in the air, but none of these meant anything to me. Still, it felt good to be there with them—to be large again, and seen. At the same time, I could never really pinpoint why it was that I, of all the girls in our neighborhood, merited the title "honorary boy." While I couldn't resist reminding the others of my important position, I was haunted constantly by a vague sense of guilt—as if I had accepted a prize I didn't deserve. I could understand why the privilege wouldn't be conferred on someone like Rachel Clark, who, with her frilly dresses and hair trimmings, was a boy's nightmare. But what about Katie Nelson? She had always been more interested in doing boy stuff than the rest of us; she could play a mean game of freeze tag, and her skill at climbing trees was unsurpassable. I excelled at none of these things. Why would the boys rather have me around than her? I could think of nothing I possessed that Katie didn't—except, of course, the perfect pair of jeans. Could that really be it? Even at the time, it seemed implausible to me. Nevertheless, it was with those jeans that I associated my power. I vowed to myself that I would wear them every day; I swore that I would never take them off.

What did those jeans mean? Looking back now, I believe they marked my entrance into a position I'd find myself squeezed in for years to come. Filling those jeans, I wedged myself into a narrow breach—the slim gap between the Rachel Clarks and the Katie Nelsons of the world. While Rachel was forced to remain outside the mystical male world of the clubhouse because she, in all her girlish trimmings, so conspicuously didn't fit in, Katie was denied entrance, it occurs to me now, because she so obviously did. The tomboy was competition, the priss was the enemy, and I, in my rough and hardy jeans tenderly embroidered with little pink ribbons, was neither.

What was I then? I was something in the middle—saucy and brash, but not so uppity that I didn't know how to smile and sit quietly while the boys performed their puzzling ceremonies. I was a figment of the imagination. Creative credit belongs in part to the originators of Daisy Duke and other early eighties female fictions like her, but, in the end, the imagination that I was really born from was my own. That summer, haunted by a feeling of absence, I stepped out of my body and imagined what I would look like through an approving pair of male eyes. Then I simply became the thing I saw. It's ironic, really; only by turning myself into the imaginary could I finally feel like a perceptible reality.

What I did that summer when I viewed myself through a male gaze was not an act specific to the time or place in which I grew up. At the turn of the century, almost a hundred years before my jeans were in fashion, Virginia Woolf was performing similar visual acrobatics in England. In her unfinished memoir "A Sketch of the Past," Woolf describes how she, after dressing for a society gathering, would present herself for inspection before her half-brother George Duckworth, a man who adhered unquestioningly to Victorian social codes:

> He at once fixed on me that extraordinarily observant scrutiny with which he
> always inspected our clothes. He looked me up and down for a moment as if
> I were a horse brought into the show ring. Then the sullen look came into
> his eyes; the look which expressed not simply aesthetic disapproval; but

something that went deeper. It was the look of moral, of social, disapproval. . . . I knew myself condemned from more points of view than I could analyse. As I stood there I was conscious of fear; of shame; of something like an-guish—a feeling, like so many, out of all proportion to its surface cause.

George's critical gaze was not enough in itself to fill Woolf with the "an-guish" she describes. The look of disapproval that came into his eyes was per-haps powerful enough to instill fear in her, but shame derives from self-condemnation. As Woolf never honored the Victorian social code as fer-vently as George, it is unlikely that she would so fervently censure herself for breaking it; shame is a sensation she could only have arrived at by stepping outside herself and judging herself from George's standpoint. And George's eye was not simply the eye of one man; it was stronger than that. George, as the product and embodiment of patriarchal Victorian England, gazed with the strength of a culture; when Woolf adopted his point of view, she con-demned herself with the force of an entire society.

Across the Atlantic, a half-century later, patriarchal America of the 1950s gazed at its women with this same patriarchal scrutiny, and its women were conditioned at a young age to scrutinize themselves right along with it. Two years ago I wrote an essay analyzing the voice with which teen magazines of the fifties addressed their female audience, focusing specifically on the drivel in advice columns. In *Seventeen*'s column of February 1956, one girl com-plained that the boys she went to school with seemed to like her but, for a reason she couldn't figure out, did not want to date her. "My problem," she explained, "is that boys don't take me seriously. . . . They tell me their girl troubles, and I help them out. They always say they're too shy to tell anyone else. . . . I'm popular in everything—except dating." The editors' response to this reader was as follows:

> Perhaps the reason you are not being asked on dates can be found by turn-ing a powerful searchlight on yourself. Don't you secretly like being asked for advice because it gives you a feeling of superiority? In a dating situation, it's the boy who likes to feel stronger, since the world will expect him to act this way later on, as husband and breadwinner. Our advice to you is to refuse gently but firmly to manage any boy's problems for him. Instead, ask him to help *you* with something.

The young girl here is assessed through a male gaze; she is spoken to in a voice derived from this gaze; and to help her better understand her egre-gious blunder, she is advised to step outside of herself and inspect herself through this gaze—with the aid of a high-beam light.

Almost a quarter of a century after this advice was given, I was born. With the help of Betty Friedan and Gloria Steinem and the radical feminists of the sixties and early seventies, who had the guts to turn that powerful searchlight away from themselves and onto the world around them, America had undergone a revolution by that time. My female cohorts and I have grown up in an era of liberty and enlightenment. Women can be strong; we can speak our minds without worrying what men think of us; we can listen to our own voices; we can be our own breadwinners; after the long hard struggle, we are finally free from the chains that bind us; at long last, we can be *ourselves*.

Or can we? The last I checked, *Seventeen* was still on the newsstands—right next to *Sassy* and *YM* and a smattering of other newer competitors in the teen magazine market. I know this because I still receive subscription renewal notices from each of these publications. I will not dispute that their contents have altered significantly since the 1950s; sex is discussed in explicit detail, slim pantsuits have replaced poodle skirts in the fashion layouts, and advice columns now offer perfect answers to stumping job interview questions. The modest, passive feminine ideal of the 1950s may, in many ways, be gone, but the voice that dictated it is not; it has simply made some changes in its demands. This voice, as it did in the 1950s, speaks from a male viewpoint. The world may change for women, and male taste and expectations may change with it, but that gaze is never diverted for a second. It is willful and tenacious. When *Sassy* encourages its readers to be their bold, clever, with-it, modern selves—when it, in short, encourages them to be "sassy"—it is usually in the context of how to land a date for the prom. This voice does not tell us to be ourselves; it tells us to be independent and savvy and smart because that's the way men like us—at least for now.

I hear this voice, and I know that the female goddess of my time resides in that chink between tomboy and priss—a lusty Athena tied up in a pink ribbon. That dreaded sensation of absence that I felt outside The No Girls Clubhouse compels me, more often than I would like to admit, to listen to it. I hammer myself into the chink. I am Farah Fawcett on "Charlie's Angels"; I plow through obstacles, outwit the world, and wave around a loaded gun, but mostly because some faceless male voice has so instructed me through a booming intercom, and mostly because I know that I'll be complimented on my performance after I'm done. I watch myself through Charlie's eyes, and I judge myself according to what I see. If I am not pleased with this, I modify my performance, because people look at what they like to see, and I know from experience that I never want to be unseen. I drive myself deeper into the chink, knowing that the tighter I'm lodged, the closer I am to standing atop the goddess's pedestal—way up high where no one's eyes can escape me.

The elements of my performance have been determined not only from such cultural distances but also by a specific pair of male eyes and a voice that I heard in my own home. As most children do growing up, I always fit into a particular, clearly delineated slot in my family. This slot, I believe, was shaped mostly by my father's point of view. "You're too smart for a kid your age," he would declare affectionately when I protested something he said. "It makes it hard for me to pretend I know better than you." The rest of my family would laugh and nod in agreement, and so it was decided; I was the smart kid, the staunchly autonomous one, a "tough cookie." But if my father determined my role, he also led me to take pride in it. If I truly possessed the traits he associated me with, then I must be someone like him, and I wanted nothing more than to be like him. With young eyes, I saw my father hovering above me crowned in a halo of brain waves and strapped with wings of self-sufficiency, and I worshipped him for it. Quality time for us was time spent tossing ideas back and forth like a baseball, and nothing felt better than impressing him with an idea. I would know when that had happened by the way he would look at me just a little, for just a second, with just the hint of a smile; that look would touch me like the tap of a magic wand. It would make me believe that, at least for that moment, he saw me the way I saw him—winged, crowned, poised in the air. I suppose my father's were the first male eyes I ever looked at myself through, and I liked what I saw through them. So much, in fact, that I have since tried to see it again and again, to recreate that magical image, to make it a part of what I see each time I step outside myself and examine myself from a male perspective.

I suppose this could be called "putting my best foot forward." But this phrase has definite positive connotations; it says "you see something in yourself of which you are proud, so you are going right ahead and showing it to the world." But there is a distinct difference between "putting your best foot forward" and turning yourself into a vision. When a woman turns herself into a vision, she puts less energy into *being* and more energy into *showing*, she puts her strengths and talents on display instead of putting them to use; she empties out all the good things from inside of her and pastes them like emblems onto her skin; she becomes a sign of herself, an empty shell. A woman who turns herself into a vision can recognize her positive qualities only as much as these are recognized by her viewer; she depends on the male look to buoy her up, and if she discovers that she is not being seen the way she wants to be seen, she plummets to the ground, crashing like Icarus in a blazing pile of feathers.

In her memoir, Virginia Woolf describes how being the object of George Duckworth's patriarchal scrutiny forced a split in her identity. In the drawing room the young Woolf was both active and detached, simultaneously performing and critically observing those "acts" expected of her by her half-brother. This split gave her attitude to George a "queer twist"; ". . . Even while I obeyed," she explains, "I marvelled—how could anyone believe what George believed? There was a spectator in me who, even while I squirmed and obeyed, remained observant." My own sense of being under the male gaze has similarly endowed me with a dual consciousness. But I believe the age I live in has torn me asunder in a way that Woolf never was; an additional feminist gaze—which nowadays has a cultural force as powerful in many ways as patriarchal scrutiny—severs me yet again, creating a third contender in the battle over my identity.

As much as feminist expectations of women have been co-opted by popular culture to reinvent the female goddess, those expectations still exist unadulterated. I know what they are, and I can look at myself from a feminist perspective and judge myself according to how well I fulfill them. When, from this perspective, I am confronted with a woman who depends on male eyes to make her feel good about herself, I know I have a long way to go. I keep a feminist gaze upon myself and monitor my progress. But still, I cannot fully shake that temptation to see myself as an object of male vision; the two opposing gazes come into conflict and, once again, I find myself wedged in a chink. To please both male and feminist viewer, I must walk a tightrope between two extremes, and this rope is a fine one. I try to keep balanced upon it, but to do so I must hold myself back, because I know there are things about it that could throw me off in an instant, sending me toppling to either side. I too often lose myself in this run-in between gazes; the conflicting sides battle it out while I am left sitting out on the bench. Then, I'm a third wheel; I've lapsed into the third person; I've become "she."

When I was younger, my mother would tell me how fortunate I was to be part of my generation. "It was different for us," she would say. "No one expected us to be anything but a good wife and mother. You can be those things, if you choose, and anything else you decide you want to be." Her words would give me the strangest feeling—an unsettling blend of sadness and excitement. I sensed that there was a void in both of us, but that hers was a hopeless, barred-off void—a vacuum that had never been, and now could never be, filled. The vacancy inside of me was an open, inviting space—

empty, but on the verge of being filled, braced to receive anything I chose to seize and stuff into it.

But packing that space full has not been as simple as I anticipated. Filling it requires forceful movement, rapid action, daredevil decision-making, and it's no easy thing to move forcefully, act rapidly, or make daring decisions when I've wedged myself into a chink or stepped out onto a tightrope wire. When I am aware of the eyes upon me, I am in a state of paralysis, petrified that movement might melt the flattering pose I am frozen in. If I consider the gazes that are fixed on me, I take itsy bitsy steps, dreading the boos of disapproval that will erupt if I fall to the ground. And so, I remain empty. However glorious it feels to be gazed upon with approval, this feeling cannot make up for the horrible sensation of going unsatiated. I want to fill that space, and I want to fill it with the best stuff in the world.

And so I make a pact with myself that I will ease up on the pressure I put on her; I will stave it off from both sides; I will loosen her belt and let her out of her jeans; I will put down my hammer and chisel; from this moment on, I will no longer survey her from a distance. I close my eyes and plow forward blindly; I take giant steps; I tread a swerving path; I charge and graze with every stride; I pack myself full. You might not want to look at me, but you will know I'm there when I knock you over. If you want to stare, that's fine with me. I have no reason to go unseen.

HAYDEN CARRUTH

Intelligence, Anyone?

———ɱ———

FIGURING BACK, I'd say it must have been 1929 when pupils in the third grade at Mitchell Grammar School in Woodbury, Connecticut, were given the Stanford-Binet IQ test. Connecticut was said at the time to have one of the best public school systems in the country, paid for with funds still accruing from the sale of the Western Reserve in the early nineteenth century; this is what we were taught at any rate. The Stanford-Binet test, long since discredited for its bias toward middle-class Anglo literacy, was then still new and well regarded. What the state expected to achieve by administering it to all its third-grade pupils I don't know and can scarcely imagine—except that it couldn't have been done in our properly egalitarian school systems today. But I believe the state was trying to do its best. Mitchell Grammar School was the least of schools, but still the teachers, all of whom I remember, were well trained, certified, devoted, convinced of the importance of their work. They took the test seriously.

I scored high, well up in the classification of genius. It was a disaster. From the first grade on my teachers hadn't known what to do with me, in part because my father had taught me to read and write when I was four years old. I always already knew what I was supposed to learn. They put me at the back of the room in a corner by myself and gave me books to read. In those days, even though Connecticut was a wealthy state and the educational system was reputed to be "advanced"—hence the intelligence tests—we still had four teachers and four classrooms for the eight grades of grammar school, a small step up from the one-room school, so that the third grade, for instance, occupied one half of a room and the fourth grade the other. When a girl or boy in the fourth-grade half didn't know the answer to a question, the teacher would call on me, and from my place off in a corner of the lower grade I'd give the answer. Not for long, however. I learned soon enough that my ostracism was only made worse by this, and I began saying, "I don't know," which probably never fooled anybody then or since though it became and has remained my standard answer to every question. Some readers of my reviews and essays, including some of my editors, have complained about it.

The teachers wanted me to skip a grade, or maybe two. But my parents, who were conscientious and trying to be up to date, wouldn't permit it. They had read in a book by some predecessor of Dr. Spock that children should be kept in their own age groups, that skipping ahead in school would lead to disadjustments. Maybe that was right. I don't know. I labored—the right word, even though the academic side of the program was easy for me—through eight grades at Mitchell Grammar School and never found a solution to that problem.

As for me, what I wanted and wanted desperately was to get rid of my specialness and bury myself in commonness. I did my best to ingratiate myself with my classmates outside of school and to some extent succeeded; I had close friends in those years. I made myself a good, but not the best, marksman with a slingshot. I made myself a good, but not the best, player at marbles, both ring taw and pooning. I became a fast skater and took my part in prisoner's base and other games we played on the ice. At the swimming hole under the iron bridge on the West Side I became a fair swimmer and a courageous, not to say reckless, diver. And so on. I spoke in the accents of my friends, the girls and boys from the farms, listening to them, imitating them. Beginning at age six or seven I dissociated myself as much as I possibly could—not enough—from my family. I never spoke with my friends about what I read in books, though at home in the attic I continued to read a good deal, and I certainly never spoke with them about the fears and uncertainties that engaged my thoughts.

Many years afterward, when I was in my late sixties, I spent a couple of weeks in a mental hospital in Syracuse, and there I was subjected to "psychological testing" that lasted two days. Most of the tests were intended to discover and expose this or that aspect of my personality, but a couple were measures of intelligence, and again, according to the report I was shown, I scored very high. In a way this was gratifying because in the intervening years I had been through all kinds of hell—alcoholism, electroshock, very long periods of treatment with narcotic, hypnotic, and psychotropic medications—and although my memory had been damaged, apparently my crude mental capacities had not. I remember saying to the psychiatrist in charge of my case that what I'd been searching for all my life was a woman who was smarter than I was, so that I could quit all the masquerade. She said: "Not a chance."

I was confirmed in my experience, which was not so gratifying. To become a psychiatrist, for instance, she had been through a course of study that appalled me—pre-med training, med school, internships, I don't know what all—a course of study to which I would never think of submitting myself, yet I was clearly smarter than she was, as she readily acknowledged. And she was a tough, no-nonsense woman who had achieved her place in life against the odds and had suffered hardships—the ones I knew about—along the way. The people I've known personally whose intelligence, which I can only define as quickness and acuteness of understanding, was superior to mine can be counted on the fingers of one hand. It would be foolish to do that, of course. But I don't mind saying that the one who dazzled me the most—I'm speaking of those I've known personally, not of artists and scholars whom I've met only through their works—was Paul Goodman. Yet I've *felt* inferior to almost everyone all my life.

No doubt the consequence is obvious to people who have read my poetry. My early experience among my schoolmates in rural New England may not have been the only reason why I've written so often in languages not my own, but it is a substantial reason. Nor is it the only reason for my life in isolation later on, away from the world of glitzy literary brilliance in Boston and New York, the world I've glimpsed through my friends, Denise Levertov, James Laughlin, Adrienne Rich, Galway Kinnell, and others, for that matter the world I often enough have wanted and in which I've even known that if I could only find an entry I might shine there as well as anyone. But at a tender age I was taught to fear myself and the least promotion of myself, and this has lasted all my life. It has been reinforced over and over again. I've fought against it and in recent years, in my sixties and seventies, have somewhat, though never wholly, prevailed. But in my middle years much of my best poetry—poems like "Marvin McCabe," "Regarding Chainsaws," "Eternity Blues," the asphalt georgics, etc.—was written in this fear and hence in common or colloquial speech. Some was in archaic or poetic speech, or in the characteristic speech of particular intellectual or professional sectors. Literary conventions, the guises of history, were important to me. Almost always and in hundreds of different ways I have submerged my ego in camouflage, fronts, deceptions of all kinds. Call it obfuscation but I hope not obscurantism. Usually I have been unaware of it. It has seemed the natural thing to do.

Well, I hope the work is honest fundamentally. But is it? I don't know.

A further note: not in grammar school, not in high school, but at some time later I came by gradual stages to see that my "I don't know" was more than mere evasion. I knew many things, I had a "photographic memory," but in issues of substance, including moral issues, I truly didn't know. And neither did anyone else, at least that was—and is—my understanding. Knowledge is a function of ego, and like ego exists in the concrete world; it has its importance. But to transcend ego, to become an authentic subjectivity, to become undetermined, was what life in its fullest potentiality was all about. Knowledge was arrogant and condescending, as I knew for years and years and then found even more indubitably when I became an academic: the university is full of the empty bluster of the cognoscenti.

The ancients were right: what one seeks is wisdom. But they were also a little naive, having never suffered the degradations of mass culture and technocracy. The greater part of wisdom is its inaccessibility. Yet I still believe in the efficacy of straight thought—when it is in the service of magnanimity.

RANDOLPH THOMAS

May Prescott

———៕៕———

AUNT MAY was twenty-five the summer I stayed with her. Her skin was dark, her hair long and fine. She had high cheekbones and brown eyes. She was my mother's only sister, and she lived alone in the farmhouse that had belonged to my grandparents, in Ellett Valley, forty miles southwest of Roanoke, Virginia. My grandparents were dead, and the remote location of the farm—the nearest village was Cambria, fifteen miles away—had given May a quiet independence that would prove dangerous in the years to come.

I was twelve. My mother had died of cancer that spring and was buried in northern Virginia where we were living at the time. May sent me a card but did not attend the funeral. I asked my father why, and he told me Aunt May had a lot to do at the farm, that she did not travel well. I accepted this answer. I did not know much about May, except that she lived on the farm that was half hers and half mine. I barely even remembered the farm or Aunt May. When I was little and my grandparents were still living, we visited sometimes in the summer, but May had been shy and standoffish around us, barely even a presence.

My father was a lieutenant colonel in the air force, and after my mother died he requested a transfer to Korea. I remained in the military school I had been attending. That summer I was to stay with my father's parents, which I wasn't looking forward to. Most of the men in my father's family had been in the military. My grandfather had been an officer in the years between the world wars. Whenever I visited, he marched me around the yard and made me stand at attention while he barked out orders from his lawn chair where he sipped drinks from glasses with umbrellas in them. I decided I wanted to spend the summer with May at the farm and wrote to my father, asking if I could go. He refused entirely, insisting that the farm was in the middle of nowhere, that I would hate it there, but I begged and begged. Finally he gave in.

When classes ended, I took a bus to Roanoke where May met me. She was wearing a flannel shirt and jeans. She looked thin and ill at ease in the crowded terminal as I came forward, pulling my trunk. We didn't hug. When I saw her come toward me whispering my name, I didn't even recognize her.

"Why don't you let me help you with that?" May said, leaning toward me tentatively, touching my sleeve.

"No thank you, ma'am," I said. "I'll be all right."

"Suit yourself," May said. She stood back, withdrew her hand, crossed her arms.

She walked in front of me, led me out of the terminal. When we got out to her pickup truck, I could barely lift the trunk. I was sweating, edging it up against the side of the truck when I felt her beside me, helping me. Together we heaved it up onto the tailgate. Out of breath, we leaned there together.

It was early afternoon, and the crowd that had left the terminal with us was dispersing. May shrugged, looked at the trunk.

"Is that full of rocks or what?" she said. Her hair was uncombed, tangled. It shined in the sun. She looked like what my father would have called a hippie.

"Just clothes, ma'am," I said.

She looked at the trunk and at me.

"Everything you own's in there, isn't it?" she said, smiling for the first time.

"Yes ma'am," I said. "Everything."

"Look," she said. "Don't call me ma'am, okay? You're not in the army yet."

I looked at her. I nodded, and she ruffled my hair with her fingers.

"Let's get a pop for the drive back," she said, and I stood by the truck, guarding it, while she went to a machine and bought us some soft drinks.

The road out to Cambria, and then beyond, even farther into the country, was surrounded by forests and pastureland with horses and cows set off by split-rail fences. From time to time there were farmhouses sitting back on knolls, at the ends of long dirt or gravel driveways. Aunt May asked me if I'd ever ridden a horse or if I liked to swim. She reminded me that there was a river bordering our land. She said that we could swim there as much as we liked.

The two-story brick house, which was built by my great-grandfather in 1884, sat on a rise. All of our pastures were rented out to neighboring farmers whose cattle and horses could be seen grazing, in groups or alone. The grasses of the pastures had been nibbled down by the grazing animals, which gave the earth—although it was bright green—a hard, barren look. There were dead trees with short, broken branches, and jagged white rocks jutting from the ground. The land reminded me of pictures I had seen of Greece. I marveled at the country which was so foreign looking and yet the only place I could honestly call my home.

I thought the house looked spooky. Much of the furniture was covered by sheets and made large, grey shadows against the white walls. May gave me a room in the basement. She explained that the house had electricity, but not in the basement. I would have to use a kerosene lantern after dark. I unpacked and took a nap after I arrived, and when I woke up May was sitting in the room with me, in a chair in the corner, watching me. At first I wasn't sure where I was, and I lay there blinking.

"I hope I didn't scare you," May said, finally. "It's been a long time since I've seen you. I just wanted to look at you."

I didn't answer her. I just blinked and nodded. May seemed to want to talk now, and her voice, which never got very far above a whisper, was deep and halting. She got up and walked around the room. "This used to be your great-grandfather's room," she said. "It was his favorite room in the house. He liked it because it was cool in the summer."

I propped my head up on my elbow. "Did you know my great-grand-father?"

"When he was old. You favor him, I must say, especially around the eyes. And the nose. I have a picture of him when he was your age. It's in my room, and I'll show it to you sometime. But we don't have to do that now. Well, I'm keeping you awake talking. I'll go now. You take your nap. We can talk later." May left the room, but I wasn't sleepy anymore. I got up and dressed and went upstairs.

"Where's the TV?" I said. May was sitting in the living room, in one of the chairs that wasn't covered with a sheet, reading. She was beside the window. The bright afternoon light made the room look dark. The house was completely quiet.

May looked up at me and laughed. "I don't—," she said, laughed again, waved her hand in front of her face, shook her head. "I've got a radio but no TV." I nodded. "Listen," she said. "Why don't we take a walk or something. I'll show you around, then we'll eat."

That night we had tomato casserole and pecan pie for dinner. Afterwards we listened to the radio. May got a big roll of paper from the attic, and I lay on the floor and drew pictures. After dark she went to a place that she said was top secret and came back with a lit candle and a cracked Ouija board with letters so faint I could barely read them.

"Do you know what this is?" she said. I shook my head, and she explained that we could use the Ouija board to talk to the spirits of the house. May set the board on the kitchen table, put out all the lights except for the candle. She turned a clear juice glass upside down on the board and touched the bottom with her fingertips. She told me to touch it too.

"Spirit," May said. "Spirit, can you hear me?"

The glass began to move, draggingly at first, as if the spirit were only beginning to remember how to speak. The glass moved over the word *yes*, and May said, "Spirit, do you have a message for anyone among us?" The glass continued, stopping on letters until it spelled my name.

I looked up at May, took my fingers from the glass. Her hair was parted in the middle and dangled down the sides of her cheeks. Her eyes were heavy as though she were sleepy, and her lips made a sly smile for me.

"Mom," I said.

May took her hands off the glass. She reached across the board and touched my shoulders. She squeezed them.

"No," she said. "No, I don't think it is."

"What if it is?" I said.

"It can't be," May said. She bit her lip. "It can't be her because she hasn't been gone long enough." She was still squeezing my shoulders, and now she was looking into my eyes. "You can only talk to people who have been gone a long time," she said. She suggested that we talk to my great-grandfather.

"Ask him about Mom," I said, and May did. My mother, my great-grandfather said, was fine.

May brought the Ouija board out almost every night. My great-grandfather told us stories about the house, and my great-great-grandfather told us stories about the Civil War. In the evenings we also listened to the radio or took turns reading each other our favorite stories from the crinkling yellow pages of books from my grandfather's library.

May had a vegetable garden. She baked her own bread, made everything we ate—rich casseroles, cakes, and pies—from scratch, and her cooking was nothing like the quick meals my mother had prepared in the prefabricated houses on the bases where I spent my early life.

Our farm had one cow for milk. It was my job, once May had taught me how, to milk it. We had two mares, which we rode to the river to picnic at least every other day, and there was a henhouse. We called it the hen hotel because there were so many vacancies.

The farmers who used our land cared for their own animals, and occasionally we saw our neighbors when we were hiking or riding along some ridge, or stopped, eating sandwiches beside a rock. But except for these glimpses and for an occasional drive to Gibbons store in Cambria, the summer was completely ours, and we did not have to share it with anyone.

After morning chores were completed, May made sandwiches—tomato and mayonnaise or ham and sweet pickles with a dab of mustard—and we rode the mile path to the river. The path was narrow. Around it, as the ground became steep, there were more rocks and willows, some of which were very tall with long, sweeping branches that rattled if the wind blew. But mostly the days were hot. We wore shorts and T-shirts. At the bottom of the hill, a line of willows ran the length of the river and leaned out over the water. Beneath the trees were rocks, and there was no beach, only a five-foot drop to the river. We would let the horses graze. We ate our lunch on the rocks and then dove into the river in our clothes.

On the other side of the river was more pastureland which belonged to a neighbor. There were always sheep coming up to the edge of the river and bleating to us. Sometimes we threw bits of bread to them. We swam and played, splashing each other, and then we lay beyond the tree line in the sun until our clothes dried.

One afternoon I was swimming against the current, upstream to a wide spot where the water ran faster. We were playing water tag. May was swimming after me, calling my name between gulps and laughter. Rounding a bend, I realized she was so far behind me that she wouldn't come into view for two or three minutes. I moved to the side, clawed at the dirt bank until I could reach a branch, and pulled myself out of the water. I scrambled up over the bank and lay with just my head leaning out far enough to see her. May rounded the bend and swam past me. I pulled my knees up underneath me, knelt, and sprang into the water behind her. I landed in a hole, six or seven feet deep in the river bottom. The water was brown, and I couldn't see anything. When I bobbed up, the current took me by surprise. It seemed suddenly stronger, and my breath was knocked out of me. The water pulled me into another hole. There was water in my mouth and lungs. I was coughing. I'd been washed about twenty or twenty-five feet when I felt May's arm around me, under my arms. I felt her legs kicking behind me, under me, between my legs as she pulled me to the side where she pressed her back against the bank and held me. I was still coughing, but she was already squeezing me from behind, forcing the water out of me. I could feel her breasts heaving against my back, her breath against my neck.

"I'm sorry," I said, my words broken by coughs.

"Thank God," she said, and I felt her wet lips against the back of my neck. "Thank God."

By the time we got out of the water, it had started to rain. The sky had been clear blue all morning, and the rain, which had arisen suddenly, was one of those hard summer rains that doesn't usually last long. We ran home through the rain. It wasn't until we reached the house that I realized I had lost my watch. It was one my father had given me for Christmas three years before. The watch was on a stretch band. After I'd calmed down, I could remember the water pulling it over my hand.

"That watch is gone," May said. We were sitting on the wide wooden porch that ran across the front of the house, watching the rain. We were still wet, catching our breath, sitting side by side. May put her arm around my shoulder and held me to her, rubbed my hair and kissed my cheek. "There's no use looking for it," she said. "You'll never find it again."

The next day I finished my chores early and walked down to the river. I believed that the rain might have washed the mud out of the river, that I might be able to see my watch on the bottom. I walked the length of our land on the rocks, looking down into the water which was still a murky brown. I didn't see anything except a dead lamb floating. The lamb was newborn. I stared at its thin, white hair, at the pink of its lips and its eyelids, which looked like they were pinched shut. The lamb washed against a rock and was caught there. I looked across the river, thinking that its mother might be watching from the other side, but that day I saw no other sheep. I heard May calling me, and turning, saw her walking down from the house. I looked back at the lamb, saw that it had washed free from the rock, and ran to May.

The next morning I awoke with a fever from a summer cold I had caught the day we ran through the rain. I ran a temperature for two days. May moved me to one of the upstairs rooms where she brought me soup and sandwiches. She read to me. At night, when I awoke from bad dreams, sweating, May was already in the room with me, asleep or reading in a chair. She gave me alcohol rubs. Afterwards, she sat on the corner of my bed, massaged my face and my hair and whispered stories and jokes to me until I fell asleep. One night after the fever broke, I awoke and found myself alone. I had become spoiled by May's doting on me. I climbed out of bed and walked down the hall to her room. The hall was dark and the house was quiet. I closed my hand into a fist and was about to knock when her door sprang open. May stood before me, her robe pulled around her. The lamp beside the bed was on, and it lighted her face. I could see sweat on her cheeks and brow. I didn't say anything, only stood there looking at her. Slowly, she smiled at me.

"You were lonely too," she said. I nodded. She bit her lip and smiled and looked at me. Then she took my hand and led me to bed. I climbed in, pulled the sheet up to my chin and watched May. She pulled her robe tighter around her, and retied the belt, and climbed under the sheet with me where she held me against her.

After that we always slept together, in her bed, which she always made in the mornings, neatly folding the simple white spread, which had been made by her mother, around the corners of the pillows. May always slept with her cotton robe tied around her and some nights after she had fallen asleep, I would turn and watch her, the curves of her body beneath the sheet that covered us.

In the middle of June, we made our first trip into Cambria to get some groceries from Gibbons store. Cambria, at the base of a mountain, consisted of two stoplights, a few stores, a boarded-up train station, and a post office. May had been talking about the trip for over a week, but she had put it off until it was absolutely necessary.

When we got into town, May parked on the street and we got out. Walking along the cracked and broken sidewalk, I saw two boys a couple of years younger than I was sitting on a bench between the post office and the store. They both looked dirty from play, their hair long and wild. I stopped walking and looked at them. May didn't stop, but speeded up. I had to run to keep up with her. When we got in the store, the man behind the counter said, "Miss Prescott, George Riley wants to come out and see if you need any fencing done." May stood and looked at him and nodded.

"I don't think we need anything," she finally said, her head bowed as if she were closely examining the scuffs of the tile floor.

"He's hard up, Miss Prescott," the man continued. "I don't know if you heard, but Agnes is laid up in Roanoke, and it looks real bad for her. I'm sure George'd do about any kind of job you could come up with."

May nodded again but didn't answer. She headed down an aisle toward the back, stopped at the wall, held herself and closed her eyes. I followed her and stood near her.

"What are you looking at me for?" May said. Then, "Why didn't you get a cart?"

I shrugged, knowing that something was wrong and not understanding what. "I'll go," she said, and she headed toward the carts at the front of the store. May had a list of things we needed, and she began gathering them from the aisles and putting them in the cart. I followed her, but she was ignoring me. I felt useless to her, and I wandered back outside. The two boys were still there. They looked like brothers, and one of them was a little taller, maybe a year or two older, than the other one.

"What are you doing?" the older boy said.

"Waiting on my aunt," I said.

"We're waiting too," the boy said.

They studied me. I glanced up the post office steps.

"What's up there?" I said.

The older boy shrugged and then the younger one shrugged, imitating him.

I wandered up the steps. Gradually, they followed me. I opened the glass door and went inside.

Except for us, the post office was deserted. I pointed to the wanted posters on the bulletin board. "Can you read?" I said, and the older boy shook his head. I read the wanted posters to them and began looking through some armed forces literature that was stacked on one of the tables. I showed them a picture of a new fighter jet, explained that my father was an officer in the air force, that once, on the base where we lived, he had taken me to see this very jet, that I had sat in it and pretended to fly it. The older boy nodded and shrugged, and the other watched him to see how he was supposed to act. I was looking down at the brochure again when May grabbed my arm. I turned around. May took hold of me with both hands and shook me. Her face was red. Looking around her, I saw the two boys dash out the door.

"What do you think you're doing?" she said. "What do you mean running off like that?"

"I'm sorry," I said. "I didn't think you wanted me around."

"We've wasted enough time," she said. "Let's go home." She pulled me, her grip tight on my arm, down the steps of the post office. May was practically dragging me, saying, "How could you?" under her breath. I turned and saw the man from the store watching us through the window. May opened my door and said, "Get in." Then she went around to her side, got in and slammed the door behind her. The tires squealed and stirred up a cloud of dust, erasing Cambria as she pulled out. May drove fast, her gaze fixed forward. We drove about a mile out of town at breakneck speed. Even after she slowed down, May was quiet. She didn't talk during dinner, and there was no Ouija board that night. Later, after we had gone to bed, I heard May crying beside me. Her back to me, I reached over her, touched her face. I held my hand against her cheek. She turned around and put her arms around me. She said over and over that she was sorry, but I was careful during all of our other trips to Cambria. I stayed close to May but tried to stay out of her way. In town she was always tense and nervous, but I never gave her the opportunity to get mad at me there again.

Our days and nights at the farm continued unchanged, but I was changing. One afternoon in late July, after we had been swimming and while we lay on the bank drying ourselves, I propped myself up on my elbows and looked at her. She was lying flat on her back beside me, her eyes closed. I watched her breasts and her flat stomach move as she breathed. Her nipples were wide and dark through her shirt. Her shirt was short. Her belly button was exposed, and I reached out and tickled it lightly with my finger.

May laughed and spoke my name. I put my hand flat against her stomach, and May laughed again.

"Stop," she said, "your hand is cold," but she didn't open her eyes, and I began to move my hand, walking it like a spider. May continued to giggle. I moved my hand faster, up under her shirt toward one of her breasts.

"Cut it out," she said. She sat up. Her brow was wrinkled and her hands were both on my arm, roughly forcing it down and out of her shirt.

"Ow," I said, because she was bending my arm backwards. "Hey, I'm sorry, that hurts."

I wrenched my arm free and looked away from her. I stood up, ran toward the house.

"Stop," I heard her say. "Wait for me."

I was confused and stumbling over rocks, not staying on the path, and she caught up with me.

"Hold it," she said. She grabbed the back of my shirt, but I pulled, stretching it.

"Wait." She grabbed me around the shoulder, circled her other arm around my waist, and knocked me off balance. We rolled on the ground and she pinned me.

"Listen," May said. "I'm sorry I hurt you, but there are things you're not supposed to do. I know you come from a place where there aren't any girls."

After dinner, May said that maybe I should sleep in the room downstairs. I picked at my food and didn't answer her. The next day we did our chores, rode to the river, picnicked and swam. At night after the stories or games or the Ouija board, May retired to her room upstairs, closing the door behind her.

August was very dry and hot. As the date of my return to school drew near, we talked about my visiting the next summer. The length of a year seemed impossibly long to me, and the rigorous schedules and assignments had now grown as foreign as the ease and ennui of life on the farm had been before I came. A few nights before I left, I caught May cheating with the Ouija board, pulling her edge of the glass to make answers that would make me laugh or be spooky and mysterious. In truth, I had known it wasn't real for some time and this night, perhaps because I was angry for having to leave, I lifted my fingers from the rim of the glass, which tipped from the pressure of May's fingers. The glass rolled across the board and dropped to the floor.

"I caught you," I said.

"What?" May said.

"You were cheating," I said.

"No."

"Yes you were. You were making it all up."

"But I wasn't making it up," May said. "How can you sit there and call me a liar?"

"I'm not." I shrugged.

May's eyes narrowed watching me. Her face became red, her voice lowered. "These are the spirits of this house," she said. "These are the spirits of these walls."

"You were moving it," I said. "Why else would the glass have gone off the table like it did, unless you were moving it."

"Because you doubted the spirits," she said, "and it made the spirits nervous."

I shook my head. May stood. She picked up the board, bent over, and picked up the glass from the floor.

"All right then," she said. "You believe whatever you want." She headed out of the room.

"Come back," I said, but she was heading up the stairs. "I didn't mean it," I called after her, but then I heard her footsteps cross the big hall upstairs, heard her bedroom door slam, and we never played with, or spoke of, the Ouija board again.

The day I left to go back to school, May was quiet but cheerful when she spoke. My breakfast was on the table when I came into the kitchen. She watched me eat, and afterwards we drove to the bus terminal in Roanoke where she put fifteen dollars in my hand, gave me a bag of egg sandwiches. We pulled my trunk inside, and both of us laughed when I bumped into a man because I wasn't watching where I was going. Before I got on the bus, she hugged me hard. She told me to write her and to mind my father. I said I would. When I got to my seat, I propped open the window just as the bus began to move out of the terminal. There was a crowd of people outside waving goodbye. I searched for May, but I could not find her among them.

That was August of 1974, and I did not return to the farm for seventeen years. When I did, I came in a station wagon with my wife and children one afternoon following a weeklong drive across the country. I showed my family into the living room, but I was overcome by the place — it was exactly the same as I remembered. I had planned to give them a tour, but my voice faltered. Melissa, my wife, sensed that I wanted to be alone. She took the boys — Michael and Todd — outside. Upstairs I found the door to May's room open. On her desk by the window, I found a wide vase full of letters bound in rubber bands. More than half of the letters were from me, and I marveled at the number of letters I had sent her.

I began writing to May the day I left, while on the bus to northern Virginia. After I returned to school, I missed May and the farm. I became bored with my schoolwork. My grades slipped to just above the passing mark. May and I wrote to each other at least once a week, telling each other about our days, and I looked forward to her letters like nothing else because they freed me, if only for a short time, from the strictness and monotony of my life. That spring my father was promoted to full colonel and given command of a base in Hawaii. Although I wanted to go to the farm and see May, my father was adamant that I should join him. I wrote to May, and she replied that my father was right, that I should be with him. She said that perhaps I could come the following summer instead.

In Hawaii I felt that May and the farm had been in some distant world. This depressed me, but I enjoyed spending time with my father. We played tennis almost every day. I wanted to enroll in a nonmilitary private school, but my father resisted, telling me I needed preparation for the Air Force Academy, which was only a few years away. He made me adhere to rigorous study hours in the evening, coached me with my homework, and, gradually, my grades did improve. One night he came into my room without knocking and found me writing a letter to May by flashlight.

"I thought I said lights out," he said, but after I told him what I was doing, he smiled. He took the letter from my hand and glanced over it.

"You know," he said, "it's very good of you to keep up with your mother's family."

I nodded and looked at the letter in his hand.

"When I was your age, your grandfather had to make me write to the relatives. He made me sit down at the dining room table and do it."

I was looking at his face. My father was a very tall man with a broad forehead and a receding hairline. His eyes, though, were small and he squinted nervously.

"This would make your mother happy." He turned his head away. He set the letter on the table, patted my knee through the sheet, then, composed, looked at me again. "All the same, I said lights out. You can finish that letter to your Aunt May tomorrow."

He cut off the light and went out of the room. I realized then that I had been close to May in a way he didn't realize. From the beginning I had known—I don't know how I knew—that I would never tell him that I had slept in the same bed with May. Now I understand that I was right not to tell him, that he would have thought that May was perverse. May had been clinging desperately to the only family she had, treating me as though I were her own child, a child she did not know exactly how to love. She had meant nothing sexual or hurtful. But I had loved May. She was the first woman I ever fell in love with.

That was the fall I turned fourteen and got drunk for the first time when I was spending the night at a friend's house. That was the year of my second crush, on a girl a few years older than me who worked as a lifeguard and who let me kiss her once after I stayed late helping her close down the pool. That same spring, my father told me at breakfast one morning that he had heard from the attorney in Roanoke who was looking after my trust. A neighbor had found May wandering in one of the pastures we rented. She spoke to the neighbor belligerently. Worried, the neighbor telephoned the sheriff, who found May in her bathtub a short enough time after she had slit her wrists to save her life. May had been hospitalized in what my father called a sanatorium.

My father came over to my side of the table, awkwardly put his arm around me and said that he was sorry. I sat at the table stiffly and didn't acknowledge his embrace.

He said that May had mental problems.

"Yes," I said. "I know that."

"She can't cope with people," he said. "She shuts herself up on that farm. Your grandparents knew she had problems, but they didn't do anything about it." He looked at me, and for lack of anything else to say, I suppose, he shrugged.

Of course there would be no trip to the farm that summer. I saw this, was disappointed by it, and at the same time felt ashamed at my selfish disappointment. I looked down at my food. Having lost my appetite, I said I wanted to go to the pool. Instead, I walked to the ocean and lay on the sand for the rest of the morning.

Sometimes as I was drifting off to sleep, May would return to me, her voice speaking or laughing inside my head, or I would see the outline of her body beside me. I thought of when we would lie beside the river drying ourselves and of her laughter during our sunny days together.

I worried about May. I continued to write her, although I didn't know what to say in my letters except what I had always said: I told her how I was feeling, described what I was doing and studying, and went back over the experiences I most enjoyed when I had stayed with her. I didn't hear from her for nearly two months, and then she wrote to me from the farm. In the letter she sounded fine. She said the hen hotel was doing better business and that the cow refused to be milked by anyone but me. The letter cheered me up. I wrote her back immediately, but May was hospitalized again and again. Gradually our letters dwindled to three or four a year.

Ultimately I failed my father by refusing to go to the Air Force Academy. I did not even apply. I eloped, instead, with Melissa, whom I had been dating for five months. We flew to the mainland, to Los Angeles, where we stayed with Melissa's sister until we found our own place. Over the next six years, both of us attended UCLA part time and worked. I got a degree in journalism and found a job working for a trade journal. I kept in touch with my father regularly. Over the years, especially after the boys were born, we grew closer again. Once, though, when we were in the midst of a heated long-distance argument, he said, "You're one of them all right."

"What?" I said. It was three o'clock in the morning. I was sitting on the fire escape with the kitchen window closed on the telephone cord, so only the neighbors, and not Melissa or her sister, could hear me arguing with my father.

"Unreasonable," he said. "You're irrational. Crazy. Prescotts."

I have since forgiven him for saying this. I know that he truly loved my mother, and except for that one angry outburst, which came from his disappointment in me alone, he has always held a silent reverence for my mother's family.

But he was right. I am one of them. Maybe not completely. Maybe only half. At the farm, while the boys played on the lawn and while I was looking through May's papers, I came across a stack of family photographs. There were only ten or eleven, some of them of people I did not recognize, but I found the photograph of great-grandfather, the one May had promised to show me but never had. He was a boy, wearing shorts and the white bib children wore then. He was sitting on a fence, and there was a hunting dog staring up at him. His hair was parted in the middle and combed neatly to the sides. Beside the styles that separated our times, we bore a striking resemblance.

I also found a picture of my mother and father, shortly after they were married, standing in the living room downstairs. They had been fishing. My father held a net in one hand, a rod in the other. I realized for the first time how much my mother looked like May Prescott when she was younger. May would have been five or six at the time the photograph was taken, and I wondered if she had been in the room, hiding behind a piece of furniture, her face buried in her hands.

My father settled in San Diego after he retired. He never remarried, and his face took on the unnatural redness of an alcoholic. When he called me one day and said it was urgent that we speak in private, I was sure he was only going to brood, complain about the world, and speak at length on the dwindling greatness of our family. I went anyway—I always go—and met him for lunch at his military club. As was the case each time I had seen him since his retirement, he was drinking gin and smoking cigars. We sat at a table in a windowless room with ceiling fans. While I ate, his bloodshot eyes watched me, and I kept expecting that a speech was imminent. When I finished eating, he said as if I wouldn't even remember her, "I have some bad news. May Prescott, your mother's sister, has drowned herself."

For me, May and this place will always be inseparable. When I finished looking through her letters, I put them back. Outside, walking to the river with a bouquet of wildflowers Melissa had picked, I saw a neighbor in the distance mending a wire fence. He waved and I waved back. The river smelled fresh, and I could smell the pungent manure of the animals. I wondered how May could have suffered here, perished here, in the first place I had felt alive.

That night, after I had settled the boys into their room, called lights out, and retired to the dark of the basement where Melissa and I were to sleep, I remembered May's voice as clearly as I remembered the stone wall at my back and the lantern that was burning beside me.

"I'm going to miss you," May had said. It was two or three nights before I left for school. It was dark. My eyes focused on her standing in my room, her face above the lantern she carried. She moved to the doorway. "Why don't you come on," she said. "I think it'll be all right." I got out of bed and followed her up the steps through the living room and the hall, up the steps to the second floor, and to her room where we got into bed and she turned out the light.

"Aren't you going to miss me?" she said.

I couldn't answer because I didn't want to have to miss her. May pulled the sheet over my head and started tickling me. I laughed until my eyes welled with tears. May laughed and later—after she had whispered my name and believed that I had gone to sleep—I heard her cry. She had turned away from me. Her cries were muffled, but I still hear them fill the house, echoing through all the rooms. I hear them by the river where we picnicked, in all the places where my children laugh and play.

ELIZABETH SPENCER

Sightings

—ᗰᘉᘉ—

MASON EVERETT, a man who lived mostly happily in his own mind, hadn't any idea why his daughter Tabitha had come to visit him. It's true they never saw much of each other. Maybe it was a shame. He was neutral on the subject. He had long loved her at a distance, but now she was close she brought back shadows. Still he was willing to find out what she wanted. Her mother, in far-off Maryland, was maybe the one to ask. On the other hand her mother might be the very reason she headed his way. She arrived about twilight in a cab from the airport.

"But I would have met you," he protested.

"Too much trouble," she answered, and came right in with her duffel. She looked like all the rest of the ones her age, but also bore a resemblance both to him and Celie. He remembered that when young he too had done unexpected things. She went upstairs to the spare room. She shut the door. Mason waited downstairs and thought about dinner.

Other ideas trundled through his head. Was she into a love affair, was she on drugs, did she drink, did she need money? If she needed money, why did she take a taxi from the airport? Everything went in a circle until he heard her step on the stair coming down. She drifted around the living room. Did not turn on TV. "How is your mother?" he inquired. Tabby said her mother was okay. He had not counted on monosyllables. He tried several other directions but finally gave up. "Is a steak all right?" She said yes. She also said, when asked, that she liked it medium.

During dinner he asked if she was in school. She replied that she had had to leave. "Had to leave?" he repeated, inviting her to explain. But she did not say anything more.

Mason wondered why he didn't push her further, but then of course he knew why. It was a habit formed long ago, not to go too deep, not to quarrel. If they quarreled, they would get back to the accident, that blue blinding flash, that had brought guilt in, and blame, wordless until her mother got into it and a real quarrel started, the kind that spiraled downward till it reached a depth charge.

He was walking his dog Jasper the next evening when old Mrs. Simpson, who occupied her front porch as a regular thing, called out, "I hear your daughter's with you."

"Yes, ma'am," Mason answered, adding, "She can walk the dog."

She had walked Jasper twice now, once with Mason, once alone. He seemed content in his private way. Airedale mix, had looked forlorn in the shelter when Mason chose him out of others. But choosing didn't change him; he still looked forlorn. Tabby didn't pet him but seemed to like him.

"What's her name?" asked Mrs. Simpson.

"Tabitha. We call her Tabby."

"Tabby and Jasper," said Mrs. Simpson.

Mason agreed that was it.

In the years since Cecilia left, Mason had framed up his life in an adequate way. He missed her but not what she had turned into. But he liked a woman to be somewhere in his life; and when passing through one of the town malls, he observed a likely one who owned a knitting and handwork shop. She was doing some sort of fancy stitching when he walked in. He introduced himself and found she knew him already. She had had some acquaintance with Celie. He said that Celie had moved away. Yes, they were separated. Too bad, she said, but things happened. Her name was Marsha. He asked if he could call her. She thought a minute and then laid aside a bright length of wool to write down her number. So it was easy as that. She had had two husbands, both long gone. He agreed that things did happen. Though he didn't see her often, he liked to know she was there.

Tabby began to catch the bus in the afternoon and to be absent until dark. He didn't ask where she went. But one afternoon he called Marsha, who didn't work on Thursdays. Mostly, he wanted to talk about Tabby.

"Can't you call her mother? Seems to me her mother should have called you."

"She did call. The evening Tabby arrived. I said, 'Yes, she's here. Yes, she's fine.' I hung up."

"You ought to have asked some questions."

"That's the very thing I don't want. I don't want Celie's side. I want Tabby to tell me what she wants to when she wants to tell it. None of this ought-to business."

Marsha laughed. "Well then you'll just keep rocking along for months and years." She sat in her big chair, doing handwork.

"It's fine with me," said Mason and added, "She likes Jasper."

"Does Jasper like her?"

"He doesn't say."

"How old is Tabby?"

He counted back. "About sixteen, I think." He grinned, sheepish. "Actually, I'd have to look it up. I forget."

"I think you just better come right out and ask her what the problem is."

He didn't really want to. He remembered the terrible day she had blinded him, the flash of blue light in his face when he was trying to fix the electrical motor for her CD player. He was threading the wires together, holding them close to squint at when she had connected the plug to the outlet. His eye streamed water and blood, and she yowled *I'm sorry* till her mother made her stop. It seemed to him every time he looked at her, she was yowling it yet, for his sight never entirely came back. Did it matter? He could read and work as he did before. The surgery had been delicate, one eye all but blind, the other intricately damaged. The accident gave him the chance to work at home instead of at the office. He wore glasses with thick hexagonal lenses and had to have special equipment to work with figures. Insurance supplied the major expense. So what did it matter in the long run? Sight-damaged people went successfully through life. It was well known. But he read it as a constant theme in his daughter's eyes whenever they met his, never to be erased. *I'm sorry, I'm sorry.* And instead of *It's okay, forget it,* his said now, *Why are you here?* No answers so far, but, as Marsha told him, he had to try.

Tabitha had volunteered to cook dinner and turned out something done with hamburger meat that was edible. When he had praised her and eaten enough, she brought out some ice cream, and he ate that too.

"Listen, honey," he started. "We've got to talk."

She looked up. He thought he heard *I'm sorry.*

"I haven't asked you yet. I was too glad to see you. But why did you come? Just to visit? No other reason?"

She played with her spoon. She let Jasper lick it clean. She leaned to pet him. "It's mother," she said.

"Well, what about her?"

"She wants to marry somebody. I think he's terrible."

"Terrible or not, I can't stop her. What's his name?"

"Mr. Bowden." She winced on the word. "I told her, if he didn't leave, I would. She got mad. I think he's an alien."

"From where?"

"Outer space alien."

"Oh." After a silence he said, "But if she's happy with him . . ."

"Nobody could be," said Tabby.

He sighed. He was a little bit jealous; unavoidable, he supposed.

"Have you heard from her?"

"I told her I was coming here. She was mad and shaking."

"She gets like that," he recalled, speaking half to himself.

The next day Tabitha got a letter. Mason, who went for the post, saw it before she did. The lettering of the address was stiffly upright, like printing. He gave it to her to open, and she read it aloud.

> *I know your mamma misses you, she says so all the time. I wish you would come back. We can all go out to restaurants and the movies. You wouldn't have to go unless you want to.*
> *Your friend,*
> *Guy Bowden*

"You see what he's like?" asked Tabby.

"Maybe he means it," said Mason.

"He's stupid," said Tabby.

They alternated cooking. Tabitha improved. Mason asked Marsha to dinner. Tabitha wore a bright blouse, brought up out of that bottomless duffel. She ironed her jeans and put on lipstick. She made a veal concoction, which was edible. Mason opened some wine.

"I'll teach you to sew," Marsha offered.

"Maybe I ought to learn," said Tabitha and got dreamy.

"She's like you," Marsha told Mason. "She's pretty though."

"Are you going to marry her?" Tabitha inquired later on.

"Nothing like that," Mason replied.

"What you mean, 'like that'? You sleep together, don't you?"

"Mainly we're just friends."

It was a week since she came. Jasper now slept in her room, lying near the door sill. Sometimes he snored.

There was bound to be a foray.

When the phone call came, Mason was alone in the house and had no idea what to say. "I can't direct you here unless you tell me where you are." It was Celie, travelling with Guy Bowden. She thought they should all get together and talk. "We've got to understand things," she said. She had forgotten how to get to the house. The new highway had confused her sense of direction. They had stopped at a minimart to telephone. Mason knew where it was.

"Tabby's not here now," he floundered. "Get something to eat and call us back."

"We've eaten already," Celie wailed. She had taken on her desperate sound.

"Everett! Guy Bowden here." The voice was commanding. "We would like to see you."

Mason hung up. He wasn't going to be bossed around. Where was Tabby? Letting Celie know he'd no idea where she was—that would cause a flare-up. He shrugged into a jacket and took Jasper for a walk, hoping to think things over.

When he turned the corner to return home, he saw the strange car parked in front of the house, also Tabby, approaching from the bus stop. And now he freely saw what he had been thinking all along without knowing it: *It's her and me. It's WE. And they are THEM.* Big question: *Did Tabby think so too?* In just one week it might have happened.

He hastened to her, heart beating with unexpected love that now came on full force, out in the open. How urgent it was. To love and to know.

"Honey," he said, "it's your mother."

"Oh, God," said Tabby and thrilled him.

He caught her hand. Jasper wagged to see her. They huddled, a party of three.

"I bet he's with her," said Tabby, adding, "Let's go somewhere else."

It seemed such a good idea that Mason almost thought it might work. But he was not entirely lawless yet, and they went in.

They were both in the living room. Celie looked as if she still belonged here and had told just Guy Bowden to sit down. That was the first thing. The next was how nice they both looked. Mason recognized that he and Tabby did not look nice. They looked scruffy.

Guy Bowden was a beefy fellow, large arms, thick legs, heavy feet. But wearing a nicely pressed grey suit, a satin tie. Celie was trim, she was a word he used to think about her: petite. It rhymed with neat. That was long ago when he was proud of her.

Guy Bowden was looking all around without approval; but when Mason and Tabitha entered, he at least stood up. Celie had rushed to Tabby, who now was getting her hug. Jasper growled.

"Leaving me!" Celie wailed. "It's been just awful, you leaving me!"

"Your mother's desperate," Guy Bowden said and sat back down.

"How about some coffee?" Mason offered. "How about a drink?"

So was he being weak? It was what she accused him of, often in the past. Tabitha got glasses and poured them out some Diet Coke.

"The lawn looks nice," said Celie, as though she had jurisdiction.

"I still have Aaron," Mason said.

"Don't feel up to it?" Guy inquired.

"Don't really like it," Mason admitted.

"Tabitha, we've come to take you home with us," Celie said firmly; and though it once may have worked, Mason saw it wasn't going to work now. She's grown up, he wanted to say, but didn't.

Tabby sat on a footstool with her arm over Jasper's neck. "Suppose I don't want to?" she said.

"Well, now," Guy pronounced, "there's been a legal agreement, as I understand it, and I think you have to, young lady." He spoke in a teasing way.

"I'm not going," said Tabitha.

They were silent.

Mason Everett regarded his ex-wife, judging that she hadn't changed all that much. He wondered to what degree he had changed. He wouldn't doubt he was showing his age. More wrinkles, a haircut overdue. Celie worked at exercises, she tried different diets, she measured her waist. She talked a blue streak about uninteresting things. She was talking now. There was a group she belonged to. They discussed single parents, problems with preschool children, problems with school-age children, problems with adolescents. They called in experts and listened to lectures. There was this interesting woman from Canada . . .

"What do you do here?" Guy Bowden asked Tabitha, leaning forward. He sounded intently kind.

She took her time about answering, then said, "I'm studying at the library. I'm going to go to college."

"Oh that's great!" said Celie. "I'm glad of that! But you can do that back home! I'll arrange it for you."

"I'm going to do it here," said Tabby.

It came to Mason that this was all a lie. He didn't know where she spent her time when she left the house, but it was the freedom sense he saw in her. He thought that was what she took with her wherever she went. It was what he wanted her to have.

Celie turned to Mason. "So you're doing that for her?" She seemed shocked.

"First I've heard of it," said Mason, "but if she wants it—sure."

"Taking things away from me," Celie said and sprouted tears.

So they would be back into it, Mason thought, and saw the whole flawed fabric of human relations form, the present now becoming like the past, the future scrolling out ahead looking just as always, torn, stained, blemished. No change. He winced.

"How are your eyes?" asked Celie.

"Same as always." Silence.

For Guy Bowden, the moment had arrived. He leaned toward Tabby as if he were right in her face.

"Tabitha, you've got to understand that your mother and I just want the best for you, and what we think is that the best, the very best, is coming back to us. I know I upset you with some things I said. I'm just a rough fellow sometimes. But my heart's in the right place. If you only knew how I mean that. More than you could ever know. I mean it! I mean it! And where is my heart? It's right with you, honey. With you and your mother, she's just so fine."

Tabitha and Jasper both looked at him. Mason tried to look elsewhere.

"Don't you see, Mason?" Celie appealed.

"I think it's up to her," said Mason.

"Unfortunately, it is not up to her," Guy said. "I mean as I understand it, you two agreed—"

Tabitha jumped up and ran into the kitchen.

Guy Bowden rose with resolution and followed her, his heavy feet like a marching drum. They could hear his voice, muffled but persuading, "Now sweetheart, you just need to listen. And think . . . you need to think. . . ."

Mason and Celie were left alone.

"Is he what you want?" he inquired.

"He's just so good to me," she explained.

Now was the moment to say, *So you think I wasn't good to you.* But he didn't. He'd had enough of that. What is separation, together or apart, but one long silence?

Two birds chirped outside the window. It did sound like a conversation, he thought, and wondered what they were saying. From the kitchen they heard something shrill, a sound as if it came from a stranger.

Tabitha ran. She shot through the hallway and was out the front door, running like a deer. Jasper was right after her, he made it through the door. Maybe he thought she was playing.

Mason jumped right in front of Guy Bowden, who was chasing her. "What do you think you're doing?"

"She's the one." Bowden was rubbing at his face. Had she hit him?

"I was trying to be nice to her. Damn it all, I'm always trying to be nice to her. She won't let me."

Mason walked out the door. He looked up and down the street, but neither dog nor girl was in sight. She could have made it around the corner, or into the next yard. But which one? He called her once, "Tabby!" then decided not to call again. It was exactly as if she'd caught the bus. He stood on the sidewalk, looking all around. Next Celie and Bowden would come to the door and start talking.

He walked deliberately away. From the door Celie called after him. "Mason! Where are you going?"

"I have to find her," he said, not looking back.

He did look for her quite some time. No Tabby, no Jasper either. He telephoned Marsha. Marsha said that Tabby was there, but she hadn't seen Jasper.

Mason got the car and drove to find them. Tabby was in the kitchen eating cake. The three of them sat and thought things over. No Jasper.

"Aren't you allowed to have her with you at all?" Marsha asked in an experienced way, two divorces and a grown son somewhere.

"It was something I could have arranged. But they let me know a fixed arrangement meant I could only see her at allotted times."

"And you wouldn't?"

"At the time I wouldn't. I was tired fighting. Celie—you see Celie can keep on fighting forever. Nothing stops her."

"Maybe they'll go away," said Tabitha.

"Maybe they'll stay and just keep the house," said Mason.

Mason's reading equipment was in his house, also his workload from the hospital. Mason's present project was research in genetic statistics as related to disease. Figures from the computer flowed under his crafted Dome magnifier, a glass balloon large as a grapefruit. Specially enlarged from his machines, they arrived sometimes in complex pairs, wavered and spread apart; at other times they approached, hesitated, then matched up and marched together. He checked results and tabulated conclusions.

When Tabitha called, Marsha had left her shop with the assistant. She had driven to her house where she found Tabitha, sitting on the steps. Marsha was a good-natured woman, tolerant of human mistakes.

She gave a drink to Mason and a Pepsi to Tabitha. Then she talked in a quiet sort of way, about a time when she had lived out west, married to her former husband. She got out some knitting. In and out, the long needles kept to a steady rhythm.

Yes, it was her second husband she remembered most. Brad. The first she had been too young to evaluate now or ever. The second she had loved deeply, but he had always wanted to travel. His business was mainly in investments for himself and other people. He could carry his office everywhere—a computer, a cell phone—set up every needed connection in fancy motels. This was West Coast life. They journeyed, up into the Northwest—Seattle, Portland, sometimes into Canada. Then he'd take a notion to go south.

Mason sat and watched his daughter with his fragile eyes. If he only had a vision device to see into her being, discern her aim and direction, for even at so young an age she must feel something of the sort.

"You didn't want to keep me," she suddenly accused.

"That was then," he replied. "This is now."

Marsha knitted on. She kept journeying on as well. In the south, Brad liked to go to San Diego and especially always took a day or so for Coronado. There was an old resort hotel out there near the beach. He would switch for once from motels just to stay there. The food was good. He never stayed anywhere there wasn't some special restaurant to explore.

"Didn't you ever go home?" Mason asked.

"Oh yes, the house. It was in LA. It was nice enough, everything in order. He left it with one of his assistants, a boy who practically lived there. Very nice young man, but then he—" Another story.

It was growing late. The rhythm of the long needles was steady. Tabitha yawned.

Mason was not supposed to drive after dark. Impressions blurred. He sometimes thought he saw someone cross the road in front of him when no one was there. Wary of arriving, he drove slowly home.

"I bet she was going to tell how they went to Mexico next," Tabitha said.

"Probably."

Tabitha said she was out of money. He said he would give her some.

He dared then to ask, "Bowden. Did you hit him?"

"No, I bit him. He bent my arm back till it hurt. He did that before. That's how I got close enough. So I bit him."

"Why do you go uptown? What do you study?"

"I don't study. I made that up. I just hang out. I met a boy I liked, but he's gone away."

Mason remembered the day they removed bandages from his eyes. He remembered blinking. Though dimly, dimly yet, he could see. He had felt a burst of joy, like a bubble.

He turned into his own street and crept nearer. The visiting car was gone. The house was dark. A shape was waiting at the door.

Tabby gave a cry of delight: "It's Jasper! He's come home!"

"And so have you," said Mason, and was happier than he could say to hear no denial.

WILLIAM HALLBERG

The Rub of the Green

—ʍ—

AT FIRST golf was only a green shade protecting me from the gathering white heat of my mother's death. Stan, my dad, wouldn't admit she was going to die and refused to make any plans for her cremation. Instead he spent the last weeks of her hospital stay rearranging all our furniture in ways that would please her when she came home. Of course, she never made it home. He wanted the sofa where she could see the boiling yellows and reds of the maples lining Fairway Avenue. The painting of fish and cheese and apples above the mantel gave way to an abstract print she'd bought at an auction in Toledo. Stan's obsession seized him and held him; finally it got to be more than I could take. One Saturday, while he was alphabetizing books in the den, I escaped to the garage where the chaos of the week before had been brought, in a couple of furious mornings, to an almost military order. Thin rolls of chicken-wire fence, bicycles, a wicker birdcage, a tent, a bamboo rake—all of it hung neatly from spikes. In the corner above the hot water heater was a corroded set of J. C. Higgins golf clubs, which I yanked from the wall and kicked so the contents of the plaid bag spilled across the floor. I picked up an iron, stood in the center of the garage and swung the club as hard as I could over and over again. The sole clicked against the cement, making a trail of sparks. My follow-through barely missed the bug light suspended from a wooden beam. Somehow by swinging the club I seemed to cool down by degrees until the process was organic and regular like a heartbeat. Uptake, downswing, and follow-through together made a wide arc resembling an invisible lariat.

That night I slept without dreaming of my mother in her orange robe and blue slippers, her body going into a furnace. I could never bear to think of her brown hair on fire. For once my dream found me standing in a patch of sunlight amidst tall pine trees, halfway up a narrow green fairway. Stan and I walked to see Mom twice every day. I'd come home from school and we would walk past the country club, through the brown leaves scattered on the sidewalk. "Your mother's quite a gal," he'd say. The leaves came in and out of focus for me. There were thirty-six telephone poles between our house and the Wood County Hospital. After pole number twenty came the small shopping center where we stopped occasionally. Lucille's Cafe was flanked by a flower shop and DiBennedetto's Grocery. On the way to see Mom we'd have a cup of coffee (Lucille had convinced Stan I was plenty tall and that he didn't have to worry about my growth being stunted) and a cinnamon roll at the cafe, after which Stan would buy some cut flowers in hopes he could convince Mom they were from the garden. But an early frost had wiped ours out, and I doubt she ever really thought those red chrysanthemums were from the garden. She wanted him to think he was fooling her, though. Her voice was low, like a man's almost, and halting. She'd say, "Oh . . . aren't they nice," and touch the stems. Then Stan would hold a plastic mirror for her while I brushed her hair.

Coming home we'd buy some frozen dinners and Coca-Colas and potato chips at DiBennedetto's. Then we'd cut across the golf course, provided it wasn't too wet. Stan would put his hand on my shoulder. "You like the turkey pies or the beef? I like the beef. Your mother likes the beef, too. . . ." The weather had turned the golf greens the color of straw, and the flags were gone from the metal poles. Sometimes it was possible to hear the greenskeeper filing the mower blades or banging at a piece of machinery inside the aluminum Quonset.

We always ate the pies from their tin containers. Then I'd go upstairs to do my homework while Stan sat motionless in front of the picture window and looked at the last golfers of the season in their fall windbreakers and heavy sweaters, pulling their carts in the last hour of grey light. Or maybe he was just watching a sluggish October fly crawl across the glass and the golfers were only blurred figures moving in the distance. From my desk in the bedroom I'd look out at the same scene. The golf course looked bleak to me. The golfers themselves seemed desperate, as if each shot were their last. It wasn't right that the swings were so choppy and clumsy or that the color was gone from the course. I'd go down to the garage and swing a golf club, imagining a white ball flying off toward a beautifully manicured green. I could feel banks of grass folding up around me like a blanket. When the garage windows went black I'd go inside to watch television with Stan. My mother finally died on the fourth of November; Stan allowed her body to be cremated, and we scattered her ashes in the garden behind the house as she'd requested.

After her death I devoted even more of my time to golf. I used the snowless November to practice. Stan was working late at the insurance office, so I'd race home from school, take the clubs out from under my bed where they were hidden, and sail out the front door to the golf course. A copy of Ben Hogan's *Power Golf* always went with me. The seventeenth tee was hidden from view of the clubhouse by an enormous barren forsythia hedge. In my cold hands I'd grip the club exactly as Ben Hogan suggested. I imitated all the diagrams of proper backswing, downswing, and follow-through—hitting five or six shots off the tee, then retrieving the balls and hitting them again. Stan never returned home from work in time to discover what I was up to.

He had a bad reputation among the golfers who played the country club course across the street. Living on Fairway Avenue had poisoned him. Those windows that looked onto number seventeen had short life spans. Fortunately, Dexter's Glass Works had a stockpile of windowpanes precut to fit our house perfectly. They were quick at repairs, and Stan was probably the best customer Dexter ever had, and no doubt the most irate. Almost every week a hacker would slice his drive off number seventeen tee. The ball would land on the asphalt road, make a grandiose leap, and, as if guided by radar, home in on one of our windows. There was the crash, and a Maxfli or a Titleist would dribble across the carpet, sometimes coming to rest at Stan's feet. When that happened his round face would contract slightly like a grape in the early stages of becoming a raisin, and he'd lift the ball to his eyes. He'd glare at the thing, then storm to the front door for a face-off with the culprit.

Every now and then he'd find a golfer, spindly legs dangling from slack Bermuda shorts, preparing to ring the doorbell. Not to apologize or offer payment for damages, but to recover the ball. On one occasion Stan found someone worming beneath our station wagon. The man was yanked by his ankles onto the grass, and when he stood up he was greeted with an awkward punch that caused a bloody lip. There was supposed to be a lawsuit, but it never came about. Enough was enough, though. Soon the house had shutters, and the stockade fence that had merely framed the house before was closed in on the fourth side so that the front yard became a kind of fort. Stan bought a Doberman pinscher that answered to exactly nobody, him included. To feed the dog he'd hurl a shank bone across the yard, and when Fritz ran snarling after it Stan would slide a bowl of Ken-L Ration through a crack in the door. It wasn't long before the Doberman was sold to an adult bookstore owner from Toledo, and replaced with an epileptic dachshund named Sally. The fence was plastered with signs, some of them handmade, others orange and black from the K-Mart.

BEWARE OF DOG. TRESPASSERS WILL BE PROSECUTED. WE ARE ARMED.

LOST BALLS ACCRUE TO PROPERTY OWNER.

Vandals retaliated by painting the words FUCK YOU in two-foot-high red letters on the cedar boards. Stan called Garlington's Lumber Company, and they sent a young man to replace those boards. The next morning a new message for Stan appeared. EAT A RUBBER.

Mom was sure Stan had gone overboard. She argued against his crusade until the day she went into the hospital. One morning about a week after her admittance, he was sitting at the breakfast table. "What sort of people live on this planet?" he asked me.

"Apes," I said, my mouth brimming with shredded wheat.

"Apes mind their own business. They eat their bananas and bamboo and do their crapping off . . . well, way off somewhere. These punks do their crapping all over everything and everybody. When I was a kid things were different, I'll tell you that."

Even several months later it was pretty clear to me that he'd never favor my taking up the game of golf. But practicing filled long vacant stretches of time when I would otherwise think about Mom. I read Ben Hogan's book from cover to cover maybe twenty times that winter after she died, and practiced on the sly.

When spring came my friends from school rode their bicycles past our yard. I could see their baseball hats skimming above the fence. They were flocking to the golf course, which was open to them on weekdays after school let out. I wanted to join them, but I didn't think there was much point in asking permission from a man who considered golf one of the great American diseases.

There was no choice but to pull myself out of bed when the sky had barely turned pink over the smokestacks of the Heinz 57 ketchup factory, visible from the bathroom window when I stood at the toilet. I'd hoist the golf bag over my shoulder, holding the cold steel clubs so they wouldn't rattle and wake Stan, and sneak down the stairs. I prayed they wouldn't creak. Sally had to be given some bologna from the refrigerator so she wouldn't whine or have one of her seizures when I went outside.

The mornings were cool and ketchup-smelling. Listening for the first birds, I would cross the street and walk up number seventeen fairway, then eighteen until I got to the clubhouse where the Miller High Life sign glowed through the curtains of the bar. From there the first tee was only twenty-five or thirty yards. But it was important to work at the practice green before heading to number one. When I putted, a little rooster tail was thrown up by the rotation of the ball on the wet grass. I'd take ten short putts, ten mediums, and ten long putts. Then it was time to go to the first tee. In the quiet of the morning I could hear Arnold Palmer breathing as he waited at the bench. The course spread out before me was Augusta without the azaleas. Bobby Jones had seen to it that the greens were mowed to a slick thirteenth of an inch. Ben Hogan, "The Hawk," watched me from where he stood off to the left. I hit my drive pretty well. It was a dark speck in the morning light.

I heard Arnie tell Ben, "The kid's going places."

"Great tempo," said The Hawk. "A human pendulum." I followed through the wet grass after a new Titleist, my only one. Dew soaked my sneakers and water trickled out of the metal shoe eyelets. When I turned to look back at the clubhouse, my footsteps were emerald green in the grey moisture that had settled during the night. Sometimes starlings would be gathered at number one green, eating ungerminated seed. My approach shot would land in their midst, and they would scatter in a noisy swarming cloud, finally blackening the branches of the big Dutch elm.

If the club went back just right, the weight of the steel club head would shift at the top of the swing, just like Ben Hogan said it should, and I was really throwing the blade down into the ball. The impact of club face against ball came just before the leading edge of the club cut through the soft turf and tossed it into the air. When everything happened just right I'd drop the club and applaud. The morning was so still that my clapping would echo inside the tunnel of elms that darkened the fairway.

I returned from the golf course one morning and found Stan already up. He looked startled when I came through the door with my clubs. "So you're a golfer, eh?" he asked me. His voice had a hard ring to it, and there was a queer pitch to his bushy eyebrows. The chair he pulled out from the table for me squeaked against the linoleum, causing Sally to bolt from the dinette into the living room.

By that time my clubs were on the floor by the hatrack. I scratched an imaginary itch behind my ear. "Can't you say something?"

"I was afraid to tell you . . .," I said. ". . . the fence and all."

"Well, there's no need to be a damned sneak. I just don't like this damned sneaking-around-behind-my-back business." He waited for my apology, and once it was given he motioned for me to come through the wide arch to where he sat. I slid onto the seat and looked at the spoon Stan was aiming like a sword at my nose. He had a habit of pointing with anything handy—a pipe stem, a pencil, a spoon—when he was feeling emphatic. It was an authoritative technique he'd picked up from selling insurance policies to unwilling buyers. I took a slice of Wonder Bread from the loaf he'd brought to the table, folded the bread, and took a bite from it. "You know what?" he asked, stirring his coffee. "I knew all along what you were up to."

I asked him how he knew, and he said that Sally would stand broadside to the front door after I left in the morning and would whack the wood with that noodle tail of hers until he got up to let her out. My footsteps in the grass of the front yard had given me away. "Teddy, I don't care if you play golf. God knows I used to play a little bit myself. You could've told me. Just don't be one of those jerks out there with half their damn clothes off, cussing and throwing their clubs and pissing on trees." I saw him digging for the spoon again. He was on the brink of a big point. "If I ever catch you being anything but a gentleman I'll put those clubs up in the attic with the exercycle and the stuffed wolverine, and that'll be that. Hear?"

So Stan was setting me free. From then on I gave up the early morning skulking, all that tiptoeing down the stairs. Spring and summer opened up like a broad fairway inviting endless golf shots. I emptied my savings account in favor of a junior country club membership.

Throughout the month of June I spent my days practicing. Shadows would swim back and forth across the grass as the sun drew from east to west. I mashed shot after shot through the mottled branches of a sycamore in the rough of number fifteen. Trees are theoretically ninety percent air, a supposition I put to the test. Twigs and leaves rained down when my ball clattered through or ricocheted off the wood. The tree was impenetrable, and the theory proved a vast exaggeration. Only darkness or throbbing hunger could drive me from the golf course, and even then I'd pore over golf magazines and instruction books and biographies of the game's greats—Guldahl, Travis, Nelson, Ouimet, Demeret, Snead. . . . On weekends when the country club was overrun with duffers I'd drag a bushel basket of golf balls, the spoils collected over the years from bushes and flower beds, to the side of the yard nearest the driveway. I overturned the basket, then placed it empty at the other side of the lawn. My game was to chip the balls from where they were spilled into the basket sixty feet away. When he could, Stan would sit on the porch with Sally and watch me. My club bit into the lawn, and there would be divot after divot. But he didn't seem to mind because he had a burlap bag of seed in the garage. Anyway, a temptation would sweep over him every now and then and he'd grab the club from me and take a few shots himself. Usually he'd blade the ball so it flew over the stockade fence into the neighbor's yard, or he'd scuff it so it would dribble only a few feet. When by some miracle one of the balls happened to rattle into the basket for him, he'd look at me and say, "See, it's a piece of cake if you do it right." In the summertime, when dusk had chased the golfers off the course, Stan and I crossed the street and I practiced short irons, moving up from seven, to eight, to nine, to a full wedge . . . arcing the ball up into the pink sky where martins bored through the atmosphere in search of mosquitoes. The ball would be a black dot falling near a particular tree or sand trap. Stan lurked just out of range, a hulking silhouette, shagging balls for me. I imagined strange penalties for every bad shot—loss of thumb, wilted ear, a life of ugly pointed shoes like Stan wore when he raked leaves. I was working for perfection, that flawless contact of club face on ball . . . drawing the iron back with the left hand to the top of the swing, pulling it down and through exactly as Hogan would, so the wrists broke into the ball exploding it skyward and down, toward the dim figure who scurried back and forth through the twilight.

Without Mom, our days together became ritualized that way. We continued to have supper once every week at Lucille's. She made pies from the sour cherries of her private orchard, and often she insisted on Stan taking a freshly baked one home with him. Every time we ate at the cafe, he'd leave a dollar bill under his plate for her. Lucille called my dad Stan, which seemed peculiar since even his clients called him Mr. Kendall, although he called them by their first names. Somehow she knew about my golf obsession. Maybe it was because my left hand was pale white from wearing a glove, or it might have been that she overheard Stan and me talking.

Jimmy, the club pro across the street, couldn't help noticing the hours I spent on the driving range or the putting green, deliberating over every swing as if the Masters were riding on it. He was an old shrunken Scotsman who'd more or less landed at the country club for what he called his "semi-retirement." Sometimes he'd come out of the clubhouse to watch me. He'd spit out his toothpick and grab the club away. "You've got to come to the inside with your uptake." His swing was slow and graceful. "Now let's see what you can do with it. Remember, inside. Inside." I aimed at a pin oak three hundred yards out, took my swing, and watched the ball land halfway there and roll another sixty yards across the baked ground.

He would ride an electric cart alongside me when I played, occasionally jumping out to kick a perfect drive into the rough, or nudge the ball into a brown divot. "Now play the bleeding thing," he'd say. "You have to make the tough shots if you're to be any good." On the next hole he might roll the front tire of the cart over my ball, squashing it into the overwatered turf up by the green where the sprinklers had run overnight. "How are you going to play this shot, Teddy boy?" Rather than ask Stan to pay for lessons, I accepted Jimmy's offer of a summer job at the clubhouse. That meant getting out of bed at 4:30, feeding Sally, then trotting in the dark to work. My job was to clean up the locker room, mop the floors, wash golf clubs belonging to members, and scrape accumulated mud and grass from golf shoes. Every now and then I would stand between rows of benches and swing a borrowed persimmon driver, grazing the rubber spike mat with the sole of the club. Or I would use someone's putter to roll golf balls from over by the urinals, through the corridor of lockers, down a concrete straightaway and into the shower, where the ball would orbit the drain grate seven or eight times before it spun dead center. There would be hysterics from the gallery, pats on the back from beautiful fragrant women . . . and I'd push aside all the microphones and autograph books in search of Stan or Jimmy. At the first sign of light outside, I'd lock up and head for Lucille's. She liked me and let me drink all the coffee I wanted. "There's the golfer," she'd say when I came inside. Lucille ate too much of her own food, and as a result she was too fat for her yellow uniform. I'd sit at the counter and she'd talk to me. "Your dad says you're getting to be a good player." She always leaned across the counter in such a way that I could see between her big breasts. There was a white hankie down there. I wolfed my breakfast so I could get back to the course before the early golfers. That way I could play unimpeded. The thing that troubled Stan most about the game of golf was its lack of quid pro quo. That was his favorite expression, quid pro quo. His poor clients got quid pro quoed every time they filed a claim or bought one of his deluxe whole life policies. We'd be watching some tournament on the television and maybe the frontrunner's drive landed in a divot. The camera would zoom in on the white ball cradled in its unfortunate brown trench. Stan would come out of his chair. "Where's the goddamned quid pro quo? The game's not fair," he'd grumble. His insurance broker's brain was adapted to the equations and immutabilities of the actuarial charts. Lose a leg: thirty thousand bucks. An eye and an ear: forty thousand. An ear, a hand, a gonad, a toe and a left occipital lobe . . . he could figure it out. Quid pro quo. I tried explaining that golf isn't something you can throw a rope around. It's a game of odd shapes and peculiar motions. A perfect drive can hit a sprinkler head and roll an extra hundred yards; or it can just as easily carom out of bounds, or into a pine forest. A thinly struck five iron, destined for oblivion, can ricochet off a spectator's wheelchair and jump into the cup. Bobby Jones once landed his approach shot inside an anomalous shoe, itself atop a pile of sand heaped in a greenskeeper's wheelbarrow just beyond the putting surface. With his pitching wedge, Jones whacked ball and shoe onto the green, freeing one from the other, sank a long putt and salvaged par. I mentioned to Stan that Palmer had once sent a lofty fairway shot into a lady's purse, and on another occasion had rolled an errant tee shot into the dark interior of a supine spectator's pleated skirt. That's the rub of the green. You brain some unlucky man in the gallery with a towering wedge shot. He dies on the spot but your ball is one foot from the hole. You tap in. You take it. You play it as it lays. On one of the first hot afternoons of that summer, Stan decided he'd like to come along while I played a round of golf. I did nothing worthy of mention on that day until I came to number fourteen, a par three reachable with a six iron. There was a deep quarry filled with water between the tee and the emerald tongue-shaped green. At the back of the green was a round white gullet of sand destined to swallow any shot flying too far. Stan, who insisted on carring my bag every other hole, handed me the six iron when I asked for it. He bent down, uprooted a few blades of grass and tossed them into the air. They floated briskly over his shoulder. I knew I'd have to lean into my tee shot. I anchored myself over the ball, keeping my weight balanced until it shifted rearward on the uptake. I pulled the club down into the ball, which sailed in a gorgeous arc toward the target. The ball landed at the very back of the green, maybe a foot or two short of the trap, biting into the soft apron and rolling lazily down toward the flag. I leaned on my club and watched. "Will you look at that thing?" Stan said. "It's beautiful. I think the son of a bitch might go in." The ball curled across one side of a swale, gathering enough steam to climb the opposing rise, but always funneling toward the pin situated in the middle of the shallow trough. "Roll," I said. "Get legs."

"The bastard's coming up short," Stan said. "No. Watch it now. It's still moving." The ball crept toward the edge of the cup and seemed to hang there in defiance of known gravitational laws. Stan slung the clubs over his shoulder and trotted around the rim of the quarry, my irons clicking together at every footfall. I followed at a walk, never taking my eye from the ball that hovered at the brink of the cup. Stan was already on hands and knees, his nose only inches from the ball, when I arrived at the green. A foursome on the nearby eleventh tee paused to watch this peculiar sight. The ball had in fact come to the very lip of the hole, where it seemed frozen, its round shadow darkening the white cylindrical liner. Stan stood up to let his wide shadow fall over the site of his anguish. (There is a theory—and where Stan had discovered it was a mystery to me—that shade causes an imperceptible wilting of grass.) Perhaps his porky penumbra would spill the ball into the hole. No luck. He jumped up and down, leaving size-eleven footprints on the soft green. "It's not going in," I said. "The wind's not strong enough." "It's got to fall," Stan insisted. He resumed his all-fours posture on the green and pushed his eyeball close to the recalcitrant, dimpled "sonofabitching" sphere. "You bastard," he whispered to the Titleist.

Players were now waiting at the tee behind us. "I'm going to tap it in," I told Stan.

"Like hell," he said. He filled his lungs and fiercely blew air like Buddha inventing wind. The ball teetered, then tumbled into the hole.

"What did you do that for?" I asked.

"It was a hell of a shot. The ball should have dropped."

"Quid pro quo, right?"

"Well . . ." Stan shrugged.

On the next hole I drilled a wonderful tee shot that seemed to hang forever above a row of cedars. A few days later, when I was washing up the supper dishes, Stan called me out into the living room and told me to sit down on the couch. "Wait right here," he said after I'd settled onto one of the cushions. He went to the closet and fished around behind some of Mom's coats and winter dresses until he'd found what it was he was looking for. It was a hickory-shafted putter with a brass blade. "This is from Lucille," he said. "Before her husband passed away it was his. She wanted me to give it to you. What do you think?" The putter had a new leather grip, and when I examined the sole of the blade I saw the word *Schenectady* imprinted there. I'd read about Walter Travis using such a putter throughout his golfing career at the turn of the century. He'd won the U.S. Open at Baltusrol with one just like it. My fingers trailed over the tiny nicks and dents. "It's a beautiful club," I said. "Probably it's seventy or eighty years old." I imagined Travis rolling a gutta-percha ball over severely undulating greens.

Through the front window I could see that Jimmy had already taken in the rental carts. He'd closed up and gone home for the day. Still, I carried the putter across the street and raced through the waning light to number seventeen green, where I practiced until it was too dark to see. Jimmy weighed the putter in his hands when I showed it to him the next day. "It's very valuable," he said. "I wouldn't use it except when you can be sure it won't be lost or stolen." I had the putter with me when I pushed into Lucille's Cafe that morning. She was serving old Mr. Farliss another cup of coffee. "Well, I see Stan gave you my present," she said. "It's a great gift, Lucille," I said, and thanked her for it. "I'm glad for someone to have it. It's been in my attic for . . . oh, I don't even know how long. It was Ernie's before he died, God rest his loving soul."

Ernie, as far as I could guess, was her husband. "Travis won the U.S. Open with a putter like this," I said, swiping at an invisible golf ball on the cork floor. "Is that so," she replied. Her eyebrows floated up under her bleached blond bangs.

"He was one of the greatest players of all time."

"I'm happy you like that old club so much." She began wiping the counter with a grey rag, the fat of her arms bouncing as she did so.

During the following week I nearly wore out the putting green. Every putt was to win the Open. Sportscasters were buzzing about the thirteen-year-old "pheeenom" who had taken the pro tour by storm.

On the Fourth of July the country club always held its bingo bango bongo tournament, and then at dusk the fire department shot off fireworks. Club members began drinking beer in the morning and didn't stop until nightfall. They littered the fairways with Budweiser cans. Electric carts rolled off bridges into water hazards. Stan wouldn't allow me on the course while the festivities were taking place. But from my window I could see the red, white, and blue pennants and the long tables set up in front of the pro shop. Late that afternoon, Lucille, who had closed up her cafe for the holiday, drove her pickup truck into our driveway. I saw Stan go out to meet her. She looked like a big yellow flounder from my high vantage point. Lucille gave Stan a bucket of sour cherries from her orchard. He carried the bucket to the front porch and set it on the top step. They chatted for a long time after that. When she finally got back inside the truck, I watched them laugh over some joke Stan had made. It was probably an insurance man's joke — maybe the one about the divorcee who wanted to insure her pet monkey. That was one of his favorites. Lucille's hefty arm came out of the rolled-down window and touched Stan's cheek.

I lay on my bed, found a green page inside a golf magazine, and pushed my face against it. Sporadic firecracker explosions sounded in the distance. I remembered my mother sitting on the front porch on the previous Fourth of July, a few weeks before the stockade fence went up, the lap of her skirt over-flowing with green beans from the garden, and her snapping them into pieces which she dropped into a metal pail like the one Lucille had delivered to Stan. When he knocked on the door of my room I sat up on the bed and told him to come in. "Lucille's going to join us for the fireworks display," he said. "How does that sound?" I told him it was fine with me if that's what he wanted. He shut the door, and I listened to his footsteps on the stairs. That night at about eight o'clock Lucille showed up at the front door with a gro-cery bag, grease spotted from the popcorn inside. I showed her into the liv-ing room and said that Stan would be down in a second. He was still upstairs smoothing his unruly eyebrows with candle wax, or at least that's what I thought.

"Well," said Lucille, groaning into a wing chair my mom had reuphol-stered a few months before she got sick, "how's that putter working out?"

"Fine," I said, and excused myself to see about Stan. He was in his bedroom, sliding a belt through the loops of his trousers.

"All set," he said. He sucked in his belly and checked himself in the mirror one last time before leading the way down to the living room. He handed Lucille a big army blanket from the hall closet. She smelled like cherries. Then Stan administered one of Sally's anti-seizure tablets, stroking the dog's throat so she would swallow it. "She's terrified of loud noises," he explained. The three of us went outside. We crossed the street, found a good spot halfway up number eighteen, and spread out the blanket. Lucille and Stan sat there smiling and waving at everybody. "Don't you want some popcorn?" Lucille asked, tilting the grocery bag toward me.

I told her I didn't want any; and of course Stan never ate popcorn because the husks bothered his dentures. While Stan chatted about humidity and mortality tables, she ate every kernel. I watched kids wave sparklers in the gathering darkness.

When the light was gone from the sky, the fireworks began with an explosion of red and green on the horizon. Lucille howled with delight after every burst, as if she were witnessing all this for the first time. She patted Stan's knee. "Aren't they beautiful?" she'd say, and Stan would nod. I coaxed Sally into bed with me after Lucille had gone home and Stan had locked up the house. I heard him humming across the hallway. It was impossible for me to sleep. Instead of going to work at the clubhouse when the alarm went off, I took the putter from my bag and plodded down the stairs as I'd done so many times before. The eastern sky was tinged with color as I crossed the street and walked through the damp grass of number seventeen. The golf course was littered with the wreckage from the day before—paper bags, beer cans, unexploded firecrackers, candy wrappers. That Boy Scouts would be arriving soon to clean up the mess was no consolation to me. The fairways seemed corrupt and strange as I made my way toward the quarry situated deep inside the back nine. I could see Stan's window, still dark, when I paused to look back. I wondered what he was dreaming about.

I walked farther into the golf course, across number eleven fairway to the edge of the quarry, which was secluded by trees from the street where only occasional headlights gleamed through the branches. The weak morning sun threw the distant swales of the doglegged water hole into relief. I'd played number eleven more times than I could count. I knew every roll from every part of that green. To my left was number fourteen, where I'd made my hole-in-one. I stood at the rocky edge of the water for a few minutes. Finally, without really thinking much about it I threw the Schenectady putter out into the mist hovering over the quarry. I didn't feel much like going to work that

morning. I performed my various clubhouse chores in a completely per-
functory way, wrote Jimmy a note that said "Thanks for everything, but I have
to quit," placed the key on top of the note, and headed home.

Stan would be at his insurance office until late afternoon. So I took
my bicycle from the garage and rode up to the Anthony Wayne Pike—
something I was forbidden to do—and pedaled west. Lucille's orchard was
five miles outside of town. When her two-story house was in sight, I got off
my bike and walked it the rest of the way. Lucille's yard was surrounded by
cherry trees whose branches drooped under the weight of the fruit. I laid my
Schwinn Corvette in a patch of long grass, longer than any rough at the
country club, and sat down. The house was much larger than ours. Across
the road were grazing cows and black oil derricks whose heads bobbed up
and down like enormous mechanical birds. The farmland was too rocky and
flat for a golf course, and the black ugliness of the oil pumps was a blight, and
of course there were no sources of water for the creation of ponds and creeks,
and except for the cherry trees the land was razed clean by the farmers and
oil drillers. I imagined living in the farmhouse, eating Lucille's food, feeding
chickens. Would we eat the chickens? I pulled myself up onto one of the
gnarled tree branches and stayed there for a long time. What about Mom's
ashes in our garden? Would we leave them behind for the new tenants of our
house on Fairway Avenue? I picked ripe cherries and lobbed them against
the side of Lucille's house, leaving stains that looked like blood. Dark clouds
were huddling over the clothesline behind Lucille's, so I decided to ride back
home. Wind was coming from the east, which always meant rain. I pedaled
hard for half an hour before the first heavy drops plummeted down on me,
stinging my face. Cars splashed past me in both directions, honked their
horns, and flicked their brights on and off.

The station wagon was in front of the garage when I turned onto the concrete driveway. Sally was standing in the wing chair at the picture window,
her black nose pressed against the glass. Her breath made fog circles that appeared and disappeared.

As quietly as I could, I opened the front door and went inside, leaving
my wet shoes in the entryway. There was no sign of Stan. I presumed he was
in the kitchen fixing hamburgers, but I couldn't smell them cooking if he
was. I tiptoed up the stairs, past Stan's bedroom. He was sitting at the foot of
his bed, staring across the room toward his bureau where there was a framed
picture of Mom. "Where in the hell have you been?" he asked when he noticed me.

"I went for a bike ride," I said. I realized that my T-shirt was cherry-
stained.

"You might have left some message to that effect. Jimmy's been calling here about every ten minutes." I told him I was sorry, and he said I'd better get cleaned up.

I sat in a tub of hot water for a long time, until Stan rapped on the bathroom door. "Come in," I said. He sat down on the needlepointed toilet seat cover. He bounced the rubber plunger on the toe of his shoe for a while. "You could have been a little nicer to Lucille last night," he said. "She's awfully fond of you, and it hurt her that you were so . . ." Stan didn't finish the sentence. He put the plunger behind the toilet. "Anyway, you might want to give the matter some thought." He got up and walked out of the bathroom.

We ate our beans and hamburgers in silence that night. I fed Sally chunks of meat under the table. When we were preparing to gather dirty dishes, Stan picked up a butter knife and peered at his reflection in the stainless steel blade. "You're worried about something, aren't you?"

"I don't know," I said.

"Well I know . . . and I can tell you what it is." But I wouldn't let him say. Before he could tell me, I ran up the stairs to my room, dropped onto my bed, and stared at the ceiling. After a while I heard the phone ringing. Stan, who'd been watching a ball game on the TV, yelled up that it was Jimmy.

I picked up the receiver of the kitchen phone and held it against my ear. "I tore up that note of yours, Teddy boy," the voice said. "You can't quit without two weeks' notice. I'm expecting you to be at work by five o'clock in the morning." Before I could get back up to my room, Stan had filled the only avenue of escape, which was the arched kitchen doorway. When I tried to push by him he grabbed my shirtsleeve. I yanked free from his grasp, ripping my shirt in the process. He pushed me against the refrigerator and held me there. His voice was shaking when he spoke. "Listen, Teddy. You have everything upside down. I'm not leaving this house, not with your mother's remains in the flower garden. And Lucille's not giving up her farm either. Anything else you can figure out for yourself." He took his hand from my chest and let me go. My eyes were wet and my jaws ached. It was long after the last house lights had been turned off that I finally fell into a dark sleep. There were dreams, probably deep symbolic ones, but my mind was clean when I woke up.

I didn't go to work first thing that morning. I walked out the front door toward the golf course and the distant quarry. With me I had my swimming mask and a yellow towel. The air felt cool in my lungs. I found a wrinkled golf glove in the rough of number five. The little finger of the glove had been sheared off by the big four-reel mower. At the western edge of the quarry the water was shallow, with cattails spiking through the surface. I took off my clothes on the tee at number eleven and waded in. Mud oozed between my toes. I secured the mask, then glided head first into the water where I came face to face with minnows, swam through them, and resurfaced near the middle of the quarry. I took a deep breath so I could dive through the barely illuminated water to the murky bottom. Within a few minutes I'd located several dozen balls duffed into the pond by some of the club's worst golfers. However, the Schenectady putter was several yards farther out, in even deeper water; so I swam out, fearful of snapping turtles and other unknown dangers. My skin felt cold in the morning water. I drew in a huge breath and dove about fifteen feet to the bottom. Bluegills schooled around an old corroded refrigerator, squat on the mud bottom like a sunken frigate. Although the sun was lending more and more light, there didn't seem to be much hope of finding the putter among the tires and bottles. I resurfaced one more time, swam a few yards farther out, and went down again. I'd been down twenty or thirty seconds when I saw it, its shaft vertical like a reed. Although my lungs were near bursting, I clutched the putter and swam toward the pale expanse of light above me. I sidestroked to the shallows and climbed up the bank, where I dried off. Without bothering to put my clothes back on, I grabbed an immaculate Titleist from the pocket of my jeans and walked toward number fourteen green. On the way, I clipped the heads off some stagweeds with my Schenectady.

I placed the ball at the fringe of the green, leaving myself a difficult fifty-footer to win the Open. I analyzed the putting surface to detect its personality. The ball would travel over a mound, through a shallow valley and down. I rubbed my hand over the grass, feeling its texture and morning dampness.

Anchoring my bare feet firmly, I stroked the ball. I could read the print as my putt moved with the rise and fall of the green. It followed the path I'd planned for it, accelerating on the downslope of a small hillock, taking a harsh inward break, gathering momentum to climb the opposing rise, in the middle of which was the cup.

As the ball painted its dark green trail on the dew-covered putting surface, the gallery came to life. Their voices formed a chorus. "Get going." "Get legs." "Go." "Roll." The putt had been struck perfectly. The line had been correctly calculated. The speed was right. The ball was destined to fall for me, dead center.

STEVEN MILLHAUSER

In the Penny Arcade

—⁓ᴍ⁓—

IN THE SUMMER of my twelfth birthday I stepped from August sunshine into the shadows of the penny arcade. My father and mother had agreed to wait outside, on a green bench beside the brilliant white ticket booth. Even as I entered the shade cast by the narrow overhang, I imagined my mother gazing anxiously after me from under her wide-brimmed summer hat, as if she might lose me forever in that intricate darkness, while my father, supporting the sun-polished bowl of his pipe with one hand, and frowning as if angrily in the intense light, for he refused to wear either a hat or sunglasses, had already begun studying the signs on the dart-and-balloon booth and the cotton-candy stand, in order to demonstrate to me that he was not overly anxious on my account. After all, I was a big boy now. I had not been to the amusement park for two years. I had dreamed of it all that tense, enigmatic summer, when the world seemed hushed and expectant, as if on the verge of revealing an overwhelming secret. Inside the penny arcade I saw at once that the darkness was not dark enough. I had remembered a plunge into the enticing darkness of movie theaters on hot bright summer afternoons, but here sunlight entered through the open doorway shaded by the narrow overhanging roof. Through a high window a shaft of sunlight fell, looking as if it had been painted with a wide brush onto the dusty air. Among the mysterious ringing of bells, the clanks, the metallic whirrings of the penny arcade I could hear the bright, prancing, secretly mournful music of the merry-go-round and the cries and clatter of the distant roller coaster.

The darkness seemed thicker toward the back of the penny arcade, as if it had retreated from the open doorway and gathered more densely there. Slowly I made my way deeper in. Tough teenagers with hair slicked back on both sides stood huddled over the pinball machines. In their dangerous hair,

187

rich with violence, I could see the deep lines made by their combs, like knife cuts in wood. I passed a glass case containing a yellow toy derrick sitting on a heap of prizes: plastic rings, flashlight pens, little games with holes and silver balls, miniature animals, red-hots, and licorice pipes. Before the derrick a father held up a little blonde girl in red shorts and a blue T-shirt; working the handle, she tried to make the jaws of the derrick close over a prize, which kept slipping back into the pile. Nearby a small boy sat gripping a big black wheel that controlled a car racing on a screen. A tall muscular teenager with a blond crewcut and sullen grey eyes stood bent over a pinball machine that showed luminous Hawaiian girls with red flowers in their gleaming black hair; each time his finger pushed the button, a muscle tensed visibly in his dark, bare upper arm. For a moment I was tempted by the derrick, but at once despised my childishness and continued on my way. It was not prizes I had come out of the sun for. It was something else I had come for, something mysterious and elusive that I could scarcely name. Tense with longing, with suppressed excitement, and with the effort of appearing tough, dangerous, and inconspicuous, I came at last to the old fortune teller in her glass booth.

Through the dusty glass I saw that she had aged. Her red turban was streaked with dust, one of her pale blue eyes had nearly faded away, and her long, pointing finger, suspended above a row of five dusty and slightly up-curled playing cards, was chipped at the knuckle. A crack showed in the side of her nose. Her one good eye had a vague and vacant look, as if she had misplaced something and could no longer remember what it was. She looked as if the long boredom of uninterrupted meditation had withered her spirit. A decayed spiderweb stretched between her sleeve and wrist.

I remembered how I had once been afraid of looking into her eyes, unwilling to be caught in that deep, mystical gaze. Feeling betrayed and uneasy, I abandoned her and went off in search of richer adventures.

The merry-go-round music had stopped, and far away I heard the cry: "Three tries for two bits! Everybody a winner!" I longed to escape from these sounds, into the lost beauty and darkness of the penny arcade. I passed several dead-looking games and rounded the corner of a big machine that printed your name on a disk of metal. I found him standing against the wall, beside a dusty pinball machine with a piece of tape over its coin slot. No one seemed to be paying attention to him. He was wearing a black cowboy hat pulled low over his forehead, a black shirt, wrinkled black pants, and black, cracked boots with nickel-colored spurs. He had long black sideburns and a thin black mustache. His black belt was studded with white wooden bullets. In the center of his chest was a small red target. He stood with one arm held away from his side, the hand gripping a black pistol that pointed down. Facing him stood a post to which was attached a holster with a gun. From the butt of the gun came a coiled black rubber wire that ran into the post. A faded sign gave directions in tiny print. I slid the holster to hip level and, stepping up against it, practiced my draw. Then I placed a dime carefully in the shallow depression of the coin slot, pushed the metal tongue in and out, and grasped the gun. I heard a whirring sound. Suddenly someone began to speak; I looked quickly about, but the voice came from the cowboy's stomach. I had forgotten. Slowly, wearily, as if dragging their way reluctantly up from a deep well, the words struggled forth. "All . . . right . . . you . . . dirty . . . side . . . winder . . . Drrrrraw!" I drew my gun and shot him in the heart. The cowboy stood dully staring at me, as if he were wondering without interest why I had just killed him. Then slowly, slowly, he began to raise his gun. I could feel the strain of that slow raising in my own tensed arm. When the gun was pointing a little to the left of my stomach, he stopped. I heard a dim, soft bang. Wearily, as if from far away, he said: "Take . . . that . . . you . . . low . . . down . . . varmint." Slowly he began to lower his burdensome gun. When the barrel was pointing downward, I heard the whirring stop. I looked about; a little girl holding a candied apple in a fat fist stared up at me without expression. In rage and sorrow I strode away.

I passed the little men with boxing gloves standing stiffly in their glass case, but I knew better than to try to stir them into sluggish and inept life. A desolation had fallen over the creatures of the penny arcade. Even the real, live people strolling noisily about had become infected with the general woodenness; their laughter sounded forced, their gestures seemed exaggerated and unconvincing. I felt caught in an atmosphere of decay and disappointment. I felt that if I could not find whatever it was I was looking for, my entire life would be harmed. Making my way along narrow aisles flanked by high, clattering games, I turned left and right among them, scorning their unmysterious pleasures, until at last I came to a section of old machines, in a dusky recess near the back of the hall.

The machines stood close together, as if huddling in dark, disreputable comradeship, yet with a careless and indifferent air among them. Three older boys, one of whom had a pack of cigarettes tucked into the rolled-up sleeve of his T-shirt, stood peering into three viewers. I chose a machine as far from them as possible. A faded picture in dim colors showed a woman with faded yellow hair standing with her back to me and looking over her shoulder with a smile. She was wearing a tall white hat that had turned nearly grey, a faded white tuxedo jacket, faded black nylon stockings with a black line up the back, and faded red high heels. In one hand she held a cane with which she reached behind her, lifting slightly the back of her jacket to reveal the tense

top of one stocking and the bottom of a faded garter. With a feeling of op-
pression I placed my dime in the slot and leaned my face onto the metal
viewer. Its edges pressed against the bones of my face as if it had seized me
and pulled me close. I pushed the metal tongue in and out; for a moment
nothing happened. Then a title appeared: A DAY AT THE CIRCUS. It vanished
to reveal a dim woman in black and white who was standing on a horse in an
outdoor ring surrounded by well-dressed men and women. She was wearing
a tight costume with a little skirt and did not look like the woman in the picture. As the horse trotted slowly round and round the ring, sometimes leaping jerkily forward as the film jerkily unreeled, she stood on one leg and
reached out the other leg behind her. Once she jumped in the air and
landed looking the other way, and once she stood on her hands. The men
and women strained to see past each other's shoulders; sometimes they
looked at each other and nodded vigorously. I waited for something to happen, for some unspoken promise to be fulfilled, but all at once the movie
ended. Desperately dissatisfied, I tried to recall the troubling, half-naked
woman I had seen two years earlier, but my memory was vague and uncertain; perhaps I had not even dared to peer into the forbidden viewer.

I left the machines and began walking restlessly through the loud hall, sa-
voring its shame, its fall from mystery. It seemed to me that I must have
walked into the wrong arcade; I wondered whether there was another one in
a different part of the amusement park, the true penny arcade that had enchanted my childhood. It seemed as though a blight had overtaken the creatures of this hall: they were sickly, wasted versions of themselves. Perhaps
they were impostors, who had treacherously overthrown the true creatures
and taken their place. Anxiously I continued my sad wandering, searching
for something I could no longer understand—a nuance, a mystery, a dark
glimmer. Under a pinball machine I saw a cone of paper covered with sticky
pink wisps. An older boy in jeans and a white T-shirt, wearing a dark green
canvas apron divided into pockets bulging with coins, looked sharply about
for customers who needed change. I came to a shadowy region at the back
of the hall; there was no one about. I noticed that the merry-go-round music
had stopped again. The machines in this region had an old and melancholy
look. I passed them without interest, turned a corner, and saw before me a
dark alcove.

A thick rope of blue velvet, attached to two posts, stretched in a curve before the opening. In the darkness within I saw a jumble of dim shapes, some
covered with cloths like furniture in a closed room in a decaying mansion in
a movie. I felt something swell within me, as if my temples would burst; at
the same time I was extraordinarily calm. I knew that these must be the true

machines and creatures of the penny arcade, and that for some unaccountable reason they had been removed to make way for the sad impostors whose shameful performance I had witnessed. I looked quickly behind me; I could barely breathe. With a feeling that at any moment I might dissolve, I stepped over the rope and entered the forbidden dark.

It was too dark for me to see clearly, but some other sense was so heightened that I was almost painfully alert. I could feel the mystery of these banished machines, their promise of rich and intricate excitements. I could not understand why they had been set apart in this enchanted cavern, but I had no doubt that here was the lost penny arcade, crowded with all that I had longed for and almost forgotten. With fearful steps I came to a machine carelessly covered with a cloth; peering intensely at the exposed portion, I caught a glimpse of cracked glass. At that moment I heard a sound behind me, and in terror I whirled around.

No one was there. A hush had fallen over the penny arcade. I hurried to the rope and stepped into safety. At first I thought the hall had become strangely deserted, but I saw several people walking slowly and quietly about. It appeared that one of those accidental hushes had fallen over things, as sometimes happens in a crowd: the excitement dies down, for an instant the interwoven cries and voices become unraveled, quietness pours into the suddenly open spaces from which it had been excluded. In that hush, anything might happen. All my senses had burst wide open. I was so tense with inner excitement, which pressed against my temples, that it seemed as if I would expand to fill the entire hall.

Through an intervening maze of machines I could see the black hat brim and black elbow of the distant cowboy. In the tremulous stillness, which at any moment might dissolve, he seemed to await me.

Even as I approached I sensed that he had changed. He seemed more sure of himself, and he looked directly at me. His mouth wore an expression of faint mockery. I could feel his whole nature expanding and unfolding within him. From the shadow of his hat brim his eyes blazed darkly; for a moment I had the sensation of someone behind me. I turned and saw in the glass booth across the hall the fortune teller staring at me with piercing blue eyes. Between her and the cowboy I could feel a dark complicity. Somewhere I heard a gentle creaking, and I became aware of small, subtle motions all about me. The creatures of the penny arcade were waking from their wooden torpor. At first I could not see an actual motion, but I realized that the position of the little boxers had changed slightly, that the fortune teller had raised a warning finger. Secret signals were passing back and forth. I heard another sound, and saw a little hockey player seated at the side of his

painted wooden field. I turned back to the cowboy; he looked at me with ferocity and contempt. His black eyes blazed. I could see one of his hands
quiver with alertness. A muscle in his cheek tensed. My temples were throbbing, I could scarcely breathe. I sensed that at any moment something forbidden was going to happen. I looked at his gun, which was now in his
holster. I raised my eyes; he was ready. As if mesmerized I put a dime in the
slot and pushed the tongue in and out. For a moment he stared at me in cool
fury. All at once he drew and fired—with such grace and swiftness, such
deeply soothing swiftness, that something relaxed far back in my mind. I
drew and fired, wondering whether I was already dead. He stood still, gazing
at me with sudden calm. Grasping his stomach with both hands, he staggered slowly back, looking at me with an expression of flawless and magnificent malice. Gracefully he slumped to one knee, and bowed his unforgiving
head as if in prayer; and falling slowly onto his side, he rolled onto his back
with his arms outspread.

At once he rose, slapped dust from his pants, and returned to his original
position. Radiant with spite, noble with venomous rancor, he looked at me
with fierce amusement; I felt he was mocking me in some inevitable way. I
knew that I hadn't a moment to lose, that I must seize my chance before it
was too late. Tearing my eyes from his, I left him there in the full splendor
of his malevolence.

Through the quiet hall I rushed furiously along. I came to a dusky recess
near the back; no one was there. Thrusting in my dime, I pressed my hot
forehead onto the cool metal. It was just as I thought: the woman slipped
gracefully from her horse and, curtseying to silent applause, made her way
through the crowd. She entered a dim room containing a bed with a carved
mahogany headboard, and a tall swivel mirror suspended on a frame. She
smiled at herself in the mirror, as if acknowledging that at last she had entered into her real existence. With a sudden rapid movement she began removing her costume. Beneath her disguise she was wearing a long jacket and
a pair of black nylon stockings. Turning her back to the mirror and smiling
over her shoulder, she lifted her jacket with the hook of her cane to reveal
the top of her taut, dazzling stocking and a glittering garter. Teasingly she
lifted it a little higher, then suddenly threw away the cane and began to un-
button her jacket. She frowned down and fumbled with the thick, clumsy
buttons as I watched with tense impatience; as the jacket came undone I saw
something dim and shadowy beneath. At last she slipped out of the jacket, revealing a shimmering white slip which came to her knees. Quickly pulling
the slip over her head, so that her face was concealed for a moment, she re-

vealed a flowery blouse above a gleaming black girdle. Gripping the top of the girdle she began to peel it down, but it clung to her so tightly that she had to keep shifting her weight from leg to leg, her face grew dark, suddenly the girdle slipped off and revealed yet another tight and glimmering garment beneath, faster and faster she struggled out of her underwear, tossing each piece aside and revealing new and unsuspected depths of silken conceal-ment, and always I had the sense that I was coming closer and closer to a dark mystery that cunningly eluded me. Prodigal and exuberant in her undress-ing, she offered a rich revelation of half-glimpses, an abundance of veiled and dusky disclosures. She blossomed with shimmer, silk, and shadow, ush-ering me into a lush and intricate realm of always more dangerous exposures which themselves proved to be new and dazzling concealments. Exhausted by these intensities, I watched her anxiously yet with growing languor, as if something vital in the pit of my stomach were being drawn forth and spun into the shimmer of her inexhaustible disrobings. She herself was lost in a feverish ecstasy, in the midst of which I detected a sadness, as if with each gesture she were grandly discarding parts of her life. I felt a melting languor, a feverish melancholy, until I knew that at any moment—"Hey!" I tore my face away. A boy in a yellow T-shirt was shouting at his friend. People strolled about, bells rang, children shouted in the penny arcade. Bright, prancing, sorrowful music from the merry-go-round turned round and round in the air. With throbbing temples I walked into the more open part of the arcade. The cowboy stood frozen in place, four boys in high school jackets stood turning the rods from which the little hockey players hung down. Two small boys stood over the little boxers, who jerkily performed their motions. I turned around: in the dark alcove, before which stretched a blue velvet rope, I saw a collection of old, broken pinball machines. Across the hall the faded for-tune teller sat dully in her dusty glass cage. A weariness had settled over the penny arcade. I felt tired and old, as if nothing could ever happen here. The strange hush, the waking of the creatures from their wooden slumber, seemed dim and uncertain, as if it had taken place long ago.

It was time to leave. Sadly I walked over to the wooden cowboy in his dusty black hat. I looked at him without forgiveness, taking careful note of the paint peeling from his hands. A boy of about my age stood before him, ready to draw. When the wooden figure began to speak, the boy burst into loud, mocking laughter. I felt the pain of that laughter burning in my chest, and I glanced reproachfully at the cowboy; from under the shadow of his hat his dull eyes seemed to acknowledge me. Slowly, jerkily, he began to raise his wooden arm. The lifting caused his head to shift slightly, and for an instant he cast at me a knowing gaze. An inner excitement seized me. Giving him a secret salute, I began walking rapidly about, as if stillness could not contain such illuminations.

All at once I had understood the secret of the penny arcade.

I understood with the force of an inner blow that the creatures of the penny arcade had lost their freedom under the constricting gaze of all those who no longer believed in them. Their majesty and mystery had been crushed down by the shrewd, oppressive eyes of countless visitors who looked at them without seeing their fertile inner nature. Gradually worn down into a parody of themselves, restricted to three or four preposterous wooden gestures, they yet contained within themselves the life that had once been theirs. Under the nourishing gaze of one who understood them, they might still spring into a semblance of their former selves. During the strange hush that had fallen over the arcade, the creatures had been freed from the paralyzing beams of commonplace attention that held them down as surely as the little ropes held down Gulliver in my illustrated book. I recognized that I myself had become part of the conspiracy of dullness, and that only in a moment of lavish awareness, which had left me confused and exhausted, had I seen truly. They had not betrayed me: I had betrayed them. I saw that I was in danger of becoming ordinary, and I understood that from now on I would have to be vigilant.

For this was the only penny arcade, the true penny arcade. There was no other.

Turning decisively, I walked toward the entrance and stepped into the dazzle of a perfect August afternoon. My mother and father shimmered on their bench, as if they were dissolving into light. In the glittering sandy dust beside their bench I saw the blazing white top of an ice cream cup. My father was looking at his watch, my mother's face was turning toward me with a sorrowful expression that had already begun to change to deepest joy. A smell of saltwater from the beach beyond the park mingled with a smell of asphalt and cotton candy. Over the roof of the dart-and-balloon booth, silver airplanes were sailing lazily round and round at the ends of black cables in the brilliant blue sky. Shaking my head as if to clear it of shadows, I prepared myself to greet the simple pleasures of the sun.

FRED LICHT

Shelter the Pilgrim

—⁓⁓—

TO MY GRANDFATHER, who was very much a ghetto Jew, charity was one of the exigencies of life. You breathed. You ate. You gave. Steadily and without having to think about it, my grandfather went every week to visit a hospital run by the Orthodox community, bringing with him cigarettes, fruit, newspapers, and a bit of money.

To my parents who prided themselves on being "advanced Jews" and brought us up to think of grandfather as honorable but picturesque, charity was a duty one performed at a distance. They wrote two checks, one at Passover, the other at New Year, and received in return a form letter of thanks from the agency that received their donation.

To me, to my brother and to my sister, charity is an equivocal institution designed to keep the poor in their place. We have read Marx and we have read Freud, and we can quote chapter and verse about charity as a form of social bribery and self-delusion for the abreaction of social and personal guilt feelings. We still write and send off checks at regular intervals, but we do so with a good deal of self-irony, as if indulging a quaint but not too harmful superstition. We clearly know that charity is patronizing and shameful and the ugly fruit of uglier injustice. But we are somewhat dissatisfied with our knowledge. We have come to be understanding of our parents and have come to venerate our grandfather and his bag full of cigarettes and oranges with which he set out every Friday after lunch. But we also suspect that we don't know what any of them was all about.

It has always been difficult to think about these things, but my brother and my sister and I are convinced that it is the only thing we ought to think about because if we could come out in the clear in this one simple matter, we could make our peace with all the rest.

When the affairs of my father's firm required our moving from Paris to Berlin in 1937, my mother for all her being "advanced" nevertheless felt that inviting the rabbi over in order to make a donation was as much part of settling into a new home as unpacking the suitcases and spreading the carpets.

The rabbi arrived thoroughly unsettled by the phenomenon of a Jewish family moving *to* Germany in those days of flight and panic. He harangued my parents on the irresponsibility of taking the family into the heart of a dangerous storm but accepted the customary check for the charities of his congregation. Mother, always anxious to win her children over to the outdoor life we despised, asked him whether there was an outing club or sports association in which she might enroll her three children. Patiently, as if speaking to a child, the rabbi explained to her that the community was in chaos and disintegration. Those who had not yet fled took every care to dissociate themselves from anything Jewish in the hope of passing unmolested. For burials, for bar mitzvahs, and for the High Holidays, he had to hunt and cajole among the remnants of a once-proud community sufficient attendance to constitute a *minyan*, the ritual quorum without which services could not take place.

My mother objected that there must be some sort of activity in which her children could contribute so that they would not feel totally disconnected from the kind of religious community that the whole family had always known.

The rabbi, a rather unprepossessing person, as I remember him, with pudgy hands and tiny, perfectly round and staring eyes, thought a while and then nodded. There was always something to be done, but he doubted that we would want to do it. The implication that we were too spoiled and too stupid to understand the situation in which we found ourselves stung us all to the quick, and even before he told us what it was he had in mind, we were determined to say yes just to have the pleasure of proving him wrong.

There was, it appeared, a home for retarded orphans still being operated by the community. Most of the healthy orphans had been resettled with the help of Dutch and American and English congregations, but, as was only logical, nobody wanted to take in mentally crippled children. There had been fairly generous contributions to keep the institute in Berlin running smoothly, but there was no getting around the fact that they were being abandoned.

Among these children there were quite a few who weren't absolutely hopeless. They could dress themselves and do some rudimentary reading and writing. The aunts and cousins who had placed them in the institution had, for the most part, emigrated, and the children were growing more and more despondent as their former contacts with the outside world dwindled to nothing. The nurses hardly dared take them out for walks anymore because there had been violent incidents. Now that Sunday visits to distant relatives had stopped, these children were limited to their dormitory and to the narrow asphalt yard in which they played. For the utterly benighted children, it didn't matter, of course, but for the others . . . In short, would we consider inviting one of these children to our house for weekend visits so that he could have a bit of family life and affection and normal childhood play? It would make an enormous difference.

We children were aghast at the notion and with the healthy brutality of childhood hoped fervently that mother, who usually objected to our bringing school friends home because they upset her tidy householder's routine, would refuse. We felt absolutely betrayed when, without so much as glancing in our direction, she said that she would be delighted to receive one of these children for weekends. Two days later the rabbi phoned to tell her that the boy he had selected was called Ernst, that he was fourteen years old, my age, of impeccable cleanliness, and that even though he had the mind of a six-year-old he would amaze us all by a curious gift he had of doing the most astonishingly complicated mathematical and algebraic problems in his head within seconds.

We children had decided beforehand that the one closest in age to the impending guest would bear the brunt of the visit while the others would help out now and then. Ernst, therefore, fell to my lot, and since I didn't have much faith in my sister's and brother's loyalty in this matter, I didn't look forward to Friday. The mathematical quirk of our imbecile guest was a personal offense. Arithmetic was my weakest subject, and I toiled over my homework in daily bitterness and frustration while my teacher kept repeating that if only I could understand the mathematical discipline of mind all the rest would come by itself. To have an idiot crassly expose my weakness enraged me, and I went into a wild tantrum when my mother told me on Friday that I was to fetch Ernst from his institution after school. Parental orders went unquestioned in our fairly authoritarian household. But at this I balked. I would go accompanied by my older sister and by my younger brother, or I simply would not go. My mother found the scene I made unreasonable but felt, on the whole, that my request, though silly, was acceptable. At school's end, therefore, I found Edith and Jonathan waiting for me, looking sulky and keeping a glacial silence. It was a drizzly day toward the end of September, and the orphanage in Moabit was accessible from our school only by a complicated trip which required changing from the underground to a bus and then to yet another bus. I tried to make up for the discomfort I had imposed on them by offering to buy hot chocolate at the corner Conditorei. Jonathan, who was always straightforward, refused outright. Edith, who was sneaky, accepted the bribe; but after she had greedily finished her hot chocolate, she still refused to speak to me.

It wasn't till we were on the last bus, driving through Moabit, that we drew together again. Moabit is an immense and squalid slum, utterly without color or the kind of devil-may-care arrogance that makes the slums of Latin countries less dispiriting. None of us had ever seen such wretchedness before. We were too young to put it into words but involuntarily and silently we put by our squabble and stood abashed at its triviality. We had suddenly come up against the extent of our good fortune, which had spoiled us and which we took for granted.

The institution, when we finally found it after losing the way several times in the mirror-maze of block after block of uniformity and wretchedness, turned out to be a low barracks, sooty and forlorn. The roof had been mended here and there with tar paper and wooden laths; the brick wall that ran clear around it bore patches of torn advertisements and was topped by a grim run of broken glass. We were not allowed inside but had to wait in the porter's lodge, which was foul with rancid smells and the fumes of a potbellied stove. The porter stared at us with unconcealed hatred while we shifted from one foot to the other, avoided each other's eyes, and felt by turns vaguely guilt-stricken and aggressively arrogant. The door opened, and an elderly lady in a white smock entered, resolutely holding on to a recalcitrant boy with a sullen and peevish look on his round and somewhat beefy face. He was taller than I and bigger, but in a bloated, unhealthy way. It occurred to me that if it should come to a fight, I would win without any great effort.

Meanwhile, with the kind of mechanical cheerfulness that scorns to hide its artificiality, the woman in the white smock was making the introductions.

"Don't they look nice, your new friends? You must be Edith, of course, and which one of you young men is Jonathan, and who is Henry? Oh good! Now off with the lot of you before it gets dark. And remember—be back on Sunday not later than six. Come on now, Ernst," she cajoled in the same artificially patient tone. "Come on, there's no reason to be shy! You'll have a marvelous time."

But Ernst seemed unwilling to budge. I was in an ecstasy of embarrassment and paralyzed with a surge of compassion such as I had never felt before. Jonathan, by my side, was also stricken; of that I felt sure without even looking up. Strangely it was Edith who saved the situation. As long as Ernst remained a weekend guest in our house, I never failed to be amazed at Edith's quick and effective sympathy for him coupled with absolutely cool detachment. Like an efficient but somewhat distraught mother helping her little daughter with her knitting, Edith would step in whenever Ernst and I reached an impasse, set things straight, and hand him back to me while she went quickly on her way. Now, rudely and nonchalantly ignoring the nurse, she broke in with one of those algebraic problems that always made me go clammy and weak inside.

"Ernst, if one car starting out here travels at fifty kilometers an hour, and another car starts from the same point seven hours later but travels at sixty kilometers an hour, when will the second car overtake the first car?"

"After three hours and ten minutes," Ernst said, just as you or I might say "Good morning," without the slightest hesitation and without a trace of triumph. Though he towered over her, he took Edith's hand as children do at street crossings and without a backward glance turned to leave the porter's lodge. Jonathan and I followed, perplexed beyond the ability to think over what had happened.

Outside, Edith resolutely put Ernst's hand in mine.

"You're going to be Henry's friend from now on," she said.

Ernst looked at her, impassive and stolid, and then looked at me. Unable to fathom what went on in Ernst's round head, I simply stared back, not daring to venture so much as a smile. Then he nodded. His hand, which had lain in mine like a passive object, closed around mine with a firm grip, and he nodded again. Edith, Jonathan, and I were seized by the same panic. If we let one minute go by, we would never find the way back to where we belonged. Like children under a spell, we would be doomed to wander about in these grey and rank streets forever. Breaking into a run and dragging a puzzled Ernst with us, we made for the bus stop and did not relax till the familiar lights of the Westend gathered about us once again.

At home we were surprised when mother gave Ernst a very summary and hasty reception. Jonathan and Edith disappeared under spurious pretexts, leaving me to show Ernst my room, which he was to share with me. I expected him to be pleased. It was a large and comfortable room filled with the oddments that I had collected over the years: a small mineral collection begun and then abandoned; stamps which I had kept at with slightly greater constancy; all sorts of sports gear; a Tahitian xylophone; books ranging from the *Iliad* to cowboy tales; a modest collection of records; and a hand-cranked Victrola. Not knowing quite what to do, I put on a record. But Ernst didn't respond one way or the other. He sat in an uncomfortable armchair by the side of his bed and stared at me, patient but obviously expectant, quite oblivious of the Victrola.

"Would you like to play a game?" I asked, wondering secretly what sort of games one could possibly play with Ernst.

His expression didn't change, and for an instant I thought he was deaf. Finally, unable to support his steadfast stare any longer, I got out a piece of paper and tried tic-tac-toe. He didn't know the game, and I tried to explain it to him. It is difficult to explain very simple matters when one is fourteen, and I was clumsy and self-conscious as I went about the business of x's and o's and how one had to try to line them up. Ernst followed me very seriously, and we tried our hand at the game for a few turns. But just as I finally thought that he understood the game, he unaccountably lost interest. Again he looked at me expectantly. It was many weeks before I realized that his stare was really blank and not at all expectant. He was quite content to sit and watch me, even if I did nothing more interesting than read a book. Once I discovered this quirk, things got easier for me, but at that moment I was near the end of my tether.

With the piece of paper between us and a pencil at hand, I decided to try another game: the one in which each participant draws part of an image, folding the paper in such a way as to hide everything but the bottom lines before handing the paper over to the next player. The point of the game is the incongruous, fantastic picture that appears when the paper is unfolded. I remember being fascinated by the game when I was in kindergarten and thought it would do beautifully for Ernst. He seemed to understand my instructions quite easily this time and turned out to be a very meticulous, painstaking draftsman. I was delighted to have hit on something that made time pass so agreeably.

"All right now," I said when we had reached the bottom of the page and it was time to unfold the paper, "let's see what sort of monster we have got here."

Of its sort, the picture was a tremendous success. My sloppy sketches contrasted vividly with Ernst's precise and sober rendering of faces, bodies, and landscape. He looked at the page for a long time and seemed to grow perplexed at first and downright angry afterwards.

"Don't you think it's funny?"

He shook his head stubbornly and handed the page back to me visibly agitated, as if he had been tricked in some way and could see no justification for the deception that had been practiced on him. But by then it was time to go into the living room where Edith and mother lighted the Sabbath candles. Ernst was very proud of being given a cap to wear while the prayers were said but didn't seem to have any interest at all in the little ceremony. He kept fingering his hat and later asked whether he could keep it on during dinner.

"Just like in a synagogue," he kept repeating cheerfully.

"Do you often go to synagogue?" mother asked, and Ernst nodded and laughed.

"I like going to synagogue." Abruptly he started to mutter a few prayers in Hebrew which he had contrived to learn by heart. But when we complimented him on knowing them so well, he was surprised and started to stare again.

At dinner he behaved better than we could have foreseen. He was clumsy with the silver, holding knife and fork at the very base of the handle, and he sometimes lost track of how much he had in his mouth and stuffed himself, but there was a great attention to detail that bore out the rabbi's prediction that he was very tidy and clean. Once, when he broke his roll, a few crumbs scattered on the floor, and he simply couldn't go on eating without first getting up from his chair and squatting on the floor till he had picked up every tiniest speck. He particularly loved apples and had a way of peeling them in a continuous spiral, which pleased him immensely. Father asked him whether he would mind peeling an apple for each one of us, and Ernst beamed with gratification. It took almost half an hour before we each had an apple, but because of father's inspiration, we all got up from the table feeling that dinner had been a great success.

Going to bed was what I dreaded most. I hadn't had a chance to get used to my manhood yet, and all the family teased me about being exaggeratedly shy. It was excruciating for me to be seen in my pajamas or my underwear, and now I would have to undress with an utter stranger in my room. For his part, Ernst had no qualms at all. With the careful, studied tidiness that marked all his gestures, he slowly got undressed while I sat on the edge of my bed wondering where I could hide and envying Ernst for his nonchalance. As in a trance, I watched him take off his sweater, then his shirt, his trousers, and his socks. His skin was very white and fine, rather like a baby's; and when he finally stood naked by the side of his bed, I saw that there wasn't the vaguest sign of that change which bedeviled most of my waking and almost all my sleeping hours. The sight of Ernst grown to the full height of a man but childish in every other way overwhelmed me with a sudden, shameful, but irrepressible wave of physical disgust. I couldn't get myself to undress in front of him. Mumbling some stupid words meant for an excuse, I grabbed my pajamas and robe and disappeared into the bathroom.

Returning, I found that Ernst had already turned out the light in my room. I was used to reading in bed before falling asleep; but out of a sense of hospitality I didn't want to turn the light on again even though I could tell from his breathing that Ernst was still awake. I lay in the dark wondering how I was going to live through the rest of the weekend when suddenly his voice broke in on me. He sounded strangely shy and hesitant, and like a child that wants something but doesn't know what he wants or how to go about getting it.

"Henry? Please ask me a question, Henry."

"All right. Here's a question: what do you want to do tomorrow?" I spoke more brusquely than I had intended. There was a silence. Then:

"Not that kind of a question," Ernst said timidly and obviously close to tears. "*My* kind of a question." He was almost whispering now. As so often in my encounters with Ernst, I felt deeply ashamed and consequently vengeful.

"What's your kind of question?"

"You know—my kind of question. The kind I'm good at."

"All right. But I'm not good at asking them."

"When were you born?"

"On February 12, 1922."

"Now ask me what day of the week it was."

"All right, Ernst—what day of the week was it?"

"A Saturday. And now ask me what day of the week it will be in the year 2012."

"Why don't you just tell me," I said, exasperated.

"Ask me. Please!"

"On what day of the week will my birthday fall in the year 2012?"

"Wednesday," he sighed happily. "Thank you Henry. Thank you for asking me."

Saturday passed easily enough. Ernst liked to stay in bed in the morning, and I sneaked from my room, dressed, had breakfast, and sought refuge with Jonathan. It was eleven before Ernst finally got up, and since it took him a long time to take his bath and get dressed, the morning was gone without my having to do anything at all. Lunch passed off easily, too. We were all a bit apprehensive about whether Ernst would want to peel apples for all of us, but he seemed to have forgotten his triumph of the previous evening. Jonathan promised to take care of Ernst till three when I was to take him to the movies. I had looked forward to having an hour off, but when I entered my room alone I found that I wasn't really in the mood for anything much and just moved about restlessly till it was time to go.

Ernst didn't have any preference where movies were concerned, and followed me with great docility to a film about car racing. On subsequent visits our Saturday afternoon at the movies was repeated religiously. In time I took him to every conceivable kind of film but could never quite make out which sort of movie he liked best. Now and then, especially during sequences that played on a ship or at the beach, he would talk to himself, saying how pretty it was, but he never seemed to disapprove of anything. Murder mysteries, which frightened me to death, and love scenes, which I thought contemptible, went past him without eliciting visible signs of displeasure. And, strangely enough, he always managed to understand the plot when we talked about the movie on the way home, even though he could never follow the thread when I tried to tell him of some incident that had happened to me or some story a friend had related to me. Maybe the acting out of the story made it easier for him to grasp the situation while episodes that consisted only of words confused him. I don't know about such things.

If Saturday had been a success, Sunday was a despondent failure. We let him sleep again as long as he wanted to, but when he did get up he was nervous and hurried and got everything wrong, and I had to make him undress again and turn his clothes right side out. At lunch he choked on his food; and after the meal it was obvious that he was already thinking of having to go back to his institution. He just sat there, fidgeting, unable to do anything, just waiting to get it over with. On the bus he hardly spoke a word and kept looking out of the window. He was breathing hard, the window fogged up, and he wiped the pane with his hand getting himself all smudgy.

"Why don't you stop wiping the window?" I suddenly said irritably.

He folded his hands in his lap, looking at them with distaste but obviously imposing his best behavior on himself in order to please me. At the porter's lodge I tried to shake hands with him, but he refused because his hands were so dirty.

"I'll be here on Friday again."

"I don't think you will come."

"Yes I will. Of course I will. Why do you say that I won't?"

He was silent, looked down, and then turned from me and went through the yard to the barracks at the far end.

After such a gloomy farewell, I expected him to be cheerfully surprised when I came to fetch him on the following Friday. But it was as if he had forgotten all about me in the intervening time, and it was several hours before we were on familiar terms again. The third week he expected me, and even though I always resented the duty my parents had imposed on me, I grew used to it. In a way I managed to get a certain amount of prestige out of the situation vis-à-vis my school friends. It got around that I played nursemaid to Ernst on weekends, and gradually some of my more inquisitive friends asked to see him. On these occasions I would sometimes be extra kind to him to impress my friends with my philanthropic tendencies. Just as inexplicably, I would sometimes show off before my school friends by being deliberately cruel to Ernst to show my comrades that I had trained him to loyalty as one might train a dog. And either way, Ernst was happy. He clearly regarded these friends who came and went as ephemeral creatures of no account while he was part of the family.

"I'm staying here," he would irrelevantly and abruptly tell these friends at odd moments of the afternoon. "And you have to go home."

He quite willingly put up with my willfulness as if realizing that both my exaggerated kindness and my equally artificial brutality to him were put on only for my friends and had no meaning as far as he was concerned. Once I pushed him so far that we came to blows. My impression that he represented no physical threat to me proved to be quite mistaken. When we began to fight, he was caught off guard. He hadn't noticed my mounting irritation when he remained good-natured and oblivious to the taunts I flung at him to show my friend that I was like a ringmaster with a beast. Taken by surprise, he fought back with far more energy than I expected, and he easily could have got the better of me. But suddenly he stopped fighting and went limp. Looking at me and at my friend, he laughed an odd laugh that was cut short in his throat. I managed to free myself and pushed him away so that he staggered against the wall. My friend, awkwardly ashamed for me and of the spectacle I had put on for his entertainment, said he had to go home.

In November my class went on a school trip, and to my surprise and also to my disappointment, Ernst gave no sign of sadness when I told him that I would not be back to fetch him the next weekend. In December the whole family was to go to the mountains for a skiing vacation, and mother decided that we would celebrate Channukah a little early so that Ernst would be able to be with us for the festivities and for the presents. Edith had knitted him socks. I gave him a little box with minerals that glowed in the dark, Jonathan got him some sweets of which he was especially fond, and my parents bought him a handsome winter coat. Ernst was beside himself with joy. He was allowed to light the candles, and even though you're only supposed to light two candles on the first day of Channukah, he asked to be allowed to light all eight and stood over the menorah in beatific enchantment, torn between looking at the presents and the glow of the chased silver candleholder.

He had never been demonstrative of his affections. Probably hugging and kissing is something that has to be learned in the cradle, and being an orphan, Ernst had never learned it. Now, not knowing how to find release for all the pent-up happiness, he ran from me to mother, from mother to Edith, and back to me and to Jonathan. He stood in front of us, tense and tremulous, not knowing what to say or do, and when one of us asked him whether he was happy he went visibly rigid with the effort of trying to tell us just how happy he was. It was Edith who again saved the situation by kissing him soundly on both cheeks. Ernst gave a deep sigh after that and went off to sit in a corner with his presents. The minerals he took to bed with him that night, and there was a soft, steady glow by his bedside when we turned out the lights. In January, when I fetched him home on our first Friday back in Berlin, he seemed to have forgotten Channukah altogether—or at least he didn't talk about it. We picked up our routine again, with Saturday movies and a walk to a good pastry shop on the Oliva Platz after supper for sweets gluttonously stuffed with whipped cream. He became so much a member of the household that we no longer made special efforts to amuse him. Often I would go out on Saturday mornings with friends and leave him at home all by himself. He didn't mind in the least but played with my things or else went into the kitchen to help peel potatoes for the pommes-frites he adored and always got at lunch time.

That every farewell brings with it a premonition of death, of the ultimate farewell, is known to all. Even children have sufficient experience of that numb, wordless sensation of grief that comes with goodbyes, a grief that is diluted but never quite dissipated by time and that surges to the surface ever more strongly each time a new turning in our lives tears us from old customs and friendships.

But I believe there is something more important involved than the mere premonition of death. I believe there is in our goodbyes also a prophecy of the manner and the worthiness of our dying. Are we able to part with friends and with life with conscious dignity or with a hasty nervousness, anxious to get it over with? When we come to partings, are we baffled and confused, or can we look steadfastly at what we can't understand and accept it nevertheless? We inevitably show color at such moments, and what really frightens us is the foreknowledge that we will do no better when the final parting comes. Such moments mark us for life.

I don't precisely know when my parents decided that their moving to Berlin in such times and under such circumstances had been an unjustifiable mistake. Or else—my parents have always avoided the subject—they had come to Berlin with a specific purpose in mind and, having achieved it, they naturally decided to go home to Paris again. In any case, we children were told late in April. The school year came to an end in mid-June, and shortly after that we would leave. There remained the business of Ernst.

Mother was of the opinion that it would be best not to tell him anything. What was the use of burdening him and spoiling the weekends that remained? For all we knew, his mind was incapable of taking in recurring events. He might miss me for a few minutes when one fine Friday I didn't show up in the porter's lodge to take him home with me, but his sense of time was confused in any case. He might not even realize that it was Friday. Father and Edith were against such a plan. Secretly I agreed with them, although mother's idea suited me better for I recoiled at the very idea of having to tell Ernst that we were leaving for good. We finally arrived at a compromise. Father was to call the doctor who ran the institution (nominally at least: I don't believe he ever looked in more than fifteen minutes once or twice a week) to put the case before him. The doctor decided that we must tell him and that it would be best to tell him a little bit ahead of time so that he would have a chance to get used to the idea. I know nothing of the clinical side of Ernst's case and cannot tell whether the doctor's advice was sound. But in mid-May, just after Sunday lunch, when Ernst and I were about to get ready to go back to the orphanage, I steeled myself and took the leap.

"Ernst, I have to tell you something that makes me sad, and I'm afraid that it might make you sad, too. But pretty soon, all of us, Edith and Jonathan and I and my parents, will be leaving to go to Paris."

He looked blank, with his head tilted a little to one side, an attitude he sometimes took when he feared being scolded.

"Paris is very far away. Look, let me show you."

I took out my atlas and showed him where Berlin was and where Paris was and how far it was from one city to the other. But I got tangled in trying to explain the map scale to him, and that a tiny millimeter on the map was much, much longer than the trip from the orphanage to our home. I suddenly had the feeling that he could understand if he wanted to—we had managed to get more difficult concepts through to him—but that he simply didn't want to understand what I was saying. I grew curt and told him that sometime in June we would go away and that was that. I gave him his jacket and put my jacket on and headed for the front door.

Outside, of course, I repented having been so short, and took his arm as we went off to the bus station.

"You see, we have to go to Paris. That's where all our family is. My grandfather and my cousins and aunts. They all live there, and we have to go live with them."

He nodded.

"But we won't leave right away. We'll see each other plenty of times before we leave."

He nodded again, but I could tell that he had fallen into that obstinate silence that was his only weapon against a treacherous world. Those silences were uncanny; you felt that he would endure martyrdom rather than make a sound.

On the Friday after that, I had some business to attend to at home before going off to the orphanage for Ernst. The weather had turned warm, sultry almost, but strong gusts of moist wind blew through the streets, and grey clouds, bloated with rain, hung heavy and low above the roofs. By the time I got to the orphanage it was getting dark, but I had telephoned ahead to say that I would be late and didn't feel that I need hurry. At the porter's lodge I sent word, as usual, for Ernst to come and meet me. Even though I am inquisitive by nature, I had never entered the institution, though I had been asked to do so quite often by the nurse who accompanied Ernst to the lodge every time I called.

I was prepared to wait, as usual, for Ernst. He was slow about getting himself together to go out. But within minutes of my arrival, the woman in the white smock crossed the courtyard alone.

"Maybe he doesn't feel well . . . I don't know what it is, but he doesn't want to come today."

"If he is sick you could have told me when I telephoned."

"Well, I didn't know at the time. But he went to bed. I think he must feel sick. The doctor comes tomorrow in any case. We'll see what he says."

"Does he have a fever?"

"No. I took his temperature first thing. That's why I think we can wait till the doctor comes tomorrow. If you'll call around eleven . . ."

Instinct—or is that just a better word for cowardice?—told me to let it go at that. But I rallied and asked her whether I might come in and see him for a while.

"Of course. Please. I am sure your visit will do Ernst good."

She led me through the asphalted court into a long corridor bleak with peeling paint. Ernst shared a room with four other boys, and two of them were in the room with him when I entered. They were mongoloids and grinned at me ingratiatingly, their heads swaying back and forth. The nurse trooped them out, but they went unwillingly.

Only one bulb lighted the room from the center of the ceiling. Through the tall windows the evening looked dark and inhospitable, the color of a bruise.

"Ernst? What's the matter? Don't you feel well?" I suddenly cursed myself. The artificiality of my tone made everything inside me shrink with a pang of shame. Why had I come?

"I don't know," Ernst said. His voice was surprisingly even. "Turn the light off, please."

The room was dark now, and I took a chair near his bed. Having started, I vaguely felt that I must go on. I don't know why. But I suppose we all want things to be orderly and tidy. When life frays and threatens to be inconclusive, we try out of sheer selfishness to mend things that can't be mended.

"Won't you come home with me? Edith has a surprise for you." He got up—I could hardly see him, it was so dark—and rummaged under his bedstead for a bit. Then he got back under the covers. In his hands he held the fluorescent minerals I had given him, and they shed a soft glow. He didn't cry. My throat tightened with tears, and I was sure that from one moment to the next Ernst too would begin to weep. But he didn't. Maybe he felt too sad for the kind of easy tears that were swelling behind my eyes, or maybe he didn't feel anything at all.

We sat in silence for a long time. Then suddenly, as if inspired, he clambered out of his bed again, cumbersomely impeded by the minerals he held aloft. Gingerly and with great affection, he placed the glowing rocks and pebbles on the floor before me and looked up at me invitingly, as if he expected me to take part in some ritual that would make everything all right. He had some important idea in the back of his mind connected with the radiant stones I had given him. I racked my brain, seized by a sudden panic because I felt quite clearly that I too knew what the ritual was—but this knowledge lay just beyond the reach of memory. For a frantic, paralyzing moment I knew how narrow are the limits of the human mind.

Like an animal, I was hard up against the electrified wire that circled my little field. I could either break through the imposed limit by risking the shock, or I could retreat. For an instant I thought I might evade the issue yet, deflecting Ernst's grave and expectant stare by throwing him another algebraic puzzle. But no algebraic problem rose to the surface of my mind. It was for me to find what x was worth—I had been given all the data that the equation demanded. With a little effort I could capture the unknown quantity.

Ernst continued to look at me as if what he expected me to do was the most natural thing in the world. The diffuse, tender glow of the mysterious little stones was matched only by the steadfastness of his inviting smile. Then, slowly, only the light of the minerals remained hanging between us as the light of his face subsided under ashen disappointment.

He climbed back into bed then, leaving the little heap of minerals at my feet. Turning on his side, he looked unblinkingly at me with every meaning, intent, or feeling totally extinguished from his eyes.

I stayed a few minutes and then cleared my throat to say goodbye as normally as I could. But my voice didn't quite obey me, and the words were left hanging more as if they were a question, a question apprehensive of inducing silence. Then I swiftly left the room, crossed the courtyard at a run, and caught the bus two blocks down the street. I met all my mother's efforts to make another try the next day and then again the next week with a steadfast refusal. Adolescent brutality? Fear of hurting Ernst some more? Cowardice? Good sense? It's too long ago for me to tell. But I suppose that it was a bit of each.

We returned to Paris and resumed the life that had been so unpleasantly interrupted. We were still there in 1940 when Paris fell. Six months later—I was nineteen then—my father managed, by means I'll never know, to arrange a complicated plan first to get us out of Paris, then to obtain false papers for us in Marseilles, and finally to bring us across the Pyrenees to the relative safety of Spain.

At first my father insisted that grandfather come with us. But the old man refused. He insisted that he would only be a hindrance, and he produced any number of Talmudic quotations that spoke of the necessity of preserving young life even if it is at the cost of the old. Besides, he wanted to be buried by the side of his wife, and nothing would stir him from his decision. Late in January we were to leave Paris by a night train. In the evening of our flight, mother made a light supper which we carried in bowls to grandfather's house. We sat about in silence after dinner till it was time to go. Then, with tranquil deliberation and with unanswerable assurance, grandfather blessed us one after the other, putting his hands on our heads and speaking a steady prayer over each of us.

During the past two or three years I had grown temperamentally and intellectually into anti-religious attitudes. But even I felt incontrovertibly that this man had the power to bless. I felt at peace but I also felt frightened at losing some small detail because I wanted to remember everything about that moment. It would have to last me to my dying day. Never again would I meet a man who could take the full force of benediction onto himself.

Having given us his blessing, grandfather stepped back from where we were standing and dismissed us with a nod. It was he who was voluntarily going from us, even though to others it might look as if we were abandoning him in our flight.

Then we slipped away and found . . . well, safety. Survival. Call it what you will.

As for Ernst and grandfather, details hardly matter. They died, and they died alone. But to the end each had retained the power to relinquish what had been his, to say farewell on his own terms. I, on the other hand, have still not learned to say goodbye—nor has anyone else I know. My brother, my sister, and I, left pondering the quick and cheerful way Ernst had with his algebraic equations, are resigned to the fact that the puzzle we shall face during our last moments will be the very one we've never been able to solve.

MAIRI MacINNES

Porrock

—w—

IN 1941, the second year of the war in Europe, with the German bombing campaign in full operation over England, and the threat of invasion on everyone's mind every day, at that very worst of times, my parents decided to move house. I was sixteen, and I'd been born down the street in a smaller house, and grown up in the house we were leaving. This was in Norton-on-Tees, a village on the verge of the ancient industrial region of southern County Durham. I did not mind leaving that particular house, though I ran through it sentimentally on the last day and blessed each bare scrubbed room for the happy times I'd known there. I might have minded more if I'd understood that we were leaving what comprised an entire interior world as well. Our lives were being dismantled, dragged out, exhibited, wrapped, packed, and presently set up in an elsewhere indifferent to us and even, to our senses, slightly superior. We were moving to Windsor, in the South, because my parents thought of bettering their lot. They believed that my father was overworking while his partner in medical practice was marking time; his wife and little boys had gone for the duration to the Lake District to escape the bombs, and he would go at weekends to visit them, leaving his patients to my father, who was senior to him. And our house had become engulfed just before the war by a tide of council houses, in which people from the slums of nearby Stockton were installed when their damp verminous old houses were demolished. So the green fields vanished, the traffic increased, and the big copper beech on the pavement outside the house was occasionally hung with boys. They were perfectly harmless boys, yet everyone except me considered them a disgrace.

"We've lived here twenty years," my mother told everyone when we prepared to leave, as if we were entering history. Twenty years was an age to me, and our house belonged to another age yet. It had the date 1902 in the stained glass of the landing window, together with Ceres with a sheaf of wheat. The lobby was lined with carved wooden panels, and there were marble columns by the big sash windows, brass fittings on the heavy doors; drawing room with conservatory off it with furnace underneath; a double kitchen with pantry and larder, tiled in red and cream, with a black cooking and heating range; cellars with tiled table for keeping food cool and with racks for wine bottles. There was also a living room in two parts with plenty of plaster swags of fruit and bunches of flowers on the ceiling and a device for communicating with the kitchen by means of a whistle and a pipe that you spoke into. Outside in the garden were two little summerhouses, a washhouse with fireplace and a vast copper for boiling clothes and drying dollies overhead; stables with loft, a big greenhouse where George, the lad who worked for us, taught me secretly to shoot at tin cans with a borrowed service revolver.

The next house hadn't nearly so much style. It was a big 1930s Tudor building with black and white pseudo-timbering over a half-story of brick. Some windows were leaded, and one room was even paneled in dark oak, but the house was no more Tudor overall than it was gothic. It is true that I was allotted a room of my own for good at last. Though pleasantly surprised at the view over the garden, I had inklings of what was later to trouble me about the new town, that it was somehow idealized, not the jumble that was Stockton and Norton, an organic heap in the mutilated landscape of the North Country. The model nature of Windsor involved imitation, as of the Tudor style, to make a statement with a lot of leisure about it. It didn't really make much difference to day-to-day living, but it seemed humbug. Witness the doctor's surgery and waiting room tacked on one end of the main house: what was Tudor about them? You wouldn't have had Tudor in dirty old Stockton. People would call it stuck up.

Even with the old things distributed throughout, the house still stayed strange, though my mother set to and polished and prettified till she was exhausted. No George, of course, no Nelly to cook and run the laundry, no Betty the housemaid. No pony, no dog. Outside the house, no friend, not even an acquaintance. My brother Iain was now at Oxford. As for me, at sixteen, I'd compounded my isolation by deciding to leave school for good and work at home with tutors for an Oxford scholarship. I wanted also, contrarily, to join the services when I was old enough, before I was called up at eighteen, so as to do my bit in the war effort. I hadn't the least idea of how lonely I would be, and in any case my feelings didn't matter when so many were being wounded and killed. Girls were irrelevant or seductive. As a girl I hid myself; people understood that, and were kind. So occasionally I struck out for myself.

Porrock was the first dog in our family that everyone thought of as mine. He was a small black-and-tan terrier, all curls, ravaged by fleas, who cost me five shillings at a door in a back street. He was promising from the start, overjoyed as he was to meet me and charmed to sit on my knee and be driven from his birthplace like a grandee. In two days he was housebroken. In three he learned his name. Porrock was an old detested nickname of my father's, now thankfully abandoned in the new habitat. The dog looked up at the sound, searching for the source of my voice, which he duly discovered in my face high above. When he saw me smile, he'd curl back his ruched lips in imitation and reveal his tiny white teeth. So I would laugh and he'd wriggle for joy.

We went everywhere together. He learned to walk on a lead in hours; he loved learning what I had to teach. Because he was just a pup and tired easily, I taught him to sit in a basket on the front of my bike and be carried to places of long grass and wild flowers where I'd lie and read one of my prescribed books while he stumbled and bumbled to and fro and eventually came back to sleep with his small hard head on my foot. For a long time — for the year and a half between my leaving school and entering university — Porrock was my only friend.

In our old town there appeared to be two sorts of people — the industrial working class and the rest in ascendancy. In Windsor we were the working class, and there appeared to be three lots set over us: the Court, who lived in the castle, the clergy of St. George's Chapel in the castle precinct, and the Guards in their barracks nearby. My mother seemed not to understand. She remembered going to Norton as a bride in 1920 when she and my father set up house and everybody in the ascendancy called on her and left cards and invited them to dinner. So every afternoon, herself freshly made up, the house tidied, she waited for people to call on her, and none did. No surprise there. France had fallen, invasion threatened, U-boats sank terrifying numbers of merchantmen, bombs flattened the East End of London, the British Army fell back across North Africa, the Japanese took Singapore. But there was a kinder tradition in the North that the disintegration of convention did not disturb and that hasn't disappeared even yet, and she looked for it in the soft atmosphere of the South as the war raged on. She was so aware of the danger that she'd booked passage in a ship for Australia for herself and me in 1940, meaning to leave me with her family there and return to England. (I'd refused to go.) But she expected people to behave in a certain fundamental way even in extremis. When people didn't call on her in Windsor she simply changed her tack, and bridge players began to crop up like mushrooms in her friendly soil, not of the Court, or the clergy, or the Guards, it is true, but decent enough, and serious enough too, I dare say, though they played cards while half the world burned. My father quickly got to know the medical fraternity and became acquainted at the hospital. My brother went on being a medical student. I alone felt the need to speak to a dog.

"In our life alone does Nature live," wrote Coleridge, and when I read his words, prescribed as they were, and therefore hallowed, I wondered what Nature lived in me, so far from the world I had lost. Even now my friends in the North would be preparing work in the sixth form, talking and arguing and attitudinizing, while I went unsteadily on by myself, unsure and unsupported except by a puppy. Of my old dense life, barely anything remained. Even my physique had changed. To look at, I was now a woman. But it felt odd to be inside that woman, housed in ridiculous splendor when I wanted something simple. Coleridge, the man of chaos, offered a revelation of how to think in orderly fashion. "Not only this," I told Porrock, "but also that. Moreover. Even yet. Let me venture to add. In the first place. In the second. A third class of circumstance." My understanding crept sideways like a crab. Suddenly it would arrive, and without a process of thought. I did not think. I jumped. I landed. I fell over. Coleridge showed me how to appreciate at least some of the ways by which one arrives at an opinion, even retrospectively. Once a process of understanding is consciously gone through, the pattern becomes easier to repeat. So I began, quite timidly, to think for myself.

My schooling hitherto had been mechanical and girly, and so it continued to be in Latin studies until I made some progress. It was otherwise from the start in English, where I began to see the skeleton under the flesh of words, and saw how certain writers manipulated the skeleton, and how the genius of language mysteriously affected us, as figures in a dance affect us differently when performed by different dancers. No one had previously talked to me about art, and no one gave the name of art to these considerations even now, but my new tutors talked frankly and openly and critically about them as if they were talking about food and drink, and smiled at me with goodwill, and an excitement breathed over me as if puffed from the mouth of Apollo himself.

For escape I walked in Windsor Great Park. An avenue bordered by a double line of elms ran from the southern gate of the castle three miles to an opposing hill on which there was an immense statue of a toga'd Roman on horseback, crowned with a laurel wreath, extending a hand benevolently over the land. The plinth bore an inscription in Latin and declared that George IV put up the statue to his father George III—fat Prinny put it up to his poor mad father. How ludicrous the statue was compared with the mythological figures I had seen dotted about the eighteenth-century parks in Yorkshire, which weren't out to dominate or impress so much as to embellish the landscape. In those parks little Grecian temples worked in the same way at the end of vistas. You could sit by one of the columns and eat a sandwich and the landscape quietly went to work on you. It was not very different from examining a poem by Wordsworth, letting it work and then seeing how it worked. The gross statue of the king was of a lower order altogether, and I allied it with the weight of gentility in Windsor compared with the mixture of frankness and tolerance in Norton, where it seemed to me that nearly everyone tried to avoid coarseness or "commonness" and condemned the "cheeky," whether they were high or low.

As I walked, the dog rabbited ahead. The country was very fine, though for me it lacked the power and reticence of the North Country. A huge castle, flowers everywhere: not my taste. Nor was the lassitude of the Thames Valley. Coleridge said, "In looking at objects of nature, I seem rather to be seeking, as it were asking, a symbolic language for something within me." That was it. And: "To see is only a language." I looked about me with anguish at the objects of nature: they were indifferent to whether I lived or died, whereas I cared passionately for them. To love and be loved, man to woman, woman to man, must be perfect. I was only slowly associating such perfection with my huge physical desire. Love I associated spontaneously with the movies, and the movies had nothing to do with my own experience, or with those of the other moviegoers, any more than the looks of the actors had to do with the looks of people on the street.

"Give us a smile, bonny lass," said the young sentry in a sweet Geordie voice as I walked past pretending to be invisible. I was pushing my thoughts in the wrong direction. So I paused and grew visible. "I'll talk on the way back, because I'm late," I said, and made sure to go home another way.

Meanwhile Porrock grew. He'd learned to catch a ball in midair, and proceeding from that to toss the ball up for himself with a jerk of the head and to leap up and catch it. This he'd do over and over, jumping and twisting like an acrobat. I'd look out of the window and see him at it even when there was no one outside to take any notice. He'd amuse himself too by hurling himself into my arms as I walked up, so I'd have to catch him. The memory of that skinny, awkward little body with its thrusting legs is still marvelously with me.

I used to take the double-decker bus into town to shop for my mother, and Porrock used to go with me, scrambling up the steep stairs to the top deck. When I came back, laden with groceries, I let Porrock off the lead so I'd have one hand free to grasp the rail, the other hauling the loot; Porrock managed perfectly well to keep his balance in the jerking and cavorting of the bus on the empty streets of those days. In fact he managed so well that sometimes he took it into his head to go into town by bus without me, hanging about at the bus stop and hopping on with people and letting himself off at the High Street before the conductor could find out whom he belonged to. So I was told by those who'd witnessed this extraordinary performance. I was told too that he visited butchers' shops and made off with scraps of bone or gristle. He would also drop in on various well-meaning householders who would feed him and make him welcome with titbits nicer than the regular stuff I gave him at home. Eventually he would come back by himself and resume a common dog's life.

"It's a pity he's so damn ugly," said my brother after Porrock had reached maturity. "He isn't a bad dog, as dogs go." Iain preferred cats. In recent memory, in the lifetime of our previous dog, an unlikable Sealyham, we had nearly come to blows. The dog barked at the cat and made to steal the cat's food. So Iain booted the dog and I screamed and squared up to him like a boxer. For two pins I would have hit him. "Look at her! She thinks she's a man!" he jeered to the audience of my mother. But I wasn't man enough to hit him. For Porrock, the cat was negligible, which in our household, where emotions ran high, was a blessing.

For months these high-running emotions became directed at Iain, who kept failing his exams. He failed anatomy and physiology three or four times and later midwifery, obstetrics and gynecology, surgery, and all the other branches of medicine you can think of. Every time failure was announced my father would roar and bury his head in his hands and ask aloud where the money was going to come from to finance another go. Medicine was hard, and Iain should work at it hard instead of reading Proust or fooling about learning to dance or listening to opera on scratchy expensive records. How ironic it was, my father said, that as a young man he dreamed that his baby son would grow up to be a famous surgeon and play rugger for Scotland. What a hope! He couldn't even pass anatomy! Then we'd all go around with long faces for a week, until we began to think of something else and cheered up.

As far as my mother was concerned, emotion expended itself in enormous measure on domesticities. She made clear that the two or three hours a day I'd mentally allotted to her were not enough. She said that the house was falling into filth and decay, the ironing overflowed the laundry baskets, the brasses were dull, the shopping had to be done, food provided, dishes put away, the lawn to be mowed, the windows washed. None of these imperatives struck me as important. There was a war on, I pointed out. People were killing each other on various battlefields and some were bombing civilian populations. The bombing had been far worse in the North, where we had lived within striking distance of the chemical works at Billingham. We'd been protected by anti-aircraft artillery manned by men and women and by barrage balloons—silvery blimps moored by cables to prevent bombers from flying in low (the balloons used to catch fire in storms and go up in vast sheets of flame). Fewer ack-ack installations here, no barrage balloons, only squadrons of bombers droning every night, sometimes dropping their explosives so the house trembled and one's ears cut out. In any case, housework bored me to death. "I don't know what's wrong with you," said my mother in utter bewilderment. "You always have your nose in a book. Let me tell you something: men don't like bookish women."

I wrote to my old school friends describing the scene. My mother lived in a frenzy, I said, preparing for visitors who never called, while my father behaved like a god whom nobody prays to.

My mother intercepted these letters and read them. "If I'd written letters like that when I was your age, I'd have been beaten."

In the midst of these domestic confusions, Cousin Mary telephoned to say that she and her husband Hector were in London on business and she'd like to call on us the next day. My father happened to answer the phone. By this time my mother and her mother—my father's sister—no longer spoke to each other. My mother therefore decided that she would not be at home to Cousin Mary either. So as the time of her visit drew near, my mother tidied the already tidy house and withdrew upstairs, forcing me to go with her. We watched from a bedroom window as a taxi drew up and a good-looking woman in a trim navy suit approached the front door. After a cup of tea with my father, she crunched away over the gravel and went off in another taxi.

"What is this farce?" I demanded. I would have liked to meet Cousin Mary again. At five or six I had been a bridesmaid at her wedding in Edinburgh, where there had been more kilts than I could count, and she gave me some pretty beads. "Little do you know," said my mother, keeping me by the window in case Mary returned unexpectedly. "Your cousin is not a nice woman."

"I don't see why you have to pretend you're not here."

"Little do you know."

"Tell me then."

"You shouldn't speak to me like that. One day you'll understand."

"Understand what?"

"Never you mind."

"What a farce this is you lead."

Presently the domestic pressures created by my mother met my resistance head on. "I don't know what you're crying for," she said. "I'm the one who should be crying."

They sent me off to stay with a friend in Yorkshire for a few days. When I came back I bought a charming black-and-white rabbit to fill a gap not entirely stopped by Porrock the dog. The rabbit escaped from the hutch I built him, and while he was eating cabbages on a neighboring allotment, the allotment holder cornered him and hit him with a stick. The rabbit was squatting by the cabbages unresisting when I was summoned to fetch him, and soon after I carried him back in the hutch he shut his eyes and died. But before natural death intervened, the desire to kill him with my two hands swept over me. I itched to strangle him, to throw his body on the ground and break its bones. Later my mother came to the door of my room and began to complain. "Go away!" I screamed at the top of my voice. My father came and sat on my bed and listened to me tell him between wild sobs how much I hated her. My mother stood at the door with a half-smile. She said she knew I didn't mean it. "I do mean it!" I shouted, so she left.

"What's brought this on?" asked my father. "Is it some man?" A startling thought. A young solicitor I'd talked to at the bus stop had asked me for a drink in a pub, but I'd not gone, and a handsome young sailor had chatted me up on a train, but I'd not agreed to meet him again either. "You're much more reasonable than your mother," observed my father, still sitting by me on the bed.

A huge understatement, I thought, flattered all the same.

"You know, you have to put yourself in her shoes," he added.

"Why? She doesn't put herself in mine."

"No. I don't think she ever went to school, you know."

The jump in reasoning brought me up short, and normally I would have leaped on him for it, and the conversation would have ended. But now I needed him, and I listened closely. He said that my grandfather did not believe in women's education.

"So she doesn't either," I said.

She wouldn't talk about it, he said. The grandfather was a difficult old man. "I've always held it against your grandfather that he never gave us a penny when we got married. He's a rich man, and we had nothing. Not a penny did he give us."

He spoke with feeling, and I understood that he was on my side and felt immensely cheered. "She's a very brave woman, your mother." In 1917, he went on, she left her home in Sydney to volunteer as a nurse with the Australian troops, with not the slightest idea of the hardships she was to undergo. Had I seen her medals?

I had rescued them from the bin where she'd thrown them more than once: war decorations with important grosgrain ribbons in moiré reds and blues dangling from a clasp, in a leather box from Spink of Piccadilly, like a soldier's. "She was very brave."

But never went to school. Must have had a governess. Probably shared the governess with half a dozen sisters. Wrote a beautiful hand, full of character. Was amazingly good at mental arithmetic. Could make my brother laugh till he cried. Sang well. Hadn't a clue about history. Didn't know the Bible, didn't think about it. Could recite Wolsey's speech from *Henry VIII*: "Cromwell, I charge thee, fling away ambition! / By that sin fell the angels. . . ." Sewed beautifully. Adored her husband. What a pain my mother was, rich man's daughter, immensely loving and lovable and unpredictable, sexy obviously and frigid probably. I much preferred my father. I think everyone did. She insisted on his perfection, too. However, he was devoted to her.

The day after my conversation with my father I painted a wall of my room with huge figures dancing in a landscape of tall thin poplars and rounded busty hills. It astonished me to see how sexual the painting was.

Within a few weeks my mother had painted it out.

We all leaned formally on the idea of compassion, especially because none of us, with the exception of my father, was compassionate. Porrock, for example, came in for a great deal of verbal abuse because he was ugly and good-natured. Kind words came only from my father, probably because he was the only member of the household who lived his life in composed and dedicated fashion. As he'd always rushed, his constant rushing didn't suggest to me that he was under a strain. Just as in the old days, I used to go with him when he paid a few visits on a Sunday morning; I sat in the car with Porrock while he dived into various houses to see how the sicker patients were doing. The streets were better kept, the gardens were neater, the houses really finer than the ones I'd grown up seeing, and there were no foundries or ironworks or men hanging round street corners waiting for the pubs to open, no slums, in fact, and the river had walks along it and flowering trees, not abandoned staithes and crumbled wharves. My father should have been happier, and perhaps he was; he kept his own counsel about happiness. In his book, hard work brought its own rewards. He used to hum or whistle to cheer himself along, and this device among others and his willfully sunny nature made me think he was someone to laugh at as well as be fond of, and my brother and I used to get hysterical at his simplicity. One Sunday the small Morris my father used to visit his patients broke down half a mile from home, and we decided to haul it to the house with the help of the bigger car he kept in the garage for better days. There was a thick rope somewhere in the garden shed. I spied it behind a heap of tools, the mower, the roller, flowerpots, string, netting, and my father—a great strong man—reached in and began to haul the rope out in powerful heaves. It wasn't a clever thing to do. The smaller objects flew about, the flowerpots smashed, the mower fell over, the rope came out inch by inch. My father exerted more and more brute strength: the shed came away from the wall and tottered. Terrible rending noises ensued. At any moment the window would pop out and shatter and the roof and walls slide down like playing cards, one on top of the other. At last the rope came free and my father staggered back with it in his hand. Porrock had long ago fled into the house. I looked at the debris of the shed and then at my father, trying to grasp what was happening. "Sorry," he said, panting and surveying the damage. By the time we'd got the other car out and hauled the Morris home, he was again calm and humming one of his two tunes, "My Blue Heaven" and a Gaelic song that goes

Hoo-roo my nutbrown maiden,
Hoo-roo my nutbrown maiden,
Hoo-roo, roo, maiden, you're the maid for me.

The words made me blush, they were so silly, and yet so sweet, and the tune was pretty. The oddity of my adorable father filled me with misgiving. Why, for example, didn't he relieve his expenses by giving up smoking? "Cigarettes cost you a fortune. Think how rich you'd be without them."

"True," he'd admit, and light up. Often he regretted how he'd sold his stocks and shares on the outbreak of war. Sometimes I think he also regretted leaving his huge working-class practice in the North for the small middle-class one in the South. The Stockton practice provided a sure and steady income, and it was a two-man practice. In Windsor he worked alone and shouldered the responsibilities alone. Certainly the National Health Service in Stockton would have paid him well by his large register of patients when it was introduced after the war, and he had a commitment to poor people that would have been amply rewarded there.

Those were exceptional times, though passionate indignation is the norm in families and exceptional times merely raise the temperature. The war grumbled away in the near distance like the weather, or at worst a dragon that occasionally bothered the neighborhood. We didn't think crisply about it, any more than we thought about fate. And yet we considered each other's conduct. If only one behaved better! If only one were kinder! If only we had more fun and weren't so glum! "You're all so glum!" my mother said repeatedly. "How I laughed as a girl! All my sisters laughed their way through life."

A depressing thought. Only Porrock was jolly, and she disliked the dog for so effortlessly displaying the cheerfulness she demanded of us.

The illogicalities of her train of thought were set off by my own routine. Twice a week I biked three or four miles for a session with my Latin tutor, which was followed in a different part of the town by a session with my English tutor. There should have been a French tutor also, but he fell away after a couple of meetings, bidding me study by myself. The Latin and English tutors were much more conscientious and demanded swaths of material — prepared texts, unseens, essays, commentaries. I knew I hadn't the slightest chance of a scholarship.

"What is the point of Latin?" my mother asked.

"I like it," I said, and my father, with authority, "Wonderful training for the mind." Ludicrous assumption. My mind was netted by the language into which I'd blithely flown. And somehow or other I was frightened that I'd be exposed as a fraud when the great moment of the scholarship and entrance exam came along. My fondness for Latin was like a fondness for sweets. I was wasting my father's money. What hard work those fourteen months at home was! We had few books at home and I had no book allowance. Nor was there a decent public library in Windsor. I remember thirty-minute bus rides to Slough Public Library to read contemporary writing: Auden, Isherwood, MacNeice, Ivy Compton-Burnett, Henry Green. The bus passed through Eton, and it is tempting to depict resentment at how well off the Eton boys were in comparison, with their rich libraries and their hosts of masters; but it did not occur to me at the time to think poorly of my situation. I did not see how I could learn any better than under my excellent tutors, who insisted principally on close study, with the library at Slough providing what breadth it could. I've never found a substitute for that primary wrestling with the subject that I was forced to undergo, and subsequently write about, regardless of whether I cared for the subject or not, or had anything to say about it.

The only real pleasure of my life was my relationship with Porrock, who would dash with me alongside the bike as I tore to Latin and back to English, waiting for me in the hour-long sessions, guarding the bike, enchanted when I emerged with my file of papers, barking with joy at the prospect of the next lap, the race with me along the pavements till I finally swerved into the graveled drive of our house with him skidding beside me.

I thought a lot about morality in those days, and the morality of loving a dog more than my family was one of the many issues that gave me pause.

I took the Oxford exams in the family drawing room with a defrocked clergyman as my invigilator. He was one of my father's patients, a thin, harsh, unfinished man who'd run off with someone's wife and now lived with her in sin. He sat on the sofa and read while I scribbled at a card table. The exams stretched over three or four days, at the rate of a paper in the morning and another one in the afternoon. One was an essay, which my clergyman read through when time was up. He shook his head: "No, no. You can't say that. It's rubbish. Go on, do it again. Go on. It's all right. Don't worry about the time. I'm not going to say anything." I'd written for all the time allowed and said everything I wanted to say about simplicity, the subject I'd chosen for its appeal in a confusing world. The clergyman made me sick because he assumed he was my superior and had better judgment. I was tired of not being taken seriously. It was clear that the man was unwise as well as dishonest. So I declined his offer, letting him cluck in dismay.

My essay was the best thing I did. It didn't win me a scholarship, but they offered me a place at Somerville. (I had applied to Somerville alone because it was the only women's college that was secular and admitted women of all creeds or, like me, of no creed yet.)

My father said: "I don't know if I can afford to pay for more than one year, but at least you'll be able to say that you've been to Oxford." So he prized what I prized? And yet he'd have me throw it away? Why couldn't he throw the house away, or the garden, or a car?

At this juncture, when the end to my time at home was in sight, something happened to Porrock that changed him. It was late spring and the front door stood open on the graveled circle inside the gates to the garden. One morning he came through it howling and yelping, tore up the stairs as I was going down, passed me and disappeared into the furthest bedroom, where I found him under a bed. When I put a hand out, he showed his teeth. Later, unable to fathom what had happened, I dragged him out in spite of the bared teeth. He was quite rigid but had no sores or contusions. Much later, he crept downstairs and drank from his water dish, but he wasn't his old self and took no notice of me. The next day he went out on the road and raced after a car and tried to bite its tires as they spun by, so I suppose he'd been hit by a car previously and was trying to punish the aggressor. I had to keep him on a lead, because he became insatiable in his pursuit of wheels. Only gradually did he come back to normal. We went out together on the bike, with him sitting in the basket in the old way, or running on a lead beside me, but several times without warning he yanked the lead out of my hands and tore after another bike, dangerously snapping at the feet of the cyclist, or after a car, yelping hysterically all the while and traveling like the wind. Once a car stopped and the driver got out and told me off for keeping such a dangerous animal. Yet on the whole, in spite of such incidents, I thought I was checking this mad new tendency and believed it would wear itself out with kind handling.

At the same time something told me that I'd let Porrock down and he wouldn't change back into the innocent creature he'd been. He was only a dog. You could not expect him to go to town on a bus or steal from the butcher's or walk alone into people's houses for a meal, or wander down the street by himself, without things going wrong. The human world wasn't geared to him. Even the dog world wasn't geared to him; he was much too intelligent to be content with its smells and meals and grooming rituals. If he were only a dog he wouldn't teach himself to play his ball game, or to smile at me with bared teeth.

So what was I to think? I didn't think. My mind had shifted away from him, as his had shifted away from me.

When I came down from the university at the end of my first term, I looked forward to the old scene: my parents, my brother, my dog. But Porrock was not there to meet me. "We had him put down," my mother said. "That business of chasing after traffic got too much for me. There was no one to look after him."

I remember not replying. A reply would not have been adequate, it would have been hurtful, and it was too late. Simplicity had arrived, like a razor. Porrock didn't belong in the house except through me, and I'd gone away. Therefore they felt free to kill him off. I had used him, and his usefulness was over. My mother said I would be thinking of other things now, and it was perfectly true, my world had become fascinating and full of friends and talk and opinion in which Porrock had no place. And yet he was the halfway point between, on the one hand, the baffling world of green places that did not respond to me and, on the other, the world of ideas. But that was not quite right. There should have been a place for him, and I should have found it, and not given up till I'd found it. "You must respect the animal," my father said once when I was younger and had dressed an earlier dog in a bonnet. So I respected Porrock. He had his own life, and it impinged on mine. He was the fur, the lick of the tongue, the heavy sigh with which he'd collapse beside me before going to sleep, the desire for physical companionship expressed by pushing against me. We were two animals with an animal world in common, but a generic barrier between us. Or we were two kin souls if there is a world of souls, as I sometimes think there is.

Many years later I reminded my mother of how Porrock used to throw balls up into the air for himself to catch on the way down. I laughed with delight at the memory, but my mother looked puzzled. Then she remembered who Porrock was. "Fancy your remembering that. After all this time." Her voice was full of reproach.

TENNESSEE WILLIAMS

In Spain There Was Revolution

FROM WHERE he lay on the end of the dock, the river was like fluctuant diamond-paned glass of two colors, olive green and steel blue, leaded together by wavering white stitches of sun. The summer was dry. There had been a long succession of these flawless, brilliant days. It was now the middle of August but already the trees along the opposite hills were turning color. Reds and oranges and yellows stood like a motionless and smokeless fire above the intense, burning green of the river willows. Things were drying up in the earth. But it was a death that wore bright colors. It looked like a flaming opulence of life. Only the desiccated patches of pale yellow corn glimpsed between folds of the Ozark hills seemed willing to admit without any bright evasion the solemn fact of things dying.

Steve heard the rasp of oarlocks and the faint plash of a leisurely moving boat. The black blades lifted and caught the white reflection of sky and dripped a thin sheet of silvery water on each side. The girl rowed perfectly. Her approach had an air of quiet inevitability unhurried as time itself. There was no swerving, no unnecessary motion. There was perfect timing and absolute poise. It was herself graceful and shining and entirely at ease and not the clumsy wooden boat that moved toward him.

He breathed in deeply and felt his body expand against the warm, moist boards he was lying on. He raised an arm in casual salute. She didn't return it, but the white gleam of her teeth became more distinct and the oars rasped with a quicker rhythm. The boat curved in slightly toward the shore.

The girl was a counselor at the Idle Wild Camp a mile up on the other side of the river from the resort where the boy was lifeguard. Every morning or afternoon she rowed or paddled down to see him. At night they met sometimes on the middle span of the new white concrete bridge, which was a lovely, unearthly place suspended between the dark water and the sky, in both of which the stars were clearly visible. Being a long bridge, it was reasonably safe. When headlights curved out of the highway on either side of the river and wrinkled the dark with fiery prismatic radiations, there was always time enough for the boy and girl to draw discreetly apart and meet the passing glare with blinking, unabashed eyes, and there were many long intervals between when the darkness was loud with cicadas and the flow of water and the silky, rippling soliloquies of owls. At about ten-thirty the double-engined Red Ball freight thundered its forty- or fifty-car chain over the railroad bridge down the river. They waited until the red and green lamps at the end of the caboose winked finally out among the swallowing hills, and then the girl raced breathlessly away to reach her camp before the bell rang for "lights out."

"How many lives have you saved this morning?" she called up to him.

"Nobody's been in yet. Wait a minute. I'll swim out."

He looked quickly around to see that the beach was still empty, then dove off the dock and reached the boat in a few easy strokes. He clung to the end of it and expelled a jet of water between his teeth. It trickled down her smooth brown legs.

"I've got the blues," she said. "I looked at the calendar this morning."

"You shouldn't look at calendars."

"I couldn't help it. It stared me right in the eye."

"What did it say?"

"Only two more weeks of this."

"Sorry?"

"Of course."

"So'm I."

"It's been so perfect here."

His eyes dropped from her face and traveled leisurely down the wet blue suit. His voice softened.

"It'll go on being that way."

"I don't know."

Her voice had lowered also, and he could feel her awareness of his eyes on her body.

"That suit's a humdinger! Silk, isn't it? I can even see your belly button!"

"Shut up! Don't be disgusting!" she laughed.

He looked up and smiled.

"*Sure* it will be just the same."

"What?" she asked, her voice still shaking and her eyes not able to meet his.

"At school. The way it is here."

"I don't know," she repeated gloomily. "School isn't like here."

"I know it isn't," he admitted. "Here it's just perfect."

He pulled himself lightly from the river and into the boat. He stood over her, dripping water, and she frowned at him without conviction.

"I've got to get back."

"Not right now."

"I'm late. They'll ring the bell in about twenty minutes."

"What's the diff."

"Both of us are holding jobs, you know."

"We don't care if we get fired."

"Yes, we do."

"That's right," he admitted mournfully. "I wouldn't see you for about three weeks."

She smiled and met his eyes. His face was beaded with water that gathered on the stubbles of his chin and looked as though he had grown a bubbly golden beard.

"You forgot to shave."

"I know. I was too lazy. I had a strenuous night."

"What doing?"

"Dreaming about you."

"Was that necessary?"

"It is sometimes."

She looked slowly across the brilliant water.

"That suit of yours takes the cake," he murmured. "You might as well be completely nude."

"You're terribly vulgar sometimes."

"But you like it."

"I certainly don't like scratchy chins."

"Yes, you do."

"How do you know?"

"I can just tell."

"Get out now, Steve. I've got to row back."

"Not right now. Let's go under the willows a moment."

"No, not this morning," she said almost sharply.

"Yes, right now."

He looked around once more, very quickly, then seized an oar and turned them in toward the bank. She leaned against his shoulder and closed her eyes, feeling the warmth of the sun and of his body. He looked down at her as he rowed. She had tanned very deeply and smoothly. There were no visible pores in the skin, and the fine hairs of the lower legs were bleached white. Rowing had pulled up the lower edges of her trunks and exposed half moons of untanned flesh. He loved to see the white parts of her body between shoulder and thigh that were supposed to be kept unseen. Their more private quality seemed to be expressed in that contrasting whiteness.

As soon as the willow shade had closed over them he caught the shoulder strap nearest him and jerked it down. His hand cupped her breast. She looked up at him with eyes half frightened and lips falling apart. It was always that way. She let things go until they had gone too far to be stopped. Then she felt herself absolved of the responsibility.

"Steve, it will be your fault."

"I don't care."

"Just suppose."

"What?"

"Something happened sometime."

"I wouldn't care. Would you?"

The wet shoulder straps dangled coldly over her legs. With a long fretful sigh, like a person twisting in fever, she arched her body and pulled them slowly away.

"Would you care?" he repeated softly. His words arched over her like the rook of a tunnel. They shut out daylight and the sky and the incandescent willows. The tunnel bored down without effort into the darkness below them. The day was left a long way behind. The sun was glittering on the other side of the world. The boat and the lake and the humming dragonflies had slid away with one complete, lubricious gesture from under and around them, and in that cavernous darkness their bodies grew larger and larger till they had outgrown everything but each other.

"Would you care?"

"Not much if you didn't," she answered without hearing her own voice. He laughed softly. Their bodies stirred a little to make a closer embrace. All the while her eyes peered dreamily through the interstices of their green-gold-curtained alcove. He laughed at her whispered protestations which she herself did not listen to and felt her breath coming faster.

From up the river he heard very faintly the tolling of the camp bell. But it was she this time who was altogether lost to the world outside. Her eyes were closed and he knew that she didn't hear. For a moment he selfishly planned not to warn her. Then he remembered what the loss of her job would mean. The sacrifice of two more weeks together. . . .

He tightened his arm.

"Darling, it's ringing."

"I know," she smiled.

"I thought you didn't hear."

"I did. I just couldn't move."

Now she sat up and straightened her blue silk suit. The lovely white parts of her body disappeared.

"I never would have thought things like this could happen to me a few months ago."

"Neither would I."

"Hmm. I bet you're an old hand at seductions."

"I learned about women from you."

"I'm just the first lesson, am I?"

"First and last."

"Get out, you liar!"

He dove off the end of the boat, and she made a wide arc from the hidden bank.

Sun and water widened between them. He clambered up the ladder and resumed his place at the end of the Bide-A-Wee dock. A fat man with an inner tube was waddling down from the shore. It was the morning swimming hour. Resorters descended behind the fat man in little clusters. Family groups and weekend parties. He knew some of them. Some of them were strangers.

He sat up alertly on the folding chair, expanded his naked chest, and adjusted his sun goggles.

The girl was nearly around the bend of the river. He could still see her body rhythmically bending to the oars and sunlight flashing on the wet blue suit. Out there in the glittering distance was the girl shadowed by willows. Then the curving bank intervened and he could see only the rippling forked trajectory of the boat.

The man with the inner tube had waddled onto the end of the dock and was seated beside Steve, waiting to be given some notice. That was mostly what they came down for, men of his sort, to be looked at and listened to. At work they were stooges. White-collar nonentities. But on their vacations, at their play, they wanted to be vital and specific personalities. They wanted to disentangle themselves from the soft, spongy webs that had grown around them, and the way they went about it was very silly. They overexercised frenziedly the first two or three days, exposing their moist white skins immoderately to the sun's indifferent burning, and then they slumped helplessly into exhaustion, smearing themselves with creams and lotions and complaining about the mineral taste of the water and the weak coffee and the uncomfortable beds. Steve looked at them with contemptuous pity, these men who lived narrow, slavish lives in cooped-up places, men caught in ruts, graves with both ends kicked out. . . .

He avoided the fat man's searching squint, kept his eyes fixed stonily on the water. He wanted to think of the girl. Nothing else.

The man was not to be snubbed. He cleared his throat.

"What do you think of this trouble in Spain?"

The lifeguard shrugged his coffee-brown shoulders.

"Trouble in Spain? Didn't know there was any."

"My God, man, what's the matter with you? Don't you read the news-papers?"

Again Steve shrugged.

"Not lately. What's going on?"

"*Revolution*," said the man. "*Next it will be the whole world!*"

He gave Steve a disgusted glance and then climbed awkwardly down the ladder and plopped into the shallow water. He waded carefully out with the inner tube girdling his middle. Water rose to his armpits. Then he pushed himself gently forward and moved out with the sidewise paddling motions of a fat turtle.

Steve looked down at him and shook with noiseless laughter.

BARBARA WASSERMAN

Spain, 1948

—ɯɯ—

THE SCREENING ENDS, the lights go on, the theater empties. I want to join
the exodus but I am trapped in my seat. By questions. The women sitting beside me want to know more. The film we have just seen is Barbara Probst
Solomon's *When the War Was Over,* an autobiographical meditation in
which the pivotal point is a trip to Spain that she and I made together in
1948, a trip that might be quaintly described as a derring-do adventure.

My friends want details. Who were the guys? How did we get them out
of prison? Did our parents know what we were up to? And most of all, how
did we have the guts to do what we did? It is hard to respond to an accusa-
tion of heroism. I am tempted to say that we were just dumb. This is clearly
insufficient, so I try to explain that what I most remember half a century later
is not any fear I may have felt, but that I was too preoccupied by a bout of
turistas to worry much about getting caught. They think I am being flippant
and are more exasperated than amused.

They let me go at last. But in my mind the conversation continues. It has
been a long while since I have given much thought to that time. The years
have layered over the event until it is deep in a substratum of my personal
history. Now bits of memory begin to surface, shards and snippets of images
I didn't know were still there. Before I realize what is happening, I am digging down. I am excavating my past.

In the spring of 1948 I sailed to Europe for the first time. My father, an ac-
countant, was in Paris, working for the Joint Distribution Committee, an organization involved in the resettlement of people displaced by the war. My
mother was going over to join him. My brother, Norman, and his wife, Bea,

had been there since the previous fall, studying at the Sorbonne on the GI Bill.

It was taken for granted by all of us that I too would go to Paris. Having been graduated from Radcliffe the year before, I was living in my parents' home in Brooklyn, since my mother considered it highly improper for me to live anywhere else. I chafed at this. I wanted to be on my own. But to go to Europe would be the realization of a dream that, as a child of the depression, I had had no large expectation of fulfilling. It never occurred to me to stay behind. Indeed, I even agreed to go first class, much as that offended my social conscience. Mother's passage, however, was being paid by my father's employer, and she was not about to renounce her first opportunity to travel in style.

In Paris, Mother found an apartment in an *haut bourgeois* building on the Right Bank. Because Parisian rents had been frozen at prewar levels, the chic woman who owned the building could only make ends meet by renting her own apartment to Americans, although what we paid was no more than our modest rent in Brooklyn. She moved in with a friend and we moved into Louis XV elegance. There was of course no refrigerator. Perishables were maintained for a day or two in an open-air closet built into the kitchen wall. And we were advised to run our hot water tank only at night and bathe only once a week if we did not want exorbitant electric bills. We compromised and took only half as many baths as we were used to. I found the lack of customary amenities part of the charm. In fact, the hot baths and the relative luxury in which we were living made me feel somewhat deprived. I hankered for the public baths where Norman and Bea went once a week because, like most of their friends, they had no hot water at all.

But that was a standard living condition, and even on the GI Bill, Americans were better off than most of the French. Indeed, it was extraordinary to be an American in Europe in those early postwar years when we were still looked upon as saviors. It was possibly the only time in history when one could be both rich and loved. Even the French treated us with a modicum of affection.

I soon gravitated to the Left Bank and the friends Norman and Bea had made in their six months in Paris. Among them were a group of anti-Franco Spanish students, exiles, and refugees. Some of them had fled Spain to avoid arrest for political activity. Others were the children of defeated Spanish Republican leaders who had died or escaped to South America ten years earlier. Some hardly remembered Spain, but they all wanted to return. Frustrated in this basic desire, and eager for even a tenuous sense of connection with their homeland, they were still talking about the car trip to Spain that Norman and Bea had made before I arrived.

Ah, the car! Desperate for dollars, the French were selling almost all the automobiles they produced to any foreigner who could fork over a thousand dollars. The only model available—the *quatre chevaux* Peugeot—was a small vehicle with cross-eyed headlights and a rear-wheel contour that intruded so far into the frame that in the back seat you had to sit with one haunch high. And as I was to learn, four horses is not a lot of power. However, the Peugeot presented one advantage. One could at any time sell it to a Frenchman for more than one had paid. So, Norman bought a car.

The Spaniards talked to him about pulling off a coup. They wanted to spring some of their friends in Spain who had been imprisoned for political activity. They hoped to get them out of the country. An American-owned car could prove a formidable weapon. Particularly persuasive was Paco Benet-Goitia. A bright twenty-one-year-old, very intellectual and passionately anti-Franco, he was the only one of the Spanish students who was not a refugee and could therefore travel back and forth. He also had a network of contacts in the small world of anti-Franco resistance that still simmered inside Spain. He would accompany Norman and Bea. They decided to go.

They smuggled in some anti-Franco leaflets, stashed inside the springs of the back seat and in the deflated spare tire. The literature was handed over to some of Paco's friends in Barcelona, but when they got to Madrid, Paco found that circumstances were not propitious for the escape. Norman and Bea stayed a few days, went to a bullfight, and returned to Paris with their mission unaccomplished.

I arrived shortly after, and in May and June, Beatrice, Norman, and I took to the road—a trip to Mont St. Michel, Brittany, the Loire Valley; then Switzerland and Italy, and back through the south of France. In late June we stopped at the American Express office in Nice and found a mountain of mail that had been forwarded from Paris by our parents. Norman's first novel having been published in May, the reviews were just beginning to reach us. We could hardly believe they were so uniformly favorable. *Time* magazine compared *The Naked and the Dead* to *War and Peace*. Letters from our friends in the States were exultant. We sat in the car, mail on the floor, on the seats, in our laps, reading distractedly as we traded choice items and passed the pieces of paper around. Until Norman offered up still another newspaper clipping. "Gee," he said in a small boy's voice, "I'm first on the *Times* best-seller list." Suddenly we were shrieking with laughter. There we were, tired and grubby from a long day's drive, the little car a mess, and my brother was creating this stir three thousand miles away. It seemed so remote as to be absurd.

By the time we got back to Paris, however, the reality had reached him, and he decided it was time to return to the States.

While he and Bea were preparing to leave, Paco learned that the conditions for an escape operation had now improved. Flush with success, Norman decided to donate the Peugeot to the Spanish resistance. However, there was no way the Spaniards could use the car themselves since most of them couldn't go to Spain and Paco didn't drive.

Norman asked me if I would like to go.

He knew I would be thrilled. While I didn't know very much about Spain, I did know that the Spanish Civil War—won by the bad guys—had been one of the catastrophes of our time. Like many other people, I had assumed that once the fascists had been defeated in Germany and Italy, Franco would also be disposed of. However, three years after the war, he remained in power and Spanish refugees were unable to return. Instead of opposing Franco's regime, our government seemed to be supporting it—in the service of the Cold War.

My politics were less militant than romantic. I would have liked to be a nineteenth-century revolutionary. In lieu of it, I had been working for the Progressive Party. And before we left for Europe, I had started an affair with an "older man" of thirty-eight, a journalist and Marxist. For a bon voyage gift he took me to the left-wing bookstore on Fourth Avenue and bought me a bunch of tracts—Lenin, Stalin, Bukharin, Clara Thompson. I dutifully toted them along to Paris, where, under the prevailing fifteen-watt bulbs, struggling to keep my eyes open, I even more dutifully read them, all the while resolutely squelching the complaint, even to myself, that it was the most mind-numbing prose I had ever encountered.

In fact, I had found grassroots political activity not much more congenial. But the proposed mission to Spain evoked an entirely different model—the heroism of the Resistance movement in France during the Nazi occupation. Just as the Maquis had struggled against the Vichy regime, I would be redressing my government's support of Franco. (Which did not prevent me from believing that my government would bail me out should I get into trouble.)

It seemed there was only one difficulty. Like Paco, I didn't know how to drive. Norman said it was no problem. He would teach me. I should also take along another driver—he suggested Barbara Probst.

At the time Barbara and I hardly knew each other. We had met in April sailing to Europe on the SS *America*, Barbara traveling with her mother as I was with mine. Our mothers met and liked each other, but I didn't pay a great deal of attention to Barbara because for most of the trip I was deeply involved in a shipboard flirtation. Since Barbara was two years younger than I, had not yet gone to college, and was still a virgin, I suspect I saw her as not quite my peer. In Paris, however, we began to see something of each other. What I did not recognize at the time was that this pretty, privileged nineteen-year-old, whose take on things sometimes seemed to me a bit fuzzy, had come to Europe possessed by an iron determination to engage the world. She was as eager to go to Spain as I was. And she had a driver's license.

As for learning to drive, I was less sanguine than Norman. I didn't tell him that a year earlier a friend had given me a couple of lessons which had been a total fiasco. I hadn't understood why I couldn't seem to turn a corner at less than thirty miles an hour, but after climbing a couple of curbs I had decided to call it quits. The residue was a year of bad dreams. The night before Norman's first lesson I had one last nightmare in which I was forced to drive a car.

He took me to a short empty stretch of road, explained a few things about the way a car worked, then made me practice starting and stopping until moving my foot from the gas to the brake was automatic. Only then did he begin on the intricacies of the clutch and how to shift gears without stalling. At last I understood what my problem had been. My friend had been so intent on teaching me the gearshift, he had never really taught me how to stop.

After four lessons, Norman decided I needed a practice run, so I drove the family to Chartres. All went well, and he dubbed me a driver.

The license, however, was another problem. My linguistic skill was hardly up to a French driving test. We decided to use Norman's international license. Substituting my picture for his, we clumsily erased his first name and wrote in mine. It was probably worse than useless.

Naturally we did not tell our parents about the purpose of the trip to Spain. I'm astonished now that they asked no questions and expressed no concern about my ability to take a long road trip so soon after learning to drive. Of course Mother, though a woman of great energy and competence, didn't drive at all. And Dad, always a bit baffled by the used Chevies we had owned during the depression, preferred to leave the driving to others. Perhaps they thought of driving as something young people just did. Or perhaps, for once, they were so deeply enmeshed in their own lives that they weren't paying a great deal of attention. We were all giddy with Europe. Since they were going off to the fjords of Norway, they may have thought it only fair that I too should be setting out to explore another country.

One task remained before Norman's departure—to change the ownership of the Peugeot. With three days left before his boat sailed, Norman and I entered the Kafkaesque world of French red tape. Nobody could believe that he was *giving* me the car. No bureaucrat wanted any part of it. They sent us from one office to another, and of course the offices were always closing for lunch. At the end of three days we were still on square one. As I remember, Norman gave me a letter signing over the car. Then Barbara and I spent the next week, all day, every day, trying in vain to get the registration changed.

One day Barbara was out with the car and got arrested for illegal parking. Since she didn't have a registration, the magistrate wanted to call me. Afraid I would be alarmed if she didn't call me herself, she refused to give him my number. Hearing the story afterward, I was greatly impressed—particularly since her French accent was as American as mine. But she didn't give a hoot about errors of pronunciation or grammar, an arrogance which had the effect of disarming French contempt. She said to the official, "Vous ne m'aidez pas, je ne vous aide pas." ("You don't help me, I don't help you.") He finally gave in or gave up. She called me and we got it sorted out. And found a bit of good fortune. Someone we met in the court that day, to whom we told the story of our troubles, suggested we contact an organization, a French equivalent of the American Automobile Association, that would, for a fee, arrange for the change of registration. I remember he said, "C'est moins cher aussi." Indeed he was right—it was cheaper. And within forty-eight hours I was the official owner of the car.

At the end of July, Barbara, Paco, and I left for Spain.

In 1948, traveling through France by car was perpetual bliss. The sky was soft, the air fragrant, and the scenery, unlike any I had known before, changed constantly—through *allées* of trees into the narrow streets of old towns; from the geometric patterns of perfectly manicured farm fields to the kind of heart-stirring mountain ravines I had seen only in nineteenth-century landscape paintings. Everything from the thick stone walls to the black dresses of the women was wonderfully old. I believed it would stay like that forever. The main routes were two-lane roads that meandered through countryside from town to village and never avoided a city. On the other hand, there were very few cars on the road, so no traffic jams—unless one got caught behind a farmer in a horse-drawn wagon.

The *quatre chevaux* Peugeot was well suited to all of this. Its cruising speed was no more than fifty miles an hour. But since the road signs and the maps and the speedometer were in kilometers, we were traveling at eighty on the European scale, and this seemed quite fast enough. The tough part was the mountains and the weather. At night we kept running into fog. And in the mountains one never knew if our underpowered car would make it up and around the next hairpin turn. I often felt as if I were coaxing a balky pet, and the intimacy I developed with that car in the course of the next two weeks has made me ever since prefer small cars on back roads.

As I recall, we reached the south of France in a day and a night of driving. We had taken along a couple of friends—a penniless painter and his girlfriend. It was August, so like everyone in France, penniless or not, they were going on vacation. Since they could not afford even the cheapest hotel, we all went without a bed. Instead, we traveled through the night. I still have a vivid image of hunching over the wheel while I peered into a mist so thick that the car lights could penetrate but a few feet, and a ghostly hint of trees was my only clue to the shoulder of the road.

We dropped our friends off in Hendaye and proceeded to the border. The contraband leaflets stuffed into the back seat of the car made us a bit nervous as we approached the Spanish side, and we probably overdid our nonchalance during the few anxious minutes it took to stamp our passports. No sooner were we into Spain than Paco informed us that we were going to visit his mother who was vacationing near San Sebastian.

Given the purpose of our trip it seemed to me unfitting to visit one's mother. I realize now he probably wanted to pick up the key to her Madrid apartment. Besides, he hadn't seen her for some months. Indeed, as I looked at the ocean from the lovely promenade along the beach in San Sebastian, I was struck for the first time by the double-edged reality I was inhabiting. I knew I looked just like any other tourist. And I loved the ocean. But given my sense of mission, I had no desire to join the swimmers on the beach.

For a couple of hours we sat in an arbored garden with Paco's mother and his brother Juan. Their mother was a beautiful woman of much presence. Juan seemed dark and brooding and not nearly as good-looking as Paco. Because I was told Juan was nineteen, I thought of him as still a kid (after all, he was half the age of my lover in New York). Meeting him again after he had become a major Spanish novelist and a stunning fifty-year-old man, I was dismayed to discover that he had been very taken with me those thirty years earlier, when, with the heedlessness of a twenty-one-year-old, I had so blithely ignored him.

Of course no conversation was easy. Barbara and I spoke no Spanish. Neither Paco nor anyone else we met in Spain spoke English. All communication, except between Barbara and myself, was in French. Paco's French was fluent, and since he loved to spin out convoluted theories, I seldom understood what he was talking about. At the time I thought it was due to the language barrier, but a few years later when he came to America and learned English, I was still never sure we were speaking the same language. All the same, he was very attractive. Fair and downy-cheeked, his boyish good looks were spiced by the manly slash of dark bushy eyebrows that ran across his forehead. I always liked him, but we were on different wavelengths. As later events would prove, Barbara didn't have this problem.

For me, that was one of the strangest things about the trip. I felt enormously involved with the people I traveled with but never felt any real rapport. Even Barbara and I did not begin to become close friends until twenty years later. To some extent this was no doubt due to the mental blinders I wore at the time. There were only two things that seemed really important to me — falling in love and saving the world. And since I didn't fall in love with Paco, I concentrated only on the job at hand — getting the guys — *les types*, as we soon began to call them — out of jail and out of Spain. What astonishes me now is the total confidence I had that Paco and his friends could handle the details. I knew that things might not work out because of forces beyond our control, but it never occurred to me that somebody might screw up.

After leaving Paco's mother we drove to Madrid, arriving so late that Paco put us up in his mother's apartment, where he would be staying. We took the car seat in too, so we could empty out the "literature." Barbara and I slept on sofas in the living room, and I remember waking the next morning to the sight of sheet-shrouded furniture and an El Greco on the wall above me. Clearly Paco's family was not poverty-stricken. In fact, it turned out that we were in the neighborhood of the Prado and the Ritz, and later that day Barbara and I moved across the plaza into the Palace Hotel which was then considered the best hotel in the city (the Ritz was closed). The Palace was being renovated, and was almost as empty of guests as the roads were of cars. We paid the enormous sum of four dollars a night for the room.

The prospect of having a bed and a bath was delicious. While I luxuriated on the bed, Barbara went to run a bath in the huge tub. A minute later she came out, laughing with dismay and holding the cold water handle. It had come off in her hand and she couldn't stop the flow of water. We called the desk, where English supposedly was spoken, and were told that someone would come. No one did. Meanwhile, the water was gushing fast, the tub was almost full. We called again, this time in French. Again no one arrived. By now the water was spilling over to the floor of the bathroom. When it began to flood the room, we waded out in bare feet and closed the door. Still no one came, and the water started seeping into the hall. I ran down the several flights of stairs to the front desk. My bare feet and English/French frenzy caused a slight ripple of shock in the management. They promised action. I ran back up the stairs to discover that the hall had become a lake. By the time a sweet little man with a wrench appeared, the water was creating havoc in other rooms, but he seemed hugely delighted by us and the mess. "Mucha agua fresca," he kept saying as he opened a little hatch in the wall and turned the water off. He had no sooner left than all kinds of help arrived and we were moved to another floor. I no longer remember whether either of us dared to take a bath that day.

Indeed, I remember surprisingly little about the week we spent in Madrid. We arrived on Saturday or Sunday and left the following Sunday, thus frustrating Paco's wish to take us to a bullfight—the *corridas* were held only on Sundays. I would have liked to see a bullfight (having read all of Hemingway and not yet forgotten the movie *Blood and Sand*, seen ten years before when I had a schoolgirl crush on Tyrone Power). But it hardly seemed important. Given the purpose of our trip, I tended to regard Paco's eagerness to expose us to Spanish culture as touchingly superfluous. Of course, most of the time there wasn't much else for us to do, and I realized when he took us to the Prado that he had a point. I was mesmerized by the Goyas.

I also realized that I liked the Spanish people. Although I had arrived in Europe with an early case of political correctness which considered the stereotyping of any ethnic group an act of bigotry, I soon discovered that "national character" was not entirely a myth. Unlike the French, the Spanish were friendly, and unlike the Italians, they seemed more dignified in their poverty. I sensed in them a reserve and a pride that made me feel they acted out of genuine curiosity and goodwill rather than in the hope of currying goods or favor. Of course, in a time when the other countries of Western Europe were struggling back to a semblance of past position and future affluence, Spain was out of the loop. For most Spaniards, life was probably not much different from what it had been fifty or a hundred years earlier. Barbara and I must have looked to them like apparitions from another planet. Two young women—girls rather, wearing clothes (light summer skirts and off-the-shoulder peasant blouses) that looked like nobody else's, and roaming around unchaperoned, going to nightclubs where men took only their mistresses. Paco explained that what we called dating was still not done in Spain. No doubt a number of people viewed us disapprovingly, but most seemed puzzled, even delighted. Paco, having lived in Paris, was fairly sophisticated, but I remember a friend of his—another young man from a well-to-do family—who often joined us. When we went to a nightclub his eyes sparkled wickedly, and he kept saying that he was going to "rrropp" me. He had a few words of English, most of which were unintelligible, and it wasn't until years later that it finally dawned on me that he'd meant "rape." I suspect he didn't quite understand the meaning of the word since his behavior was otherwise "perfectly proper."

One day Paco took us to meet some people who were too poor to afford any regular housing and lived in caves on the outskirts of the city. It was a hot, barren place, devoid of grass or trees. While Paco went inside a cave to confer, the two American girls waiting outside were objects of curiosity to the children who milled around. I was filled with pity for a life I could not quite imagine, and with shame for feeling grateful that it wasn't mine. It was the first time I experienced that dichotomous sentiment, which is now often evoked on the streets of New York.

The family living in the cave was harboring a man who had just broken out of prison and, as I later learned, Paco's purpose in going there was to propose that he join our escape party. He refused. Sick and skeptical, he didn't believe we'd make it. He was caught soon after, and died in prison.

When he wasn't shepherding us around, Paco was making arrangements through his contacts. We did not inquire closely into the details. It was agreed that the less Barbara and I knew, the better. In case things went wrong. Toward the end of the week we learned that the plan was a "go." We would leave on Sunday.

The guys we were going to free were in a forced labor camp about thirty miles northwest of Madrid. The camp's inmates, most of whom were there for their anti-Franco activities, were being used to construct the monument in the Valley of the Fallen that was to be both Franco's future tomb and a memorial to his soldiers who had died in the civil war. While their politics were being thus punished and their bodies exploited, this was a Catholic country and the prisoners were encouraged to save their souls. On Sunday they would be going to noon Mass at the Escorial, just a few miles from the labor camp. I wondered, but did not ask, how we were going to hook up with them.

Sunday morning arrived. Barbara and I checked out of the hotel. Paco put our bags in the trunk of the car and threw into the back seat a package containing two sets of men's clothing. He was also carrying two sets of false papers.

We reached the Escorial well before noon. As we wandered through corridors and rooms and gazed at paintings, Paco would occasionally disappear to case the situation, and I believe he cached the packet of clothes in a bathroom. But most of the time he spent giving us a guided tour of the art, architecture, and history of the Escorial, an enormous palace complex built in the sixteenth century by Philip II to house not only the royal quarters but a museum, a library, a mausoleum, a monastery, and a very large chapel. Perhaps Paco's purpose was to make us look like tourists for the benefit of anyone who might see us. But as always, with regard to things Spanish, his lecture was genuinely enthusiastic. I absorbed none of it.

At last he told us to go back to the car and wait. Barbara sat in front, I sat in back, as Paco had instructed. The sun was hot. The air was dry. The oppressive bulk of the Escorial stretched endlessly along the empty street. Not a soul. Silence. I was beginning to think it just possible we might never see Paco again when he emerged through the entrance door with *les types*. Whatever we might have been expecting, it was a shock to see three college boys sauntering down the steps looking like — three college boys.

Les types, Nicolas and Manolo, jammed into the back with me. Just how they separated themselves from the other prisoners I'm not sure. Presumably they got permission to go to the bathroom, where they changed into the clothes Paco had left for them. Paco jumped into the front seat. "*Vite, vite, vite*," he said, and we were off, laughing a little hysterically. It all seemed so simple, so unremarkable. Not unlike a jaunt to the beach.

Les types and I looked at each other, smiling with the helpless amiability of strangers who have no language in common. They knew no English or French. Conversation had to be mediated through Paco, which made every question or comment weightier than one may have intended. And though I wasn't aware of it then, it was my first experience of how difficult it can be to talk to people with whom you have in common no friends, no work, no past.

Perhaps for that reason I was acutely conscious of sitting thigh to thigh with two young men who had just spent a couple of years in prison and for whom this must be the first physical contact with a woman since they had been arrested. I felt they were as uncomfortable as I was.

I mentioned earlier that Paco spoke no English. In fact he did know a couple of words and kept using them incorrectly. He always said, "Right," when he meant straight ahead, and "Stret ahead," when he wanted us to turn right. So we had to keep double-checking his directions. Or ignoring him when he would cry out, "*Vite, vite, vite*," every time we saw a Guardia Civil. We knew it would have looked suspicious if we had speeded up, even if we could have, which usually we couldn't because we were already going as fast as four horsepower could carry five people.

We were stopped a few times, but the false papers worked. The guards seemed to find us curious, yet not suspicious. Whether this was because Barbara and I were American, or because we looked like a bunch of rich kids, I do not know. After we passed Madrid there were few checkpoints. And almost as few cars.

We began to talk about lunch. Paco suggested an excellent restaurant that we would soon be approaching. It was a few miles off the road, but it had, he promised, a spectacular view. We were hungry, and it seemed like a good idea to hide ourselves in an elegant establishment where no one back at the prison would think to look.

Then the accident happened.

Barbara was still driving. We were in the mountains, the road climbing, dipping, curving. Suddenly we went into a skid, careened a bit, and ended up, fortunately, sliding into the mountain rather than off it. The car jumped a small rock and stopped.

We were pretty shaken up, particularly when we looked at the sheer drop at the other side of the road. But we weren't hurt. We lifted the car back onto the road, and to our relief the motor started. But we soon realized something was seriously wrong. The tires squealed continuously, even on straightaways, as if the car were in a never-ending curve that it was taking too fast. Since it was still hundreds of miles to Barcelona, we decided we'd better find out what the problem was. We stopped at the first town that had a service station. They only sold gas but told us there was a good mechanic in a village a couple of miles up the mountain. We turned off the road. The car wheezed and shrieked up a rutted and rock-strewn dirt path. Less than a half-mile into it, I felt as far from civilization as the moon, and the village we finally arrived at looked as if it had grown from a landscape as barren. The mechanic, it turned out, was the local expert on oxcart repairs. Our arrival was possibly the most exciting event of the year.

My urban middle-class prejudices and assumptions surfaced quickly. I was more appalled than impressed by the way they raised the car and diagnosed the damage. With only one jack, they hoisted up each wheel, then piled stones under it so they could free the jack to raise another. A couple of times the stones slipped and the hubs came down with an ominous clang, but eventually the whole car was raised and all the tires removed. By now the entire village population was circling the car, and someone pointed out the problem. One of the connecting rods between the axle and a wheel had been bent into a right angle. After a little discussion, none of which I could understand, the "mechanic" got an iron mallet and began to hammer the part back into shape. I could hardly believe what was happening. And I couldn't bear the sound. It was a little like watching a friend get his leg sawed off. I walked away with my hands over my ears, sure the axle would break and we would be stranded.

I was wrong. Primitive surgery worked. *La direction*, as the wheel alignment was called, was hammered pretty much into place, and we set off. But having lost a couple of hours, we gave up on the elegant lunch. I don't remember what, where, or if we ate, but my stomach, which had been suffering from occasional *turistas* all week, began to kick up again. For the rest of the drive to Barcelona I worried not about the Guardia Civil so much as I lived in fear that I would be humiliated by my own gut. It was long after dark when we stopped for dinner at a local cantina in a small town. I tried using the privy in back but was routed by the dirt and the smell. At some point that night I think I simply took the only remaining option and squatted in a field.

Driving was infinitely preferable to sitting three in back, and Barbara and I took turns. As the night wore on, I tried to sleep while she drove, but only managed to nod off for a few minutes at a time. Therefore, at three in the morning, when Barbara turned the wheel over to me again, I was bleary. Not quite awake, I drove. And drove. I don't know which was more agonizing— trying to keep my eyes open or trying to control my sphincter. Comparing notes thirty-nine years later, when Barbara and I were once again traveling together through Spain, she discovered for the first time that I had been more afraid of embarrassing myself than of landing in a Spanish jail, and I learned that she had been in a low-grade state of terror through all the hours in the mountains because she was afraid of heights.

Everyone else fell asleep, and the car was deathly quiet. However, I managed to open my eyes often enough to stay on the road until daybreak, when I had the sense to tell Barbara to take over again. Paco, who was getting a little nervous about how far a police alert would have reached by this time, decided we should turn south on a back road and enter Barcelona by way of Tarragona. This route was barely distinguishable from a cross-country trail, and as the car bumped along those last couple of hours, I lapsed into a miasma of half-sleep, waiting for the next sick spasm and only vaguely aware that Paco was helping another very sleepy Barbara to steer.

We reached Barcelona around mid-morning. I remember waiting on a little beach while Paco went to look for a safe house. He found something for the guys and himself. Barbara and I went to a hotel on the Ramblas. I have never been so happy to find myself in a room with a private bath.

The next day Paco took us all up to the unfinished Gaudi cathedral. He was very proud of it and expounded for a while on its architectural significance. Contemptuous as I was then of any esthetic of modern architecture which did not adhere to the Bauhaus, I'm afraid I didn't appreciate the building. I did like the setting—a lovely wild hillside. I seem to remember that we brought along a picnic lunch, which we ate while we studied the map on which Paco had outlined the escape route. While he remained in Barcelona, the rest of us would leave later that afternoon and travel north. About thirty miles before the French border we would come to the first of four checkpoints. They would look at our passports and IDs, and list all our names on an official form which we would have to show at each checkpoint, and which would be collected from us at the last one, just before we reached the Spanish border town of Puigcerda. Between the third and fourth checkpoints— Paco gave us the exact mileage—the road ran for a bit along the border. At that point, all that separated Spain from France was a high hill. Nicolas and

Manolo were to get off there (by this time it would be well past dark), go over the hill, and, *voilà*, they would be free. Barbara and I were to stay the night in Puigcerda, then cross in the morning to Bourg-Madame on the French side. From there a back road in the mountains would take us to the village of Osseja, which, as the crow flies, was not more than five kilometers from where the guys would have left the car. With any luck, they would be there waiting for us by the time we arrived. Then we would all drive to Paris.

Amazingly, it almost worked. We said goodbye to Paco and started out. At the first checkpoint we held our breaths but had no trouble getting the necessary piece of paper. We even had a giggle when we discovered that they had listed Barbara as Great Marsh, the name of her family's home in Westport. Near midnight we reached the stretch of road at which to debark. We slowed the car. To the right the hill loomed but did not look impassable. We turned off the headlights, stopping for a moment. Goodbyes were hurried. The guys got out, and for a brief moment before they disappeared I saw them scurrying up through the brush.

Barbara and I continued, driving very slowly, wanting to give them as much time as possible before our arrival at the last checkpoint set off an alarm. We were to say we hadn't known the guys, had simply given them a lift and they had wanted to get off.

Barbara said thoughtfully, "Let's try not to give them the paper. Let's pretend we don't understand."

The checkpoint was manned by two young soldiers. They may have been even younger than we were. We just kept speaking English and shrugging our shoulders. They began to laugh. Two girls. In the middle of the night! Driving a car! Americans! We laughed too. And finally, as if we understood what they were asking for, we handed them a partially used pack of cigarettes that we had. At that moment my admiration for the Spanish went up another notch. Instead of taking the whole pack, as we had meant and expected, they each took one cigarette, handed back the pack, and waved us on. I've sometimes thought of those two boys and hoped they did not get into trouble because they did not obtain that official piece of paper.

We drove into Puigcerda giddy with relief. And with exhaustion setting in. Driving slowly through the deserted streets, we searched vainly for a hotel. At last we saw one lone soul, and stopped to inquire. He took a look at us and his eyes lit up with that by now familiar gleam of curiosity and good will. He must have spoken French since we were able to communicate. It would be difficult, he said, because at this time of year the few hotels were crowded, but he would help. Dismissing our invitation to get into the car, he hopped onto the side, and, canted out like a figurehead, he waved his free arm to direct us from one hotel to another. It was nice to see him enjoy himself so much, but indeed all the hotels were full. When he had no more suggestions and we were contemplating sleeping in the car once again, we noticed another hotel sign down the street. What about that one?

He looked unhappy. They'd probably have room, but we really didn't want to stay there, he said. We said anything would do. Reluctantly, he went in to inquire and came back with the news that yes, we could have a room—pay in advance.

The hotel was seedy. As we climbed the stairs we heard voices and squeals, doors opening and closing. "A whorehouse," Barbara said. Which made us giggle. Until we saw that the sheets on the bed were filthy with the remnants of numerous couplings as well as a few squashed bugs. I couldn't care. I lay down and my eyes closed. Barbara tried to wake me, saying, "How can you sleep on this?" But she too finally fell off.

It was not hard to get out early the next morning, and we arrived at the border office as soon as it opened. Here we were told by the customs official that we hadn't changed enough dollars and would not be permitted to leave until we did. Spain's monetary policy at the time required foreign tourists to change something like ten dollars at the official rate for each day spent in the country. Since the official rate was a fraction of the black market rate, and we had been told that the rule was generally not enforced, we had bought only a couple of days' worth when we arrived. We tried to plead ignorance, said we'd stayed with friends and hadn't needed much money, and how could we use pesetas now that we were leaving Spain? He knew we were lying and was adamant. We considered going to another border town where we might find a more lenient official, but we didn't want to keep the guys waiting. Already we felt we had wasted too much time. So we changed the money—probably fifty or sixty dollars apiece, a goodly sum at the time. I can't remember what we did with the pesetas.

Then we crossed to Bourg-Madame, and drove on to Osseja.

They weren't there.

It was hard to believe it could take so long to walk a few miles, even in mountainous terrain. A small bud of dread sprouted in my belly.

Thus began the two longest days of my life. I read once that the most difficult part of partisan resistance was not fighting but waiting. Indeed, the minutes were longer than any I'd ever known. There was nothing to do but wait. Impossible to read. We didn't even talk much. What, after all, was there to talk about when everything else in our lives seemed insignificant? With each hour I sank a little further into the realization that we might not be living charmed lives. For the first time in my life I began to recognize that my actions could have enormous consequences not only for myself but for others. Nicolas and Manolo had probably been caught. They might even be dead.

When the waiting became unbearable, we took to the car. We would drive the couple of miles from Osseja to Bourg-Madame, then double back through Osseja and on another couple of miles to the village of Valcebollere, where the road ended. Driving slowly, the whole route took maybe twenty minutes, but it gave us a small sense of action. Most of all, it allowed us the ever-dimming hope that if we did not find the guys on the road, we might find them in Osseja upon our return.

The second day was worse. We decided to call the telephone number in Paris we had been told to contact in case of a problem. We reached Carlos, one of the Spanish refugee students. The connection was terrible, as was usual in Europe in 1948. Finally we eked out a few instructions. If the guys did not show up, we were to go to an address in Perpignan and say that Juan had sent us. The people there would tell us what to do next. Static surged on what might have been Juan's last name.

Soon after the phone call Barbara became unaccountably obsessed with a house in Osseja called "Beau Soleil." She kept repeating it over and over and saying, "There's something about that name." I thought she was being a bit peculiar.

On the third day we gave up waiting and drove to Perpignan. Awful as we felt, it was a relief to be on the road again.

It was dusk when we arrived at the Perpignan address. "Juan" didn't work. The young woman at the door said, "There are lots of Juans." Dismayed, we went off to get some dinner, and as we sat discussing what to do next, Barbara suddenly said, "That house. That's it. I think Carlos said Juan's name is Bellesoleil." Thus armed, we returned to the house, were taken in, and told we must make contact with still another person in another place—Pallach in Collioure, some twenty miles or so down the coast. We set out right away.

I'll never forget the drive to Collioure. There was the intoxicating smell of the sea, and a warm, wild wind blowing through the trees. I would have been euphoric had I not been feeling so wretched. The dichotomy intensified when we reached Collioure. It was a beautiful old walled town, a festival was going on, and it seemed as if the entire population was dancing in the central plaza. What made it particularly poignant was that the band was playing what I thought of as the theme song of that summer in Europe. It was a marvelous bouncy samba that I had heard for the first time on the ocean crossing. We heard it all the time in Paris and everywhere else we went. I loved it, and despite a dismal musical memory—I may forget the theme of a Mozart sonata I was playing last week—I can still sing "Maria dõ Bahia."

We soon found our address. I have a memory of climbing several flights of ancient stone stairs to an apartment that seemed dark and bare—in France that year no one but Americans used electricity freely. A pretty but cautious young woman told us that Pallach was out and not expected back for some time. So we wandered aimlessly in the square, feeling remote from the holiday frenzy around us. To our surprise, Pallach found us—not very many minutes later. It amuses me now to realize how easy it was to spot us in the midst of that throng.

Pallach was somewhat older than we were, and he had a sweet, comforting presence. He said there was a good chance the guys had been taken by the French border police, which would mean that they were alive and safe. In the morning he would check through a contact he had, and get word to us. As we drove back to Perpignan we were somewhat more sanguine.

But the news in the morning was not good. Nicolas and Manolo were not in the French internment camp. It was agreed that there was nothing left for us to do. Convinced that the guys had been captured by the Spanish, we drove back to Paris in a blue funk. I remember nothing of the trip, or how long it took, probably no more than a couple of days. I do remember driving into Paris on August 15 or 16 to find the city empty and morguelike, hushed and melancholy enough to mirror our mood. In the late afternoon, in the late summer light, it was also more beautiful than ever. We had returned on the one weekend of the year when every Parisian leaves town.

Some days later the news came that Nicolas and Manolo were safe in France. Without a compass, they had lost their bearings almost as soon as they left the car. Afraid to travel during the day, they had wandered by night for all of that week, and probably back and forth across the border. Weak and famished, they finally stumbled onto a road where the signs were in French, and they gladly followed it into the arms of the French police. The next few weeks they spent in an internment camp.

Paco, too, had trouble getting out of Spain. The authorities soon traced the escape to him and put out a warrant for his arrest. His mother warned him not to come back to visit her, and, awesome woman that she was, arranged for a small fishing boat to take him back to France.

By the time Paco and Nicolas and Manolo reached Paris, I had returned to New York—to my unfinished romance and to work for the Progressive Party and Henry Wallace's presidential campaign. Eventually Nicolas went to Argentina to join his father, the president of the Spanish Republic in Exile, and Manolo went to England for a while before he too left for South America.

Barbara remained in Europe for a couple of years. She and Paco became lovers and put out a Spanish exile magazine, *Peninsula*. Almost twenty-five years later she would write about that time in her memoir *Arriving Where We Started*.

I never again saw Manolo. Recently I learned that he had died. And it was twenty years before I met Nicolas again. Barbara called one day and asked if I was free that evening. Nicolas had arrived in New York for the first time and very much wanted me to join them for dinner. Naturally, I was eager to see him, but having a date for that evening with the man I would soon marry, I suggested the next day. Barbara was most insistent that it could not wait, so I persuaded Al to come along. Nicolas had been married and divorced and was traveling with a "fiancée."

That first meeting was strange. In a way, almost comic. We met at a small Spanish restaurant on Houston Street. Nicolas now spoke English, his lady knew none, and she was, for some reason, furious. I don't think she said a single word throughout the meal, but she was completely successful in throwing up a stone wall between the men and the women. Barbara and I talked nervously to each other—I now understood why she had so badly wanted me to be there—while Nicolas talked to Al the entire time. Al marveled afterward at how odd it was that he, not I, had been the one to spend the evening with Nicolas.

Nicolas eventually married someone else, moved to New York to teach at NYU, and some time after Franco died went back to Spain. While he lived in New York, we would occasionally see each other at parties, but we were never easy with each other, and I never asked if he has any regrets about the way he has spent his life. But something Barbara told me has made me wonder. She said there had been a third man in the prison whom Paco had wanted to free, but who had decided not to come with us. He was released a couple of years later and continued to live in Spain. Which of course was what they all wanted—to live in Spain. Instead, Nicolas and Manolo, who had probably expected that they would soon be able to return, spent the next thirty years as exiles. And Paco, who died in an automobile accident in 1966, was never able to go back. So I cannot help but wonder if their lives might have been better if we had not been there to help the guys escape.

The passing of the years has developed my taste for irony, and so I am not exactly surprised to realize now that this one act in my life about which I have always felt so virtuous, is still subject to a most basic lesson—that one's deeds, no matter one's intentions, almost never result in unambiguous returns. I'm grateful, however, I did not know this fifty years ago. I only knew that given the chance to rescue a couple of political prisoners, I had to go to Spain.

STEVE YARBROUGH

Sleet

—ᴍ—

WHAT SHE remembers, in the time she allots for remembering, is how cold the house got in winter. She would question the authenticity of that recollection, since she thinks of Mississippi as a hot sultry place; but her sister, who is a year older than she is, remembers those winters the same way. "It must have been the wind," her sister says. "Remember, there was that big empty field to the west?"

"I thought it was south of the house," Kendra says.

"It was west," her sister says. "On the other side of the road. The wind just came howling straight across that field, and I don't think the windows and the doors were well sealed."

They had space heaters. She remembers how she sometimes climbed out of bed, after Mary Jo had fallen asleep, and sat in front of the heater in their room, staring at the flames. The fire flickered behind radiants made of ceramic fire clay. The radiants were arched like the windows in the sanctuary at the Methodist church, and each one had many little diamond-shaped openings. She remembers sitting there in her pajamas for hours, watching the fire patterns, feeling warm, while a few feet away her sister slept. Sometimes, on nights when their father was home, she'd hear him roll over, the heavy weight of his body making the springs groan.

She remembers the traps they set out, the way they loaded them with stale cheese. Some of the traps were small, maybe three inches long. Others, the ones they placed in the attic, were almost a foot long. She knows that today she would not be capable of removing a furry little body from any sort of trap, no matter what size, but Mary Jo swears they both used to check the traps every morning and that when they found something dead there, they took it out, tossed it into the green garbage barrel out back, and reset the trap.

One night—one cold night—when they'd just gone to bed, they heard their mother scream. Both of them bolted for the door. Flinging it open, they saw their mother run naked from the bathroom, water dripping from her heavy breasts, water streaming down her back, her legs. Their father followed, a greyish ball dangling from his hand by what appeared to be a string.

He chased her into the living room and, while they watched, he cornered her near the television set. "It's just a mouse," he said. "A dead one. Don't you want to touch it? You like fur."

Their mother stood there dripping, shaking from cold or fear or both. Their father grinned. He took a step closer.

Suddenly the mouse twitched. Hollering, their father dropped it and jumped backwards.

She remembers the way the four of them stood there studying the mouse, which lay, almost flat, on the floor. Its neck had been crushed, the hair behind its head was matted with blood. Yet while they stood there, it twitched again.

You can be moving but dead, she remembers thinking. She believes this was the moment when she lost faith in boundaries, seeing life and the lack of it merge in a ball of fur.

Their father was gone so much because their farm, like a lot of small farms in the Delta, had failed, and he'd taken a job selling dictionaries for a company based in Jackson. They still owned their house, though they'd lost the rest of the land, so they were staying there until he could afford to move them down. He came home every third or fourth weekend, bringing his samples with him, one big brown dictionary for grown-ups and a smaller red one for children.

He was renting a room in a big house on North State Street in Jackson. The people who lived there, he said, were all characters. He'd set Kendra on his knee when he came home and tell her about them.

"There's this one fellow that's the chaplain at Millsaps College," she remembers him saying, bouncing her, running his fingers through her curls. "He's about sixty years old now. You know what happens to you sometimes when you get to be about sixty?"

"You die?"

"Well, you could, but there's other less drastic stuff that happens."

"Like what?"

"You could lose your teeth."

"*I've* lost a tooth," she says. She opens her mouth to remind him of the gap there.

"Yeah, but you'll grow another one," he says. "When you're sixty and you lose them, that's it. All you can do is get fake teeth, and that's what Reverend Dooley went and did. But you know what happened the other Sunday?"

When she turns around to say *what?* her face grazes his. It's rough, stubbly. She wonders now if that's why stubble on a man's cheek never bothers her. Mary Jo says she can't stand it. Most women can't.

"Reverend Dooley was up preaching his sermon at the campus chapel, talking about sin and damnation, and he got carried away. He started pounding the pulpit and shaking his head, and the next thing he knew, his dentures—that's his fake teeth—were flying through the air. He said they landed right in the organist's lap. He claims he's fixing to retire."

He tells her about Hardy the mechanic. Hardy's wife doesn't like him anymore, he says, so he's had to move into the boarding house. Hardy has problems at work. Her father tells her that the other day Hardy forgot to tighten the oil plug on somebody's Rolls-Royce, a car that costs thousands and thousands of dollars, and the lady who owns the car drove it onto the highway and all the oil emptied out and the engine caught fire. Hardy gets grease on people's brake shoes, and when they try to stop their cars they have wrecks.

"Hardy's a mess," he tells her. "Hardy hasn't had a whole lot of success."

She asks him what success is. The black satchel he totes his samples in is standing by his chair. He reaches into the bag and pulls out the red dictionary, the one that's meant for kids. He flips pages until he finds the entry.

"Success," he says. "'When the plans one has made work out.'"

"Have you had a lot of success?"

"I guess I've had my share."

He says it in what she will come to think of as a matter-of-fact way. It's as if the statement is a straight line running through the middle of his life, like the center stripe on a highway, separating what has worked out from what hasn't. He says it as if he thinks that, on the whole, things have balanced.

In her recollections, when she's sitting on his knee, listening to him and occasionally asking questions, Mary Jo and her mother are somewhere close by, in the house certainly, though never visible. It's possible that they're in the kitchen. Today Mary Jo is a terrible cook, at least as bad as Kendra; both of them prefer to eat out, and most nights they do. But Kendra remembers that at one time Mary Jo liked to help her mother cook, and she remembers that her mother cooked a lot of different things and cooked them well, particularly on those weekends when their father came home.

Her mother was at that time a woman who still dressed well, who never went out in the morning until she'd had a bath and put on a nice dress. The pictures taken in those days suggest that she dressed conservatively. Her skirts are long and full. The snapshots are black and white, so colors are hard to distinguish, but it doesn't look like she favored loud shades. She's never wearing a lot of makeup in those photos. What she is wearing, more often than not, is a frank friendly smile. She sang in the choir at the Methodist church, and she had friends, other women who always stopped and spoke to her when she and Kendra and Mary Jo went to shop in the Piggly Wiggly. They talked about the things women talked about then—about the need for a traffic light out on 82, the prices of various foods, the new toupee the choir director had worn last Sunday. They talked for hours, it seems like, though it couldn't have been that long.

Every now and then, a really good friend would glance down at her and Mary Jo and then lean close to their mother, her hand held up by her mouth like a shield, and the friend would say something in a low voice. Their mother would glance at them too, and then she'd shield her mouth and lean toward her friend and say something back. And afterwards, when Kendra—never Mary Jo—would ask what they'd been talking about, their mother would say, "Oh, we were just discussing some folks that we know."

"Who?"

"Just some people," their mother would say, paying most of her attention to the shopping cart, which she always pushed down the middle of the aisle, even if someone else was coming toward her; she would hew to the center until the last second, then veer reluctantly off to one side. "Just some people who are having a hard time."

The beginning of their own hard times is difficult to place.

Kendra knows when she became aware that something drastic had happened. But she also knows that before the drastic event, there were other, more subtle indications of what Mary Jo calls "drift."

"It's like that Honda I had a few years ago," Mary Jo says. As an adult, she's developed deep attachments to all of the cars she's owned; her estranged husband, with whom she's had an on-again, off-again relationship for almost thirty years, is himself a car salesman. "It got to the point," Mary Jo says, "where you couldn't steer that car at all. The second I realized it had a problem, I knew I'd been seeing signs of it for more than a year."

How long Kendra was aware of similar signs in the life of their family is hard to say. When the bank told her father that it would have to seize most of his land and all of his farm equipment, he didn't seem particularly distraught. The night he came home with the news, they all sat out on the front porch, eating fresh strawberries from their garden and laughing.

"Maybe," she hears her father say, pink juice dripping down his chin, "I'll become an evangelist." He winks at their mother. "Don't you think I'd make a good one? The main thing an evangelist needs is the ability to believe the stories he tells. I can do that. The only other thing he needs is a little bit of charm."

There's a picnic table on the front porch—a table that appears in many photos—and that's where they're sitting. She's on the bench beside her father, Mary Jo and her mother are across the table. It's raining, big drops thudding on the roof like rocks. Their mother reaches over to clasp their father's hand.

"You could charm the fur off a fox," she says. "You could charm anything off anybody."

"I could be a truck driver," her father says.

Her mother says, "Gitty-up-go."

He snaps his fingers. "I know," he says. "Remember what a curve I had in high school? I could take up pitching. I'm still young enough to make the major leagues. Wouldn't you girls like to see me on TV? Imagine how I'd look on the mound at Yankee Stadium. Dizzy'd be calling my name out every week."

For a long time Kendra offered up the memory of this evening to herself as evidence that things were still okay at that point. But after a while the evening became evidence of something else altogether. Every occupation her father facetiously proposed involved travel. Each one would have taken him away from her and Mary Jo and their mother, just as surely as the one he finally hit on.

When he first took the job selling dictionaries, he came home every weekend; he phoned at least every couple of days. Later he began coming home every other weekend, and the phone calls became infrequent. Later still, to save money—toward buying a house in Jackson, he said, a place where they could all live together—he suggested they have their own phone removed. Their mother reluctantly agreed.

As for their mother, Mary Jo says she's like Nixon: the question is what did she know and when did she know it. But in Kendra's mind, the question is not what their mother knew and when she knew it. The question is how she knew it. Kendra sees her knowing as a dark heavy thing, a coldness that crept into her and made it hard for her to move.

At a certain point in her recollections, her mother begins to move in slow motion. Lying in bed beside Mary Jo or sitting on the floor in front of the space heater, she hears her mother's footsteps in the kitchen. The interval between one footstep and the next starts to seem absurdly long, and as she waits to hear it, she sees her mother's ragged pink slipper descending slowly, almost as if a parachute were attached to it, asserting drag. Meals take longer for their mother to fix; dinner, which at that time they call supper, begins to come from cans and boxes. Washing dishes, she sometimes pauses, a saucer in one hand, a soapy sponge in the other, to stare out the window at the field across the road.

One day she walks out onto the porch while they're doing their home-work; they've just returned from school. A storm is banking up in the west. "A cloud's coming," she says. It moves in fast, sudden gusts of wind rake the pecan trees, brown-hulled nuts shower down, and then the rain itself. It's heavy rain, Mississippi rain, silver sheets that ripple like stage curtains.

The storm lasts only ten or twelve minutes. But there's a lot of thunder and lightning, and the whole time it's going on their mother is out there on the porch. Kendra believes they must have worried about her, that they would have begged her to come in unless they somehow knew that she needed, right then, to be alone with the wind.

Afterwards, she walks in and says, "Let's go get in the truck."

They're using the truck because their father has the car. The truck is an ancient black International pickup with running boards like you see on the cars in gangster movies. Starting it can be a problem, but today it cranks right up.

Kendra's next to the door, Mary Jo is in the middle. Their mother doesn't say where they're going; in fact, the way Kendra remembers it, she doesn't say a word for the entire trip, and for once Mary Jo can't contradict her because Mary Jo says the trip didn't take place. Or to be more precise, Mary Jo says the trip took place later—at least three months later, possibly more—and she says it took place on a Saturday morning.

In Kendra's version it's late afternoon, probably the third or fourth week in October. From the distance of forty years and two thousand miles, every-thing appears in soft focus. The barn beside the highway lacks line and def-inition; a red farmhouse, set farther back, bleeds color. There's cotton in the field, there must be. White splotches appear in the picture.

Their mother parks the truck in a gravel lot before a small brick building at the edge of a field. Other pickup trucks are parked here too. A couple of men wearing muddy overalls are standing in front of the building, gesturing at the sky, then at the ground. They must be farmers. They were probably out in the fields picking cotton when the storm hit.

Their mother gets out of the truck. The men stop talking. They stare at her. She walks past them, into the store.

Because that's what it is: a store. On the window, white letters with red borders spell LIQUOR. Their mother is inside for a couple of minutes. While she's in there, the two muddy farmers look at the pickup truck, at Kendra and her sister, and then they shake their heads.

Their mother comes out toting a brown paper sack. She gets into the truck and starts it, and they turn around and go back.

For a long time, Kendra believes that her mother has driven some distance away from home in order to avoid being seen by anyone who knows her. This, in an odd way, offers comfort, further proof of propriety.

Then, years later, while she's prowling around the library at UCLA, her mind half numb from trying to focus on the notecards she's been filling out for five or six hours, the title on the spine of a book catches her attention. *Fevers, Floods and Faith*. It's a history of Sunflower County, Mississippi. Sitting down and flipping through it, she learns that the county she grew up in was dry until 1968.

What her mother must have done that day was drive across the line into Leflore County. What her mother must have done, even then, when she was still going to church on Sunday and saying amen and other women still spoke to her in the aisle at Piggly Wiggly, was buy her booze the first place she could find it.

There are certain things, Kendra understands, that perceptive men figure out about her.

A perceptive man learns that when he's with her, he's the only other person in her world; when he's not with her, he can expect to feel as if for her he no longer exists. Phone calls will go unanswered; messages will seldom be returned. From time to time, she will simply disappear.

Many of the men she's known have been married. A few have tried to leave their wives and children for her. But perceptive men know or figure out that you can't leave your wife and children for Kendra.

Children—she knows this from experience—feel it when you pose a threat to them. They feel the threatening fact of your existence, even if they never know your face. They feel you in the faraway stares on the faces of those who matter most.

Children—especially the children of the men she knows—love Kendra, to Kendra they come running. They perch on her knee while she whispers to them. Tiny fingers find their way into her hair, little arms wrap themselves around her neck.

People shake their heads. It's a pity, they say, that she never had a few kids of her own.

The Christmas tree looks threadbare. Her father notices it the moment he walks in.

He's been gone again, this time for almost a month. It's a few days till Christmas. They picked the tree up the other day with their mother. It's a cedar tree, and except for a single string of lights and four or five glass ornaments, there's nothing on it.

There's not much under it either. Two packages for Kendra and two for Mary Jo and one for their father. They're not expecting a lot this year, they know times are hard.

"This tree's almost naked," their father says. "This tree belongs in *Playboy.*"

Not too long ago their mother would have come back with something snappy like *It's too skinny for that.* Now she says nothing. She's sitting on the couch, drinking hot tea from a white cup that has a drawing of a magnolia on it. The tea smells funny. Kendra knows it does because sometimes her mother leaves that cup standing around, and more than once Kendra has picked it up and sniffed it.

"Who wants to go with me to town," their father says, "and get some decent duds for this tree?"

Her voice is the only one that says *I do.*

It's raining again, and the rain is cold, so cold that her father says he bets it will turn into snow or, at the very least, sleet. Sleet is something she knows about then, though the word will soon disappear from her active vocabulary. Words like *surf* and *freeway* will replace *sleet* and *defoliant.* Her surroundings are about to change, the blacktop road she's riding on will at times seem so far away that her distance from it can't be measured by any known means; at other times she'll travel down it again, through cold rain turning into something hard and icy, through darkness that seals her up forever into these moments with her father.

The wipers squeak back and forth across the windshield. Her father keeps his eyes on the road. He's a careful driver. Tonight they travel slow.

"Doing okay in school?" he says.

"I'm doing fine."

"You'll always do fine."

The way she will remember that line, the first word is italicized.

"You're an awfully smart little girl," he says. He reaches across the seat and takes her hand in one of his and gives it a squeeze.

"Mary Jo's smart too," she says.

"She sure is. But she's smart in a different way."

"What way am I smart?"

"You're smart in ways that may not always make life easy."

The lack of syntactical clarity in this statement is not, she knows now, what causes him to pause for several minutes. When he speaks again, he says, "I mean, let's think about explorers. You know what explorers are?"

"People that discover something?"

"Yeah. Sometimes what they discover causes them trouble. You probably haven't heard of a guy named Copernicus, but he's the fellow who pretty much proved once and for all that the sun was at the center of the solar system. And he got into all sorts of trouble for saying so. People thought he was way out of line."

Her father says he thinks she might be an explorer. He says she may not ever discover new continents or galaxies, but she may discover other things that people might not want to know. She may not even want to know them herself, he says.

Through the rain, the lights of town, slanted and distorted, begin to appear. Where the road crosses the highway, there's a red light. They stop there, waiting for the light to turn green.

When the light turns green, they'll turn into the highway. They'll drive along the highway for a mile or so, take a right onto Sunflower Avenue, and head for downtown. Once there, they'll park on the street, in front of Piggly Wiggly, right beneath one of several big candy canes that dangle over the sidewalks at Christmas. They'll get out of the car and hurry through the rain to Woolworth's, and they'll rush inside and buy two strings of Christmas lights, a package of tinsel, and a box of ornaments made of colored glass.

But before all of that happens, while they're still waiting for the light to change, her father has one more thing to say.

One day, he says, in the not-too-distant future, he'll be going away. He might be gone a lot longer this time, so long that Kendra's mother and Mary Jo may think he's never coming home.

"But you won't think that, will you?" he says.

She recalls shaking her head.

"That's good," he says. "Just remember that you're an explorer. It just so happens that I am too. We'll find each other again, you and me, and then we'll find your mother and Mary Jo. Just as sure as that red light up there's about to turn green."

The light changes colors, and then they're gone.

And then, several days later, on December 27, a date she and Mary Jo never disagree about, she wakes to find him gone.

A couple of hours later, around ten o'clock, he's really gone.

The Mississippi Highway Patrol car that she remembers is a black-and-white creation. Mary Jo says it was blue, that the car Kendra has in mind is the one Barney Fife drove on *The Andy Griffith Show*. Kendra doesn't say so, but she knows it isn't a car from TV she has in mind. The truth is that she sees the entire scene in black and white, so there's no other color the Highway Patrol car could be.

The state trooper climbs the front steps. He's wearing a raincoat—black in the picture—and the raincoat is wet and shiny. Her mother carries her cup to the front door. She's been drinking from it all morning, the funny-smelling tea.

She opens the door, and there the trooper stands, a wide-brimmed hat, wet also, in his hands. He asks if she's Mrs. Nelson.

They're behind her now, Kendra and her sister; Mary Jo clings to her mother's bathrobe. Kendra keeps her hands to herself. She touches no one, no one touches her.

For the longest time their mother fails to answer. Later, it will occur to Kendra that she's had to consider the question, whether or not she's really Mrs. Nelson; it's almost as if in this moment she's become aware that her identity has changed.

She nods, but the nod is something less than a yes.

The trooper says he's sorry to bear bad news. The rest passes in a grey blur, one fact colliding with another: how 49 South has a glaze on it this morning, the trouble some motorists have had with visibility; the way her father lost control of his car, how he slid out of his lane and into the other, what happened when he hit the bridge abutment. How very sorry the state trooper is, how he wishes he had better news to bring her and her beautiful girls.

"They look so much like you," he says, this big awkward man who is the first among many men to express sympathy for their mother, to be moved by the sight of this lonely woman, these fatherless girls.

In the next five years she lives in six states, in rented houses, run-down apartments, and once, on the outskirts of Freeport, Texas, in a motel. Her mother moves westward, drawn on by men who always seem to be headed in that direction. The last one leaves them within sight of the Pacific, in a walk-up apartment in Long Beach.

Her mother quits going to church. She works from time to time as a waitress, at other times as a desk clerk at motels. She loses one job after another, very often for drinking at work. She's happiest when there are men around to take care of her. A lot of them do but only for a while.

When she looks back on this period in her life, Kendra remembers walking home from school—walking from many different schools, to many different homes. She remembers some of the sights she saw along the way: the barbecue stand beside the street in Freeport, where the woman who did the cooking sometimes motioned her in and offered her French fries and a running commentary on the lives of the characters in *General Hospital* and *The Edge of Night*; a junkyard in Phoenix, the tiger-striped cat who prowled there, crawling among the wrecks in search of mice; a drive-in in Banning, California, where teenagers parked for hours, rock and roll blaring from their radios, the guys trading innocent threats, the girls jumping out of one car and into another, giggling, their ponytails flying.

But mostly what she remembers from that period are the walks she took with her father. She met him almost daily, he had never been more real. He turned up in every city she lived in. She told him of the various discoveries she had made since that morning when Highway 49 glazed and he strayed from the southbound lane. She told him that by Christmas of the first year in Jamestown, only thirty-two of more than one hundred colonists were still alive; they'd built their village in a swamp, she said, and mosquitoes had bitten them and made them sick. She told him that Mozart had been a prodigy, that he'd composed music on the piano when he was only five years old.

The highest mountain in the world is in Asia, she said, the world's longest river is in Africa. The greatest lake is the Caspian Sea. The first chief justice of the Supreme Court was John Jay.

You weren't really selling those books, she said. You hadn't been selling them for almost three months. She told him how their mother loaded them both into the truck, how the truck quit in Belzoni and their mother got a garage mechanic to make it run by promising to come back on the weekend for a date. She told him Mary Jo looked the other way when they came to the bridge over the Yazoo River, but she and her mother saw the blue paint on the abutment, and her mother sobbed silently all the way to Jackson. She told him about waiting outside in the truck, while her mother carried his black satchel that contained the dictionaries into a little office within sight of the capitol dome, how she came out moments later, her face white and dead. You can't trust a man, she said, this woman who would spend the rest of her life entrusting herself and her girls to one man and then another.

She told her father she believed the boardinghouse existed, but only in his mind. She told him she believed that somewhere there was someone else, someone besides her mother, and that this was whom he had gone to. She didn't know why he hadn't made it the last time.

Her father never answered, he never said a word, but answers were not what she sought. She poured herself out to him. In return he gave her his attention, and right then that was enough.

The year she turns fifty, she goes back.

It's January, and she's on winter break from the university where she teaches. She and Mary Jo fly into Memphis, rent a car, and drive down into the Delta.

They spend the night at a Comfort Inn in Indianola, the town where they grew up. In the morning they eat breakfast at McDonald's. They drive through the downtown area—the Piggly Wiggly's still there—then they cross the highway on a blacktop road that heads north.

It's a cold grey day; a brisk wind is blowing. In the fields, dead cotton stalks bend double. She remembers the way those stalks whistle when the wind blows hard. It's a sound she hasn't thought about in years.

These days a lot of the land is given over to catfish ponds. They see them now, muddy rectangles that spread out on both sides of the road, breaking the countryside up into watery sections.

There's a pond across the road from their house, where the empty field used to be. The field, as it turns out, was on the north side of the house, not the west or the south.

"We were both wrong," Mary Jo says.

Somebody has turned the front porch into a room and added on another structure to serve as a porch. There are trees all around, more than either of them remembers, pine trees as well as pecan. A Ford pickup is parked in the driveway.

A swing set stands in the yard. Near the front porch there's a pink tricycle; a white basket is attached to the handlebars, red streamers dangle from the grips.

Looking at the house, Kendra wonders if the space heater remains in the bedroom where the little girl who owns that tricycle sleeps. She wonders if the child ever sits before the heater like she did.

Once again, for a few seconds, she lets herself remember the way the radiants split the fire into diamond-shaped bits. When she was two or three, each of those pieces seemed separate and distinct; she thought she was looking at many different flames, not a single burning thing.

Back then the world was new, and she believed, as children do, that lines possess the power to divide.

LIZA KLEINMAN

What Went Wrong

CHILDHOOD, as I remember it, is a tangle of shifting allegiances. It is a series of passionate friendships, each as heavy as the last with the promise of immortality. It is, in short, a long, low ramp into adulthood.

When I was ten, my best friend was Jenny Pintoff. We spent most of our time together huddled in my room, enacting television shows we'd seen, inventing dances, practicing imitations of our classmates. The fact was, my mother frowned on my going over to Jenny's house.

"Her mother has enough trouble, raising a child herself. I don't like to impose upon her," she said. Bobbie was the only divorced woman I knew, and the impression I got from my mother was that divorce was a sort of disease, pitiable, avoidable, and possibly contagious. When I talked about Bobbie at home, my mother's mouth tightened and she shook her head.

"Poor woman," she said. "Poor Jenny, growing up without a father."

Jenny did, in fact, have a father, whom she saw on occasion. He took Jenny to a lot of movies and on trips to the aquarium.

"I'm telling you," Jenny would say Monday mornings at school, "if I see that ninety-year-old turtle one more time, I'm going to vomit in a really big way."

Jenny and I were in the same class, prisoners of Mrs. Danahy, a sweet, fading woman who had taught second grade for years before getting switched to a fifth-grade classroom. Mrs. Danahy had never quite made the adjustment. Unlike the other two fifth-grade classes, which sat in rows, we had our desks clumped into groups like the little kids did.

"Teamwork," Mrs. Danahy announced with regularity, "is something you can't learn too early." Jenny and I had known each other slightly for years,

259

the way everyone did in our small suburban town. We had never paid much attention to each other until we were placed at adjoining desks in Mrs. Danahy's class.

United in hardship, we quickly formed an alliance, rolling our eyes at each other when Mrs. Danahy announced story time, feigning gagging whenever she called a student "honey."

"I'm very mature for my age," Jenny explained to me the first time she came to my house. We were applying makeup to a life-size plastic Barbie head she'd brought over. "So my mother really relies on me. I always tell her what to wear if she has a date or something." Jenny let the information drop casually, as if everyone's parents dated. I selected blue eye shadow and played it cool.

"She asks you what to wear?" My own mother picked my clothing out from Kid-Go-Round.

"Sure—clothes, makeup. You know." Jenny watched me smear color over Barbie's plastic eyelids. "Let me show you how to do that," she said. She took the brush from my hand and swept it in quick, upward strokes.

"I think she still wants to get back with my dad, though," Jenny continued. "She went out with this really nice guy—good-looking too, and she messed it all up by talking about my dad the whole time." Jenny paused, anticipated my next question.

"She always tells me about her dates the next day. Except if the guy's still there—then I have to wait for him to leave." "Still there?" I said. Jenny put the eye shadow brush down and surveyed her work.

"You know," she said.

My mother knocked on my door, which was open, and peered into the room.

"How are you girls?" she asked. "Jenny? Nina? There's cookies downstairs if you want them." We thanked her and waited until she left.

"I can tell you can't talk about stuff with your mother," Jenny told me. "I don't know what my mother would do without me. We really have an amazing relationship."

Later that evening, after Jenny had gone home, my mother stopped by my room to hand me some clean laundry. She glanced at the bright-lipped, sultry-eyed Barbie that Jenny had left behind, and I saw her mouth pinch.

"You've been talking a lot about this Jenny," my mother said. "What about other girls? Don't you want to invite other friends over?"

"What's wrong with Jenny?" I asked. She and I had already begun laying plans for a sleepover sometime soon, and I didn't like the sound of this conversation.

"Nothing," my mother said. "Nothing's wrong with Jenny. I just think you might spend more time with people who are more . . . similar to you. That's all. How about Evelyn What's-her-name? Whose father rides the train to work with Dad? What's wrong with her?"

Evelyn Polinsky was famous throughout the fifth grade for carrying around in her book bag a stuffed cat, who she claimed talked to her. No one else would.

"Mom," I said. "Evelyn makes me want to vomit in a really big way." My mother's eyes narrowed.

"I don't want to hear that kind of language coming out of your mouth," she told me. She paused.

"I saw that mother of Jenny's, that Bobbie, in the supermarket. You know what she was buying?"

I shook my head.

"Two cartons of cigarettes, a single box of macaroni and cheese, and an issue of *Cosmopolitan* magazine. That was her shopping." My mother raised her eyebrows and allowed her point to settle.

"You should give that Evelyn a call," she said.

That next weekend, Jenny telephoned me.

"Listen," she said into the phone. "It's my weekend with my father, and he's taking me to the zoo. He said I could bring a friend—you want to come?"

If my own parents had offered to take me to the zoo, I would have bristled and told them I wasn't a baby.

"Yes," I said. "Let me ask my parents if I can go." I put the receiver down on the kitchen table and ran outside. My mother was on her knees, shoveling holes in the dirt in front of the shrubs.

A line of potted impatiens stood ready for planting.

"Mom, Jenny's father is taking her to the Bronx Zoo. Can I go?"

I hopped from foot to foot, worried Jenny would hang up and leave without me.

My mother looked up from her flowers and studied me. She brushed a string of hair from her eyes with the back of her arm.

She placed her hands, covered in thick, dirty gardening gloves, on her hips.

"Who's this father?"

"Jenny's father. He lives in Queens. He comes and takes her places on weekends."

"Nina, why don't you stay here and help me with the gardening? I could really use some help here. Jenny probably wants to spend some time alone with her father, if she doesn't get to see him much. Why don't you spend some time with your father today?" We both knew that my father planned to spend the day watching televised football, whether or not I was in the room with him.

"Mom," I said, "Jenny's on the phone waiting."

My mother shook her head and picked up her trowel.

"All right," she said. "Go. I want you home for dinner."

Jenny and her father arrived half an hour later to pick me up.

I sat waiting on our front stoop, and when a small red car with rust spots pulled up, Jenny waved out the back window. I ran to the car and climbed in the back next to her. A bald man with a dark moustache sat with his left hand on the steering wheel, his right draped over the shoulder of a young woman in the passenger seat. The woman wore a pink sweatshirt, and she had long red hair.

"Dad, this is Nina. Nina, this is my Dad and Gloria."

"Hello, Nina," Jenny's father said. "I'm Anthony." Gloria turned around and nodded at me, then looked back through the front window. She was chewing a piece of gum, and I hoped she'd offer me one.

My mother eased herself up from her yard work and crossed our small lawn to the curb.

"I thought she wasn't going to let me go, at first," I whispered to Jenny, and we gripped each other's shoulders, grinning. My mother peered inside the car.

"Hello," Anthony called. "Don't worry about a thing. We're going to have a great time. Right, girls?" He looked back at us, then ran his fingers up through Gloria's hair. Gloria sighed and shifted in the passenger seat. My mother looked at her, then at me.

"Be careful, Nina," she warned. "Don't get separated." I saw her face fold in embarrassment—separated, like divorced—and as she worked her mouth to make amends, we pulled away.

There are two things I remember about the rest of that day: one is that Anthony's friend Gloria didn't talk to Jenny and me at all except to tell us not to buy bras before we needed them. The other is that Jenny and I rode an elephant. It was Anthony who got excited about it when we walked past the ride.

"Look, girls! Have you ever ridden an elephant before? There's something to tell your classmates about."

A rumpled, tuskless elephant stood sleepily inside two low walls that formed a ring. The elephant wore an elaborately harnessed box with two seats, one in back of the other. An attendant in a zoo T-shirt stood outside the ring next to the elephant, holding a lead. The attendant glanced at Gloria, then at Jenny and me.

"You girls coming aboard?" he asked.

"Go on," Anthony said, reaching for his wallet. "This is a once-in-a-lifetime opportunity, here."

Jenny and I looked at each other. We both knew we were a little too old for elephant rides—it was the sort of thing Evelyn Polinsky and her stuffed cat would do and then tell the whole world about. Still, we wanted to ride on that elephant.

"Fine," Jenny said to her father. "We're only doing this to make you happy."

"I'm such a tyrant," Anthony said. "How do you stand it?" Jenny and I laughed, but Anthony was looking at Gloria, who stood with her arms folded over her chest. She glanced at the elephant attendant, then off toward the parking lot. She smiled briefly at Anthony without looking at him.

"Let's go," Jenny told me. Anthony handed a few bills to the attendant, who motioned Jenny and me to a set of steps outside the ring. He led the elephant over to the steps and we climbed into the box on the elephant's back. I took the front seat and Jenny sat behind me. The attendant walked the elephant in a slow circle.

The ride was bumpy in a slow-shifting way. We sat high off the ground, but not as high as I'd hoped. It felt more like riding in a box than actually riding on an elephant. Jenny leaned in from behind me.

"I can't believe this."

"I know," I said. "We're totally crazy. We're riding an *elephant*."

"No," she said. "Look."

Outside the ring, Anthony and Gloria were kissing. The pink sleeve of her sweatshirt bunched where Anthony gripped it, and I wondered if she still had her gum in her mouth.

"You can bet I'm not telling my mother about *this*," Jenny said. "She's just better off not knowing." I turned away from Anthony and Gloria and tried to concentrate on the elephant ride. I tried to pretend that Jenny and I were on safari in deepest Africa, with wet leaves brushing at our faces and danger lurking around every corner.

After that day, Jenny came to my house regularly. Although I could tell my mother still felt wary, she was nice enough to Jenny. I knew this was because she preferred, if I had to play with Jenny, that we do it where she could keep an eye on us, monitor any bad influence Jenny might drag in from her broken home.

The times we spent at Jenny's house—times my mother relented, or couldn't think quickly enough of a reason to prevent it—were infrequent, and I lived for them. Bobbie let us go through her closet, and Jenny and I figured out new ways for her to assemble her clothing. My mother's closet was carefully arranged: skirts here, blouses here, slacks on this side, shoes lined up neatly below. Bobbie's clothes tumbled willy-nilly against one another, slippery tops, clingy pants that started out tight down to the knees, then swirled out over thick-heeled boots. While my mother wore small, well-behaved prints or unobtrusive solids, Bobbie favored bright clothing. She owned a yellow-and-green paisley blouse, a short electric-blue skirt, a long pink scarf punctuated with red swirls. We went through her makeup and tried on false eyelashes, painted thick black streaks of liner onto our lids. We sprayed her deodorant like it was cologne, imagining we were dressing up for an evening out.

One day in late spring, the last day, as it turned out, of our friendship, Jenny and I were at her house digging through Bobbie's record collection. Our favorite record was "Girl from Ipanema," and Jenny slipped it onto the turntable. I played the man singer, mouthing the Portuguese part as nearly as possible, and Jenny played the woman, who resang the words in English.

The standing rule was that whoever played the woman got to dance. That day, Jenny swiveled her hips and pumped her arms forward and back, palms toward the floor. She rolled her neck and smiled at the ceiling as if it were the hot Brazilian sun on her face. She placed her hands on her waist, fingers tilted inward, and swayed like a palm.

Bobbie was rarely home when I was over—she sold costume jewelry at a local department store and worked erratic hours. Today, though, on a cold May afternoon that felt more like March, she had off, and when she passed through the living room she started dancing too. She held an unlit cigarette between her lips and moved like Jenny, only there was more of her to move. She nodded her head so that her dark hair swung over her arms. She wriggled her shoulders back, one at a time and then together. *Tall and tan and young and lovely*, she sang along. She grazed her fingertips up the side of her body to indicate tall and lovely. *The girl from Ipanema goes walking*. Bobbie deliberately placed one foot in front of the other, hands on her ticking hips. She swiveled past the tweeded couch, around the coffee table. *How can he tell her he loves her?* Bobbie's face tilted upward in a show of haughty indifference. I watched her move, and then that wasn't enough. I wanted to dance too, alongside her, but I feared I'd look clumsy and ruin the song. When she stopped, Jenny and I begged her to keep at it.

"Come on, Mom. Just once more," Jenny said. Bobbie refused.

"Nope," she said. "I'm old news. I'm yesterday's headlines. You girls have to carry on without me."

Bobbie left the room, and Jenny picked up the needle and placed it at the beginning of the record. We tried to imitate Bobbie, running our hands over our sides and shimmying our shoulders, but the game had gone hollow. Jenny flipped the record player's off switch.

"Let's get something to eat," she said. I agreed. Bobbie kept an assortment of chips and snack cakes to which Jenny had unregulated access.

Their kitchen table was orange, with a white Formica top, and brown tiles lined the floor. Stacks of papers covered most of the table—unopened mail, old drawings of Jenny's, newspapers gone brittle. The uncovered surface included a sticky patch where orange juice had been left to dry. A calendar from the previous year hung above the stove, open to a drawing of two kittens working string. The kittens had enormous green eyes and worried expressions. I knew my mother would never allow such a picture in her own kitchen, which shone clean after dinner every night.

Our kitchen had three framed prints of flowers with the English and Latin names beneath each one.

Bobbie sat at the table, her eyes dull. She held the telephone receiver in her hand, resting it on a stack of papers. She didn't look like the same person who had been dancing with us. Her shoulders hunched and her hair spilled over the tabletop. A coffeemaker steamed on the counter behind her, and she curled her other hand around a mug.

"Mom," Jenny said, "we're hungry."

"Eat, then," Bobbie told her. She regarded the phone receiver in her hand, then moved to hang it up.

"Do you girls want some coffee?" she asked.

"Sure," Jenny said quickly. She rooted through a cabinet for two mugs, and poured from the pot.

"You should put some sugar in that," Bobbie instructed. Jenny spooned sugar in our drinks and splashed each one with milk.

We sat at the table and placed our mugs on top of the papers. I sniffed at the steam. Jenny picked her mug up and blew on it. She sipped from it, and her mouth stretched to a grimace, regained control.

"Good coffee, Mom," she said. She looked at me, and I bent my mouth to the rim of my drink. I slurped faintly and swallowed.

Even sugared, the coffee was thick and bitter.

"I think I'll wait for it to cool a little," I said.

"So how's it going, Mom?" Jenny asked. She kept a hand on her mug and crossed her legs.

"Let me give you girls a word of advice," Bobbie said. She looked grimly at the phone on the wall. "Never date. Never marry. If you have to have sex, do it with someone you don't give a shit about, or else you're asking for disaster."

Jenny laughed loudly.

"Men," she said. "What can you do with them?" She looked at me across the table. I concentrated on picking at my mug. There was a patch of rough ceramic beneath the handle. When I looked up, Jenny was still watching me.

"Nothing, I guess," I said.

"You can say that again," Bobbie said, and again Jenny laughed.

She took another sip from her coffee.

The phone rang, and Bobbie leapt to pick it up. Her voice went immediately sharp.

"Anthony," she said. "I've been trying to call you." She stood up and moved into the living room, stretching the phone cord as far as it would go.

"I wonder what my father wants," Jenny whispered to me. "I don't think he gets me this weekend." Bobbie's voice carried into the kitchen.

"Where the hell were you last night? Where were you just now?" she said. "I called you ten times." There was a pause.

"What do you want to do?" I asked Jenny. I was thinking we could make her Barbies get ready for dates. Jenny held up a hand.

"We have to listen," she said. "This could be important."

"Ten times!" her mother said again. "Where the hell were you? Who were you with?" Another pause.

"Goddamn it, I have a right to know!" she yelled. "Ten times! Ten times!" I had an image of Bobbie appearing on one of the educational shows I watched when I was a little kid, doing a segment on counting. "Ten times!" she would yell, and Jenny would appear in a leotard and spangled top hat to count the telephone rings.

Across the table from me, Jenny shook her head.

"She's really pissed," she told me. "She's been asking me if he has a girl-friend, and finally I had to tell her she should ask him herself."

"Yes, I do have a right to know!" Bobbie screamed. Jenny listened with interest.

"It doesn't matter!" Bobbie shouted. "I still have a right to know! I still have a right! I still have a right!" She paused again, and we heard the flinty sound of her lighter. The air grew sharp.

"She's not supposed to do that," Jenny said, shaking her head.

She coughed loudly, so Bobbie could hear.

"Cough," she said to me. "She needs to know she's polluting our air too."

"I don't want to," I said. I dipped a finger in the lukewarm coffee in front of me and swirled it.

"Just cough with me," Jenny told me. "It's okay. We won't get in trouble." She hacked dramatically.

"Shut up, Jenny," Bobbie yelled from the living room, then, "I'll say whatever the hell I want to her. What right do you have? You asshole. You fucking fucking fucking asshole. Who were you with? Who were you with? She's not going anywhere until you tell me who you were with!" We heard her fist slam the table.

"I think I have to go now," I told Jenny.

"Don't be silly," she said. "It's early."

"The hell you are!" Bobbie screamed in the living room. Her voice was high, hysterical. "The hell you're going anywhere near her. You have no right! You have no right! I don't give a shit about that. You can't see her to-day. Anthony! Anthony!" We heard the phone slam down with such force the air rang. Jenny and I looked across the table at each other. Bobbie stormed into the kitchen.

"He's coming," she told Jenny. "Get up. He's coming right away." Bobbie's face was blotched and her eyes were bright with anger.

"What should I wear?" Jenny asked.

"Wear the nightgown that looks like a dress," Bobbie said. "No. No. You're not going anywhere. Get upstairs." Jenny got up from the table. I started to follow her. "Hurry!" Bobbie said. "Jenny, you're my good girl. You're my best friend."

"Mom, wash your face," Jenny said. "Your mascara smeared."

She headed for the stairs.

"Hurry and get up there," Bobbie said. "Don't you dare come down while he's here." She scrubbed under her eyes with an index finger.

"Nina!" I turned around. "You stay down here. No, go upstairs with Jenny. No, stay down here. I need you down here."

Jenny lingered in the room.

"I need to go home soon," I said. "We're going to be having dinner at my house."

"Here's what I need you to do," she said. "I need . . . I need . . ."

Bobbie breathed hard. She cast frantically around the kitchen as if she were missing something.

"I'll go play with Jenny," I said.

"No," Bobbie said. "This is what we're going to do. We're going to tell your father you're dead, Jenny. We're going to teach him a lesson."

"He's not going to believe that," Jenny said. I could tell she liked the idea.

"Yes," Bobbie said, speaking more quickly. "He'll have to. He's not seeing you. We're going to tell him you're dead, to teach the fucker a lesson. Get upstairs. Do not come downstairs, Jenny. I'm telling him you're dead."

Jenny climbed up the stairs. I turned to follow.

"No!" Bobbie shouted at me. "Jenny's right—he's not going to believe me. You're going to have to tell him. He's not going to believe me." Bobbie looked closely at me.

"Can you pretend to cry?" she asked. I shrugged.

"I don't want to," I said.

"Nina," Jenny shouted from the staircase. "It's an emergency!"

"I said get UP there!" Bobbie screamed. "Jesus Christ, he's coming. He's on his way. Nina. When he gets here, you're going to be crying, okay? And I'll be too, I'll be saying, 'Oh, my God, oh, my God,' and you say like this, you say, 'Jenny's . . . dead!' Can you say it like that, like you can barely say it?"

Bobbie peered into my face. Her mouth opened slightly, ready to form around the words as I spoke them.

"Say it," she said. "Jenny's . . . dead. God. I can barely even say it." Her voice lurched like a record skipping.

"Teach him," she said. "Teach him. Jenny's dead. Jenny's dead. Say it."

"Jenny's dead," I whispered.

"Okay," she said. "Okay. Now say it like you're crying, like you mean it. He's got to believe this."

"No," I said. "I want to go home."

The doorbell rang.

"My God!" she cried. She reached to tuck her hair behind her ear, then stopped herself. She rubbed a finger over her eyes to further smudge her makeup. The doorbell rang again.

"I'm COMING!" she yelled at it. She turned to me and gave me a small, tight smile. She placed a hand on my shoulder.

"Nina," she said. "You're saving our lives." She turned to the door and opened it.

"Anthony!" she said. She turned from the door and looked at me, blackened tears rolling down her face. Anthony wore blue jeans and a brown leather jacket. He nodded at me, then looked past me into the room.

"Where is she?" he asked Bobbie. "I left the car running."

Bobbie looked at me. Her eyes were bright, and her mouth curled into a strange half-smile. Her fists were clenched and she trembled.

"Jenny . . ." she said to me. "Nina. Oh, God. Oh, God. Tell him, Nina. I can't say it. I can't even say it."

"What?" Jenny's father said. He fixed a look on Bobbie. "What's going on, here? Where is she?" He looked at me, then toward the stairs.

"Don't play any games with me, Bobbie," he said. "Jenny! We're going! Jenny!"

Bobbie stepped in front of Anthony so he couldn't walk toward the staircase. "You can't see her!" she yelled. "You can never see her! Tell him why, Nina. Tell him why. Tell him why."

Anthony leaned down and put a hand on my shoulder. He seemed suddenly relaxed.

"Nina?" he said. "Will you please go and tell Jenny that her father is here to take her to dinner? You too, if you want. Do you like pizza?"

"She can't she can't she can't!" Bobbie said, her voice so high it was barely audible. "Nina, tell him why she can't. Nina, tell him."

"No," I mouthed. Sound wouldn't come.

Bobbie's eyes widened, lines radiating from their corners and across her forehead.

"Tell him! Tell him!"

"What?" Anthony folded his arms over his chest. The leather of his jacket creaked.

"Tell him!" Bobbie said. "Nina, tell him now." She brought her fingertips to her lips and steadied them with pressure. She gave a tiny cry that may have derived from laughter, might have been a sob. I looked toward the door. Anthony leaned in toward me.

"Help me out here," he said.

"Jenny's dead," I whispered.

"It's true!" Bobbie shrieked. "She's dead she's dead she's dead and you can't see her! You can't take her from here!"

"What the hell are you talking about?"

I'd never heard a man's voice like that, sharp and thick, both at once. Suddenly I was frightened, not just a little bit but deeply, achingly. I ran to the couch and curled into the corner. I buried my face in the space between the green tweeded seat cushion and the back of the sofa. It smelled of cigarette smoke and of something murky, like abandoned fruit. I could see grit on the base, where the cushion had slipped out of place. I closed my eyes.

"Jenny!" I heard Anthony running for the stairs, I heard Bobbie trying to stop him.

"No!" she screamed. "No!"

"Jenny!" Anthony yelled. I heard his feet pound up the stairs; I heard Bobbie go after him. I could barely breathe in my position on the couch. I lifted my head out and stood up in the empty room. There was scuffling over-head and angry voices. Then there were quick, light footsteps on the stair-case, and Jenny ran into the room. We could hear her parents' voices upstairs.

"He found me," Jenny reported, breathless. "She's so mad she's going to kill him."

"I have to leave," I told Jenny. I firmed my voice. "I have to go now, no matter what. It's time for me to go home. Your father has to take me."

Anthony came down the stairs into the living room, followed by Bobbie. Anthony's face was grim, white. He looked only at Jenny.

"Get your coat," he told her. "We're going."

"Stay here," Bobbie said. She too was pale. The muscles in her neck jumped.

"I'm dead," Jenny said. "I can't do anything if I'm dead."

"Get your coat," Anthony said. "You've really gone too far this time, Bob-bie. You have really gone too far. Get your coat, Jenny."

"I'm dead," Jenny told him. "Right, Nina? I'm dead. I can't do anything."

"We're getting out of here," Anthony said. He grabbed Jenny's arm and yanked her to the door.

"Bye, Nina," Jenny said. She allowed herself to be led outside.

She shut the door behind her.

"My God," Bobbie said, looking past me. Her eyes were shadowed, her forehead drawn. She inhaled forcefully. We heard the slam of two heavy doors, and the roar of the car down the street, away.

"My God," she said again. "My God. I can't take much more of this." I stood as still as I could. I held my breath. Then her gaze shifted, landed on my face.

"Liar," she said to me. "You said you'd help." I opened my mouth and couldn't produce sound.

"You stupid little bitch liar!" she shouted. "Standing there like you had all the time in the world to say whatever the hell you felt like! You said you'd help me! You said you'd help me!"

I turned my head from side to side and tried to push words from my throat. I felt my eyes film. Bobbie watched my face for a long moment and suddenly became aware of herself. She raked fingers through her hair, straightened her clothes. She shook her head.

"I'm sorry," she said then. She pulled me to her, so that my mouth lay, still open, against the flimsy purple knit of her sweater. I breathed her hot, sharp smell: cigarettes, the sweet spray deodorant Jenny and I pretended was perfume.

"I'm so sorry," she said, pressing a palm against the back of my head.

"I understand," I said. I knew it was what Jenny would say. It was what another adult would say.

"I've had a very hard day," Bobbie said. "You're sweet to understand. I've had a regular bitch of a day."

The pressure from her hand relented, and I did not step back. I could feel my breath dampening her sweater. A fervent wish ripped through me: I wanted to switch the record player back on.

I wanted the past hour to peel from my memory; I wanted us to throw our heads back and dance. Bobbie trembled against me.

"Tell me about your day," I said. My mother would say that to my father when he came home from work bad-tempered. "Tell me what went wrong."

Bobbie ran a hand over my neck, pushed it through my hair.

"You're an okay kid," she told me. She closed her fingers around the hair close to my scalp and shook it gently. "It's good Jenny has a friend like you." She stepped back, and I felt the coolness of halving.

"You should never know from loss," Bobbie said.

When I got home that night, I was silent throughout dinner.

The next day at school Jenny and I were distant from each other, and we remained that way. I wanted to tell her that it was okay, that we could still be friends, but it wasn't true. I had seen Jenny's own mother pronounce her dead, and although I didn't have the words for it then, I knew that our real friendship, the heady love that comes of mystery, had ended. We spoke to each other at school, still, but with the polite reserve I heard in my mother's voice when she chatted with strangers. One day when we were putting away our books to go to lunch, I asked after Bobbie, and Jenny looked me square in the face.

"She's fine," she said. She lifted her hands from her sides, spread her fingers to gesture a question. "She's my mother."

The rest of that school year I passed my time with one friend or another. Jenny took up company with Adelle Stout, a thin, pale girl whose father had died suddenly the previous year. Lunch times I watched Jenny rise to the balls of her feet to whisper to Adelle, watched Adelle break into slow, uncertain laughter.

Adelle's limbs swung wildly from her body; and often when she stood still, she grasped her own shoulders, keeping her arms in check. She ran awkwardly, missed every kickball rolled her way. I wondered if she spent afternoons at Jenny's house, if they played records. I tried to picture Adelle sitting at Bobbie's kitchen table sipping coffee. That summer I began hanging around with a slightly older girl, a neighbor whom I'd known all my life but never much liked. Her mother made ice cream from scratch and encouraged

us to organize a neighborhood litter patrol. When the next school year began, we parted company without regret.

There is a reason why now, years later and from the other side of the
country, I recall these events. Recently I heard the song Jenny and I used to
dance to, heard it by accident, sighing overhead as I shopped for towels. I was
in the housewares section of a department store, rifling through sale bins.
The towels I found were ugly but cheap—once they must have been brown
but they'd gone over to a sick beige. "Good enough," I thought.

"Serviceable." I was headed to the checkout line when the song came on:
Tall and tan and young and lovely . . .

As it happens, I've lately parted ways with someone I still love. Although
I've been telling myself to get over it, that song, that ridiculous, dated song,
allowed an old layer of sorrow within me to surface. As I took my place in
line I felt a rush of memory, and I thought about Jenny, whom I hadn't seen
in years. I thought about the two of us draping ourselves in Bobbie's clothes,
and I thought about Bobbie herself, dancing, lips closed around a cigarette.
The girl from Ipanema goes walking . . . This is a fact: I've never, until now,
told anyone what happened at Jenny's that day. I always allowed my mother
to believe I trusted her advice and dropped Jenny for more appropriate
friends. If Adelle Stout or anyone else ever witnessed something similar to
what I saw at Jenny's, I never knew about it. I hadn't thought about Jenny in
ages until I stood in that store clutching folds of terry cloth. That song
brought everything back, reminded me that when it comes to loss, we're all
old pros. We've all been in training since childhood, and we are armed—
such strong, terrible shields!—we are amply armed to cope.

PETER MAKUCK

My '49 Ford

—∿—

THOUGH MOM kept telling me I was lucky, that these years would be the best of my life, I didn't feel lucky at all, only glad to be driving. After three hours on the road, rain had sheeted down and left the pavement silver and black. Beads of water stood up nicely on the new wax of the louvered hood, but my rocker panels and bubble fender skirts would be filthy by the time we arrived. My father, clean-shaven, in a white shirt and tie, nodded sleepily in the back seat. My mother sat in front. She was crocheting as we sped past tall northern spruce. Her long piano fingers and crooking wrists used a single strand of black yarn to enlarge a pattern that rested in her lap. Suddenly she let out a bark of a laugh that tapered to a soft chuckle. I knew why: the restaurant where we just had lunch.

"Now don't look at me that way," she scolded. "You'll have an accident. I can't help it if I get a kick out of people." She tilted her head back, closed her eyes, and laughed again, the last part slurping like water down a drain. My expression must have made her laugh again. "Oh, you're just a sourpuss like your father."

"Ma, I didn't say nothin'."

"You didn't say *anything*. You're not with that stupid Road Devil gang now."

"Come on, Ma."

"You didn't say *anything*."

"Fine." I took a deep breath. "I didn't say *anything*."

"Ver-y good!" she sang. "Speech describes the mind. Keep talking like that and they'll think you're a nitwit before you even take a test!"

She was in a good mood. I wasn't—I was nervous about the general and immediate future. Out of the corner of my eye, I watched her lean forward for her purse and begin to search it.

"Ma?"

"What?"

"Don't take it wrong but—"

"Enough preface."

"I'd appreciate it, Ma, if you didn't smoke."

Her eyes got black as hornets; the mouth became a straight seam. "Ma, everybody knows what those things do. Look at Uncle—"

"You look! You say you worry about my health—"

"I do."

"And I don't seem to listen, do I?"

"No, you don't."

"Now, do you ever listen to me? do what I want you to do?"

"Ma . . . you always pull this."

"Answer me."

"I try."

She laughed in contempt, the laugh becoming a long string of ratchety coughs.

"See, see," I said. "We both know what causes that cough."

"Oh, do we?"

In the back seat, my father cleared his throat, a signal that we were getting on his nerves. God, why had I started this? But I hated smoke, I always had. At home, to some extent, I could at least escape by going into another room, yet even there the stink always found me.

"Oh you're an expert on causes. What caused the ten stitches in your head last Christmas? What caused the cops to bring you home at four o'clock in the morning that night last summer?"

"Ma, that's a smokescreen."

"Ha! I've raised a punster."

"Ma, we're not talking about the same thing, and you know it."

"Hey, knock it off," rumbled my father. "All you two ever do is go around in circles. Lay off."

She glowered, turned, and shot a black look at my father, but nothing more was said. We drove in silence. She lit up—she had to now. I knew that. And I knew the little perfumed pine tree of cardboard dangling under the dash was no match for the volume of smoke she would produce. I cracked the vent window.

Smoke—it infuriated me. Once, I had made Peggy walk home from our parking place by the ocean because she thought she had me under her thumb and lit up when I told her not to, at least not in the car. What she was giving me wasn't worth the eye-burning smoke, and the lousy taste when we made out. And to top it off, she put her feet up on the dash, on the twenty coats of lacquer and custom pinstriping. She thought I was joking, but the look on her face changed when I began to drive away. It was dark and started to rain, and I should have gone back for her, but I couldn't. Maybe it had something to do with "Cathy's Clown," a maudlin tune often on the radio then, because a few days earlier I had let her borrow my car, and she left me stranded in town while she parked in front of the A&W with a few of her girl friends. She was seen. I was seen. She needed straightening out. I wasn't going to be anybody's clown.

Next time I saw her I was in wood shop, and classes were passing down the aisle between the open metals and woodworking areas. Dumfy said, "Here comes Peggy," but she paused only long enough to kill me with a look, and say with deep conviction, very deliberately, "You lousy shit!" A great chorus of "ooos" and "ahhs" went off with laughs and hoots from the guys.

All over a cigarette. And here I was in my own car, my mother puffing up a storm. Most often she smoked only when she read. She loved reading more than almost anything. A weekly trip to the library. Always books on the coffee table or nightstand. Reading engendered her best moods. When I wanted something, I always waited until she was reading. Interrupted, she would lift her gaze, the eyes clear and a bit dreamy, and her answer was most often yes. But when she was angry, her eyes seemed to blacken. Like the sky before a storm, like the sky we watched an hour ago at the knotty-pine restaurant with its elk-antlered walls.

While my mother was being chatty and outgoing with the waitress and with the couple in the adjacent booth, I stared out the window at the inky sky and the shiny black asphalt, at my car—aquamarine, lowered, decked, frenched headlights, electric doors, customized floating bar grill, and '49 Plymouth bumpers, pleated and rolled Naugahyde interior. Last week Donna had her hand on my thigh. Bouncing rain seemed to cover the ground with smoke; it tattooed the roof of my Ford as we talked of my leaving town, talked and kissed, kissed and stroked, our heads descending and coming up again in the faint light. It got hot, the windows steamed. Our clothes came off. Time, as in a film, took a leap. Sweating, I rolled down the window and felt the cool night air on my bare skin, confident that I had pulled out in plenty of time. But the last quarter turn of the window crank seemed to trigger a bright light that blasted me in the face. I lurched in the seat, bumping my head on the roof. Somehow, even in this scary moment, I realized that the perforated, white, Naugahyde headliner was probably stained from the stuff I used on my hair. Donna cried out and clutched loose clothing to herself so that I had to yank my trousers away from her. There was a silver badge; it hovered in the dark above the light, a patch of skin and a pair of eyes.

"Okay, Romeo," said the gravel voice. "Get dressed and get out your driver's license." Mercifully, the light went out. I wiped the glass with the back of my hand and saw a black-and-white squad car blocking the tree-tunneled alley I had backed into. Donna giggled, but I didn't find it very funny. We were almost dressed when the cop came back. He held my license under the beam of a huge silver flashlight with a red plastic collar. Above the light beam floated a thick face with a bulldog mouth and bushy eyebrows that ran together above a flat knuckle of a nose. His name, I knew, was Hearn. I had seen him around, once or twice at the YMCA, grunting in the handball pit or hitting the heavy bag. And once I had seen him on Main Street with Cowboy Sheen. The Cowboy was a drunk in his fifties, a local character, harmless, who got into arguments with parking meters. I saw Hearn punch him in the face one April afternoon, drag him to the squad car unconscious and bloody, and heave him onto the floor of the back seat. Hearn was tight with another cop who lived only two houses away from us.

"I know your father," Hearn said.

I said nothing.

"Hey, Romeo, you hear me?"

I said yes.

"Has the Flying A station over on Tenth, doesn't he?"

"Yes, he does."

"What would he say to this?"

I didn't answer.

Hearn shined his light in my eyes. "Anh?"

"He wouldn't like it," I said.

"You damn straight he wouldn't like it." He shined the light on Donna's breasts. "What's your name, ah, young lady?" The light beam slowly descended to her crotch, lingered, then swung away.

"Donna Rodina." She folded her arms against the light.

"Rodino, anh?"

"R-o-d—"

"Don't worry, I can spell it. You want me to write it on the blottah, want to spell it for me down at the station?"

"No, I don't. I only—"

"I don't care what you *only*." He stood up for a moment so that only his belly hung in the window, yellow undershirt showing where a button had popped. "I know your fathah pretty well," he said, leaning down again and resting a ham fist on the window. I caught an odor of beer on his breath.

"Your father, Angelo, and me went through hell together. You didn't know that, did you?"

Donna said she didn't. I thought of the war, of foxhole buddies.

"We was suspended between floors down in New Haven. In a elevatah. Twenty of us. One of the guys goes bananas, like he's got costophobia. But not really. He was a priest, planted there to test our mettle, see if we deserved to be Knights of Columbus. Your fathah's got mettle, young lady, you know that?"

Donna nodded.

That was a hot one, but I was glad she played along. Metal—that's what he had all right, a metal appendage to his right hand, a constant, patriotic can of Budweiser red-white-and-blue. The proof of his metal was a huge underslung belly like Hearn's. And those fuzzy Friday night K of C eyes. Yeah, a man of metal.

"What do you think Angelo, your father, would say about this business?"

Donna said nothing.

"I know what he'd say. He'd wring Romeo's neck here."

My face felt like the color of stock pulled from a forge in the metal shop. Hearn. I imagined applying a piece of red hot stock to his belly button. Hearn played the light over my pleated and rolled interior, the high pile carpets, the white headliner. "Nineteen forty-nine Ford. Hah! What color is this, green?"

"Aquamarine."

"Ooooh, aqua-marine," he mocked. "You think you're something with this niggermobile, don't you?"

I gritted my teeth. With the Corvette engine, Isky cam, and twin Edelbrock four barrels hidden under the hood, I knew I could blow that squad car off the road. I'd have loved to get him out on Cemetery Road and run him into the wall at the turn. Suddenly I thought about my Road Devils jacket and hoped it wasn't on the back seat. Hearn spoke again. "Some cops," he said, "would take you home in your birthday suit for mama and papa to see. But I don't work like that. First time, I like to give a guy an even break. But I might just have a talk with ya parents." He waited for a reaction, then jerked his head forward into the window space to give us a final glare and blast of beer breath. "Get ta hell outtah heah, and don't ever let me catch you in one of these Lovers' Lanes again. You hear me?"

I said yes but would be damned if I'd say *Gee wiz, thanks, Officer,* or something like that. Donna and I watched him waddle back to the squad car. I was grinding my teeth. Donna deepened her voice: "Hey, Romeo, am I an asshole or what?" Then we began laughing.

As I thought about it now, in the car with my parents, the episode was less funny than ever. Donna told me she would write to me when her "friend" arrived at the end of the month. The sex part of it would turn my mother's mouth into a downhooked didactic scar. And my father would be more furious if Hearn showed up at the station, swaggered into the office, hitched up his holster, and leaned against the cigarette machine, squad car idling outside, antenna still twitching. My father had little use for the police and what they did, the way they loved to loom in your path. What they did, my father once said in disgust, was take: free this, free that. And during the war when tires were rationed, our neighbor, a cop, sold them out of his cellar. And where did they come from? My mother protested: "He'll have no respect for the law if you go on like this." My father scoffed: "*They* have no respect for the law. Anyway, they're just people," he said, softening things. "Some good, some bad. Just like the nuns and priests." I watched my mother's face redden. "You leave the Church out of this!" Her face was stricken, jaw slack. But when the words came and rained off his back, I watched my father retreat to his basement workshop. That was his sanctuary. She never followed. The workshop with its fragrance of freshly cut wood ended most arguments, my father conceding the last word to my mother. His tools hung neatly from brass hooks. My mother's tools were of a different order.

Again, as we rolled past a lake with a distant horizon dark-pointed with fir and spruce, my mother closed her eyes and laughed, breaking a long silence. I knew she was still thinking about the knotty-pine restaurant. "Boy oh boy! Those people were real doozies." She snickered quietly. "Weren't they, Fred?"

I saw my father straighten in the rearview, adjust the starched white collar tight around his neck. My father's name was Leo, but years ago, as a joke, my mother began calling him Fred and it stuck—with almost everyone but my maiden aunts. My father looked uncomfortable, not from the joking but from the clothes he was wearing. I rarely saw him dressed up, except for Mass, but most often he went to church early, alone, in work clothes, for Sunday also saw him at the garage.

"Timmy, your father has no sense of humor." Turning in her seat to see his unsmiling face, she laughed again, seeming to find something more deeply humorous. I could scarcely believe what humor my mother found in such minor incidents, but humor, of course, is subjective, my father and I often laughing ourselves to tears at the Three Stooges. My mother, though, would be on the phone as soon as she and Dad returned home, was probably already rehearsing for her friends the story about the man and woman with the dog in the knotty-pine restaurant. "Is that a poodle?" my mother had asked.

"No, a snoodle."

"A what?"

"A snoodle. It's a cross between a poodle and a schnauzer."

I saw her bite the corner of her lip to keep from laughing. Then she said: "Dogs are wonderful companions."

"Ain't dat da troof."

"They're nicer than a lot of people I know."

The man and his wife beamed in agreement.

"They're grateful, and they won't argue with you."

"You can say that again." The woman wore a red turtleneck sweater like the one on the dog; she was warming to a favorite subject and said they had another dog, a Lakeland terrier, that was registered, had fine bloodlines, and was very expensive. I knew my mother was delighted because she thought anyone who spent a lot of money for a nervous, unfriendly thoroughbred was a damned fool. The woman held the dog in her lap, and there was something oddly similar about their faces: the moist sad eyes, a pompom of grey hair. The woman leaned forward and in a high voice not her own began to ventriloquize: "You just say, My name is Mimi. You say, I'm four years old. You say, I'm just the sweetest little snoodle in the world. Say—" The dog didn't, of course, say anything, but it began barking and jumped on the table, upsetting a bowl of New England clam chowder, dumping it into the man's lap, making the couple argue, the husband saying they should have left the damned dog in the car.

"Fred?"

"What?"

"Didn't you like that little snoodle?"

"Loved it. We ought to get two or three just like it."

She began gasping with laughter. My father, raised on a farm, wasn't sentimental about animals. In fact, every time my dog Sargent puked in the house or left hairs on one of the good chairs, Dad swatted him with a newspaper. Then he'd declare that my mother and I were damned fools. Each time Mom and I would share hushed, conspiratorial laughter because we knew my father's annoyance was no joke.

"You know, Fred, I think you don't like it because that man said 'troof' for 'truth' and 'dat' for 'that.' They probably say 'stoonz' for 'students' too, you know, like your relatives from New Britain."

"Lay off my relatives, will ya!" My mother, getting the rise she was after, covered her mouth with her hand and gasped with laughter that turned to violent coughing.

At a smooth, plenty-in-reserve sixty miles per hour, I took the Ford over a great high-humped bridge of verdigris-covered ironwork with lots of X-ed girders. At the far side was a sign: WELCOME TO MAINE: VACATIONLAND. But this was no vacation. I had never been this far from home, and a sense of distance and unfriendly space began to haunt me. The color of the bridge was like the copper-green waterdrip tail on the porcelain of our sink. And the same color on the license attached to Sargent's collar. The dog was old; it might die while I was gone. I downshifted at the traffic circle, noticing the state trooper parked on the median, and kept the rpm's up so that the dual glasspacks wouldn't back off and get me stopped.

"Don't take the turnpike," my father said, and I smoothly swung to the right, dropping it into third long before the engine peaked to keep my father happy. And quiet. "Maine," my mother sighed, her eyes misted. "'Beginnings are always delightful,' the poet says."

My father made a chuff sound through his nose: mockery. "Years ago, when I left the farm, my mother and father, brothers and sisters, to go to work in Rhode Island, the beginning wasn't delightful. It was the depression, and I didn't know what the hell I was in for."

My mother went on as if nobody had spoken. "Yes, delightful," she said. I felt her eyes on me. "Timmy, this is a beginning for you." She sniffed. "And for us."

Suddenly my mood felt fragile. "Come on, Ma. Knock it off. You said you wouldn't start."

"Timmy, there is nothing wrong with having emotions."

"Ma."

"Okay, okay, but it's going to be awfully hard for me. Your father goes to work. He'll have things to do but—"

"Ma—"

"All right, that's it, no more." She blew her nose. "The philosopher says it's better to be a *monstre gai* than an *ennuyeux sentimental*." She blew again. "Right, Fred?"

"Of course."

My mother asked me if I knew what those words meant. I said I didn't, and she explained the phrases. "You better be ready to hear some French up here," she said. Her eyes were gleaming again.

"Yeah, I know."

She said she'd control herself from now on, but I knew better. She always gave in to the relief of sentimentality. I considered my parents and sensed their absence would be a great relief. I was supposed to miss Donna, but didn't. Not yet at least. With her, in the car, I was charmed by her every movement. But if I loved her, why did I feel so good when she got out of the car at midnight? High, excited, her scent still on my fingers when I pulled from her house, a good tune on the radio? Alone, how good it was to stop on a back road, look up at stars, the air fresh, pressure easing on my bladder, silence amplifying the hiss and sizzle of the asphalt. Moments like this wore a great halo. Moments of true feeling. But then, in the parking lot behind the A&W with the guys, a beer in hand, could it really be me, the same person, who told the anecdote about Hearn surprising me and Donna? And wasn't there a slimy sense of betrayal?

I looked at my father's serious face in the rearview. My father rarely told stories, and if he did, they were very short. One thing I knew I would definitely miss was the Ford. At State U a car would have been permitted. But my parents decided, me being me, not to send me to State where I would be with guys I'd gotten in trouble with, where I would be too close to home and Donna—everything just an extension of high school, especially with the car I lavished so much time on. "We are not," they said, "going to flush our money down the toilet." So the aquamarine Ford that I had customized in auto mechanics class and at my father's station, the Ford I had powered with a Corvette engine, would be returning home. I didn't want to think about it. I was, the farther I drove, becoming detached from my normal self.

"Tim, honey, what's the matter?"

"Nothing." *Timmy, honey, dear, sweetheart*—those words set me off for some reason.

"Nothing? You're scowling, you're forehead's all wrinkled."

I looked at her, then back at the road.

"You haven't said a word in ten minutes."

"Hey, Ma, change the record, huh?"

"Listen, Mister Mouth, you're not talking to Fagan or Dumfy. Or,"—she changed her tone—"Donna for that matter."

"What are you dragging Donna into this for?"

"Don't tell me you're not thinking about her?"

"What if I am?" God, I hated having somebody, especially my mother, tell me what I was thinking about, hated having to surrender my car, wished I could have traveled up here by myself, arrived on a Greyhound, emerging in the strange little town with a suitcase in one hand, jacket slung over my shoulder. Like the movies. But this wasn't the movies, and once I agreed to the plan I had to play by their rules because they were paying the bills. For now at least.

"Donna's not"—she stared at the pattern of yarn in her lap—"she's just not the right girl for you, and I hope I don't ever have to say *I told you so*."

I began to object. "That girl's mother, Timmy, went to school with me and—"

"And what?" I couldn't believe I was having this conversation; I had a panicky feeling of being trapped in an endless car trip with my parents, doomed forever to be told of mistakes I *had* made, mistakes I *would* make, pride preventing me from admitting certain things about Donna, her mother.

"That girl just wants to get married."

I asked if there was something wrong with that.

"Not at the right time, not after you've got a decent education. Let that girl get her hooks into you, and you'll be working at the shipyard like everyone else. Day after boring day. Your father worked there, but he had the courage to quit. He can tell you what it's like over there. Can't you, Fred?"

"Your mother's right."

"Money isn't everything."

"Ma, I've heard this record before."

There was a moment of silence. I thought she might let it pass. Then: "That's the second time you've used that expression."

"What?"

"About changing the record."

"I'm sorry."

"You ought to be. It shows lack of imagination." She looked at the slow back-sweeping salt marsh already touched with seasonal brown. "You do what you want. I won't mention it again."

I looked at my father in the rearview. His eyes were grey and soft and had crow's-feet at the corners. Very infrequently he smoked a pipe in his workshop, and somehow I didn't mind the smoke, which was richer; and the pipe gave him a meditative look. Sometimes, as now, I felt the full weight of his silence, was troubled by it, admired it, and sometimes tried, when with my friends, to affect it. My father seemed to be enjoying the shore route that was punctuated with small towns, antique barns, clam and lobster stands. On a bridge, my mother noticed another bridge off to the left and the faster flow of turnpike cars. She was annoyed and said scenery was just the kind of thing my father would want when they had no time for it. She shook her head and sighed heavily, filling the car with tense miles of silence.

The curving shore road gave me something to do, allowed me to downshift and feel the car, enjoy it one last time. But soon the rocky coast which I had never seen, the wave crash and high-flung spray took my attention as well. I wished Donna could see it. The ocean and coast were much more dramatic than the coast at home, protected as it was by that long low smudge on the horizon: Long Island, visible on clear days. The road was winding past natural coves and harbors where lobster boats with squarish cuddies and twin booms swayed on their reflections next to dockside fish shacks the color of driftwood. There were hanging nets and stacks of traps, and the late-summer air screamed with gulls. The hooking road pushed a different seascape before us at every turn; it would be a village and salt-stunted trees, and suddenly an endless spread of whitecaps on curling blue-black. Along one stretch of beach there was a tall tree all by itself, its branches and trunk twisted by the great offshore wind; it was odd and lonely because larger than anything I had seen for miles. The houses too seemed lonely, widely spaced, and encircled by their white picket fences; they were like the shells of quahogs randomly arranged by children on a treeless hillside, dormer window staring blankly at the changing sea. Out on the tidal flats was a high-sided truck where a family of kelpers was forking up seaweed to a figure standing on top of the pile.

"Harvesting the sea," said my mother.

"They must sell it," said my father.

"Looks like a painting," said my mother.

"Reminds me of haying as a kid," said my father. "Break your back."

After another mile or two was an arrow and a sign which said: COLLEGE SAINT ANTOINE.

My mother was satisfied. "It's as pretty as the pictures in the catalog, don't you think so, Timmy?"

I said yes, though I hadn't really studied the catalog. My father and I lugged my footlocker up to the third floor of Padua Hall, met the prefect, a young Franciscan robed in brown with a white knotted cord for a belt. His name was Father Andre, and he spoke English with an accent. He introduced me to my roommates, Bernard and Jacques. Bernard pointed to a bulb-less socket in the ceiling. All three spoke French until Father Andre turned to me with a big smile and asked if I understood. I said no, I had studied Spanish. He laughed and teasingly said Spanish wouldn't help much around here. I vaguely knew about the ethnic character of the college but was now overwhelmed with a sense of the foreign.

I walked with my parents out to a point that hooked into the river and made a small harbor. I looked back at the green water tower we drove past near the entrance to campus. There was a gazebo and a boathouse at the point, and to the east, at the mouth of the river, the dark fluting of the Atlantic visible beyond a long stone jetty.

Back in the parking lot, I noticed two students appraising my Ford. "Hey, I bet dat car she really go." It was the same accent Father Andre had when he spoke English.

My mother said, "Your father's right. We shouldn't argue. God forbid we should have an accident on the way home."

I told her not to talk like that.

"I can't help it. These thoughts just come."

I took a deep breath. The sky, still flocked with clouds, seemed suddenly sullen again. There was little left to say, yet no one seemed ready to say good-bye. My father finally said, "Well, we better be getting back. Long ride. I gotta work tomorrow."

I looked at my mother. For the first time I noticed faint lines of crow's-feet, a thread or two of grey in her hair. Behind her glasses, the eyes swam into focus, then went distant. She gathered me in a strong hug and kissed me. When she spoke, her mouth, from a breath mint, was an alarming green. "Timmy, be a"—tears slid down her rouged cheeks—"a good boy. Stay out of trouble. Your father and I love you very much."

I said I'd be good but, what with my track record, I wondered how they could believe me, let alone tell me they loved me. It surprised me that my voice came out strangely, sounded wrong, as it had when first changing. My breath came hard. I tried to smile, but my face wouldn't obey. My nose felt sneezy and began to run. "Just do your best," said my father, extending a big shovel of a hand. I could not look him in the face. My heart knocked in my ears as it did when I knew a fistfight was close. I tried hard to concentrate on what my father said. "Your best is all we ask. Nothing else matters."

The electric doors popped, and my father got behind the wheel. Nervous phrases flew back and forth. My mother's green mouth opened and closed. Tears ran. The big Corvette engine vroomed. I watched the aquamarine Ford rumble out of the lot; it was eclipsed by the white administration building on the knoll and reappeared on the long straight high road into town, flashing before a wall of huge green firs. As I watched the bright piece of color growing small, all that horsepower elsewhere, I felt myself shrinking, weak. I watched until it was totally gone and after a time discovered myself looking at the sky and a flotilla of clouds moving seaward on a high blue journey. Like them, I felt blown along, felt myself caught in a wild gust of unknown feeling.

"Jesus," I said, "O Jesus."

ROBERT SCHULTZ

Hardball

—◊◊◊—

WHEN I WAS an infant in the crib, my first toy was a blue rubber baseball glove. By the time I was seven I was accompanying my father to small Iowa towns where he conducted clinics for young ballplayers, mostly Little Leaguers. We would park the station wagon, gather the bags of bats and balls, and walk together to the sunbaked, crabgrass-pocked diamond. My dad always strolled to the field in nothing but a pair of white athletic undershorts and his baseball undershirt with the white body and blue sleeves. He carried his outer uniform draped over his shoulder, and I heard him tell a friend once, "When the parents see me in my boxers they decide to stick around." The first lesson of each clinic was how to look like a ballplayer.

"Whether you're a regular or you sit on the bench, everybody can look like a ballplayer," my father said. He stood in front of the sagging wooden bench next to the field with the boys ranged around him in their worn jeans and T-shirts. The bills of their caps were creased in the middle or sometimes at each edge, forming a shape like the hood scoop on a GTO. "First I'm going to show you how to roll your socks," he said. He sat and pulled on the long, white sanitaries that rose all the way to the knees and above. "Pull them smooth," he said. "Creases cause blisters." He slipped on the dark blue nylon stirrup socks and pulled them tight over the thin sanitaries. Then he stood and stepped into the pinstriped pants, drew them up to his waist, and pulled them back down, leaving the legs inside out around his calves. "The first step in rolling your socks is to pull the tops of both socks—the sanitaries and the stirrups—down over the pant leg." He demonstrated as he spoke, pinning the bottom of the pant legs to his calves with the turned-down socks. "Now fold the ends of the socks back up once, and you're ready to pull up your pants." When he pulled his pants up, the bottoms were neatly turned under, held in a tidy roll at the top of each calf. "If you roll your socks properly, they won't come undone when you run or slide, and you'll look like a pro through a whole doubleheader." It seemed to me that the boys regarded him then with a kind of awe. He had established his credentials, and they would now believe whatever he told them about pitching, hitting, fielding, and baserunning.

It was probably watching this demonstration repeatedly at an early age that engrained in me the knowledge that baseball is a game of mysteries and rituals. As I grew older, my father introduced me to the higher arcana— executing the drag bunt, throwing the change-up, reading a pitch by the rotation of the seams. But to my mind the most intricate and beautiful thing in all of baseball was the double play, and so I became a shortstop. I followed the White Sox and idolized Luis Aparicio, the slick Venezuelan who teamed with Nellie Fox up the middle. I wrote his name in magic marker across the shoulders of a white T-shirt and wore it to the playground where we played ball all summer. We were eight or nine then, and a double play was beyond us, but I dreamed of gliding across the bag like him, launching myself into the air, and firing the relay over a runner sliding harmlessly beneath me.

By the time I reached high school I knew that it was the runner's solemn responsibility to dump or distract the fielder turning the double play, and my father had taught me to slide late and hard. He told me to watch the shortstop and second baseman during pregame warm-ups to see where they came across the base so I'd know where to slide to have the best chance of taking their legs out from under them. "And if you can't reach him," Dad said, "raise your lead leg as you slide. If you show him your spikes he might pull up and take something off the throw."

This was not playing dirty. This was playing the game according to its time-honored conventions. The runner had a job to do, and the fielders knew what to expect. And a shortstop coming across the bag had ways of protecting himself. My father showed me.

He was baseball coach at the University of Iowa now, hired away from his job at Humboldt High. We worked out on the university field after Hawkeye practices or at home in the backyard with a shirt thrown down as second base. There were three basic moves. To keep the runners guessing, I should vary them, coming across second to the outside, the inside, or right down the baseline. We drilled on these moves—the footwork, the ball handling—until they were instinctive. I learned to make the outside move by stepping across the base with my left foot as I caught the throw, dragging my right foot over the bag, planting, and throwing. The inside move meant planting the left foot on second as I caught the throw, then bouncing to the inside of the diamond to make the relay. The fastest way, of course, was to come across second and drive down the baseline toward first. It was also the move that brought me straight toward the oncoming runner.

Facing a charging runner, I had three defenses, the first of which was a quick release. With practice I could catch and throw in a fluent motion, usually releasing the ball before the runner arrived. The second defense was to get into the air after the throw. "If he's going to get you," Dad said, "get both feet off the ground. You usually won't be able to jump over him, but if your feet aren't planted he won't break your ankles." Getting spiked was one thing. If it happened, you threw away your shredded sanitaries and made sure your tetanus booster was up to date. But a broken bone or a blown knee was serious. You jumped to tumble harmlessly with the blow.

The shortstop's third defense was the most effective. "Come straight down the line and throw through the runner's head," my father told me.

"What if I hit him?" I asked.

"Don't worry, he'll get down," my father said.

"What if he doesn't?" I asked.

"Well, he'll only make that mistake once," he said and grinned.

And so I came to recognize the violence within baseball's most elegant play, and the hardball understanding between runner and fielder. It was a kind of contract with a chain of subclauses activated by split-second decisions in the game within the game. If both parties understood the contract and reliably played their roles, the game unfolded with sudden outbursts of beauty along the razor edge of competition. And if a shortstop got dumped or a runner was forced into an early slide by a ball whizzing at his face, there were no hard feelings. There was, in fact, mutual respect within a common guild. Baseball knowledge and anticipation usually prevented serious injury. If everybody knew what he was doing, getting hurt was just bad luck.

In the summer after my sophomore year of high school, I worked on a Johnson County road crew and played six to eight games a week. Mondays through Fridays I drove a truck from seven to four, then played at night on the City High sophomore and varsity teams. Saturdays and Sundays there were American Legion doubleheaders. Working and playing ball outdoors all day, I sank deeply into the life of the body. My skin tanned dark, and my flesh felt sweet around my bones. At night games the scent of cornfields drifted over the glowing diamond as clouds of bugs swirled around the lights on their high poles. I slid hard and broke up double plays; I turned double plays, protecting myself with agility and guile. The summer wheeled by with the procession of the sun and the rotation of the batting order.

Three years later, in my first spring of college ball, I earned the starting spot at shortstop. Midway through the season I was in the field late in a tight game. There was a man on first, one out. I took two steps back and two steps toward the bag, positioning for a possible double play. The hitter cracked a routine grounder to the second baseman, who fielded it cleanly and flipped to me. I took the throw and pivoted at the bag. The runner from first was upright in the line of my relay. He seemed to think that obstructing my sight or placing himself between me and first was the way to break up a double play. I believe he was yelling. I think the word "idiot" flashed through my mind.

The instant of decision seemed to stretch out, and I registered in swift cascade the essence of a dialogue: "Throw through his head," "What if he doesn't slide?" "Don't worry, he'll get down," "No he won't, I'll kill him." Everything slowed and there seemed to be time to examine the runner as if he were a photograph. He ran straight up, his shirt was untucked, his socks were not properly rolled.

I made a little jump and lofted my throw over the head of the runner, too soft to complete the double play. The runner turned aside and went by me. Immediately I felt a deep pang of shame.

The play, as it turned out, was inconsequential to the game's outcome. I don't even recall who won or lost. But I do remember the way I brooded on what I thought of as my loss of nerve. I felt intense contempt for the bush-league runner, and my complicity in the ruined play stung me. He probably thought he'd made a smart move, and I'd let him get away with it. Nobody had taught him the proper way to play the game, so he'd have to learn the hard way. Someday somebody would plunk him. It should have been me. "I should have nailed him," I said to myself. The thoughts rolled around and around in my head.

I showered and went to supper. I went to my room in the dorm, listened to some music, spent some time with friends. One of them who had drawn a low draft number was reading a Canadian novel. He said he wanted to feel at home if he had to go. It was 1971.

My mind kept turning back to the play. I saw the runner's face, round as a pie, coming at me like a target. I knew with certainty he couldn't have dodged the throw. I didn't know what my father would have done, but as a college freshman in my first year on my own, I suspected he'd have made the good baseball play. You throw through the runner and he's got to get down. You feel sorry if somebody's hurt, but that's his responsibility. That's hardball.

In my instant of decision, however, there had been a recognition. There are moments, I saw now, when the rules outside the game flash into it. Mercy is not a part of baseball. But that runner, in his ignorance, had blundered outside the lines, and at that moment he'd become just a dumb jerk I could hurt or spare. By the time I released my throw he'd have been only a couple of feet from the end of my arm. I really could have killed him. I had drawn a high number myself, so I probably wasn't going to Vietnam, but the war was all around us. It was a time of taking sides, a time of decisions, a time when fathers and sons regarded one another across a generational divide exaggerated by issues of life and death.

I had not done as my father taught me, but in the end I didn't feel ashamed. Instead, a small coal of pride began to glow in the middle of my chest. In that instant of decision I had hit upon a value of my own, subversive and true. There was still regret. Regret that the runner and I had not been Maury Wills and Luis Aparicio sliding under and floating over. It had been a botched play. It was bad baseball. But, as my friends and I were learning in those harsh years—in the wide world outside the lines—there were worse things.

DENA SEIDEL

Good Times

—ɯɯ—

IT'S ALMOST eight o'clock, and I'm watching the TV reflection in his glasses. *Sanford and Son* and *Good Times* are his favorites; those people are real, he says. My face rests against his chest, and his left arm strokes my hair. I'm ready to snuggle here for hours. All we have is each other, he tells me.

On the couch's worn ribbed arm is Daddy's stash. He picks up a small gold pipe and scoops from a plastic film canister. Then he raises his lighter to his bearded lips. I hear flick, flick above me and hold my breath till the smoke rises.

Orange Marmalade sleeps at our feet on the rug samples stapled to our trailer's living room floor. Her shed blond dog hairs blend the different-colored squares and rectangles together. The samples come from Ray the rug man with the Elvis toupee who works in the basement of Daddy's home improvement store. Daddy hates his job and says so a lot. He's wasting his life selling nails to rednecks. He works there because he'll lose custody of me if he doesn't.

Good Times will start any minute. The neighbor kids are in front of their TVs too, but they're waiting for *Happy Days*. Tomorrow they'll be talking about Fonzi on the bus—they'll say Ayyyy! and hold out their thumbs. Once I told Roxanne that we watch *Good Times* and she told Geegee and the greasers and I got called a nigger lover. When I asked Daddy what a nigger is, he said it's what dumb white trash call black people to make themselves feel better about being dumb white trash. Don't ever say that word, he said. But now on the bus I sit in the back with the greasers and say "Ayyy" and "Sit on it" and listen as they talk about Fonzi and Richie. Then later I can say wasn't it cool when this or that happened on *Happy Days*. I'm nervous to get found out, but the greasers don't pay me much attention. It's 'cause of Roxanne that I get to sit in the back.

When I ask Daddy if we can watch *Happy Days* instead of *Good Times*, he says *Happy Days* is crap. The people on that show are fake. Just 'cause the ignorant hillbillies 'round here watch shit, doesn't mean we're going to.

Daddy of course is right about just about everything. I used to think the answers to all the questions in the universe lived in his brain, but only recently did he tell me that wasn't so. It shook me up a bit, to think there were things Daddy didn't know. I think it shook him up a bit, too. You see, I had told Roxanne that Daddy knows everything. She said nobody knows *everything*, so I went to Daddy who said, she's right, I don't know everything. Now I understand. Take *Happy Days*, for instance. It's not just the kids around here who watch it. Hope Jones loves *Happy Days*, and she's real smart. She's my best friend.

Hope lives in a two-story house with a pool and two bathrooms. She has wings. She keeps a comb in her back pocket to feather her wings when they turn to bangs. Olivia Newton-John has wings, and Hope loves Olivia Newton-John. Hope is ten like me. She's in fifth grade with me and Roxanne. So is Lizzie Brady. Lizzie also has wings and also watches *Happy Days* and lives near Hope in an even bigger house. Daddy says this wing thing makes a girl look like some overprimmed homo boy streetwalker. I don't know what he means, but Daddy tells me I look better natural which I know means we don't have the money for a beauty cut, and he'll keep trimming my hair with his beard scissors.

Hope is also Lizzie's best friend. Lizzie and I hate each other. Lizzie says I'm trailer trash. I say Lizzie is spoiled and stuck up. Hope and Lizzie and I met yesterday with Principal Holden on account of our screaming in the hall. The principal said Hope must play one day with Lizzie and the next day with Willow. A Lizzie day and a Willow day.

Today was a Lizzie day. I couldn't sit next to Hope at lunch or during class. At recess I played football with the boys. I saw Hope and Lizzie sitting on the hill combing each other's hair. Tomorrow will be a Willow day. In between periods and at lunch, Hope will want to talk about *Happy Days*.

Our TV sits on a shelf next to the needlepoint duck with the cardboard frame that I made for Daddy, the hand-stitched pillow that reads I Love You Daddy, and the plastic statue of a man in a toga with a leaf wreath and a gold medal that reads World's Best Dad. The TV shelf is mounted to the sliding wall that makes my bedroom. My bed can also fold into the wall but now rests on two cinder blocks. Above my bed is a shelf with books and stuffed animals my foster mothers gave me including *God Is Listening Daily Prayers*, even though Daddy says God is for daydreamers. This is my seventh bedroom in more than two years if you count the loft in the potato chip truck we lived in after Daddy kidnapped me. But this bedroom is really mine. I've been living here with Daddy now five whole months.

Daddy says move the TV trays, and I do. Every night I have supper ready when he comes home. Every day after school I call Daddy at work, and he tells me what to cook. Wash the chicken, chop potatoes, set the oven to 350 and put it in by 5:30. Sometimes it's just Spam and eggs and a can of creamed corn, but the pots are hot when he comes in the door. It's an easy night when he just wants raw hamburger and salt on white bread. Every night we eat dinner in front of the TV and then push the trays away, snuggle close, and watch.

Good times, any time you're out of money. / Good times, any time you're feelin' free. I start thinking about Hope and Roxanne and the bus ride tomorrow. Roxanne lives in the upstairs apartment of the old white farmhouse that's in between our trailer and the highway. Daddy says Roxanne's mom Shannon is straight out of Crownsville, which kids at school call the crazy farm. Frank and Kiki live in the white house's downstairs. Daddy says Frank's got a wife and kids and that's why we don't see him much. Daddy says Kiki's just out of Crownsville too, that we are surrounded by loonies. We only see Kiki come out when Frank is around. Daddy says Kiki would die of hunger if Frank didn't show up.

Every day after school, I climb the stairs stuck to the outside of the white house, stepping over the broken planks, to Roxanne's apartment. I play with Roxanne and her friend Geegee and we act out the words to "Bohemian Rhapsody." We take turns getting the bullet in the head, each time falling on the rug in a new way. We have to stand in the center of the room because the ceiling slopes on all sides. Shannon watches us from her foldout cot in the corner. She makes me nervous the way she just stares; but when we ham it up, she laughs. Then there's times when she just cries and cries. That's when Geegee and I wait outside on the steps while Roxanne holds her mom till she falls asleep. Then we play at Geegee's house. Geegee's mom has a life-size poster of John Travolta in his underwear.

Roxanne says I'm a goody-goody. She'll play with me at home, but at school she hangs with the greasers. All the greasers like her. Even Hope thinks she's cool. I *am* a goody-goody, but it's not my fault. Daddy says if I get just one B, he'll lose custody, and I'll go back to foster homes. He says if I get just one B, he'll give me something to cry about. So Roxanne says I'll never be cool, but I'm all right. She lets me play kickball with her and Geegee in our driveway.

If Frank's around, he'll break up our game and spin us by our armpits till we're too dizzy to stand. When he does this, Kiki watches from her window, and Frank says don't be jealous, they're just little girls. Frank's black and Kiki's white, but Roxanne and Geegee like Frank. He makes us laugh. Daddy also likes Frank, a lot, I think. He says we need a little *Soul Train* around here to water down the *Hee Haw*. Sometimes Daddy and Frank go catfishin' and they bring me along. Frank helps me put a worm on my hook even though I can do it by myself. It takes a long time for a catfish to bite. I sit and listen to Daddy and Frank talk about foxy ladies.

Jay Jay just told Flo he found cat food cans in their neighbor's trash but their neighbor doesn't own a cat.

"What's that mean, Daddy?"

"She's poor, she's eating cat food," Daddy says, refilling his pipe. I'm thinking people don't do these things on *Happy Days*. At a commercial, I ask if I can turn the channel. "I don't care, I gotta take a crap," Daddy says.

When Daddy comes back to *Happy Days*, he says, "Why do you watch this shit soap opera? You're rotting your brain. Don't you know people were pigheaded in the fifties." I try to keep watching, but Daddy says time's up. I turn the dial, click, click, click, back to the ghetto with Jay Jay and Flo.

Jay Jay's telling Thelma she's ugly when we hear a loud knock on our plastic trailer door. Daddy turns quickly.

"Who is it?" Daddy asks loudly.

"Police. Is Harvey Weinberg in there?" says a deep voice through our door.

Daddy jumps to turn up the TV sound. "Just a minute!"

Daddy grabs his stash and his pipe and runs to his room. I look down our trailer's rug sample hallway at Daddy pulling a large bag of weed from his closet and pushing it under his bed. My legs shake. Daddy sprays air freshener, pssssss pssssss, and I know the police are here with handcuffs to take him away like they did before. Then Daddy walks slowly to the front door and reaches for the handle. Before he turns the knob, he looks up at me with eyes that say I'm sorry you're gonna watch your daddy busted. He lifts his left hand to punch the top corner of the door, which always sticks, and then pushes the door open with his right. I see him put his hand to his chest and let out a sigh. Then Daddy laughs real hard.

"Man, you tryin' to give me a heart attack?"

I walk to the doorway and see a sunburnt man with a large nose and small, dark eyes.

"Just havin' some fun." The man gives me his hand. "Hello, Willow, I'm Adrian." His hand is wet.

"Come on in man, I wasn't expecting you till tomorrow."

"I got an earlier flight."

"Well sit down, I've got some primo Colombian for you to try."

I start breathing normal. Daddy and Adrian sit at the kitchen table wedged between the back of the couch and the refrigerator. Orange Marmalade starts sniffing Adrian's pants and shoes. Adrian scratches her ears with one hand and takes a joint from Daddy with the other. "Nice dog," he says as he takes a hit and holds it in. Daddy is watching Adrian, waiting for him to say something.

"This is good shit," Adrian says and hands the joint in my direction.

"She doesn't smoke," Daddy says. Orange Marmalade walks to the toilet for a drink. We hear slurp, slurp from the bathroom. "She's a dog," Daddy says, "that's what dogs do, and we don't have room for a water bowl."

I look at the clock. *Happy Days* has ten minutes left.

I keep Orange Marmalade's dog food cans in two compartments of my dresser drawer; and each night, as I take out her dinner, I move around the cans still left. I make sure there's an even number of cans in each compartment so that each can has a friend. I never leave one can alone. When there are only three cans, I worry—two might like each other better, and one might feel left out.

In the morning, Adrian is snoring on the couch. His blanket is wrapped around him so I can't tell his head from his feet. Daddy and I sit at the kitchen table and eat Count Chocula. In between spoonfuls, I look over the back of the couch at Adrian's lump.

"Adrian will be staying with us for a while," Daddy says, not lifting his eyes from his bowl. "We have business."

Adrian's covered shape sits up. He yawns a loud yawn and says, "Willow, I'm your lucky star." He unwraps himself. His black hair seems damp and stringy and stuck to his forehead. "Harvey, why'd you name this girl Willow?" he asks.

"There was a big ol' willow tree at an ashram in the Catskills. Always a good place for a lay."

Adrian laughs. "Well, little girl, it's always good to know your roots." I've heard this joke before. I look down at the brown marshmallows floating in my milk. I want to say my mom once told me willow trees look like silver-sequined dancers in the wind. But I don't. Daddy says there's no point in getting hung up on a name. You're born, you shit, and you die—don't take yourself too seriously.

When Daddy leaves for work, I leave too. I walk down our wood-planked cinder block steps knowing that Pinky Tuscadaro and Fonzi rode their motorcycles into the sunset last night. I heard Richie say he thinks Fonzi is really in love this time. I run to the bus stop. At the end of the driveway, Roxanne is making vroom, vroom sounds, wringing her hands like she's doing wheelies.

"Wasn't Pinky cool last night?" I say out of breath.

She doesn't answer. Just Vroom, Vroom, Vroom, as she runs in circles on her invisible Harley.

The bus pulls up, and I follow Roxanne on, past Yolanda and the other black kids who sit in the front. Yolanda looks up at me and smiles. I smile back before the greasers see. Yolanda is like me, she's also a goody-goody.

"Yo Roxanne!" the greasers call. Roxanne walks real cool to the back of the bus in her tight bell-bottoms and Lynyrd Skynyrd T-shirt. "Ayyy," Roxanne shouts, and a dozen thumbs raise "Ayyy!" If the greasers ask me about *Happy Days*, I'll know what to say. I look back at Yolanda. She doesn't know I watch *Good Times*.

In class, I keep my arms folded across my chest. I don't want Mrs. Jackson to see my boobies. Daddy's never met Mrs. Jackson. He's only seen her picture in the fifth grade class photo taped to our fridge. Daddy says Mrs. Jackson is sweet like brown sugar cause of her dark skin. He says he could eat her up. But one day Mrs. Jackson called me to her desk and said, "Child, do you notice your body changing?" She told me to walk up and down the hall paying attention to the bounce of my breasts. She wrote a note and told me to give it to Daddy.

Dear Mr. Weinberg,

Your daughter Willow is in need of a training bra. If there is no adult woman in her life to take her shopping, I'm willing to help.

Daddy read it and said tell that hot, nosy bitch you don't need a titty harness and you don't need a mother. I'm your mommy and daddy all rolled into one.

At school, I do everything I can to make Hope happy. At lunch I give her the pizza and chocolate pudding off my tray. After school, Hope and I walk to her house. I offer to carry her books, but she says that's silly, you're not a boy.

It feels good to walk next to Hope. Hope's perfect, with her feathered blonde hair and blue eyes, her butterfly shirt and new Levi jeans with rainbow stitching. I sometimes can't believe I'm her friend.

In Hope's house the carpet is all one color. In Hope's room the bedspread matches her curtains, and she has her own stereo. At dinner we sit at a large shiny table in heavy chairs with cushioned seats. Hope has a mom and a dad and an older sister and a younger brother. They pass macaroni and cheese. I don't take much. I don't want to be greedy. Everyone is listening to Hope's dad talk about the train set he's building in the family room. Hope's mom is eating a hot dog with a knife and fork. I pass on hot dogs. I eat one macaroni at a time. I say, "Mr. and Mrs. Jones, you have the most beautiful house I've ever seen in my whole life." They must hear this a lot because no one says anything.

After dinner, Mrs. Jones and Hope drive me home. Once in our driveway, Mrs. Jones drives slowly to avoid the potholes filled with rainwater. She passes the peeling white house and the dogwood trees that hide the trailer. She parks behind Daddy's car but keeps her engine running. Daddy opens the trailer door and waves and says thank you for driving Willow home. I get out of the car and run to Daddy.

"Can Hope spend the night this weekend?"

"Sure," he says and then calls to Mrs. Jones. "Would Hope like to spend the night this weekend?"

Mrs. Jones says they have company this weekend but maybe some other time. We wave goodbye, and I say I'll see you tomorrow at school even though I know that tomorrow is a Lizzie day. As we watch them drive away, Daddy says that Hope's mom will never let Hope spend the night. "Just forget about her, you're only gonna get hurt."

"But, Daddy, she's my best friend," I say, following Daddy into the trailer.

I haven't finished my homework, but Daddy says we're going for a ride, and we climb in our brown Chevrolet with Orange Marmalade and me in the back. Daddy starts the car and slips Charlie Parker into the eight-track. At a stoplight he takes out a joint, lights it, takes a long toke, and hands it to Adrian.

"Man, in Amsterdam you can smoke weed this good right on the street," Adrian says. "And all you'll get are looks of jealousy. That's the life."

"Not for me," Daddy says. "I'm stuck here. I'll lose custody if I leave."

I realize I'm chewing the side of my finger because it starts to hurt. Daddy's looking at me through his rearview mirror. "But Willow's an easy kid. She makes me look legit, so in the long run she's good for business. Aren't you, Lovey Dove?"

"And she doesn't talk?"

"Course not, she protects her daddy. What's good for her daddy is good for Willow."

Daddy's smiling at me and then turns to look at three high school girls on the sidewalk. Daddy watches them get smaller in his side mirror.

Our car slows down for traffic, and Daddy says, "It's a roadblock, see the cops way up there? Shit!" Daddy puts the joint out in the ashtray. He reaches under his seat for a bottle of mouthwash. He makes swish, swish in his mouth and moves his feet over to spit on the floor by the gas pedal. I continue peeling the skin off my fingers till we get to the cops, who look at Daddy's registration and wave us by.

As we enter the basement of Gary's house, the first thing I see is centerfolds pinned to the walls. The ones without opened legs—*Playboy*, not *Hustler*. Daddy says to Gary, "This is Adrian from Amsterdam, he's cool and his connections are for real." Gary's tall like a basketball player, but his head droops over his chest like a vulture on "Bugs Bunny." Gary takes Daddy and Adrian to a stuffed garbage bag and unties it. He takes out a stem, puts it under his nose and breathes hard. Then he hands it to Adrian to do the same.

Gary's wife Sarah comes down the stairs and says, "This is no place for a little lady. Come with me, hon," and she leads me up to the kitchen. Sarah's hair is big and yellow like Farrah Fawcett. I eat cookies and milk and tell Sarah I like her hair.

"It's easy, just stay where you are, and I'll show you how to do it." Sarah gets a curling iron and plugs it in next to the kitchen table. She runs her fingers through my hair and says it would curl easier if I had layers.

"You got a curling iron?"

"No."

"I've got an extra one you can have."

I swallow hard. I can't believe it. "Wow, thank you," I say to Sarah, but I'm thinking about Hope. I can't wait to tell her. Tomorrow. I'll tell Hope tomorrow. Even though it's a Lizzie day, I'll pass Hope a note in the hall. The note will say that I have my very own curling iron. I can do her hair and she can do mine. Lizzie will be jealous.

"Does your mother do your hair?" Sarah asks, and I feel the hot rod against my scalp.

"No."

"Do you see her much?"

"No." I hear the click, click as Sarah opens and closes the curling iron's clamp.

"Willow, your mother, is she Jewish?"

"I don't know."

"She's a shiksa, a goy," Daddy shouts, as he climbs up the basement stairs. I feel the skin of my head burning but I say nothing.

"So Harvey, you gonna raise this girl Jewish?"

"Yeah, sure. She'll have a bat mitzvah."

I raise my hand to touch the warm, curly waves. Sarah says come with me, and I follow her to the bathroom mirror. "Don't you look good?" she says as she runs her fingers through my hair.

"Yeah, I can't believe it." My hair is big, wavy and fluffy. I touch it real careful like I'm touching cotton candy.

Sarah picks up the little pink mirror sitting on the fuzzy pink toilet tank and hands it to me. I'm looking at the back of my hair when Daddy shouts "Willow!" and I know we're leaving. Daddy walks into the bathroom, smiles and says, "Don't you look fancy." I want to tell Daddy Sarah's gonna give me my very own curling iron when Gary walks over to Daddy looking real serious.

"I'm trusting you to make good," Gary says to Daddy.

Daddy laughs. "Don't worry, Adrian's a sure thing."

Gary grabs me, wraps his long arms around me and says, "'Cause I can just keep this little girl as collateral—we'll be able to make some money off her if the deal falls through." I tilt my head back into Gary's chest and smile up at him, happy that he thinks I'm worth money, but then Sarah says, "Don't say ugly things, Gary."

Daddy says come on to me and starts out the door with Adrian, and I turn to Sarah. I hope she remembers. Sarah says "Bye, bye, hon" and gives me a quick hug, and tears start to come to my eyes, and she says, "Hurry, your Daddy's calling."

In the back seat I'm crying. Why didn't she remember? What did I do wrong? Daddy and Adrian are up front talking business. They don't hear me. That's a good thing 'cause Daddy would say, "Quit bawlin', you've got no reason to feel sorry for yourself."

After a while, it's quiet. From the back seat I say, "Daddy, what's Jewish?" and Daddy and Adrian just laugh. They laugh a long time, and I don't know why. Then Daddy says, "Jews are the niggers of white people."

The next day is a Lizzie day, and I'm not too happy to go to school. At the bus stop Roxanne is singing:

Is this the real life—
Is this just fantasy—
Caught in a landslide—
No escape from reality—

She spins on her heels with her arms open wide. When she sees me, she stops.

"Hey, Willow, who's that man in the trailer?"

"My Dad's friend."

"Is he living with you?"

"For a while."

Roxanne's eyes look excited. "Willow, people say your Dad walks around naked in that trailer."

"Who says that! It's not true!" I've never shouted at Roxanne before.

"People say he has sex with you in there. Now, don't get me wrong, I don't believe it, but now there's another man. It's like a manage a twaz, you know what that is? I do. It's when three people fuck each other in the mouth at the same time, and that's what people are gonna say you and your daddy and that man are doin' in your trailer."

I'm shaking. I want to hide. Roxanne starts humming.

"You know it's not true, Roxanne."

She smiles and tilts her head back, spreading her arms out wide again:

Too late, my time has come,
Sends shivers down my spine—
Body's aching all the time,
Goodbye everybody—I've got to go—
Gotta leave you all behind and face the truth—

I start crying, and I hold my breath to try and stop.

Roxanne looks at me, "Hey, chill out. You know there's gonna be a rumble at recess on Friday, blacks against whites, everybody's bringing knives. It's gonna be cool." Roxanne's trying to make me feel better. She doesn't want to see me bawl. We hear Frank's Cadillac pull around the corner of the white house. He spent the night with Kiki and made her happy. We wave to him as he passes and watch as he pulls out of the driveway.

In every class that, yesterday, Hope sat next to me, today she sits next to Lizzie. At recess, Hope and Lizzie play hopscotch. I lean against the side of the brick building and watch. The boys come up to me and ask if I want to play football. I say no, that I'm always the last one chosen for teams and I don't like that. I say, you don't really want me to play anyway, and they just walk away. I keep staring at Hope. I want to run to her and tell her what a good time I had at her house last night. I want to run and touch her arm and tell her that she's my best friend, that I would do anything for her. I don't know what to do with this sickness I feel.

I turn away and see Yolanda sitting on the grass. She's watching the black girls jump rope. I go and sit next to her.

"You like to jump rope?" she asks.

"Sure."

"It's my turn next. You can jump with me."

I follow Yolanda. She stops before the circle the spinning rope makes. She counts 1-2-3 and we both jump in, miss mary mack, mack, mack, all dressed in black, black, black. I trip and the rope lands around Yolanda's neck.

"Yolanda, whatcha doin' bringin' fat four-eyed white girls into our game?"

"She's okay, she'll learn."

"Never mind," I say and walk back to the brick wall and stand there. Yolanda smiles at me. I smile back. Maybe Yolanda can be my new best friend. I start thinking about things that she and I can do together, just the two of us. I could learn to do her hair—it's different, lots of tight braids. And she could learn to do mine. Maybe she could spend the night.

The punch is hard, and it knocks me onto the blacktop. I see Roxanne and Geegee standing above me until the spit lands in my face.

"You're a squealing pig, that's what you are," says Roxanne.

"Oink, oink, oink," says Geegee.

"You told Holden about the rumble, you nigger lover," says Roxanne.

"I didn't, for real," I say, wiping the spit out of my eyes with the hem of Daddy's old T-shirt I'm wearing. "I wouldn't do that."

"Well, who then? You have no real friends, and you kiss ass with the teachers," says Roxanne. "You make me sick."

"I swear I didn't."

"I'm gonna kick your ass," Geegee says real angry and spits at me again. Then the kick comes with all Geegee's might and makes me double over. "Cool it," Roxanne says, "or she'll rat on us again."

I stay in my seat till Roxanne gets off the bus. I wait for Rusty, the bus driver, to yell "Hey Willow, this is your stop too." I watch Roxanne from behind. Her walk is strong and her arms swing at her sides. At the white house she stops to sit on the bottom step with her elbows on her knees and her head in her hands. She's waiting for me to walk past.

"Yo tree-girl, I thought you might like to know I don't think you was the squealer after all."

"I wasn't."

"But you still better watch your ass."

"Are you gonna tell Geegee it wasn't me?"

"Maybe," she says with a smile and jumps to run up her stairs. I hear the slam of her screen door.

I look over at the trailer and wonder what people think. The rust is dripping from the roof, making lines down the aluminum siding.

I wrap the phone cord around my finger as I call Daddy. I feel Adrian watching me. Daddy says, "Forget about dinner, Adrian's cooking while he's with us."

"Okay."

"And pretty soon, when me and Adrian get finished with business, we'll have so much money we'll be eatin' out every night."

"Really?"

"Really, and we'll buy ourselves a big ol' house, and I won't have to work at this shit-hole no more. So, don't worry about dinner, Baby Doll, just do your homework."

"Okay, Daddy," I say, and I hear him hang up. I head for the door.

"Where you goin'?" Adrian asks.

"Outside," and I punch the stuck corner of the door with my fist.

"Hey," Adrian says to me, "do you know the Pygmy word for elephant shit?"

"No."

"Bwa!" he says laughing. "So if kids at school piss you off, tell them they are full of bwa!"

"Okay."

"You know what else?" He smiles and his eyes get all squinty. "You're gonna be a looker someday, I can tell. I'm watchin' you."

Orange Marmalade and I walk behind the trailer to the rusty swing set that used to belong to Bucky, the boy who lived here before me whose father, Daddy says, belonged to the KKK. Daddy says they split the day Frank showed up. Daddy says he thanks Frank for us getting the trailer for a dime even though I never heard him thank Frank for real. I sit on a swing with Orange Marmalade at my feet memorizing my spelling words, enlighten, erratic, erase, escape, till Daddy comes home.

In my head I place one letter next to another, forming each word, but I'm too excited to concentrate. "Marmalade, we're gonna live in a big house," I say out loud. She slaps her tail against the ground. "We'll have a sit-down bathtub and enough room for a coffee table. Maybe we'll live near Hope, and she can spend the night anytime she wants. You'll like Hope. And Roxanne and Geegee will come. When they see our house, no one will say bad things about Daddy."

"Hey little girl," a man's voice says.

I look up. "Hi Frank."

"Whacha doin' all alone back here?" Orange Marmalade gets up and rubs her face against his leg. Frank leans over and scratches her back, his gold chain bracelet dangling onto his fingers. Frank's dressed fancy in a purple shirt, tan polyester pants, and shiny black shoes. No one else ever dresses nice like that around here.

"Why don't you do your schoolwork inside?"

"It's nicer outside," I say, not mentioning Adrian since Roxanne says people will think bad things. Frank's never seen Adrian as far as I know.

Frank smiles at me. "You were waitin' for me, weren't ya?"

"No."

"Come on, you know I come around on Fridays, you've been waitin' for your Frankie. Let me give my honey a push on that swing," he says with a laugh. Frank walks behind me and puts his arms on my back. I wait for the push but instead he slides his arms around my waist. I stiffen and drop my notebook. Frank pulls me and the swing against his stomach, and I feel his hands reach up under my shirt. I try and jump out of the swing, pulling his hands off me, but he grabs my arm. He holds me tight.

"You know you want this." He pulls me against him and squeezes me hard. All I see is a gold necklace in his curly chest hairs. He sticks his tongue deep in my throat. I can't breathe. It's like being caught under a scary wave crashing me into the sand. Out of the corner of my eye, I see the curtain move on the trailer's window. Adrian's face is looking out. Orange Marmalade's jumping on us barking and wanting to play. Frank's arms are on me from all sides. Then I feel Frank's hand go in the back of my pants and in my underwear. I'm trying to kick him, but I can't. Then I feel my knee dig into him, and Frank lets go and yells "Shit!" Frank falls to the ground with his hand between his legs. Orange Marmalade's licking his face. "You little white trash bitch," Frank says, looking up at me with angry eyes. I start running to the white house. Orange Marmalade follows me, all excited.

As I climb the stairs, Orange Marmalade passes me and enters Roxanne's apartment through the rip in the screen door. At the top of the steps I ask if I can come in and Roxanne turns and sees me crying. "What happened?" she asks, really wanting to know. I start telling her but the words come out in chunks.

"He touched your pussy? Ooh, your daddy's gonna kill him, right? I wanna be there to watch your daddy and Frank go at it," she says, punching the air with her fists. "Stay here till your daddy comes home. I gotta see this."

I sit on Roxanne's couch with Orange Marmalade at my feet and start combing through her fur with my fingers, looking for blood-filled ticks. Then Geegee shows up and Roxanne says, "Something bad happened to Willow. Willow, tell Geegee what happened!"

I hear Daddy's car and run down the stairs and walk next to the Chevrolet till he parks.

"Daddy! Daddy!" I shout as I stroke his arm resting in the open car window. He looks over and smiles. "Hi Baby Doll."

As Daddy gets out, he sees my notebook and papers scattered under the swing set. "What the hell happened?" he asks. I also look at the swing set and feel Frank's hands all over again. Then Daddy says, "You can't treat your schoolwork like crap. Were you at Roxanne's?"

"Yes."

"Did you finish your homework first?"

"Not all of it."

"Then you've been fucking off, and you're grounded." I start to cry. "I don't want to see tears, stop feeling sorry for yourself." He slams the car door. "I'm sick of this shit. I work all day and I have to come home to this. You have work to do, and I depend on you to do it and stop crying; you're making me sick. Now go get your papers."

I pick up my books and papers and put them in my backpack. I walk back to Daddy with my eyes on the ground. I follow him as he starts up the trailer's steps, but then Daddy stops and looks through the dogwood trees. "Hey Frank, how's it goin', man?" Daddy shouts.

I see Frank across the driveway, coming out of Kiki's apartment. I step behind Daddy, trying to hide.

"All right, man," Frank shouts back, "how 'bout you?"

"Hangin' in there," Daddy says. "Good to see you, man."

"Good to see you too," Frank calls back.

Above Frank I see Roxanne and Geegee standing on the landing at the top of their stairs. They're watching, but I avoid their eyes.

"If you're around some weekend," Daddy says to Frank, "we should go catfishin'. Willow here will dig us up some worms," Daddy says, laughing and pulling me out from behind him.

"You bet," Frank shouts as he waves and goes back inside. And then Daddy turns to me. "But there'll be no catfishin' till you get your shit together with school. Remember, you're grounded."

Daddy walks in the trailer and I follow. Adrian is sitting on the couch, smoking a joint and reading *Sexual Energies in Indian Art*. The trailer smells of pot and fried fat. "Tonight we're having potato latkes and homemade chopped chicken liver," Adrian says with a smile. Orange Marmalade walks to the stove, sits, and looks up at the frying pans. She smacks her tail against the cracked linoleum floor.

"None for Willow," Daddy says. "She's gonna spend the rest of the night in her room."

"Oh," says Adrian.

I look at Daddy knowing I can never explain. He opens the fridge and pulls out a Rolling Rock. "But, first, Willow, feed the dog."

I go to my room and take a can of dog food from my dresser drawer. There is only one can left, sitting in the drawer by itself.

I carry the dog food out of my room and Daddy says to Adrian, "You're here all day, can't you keep an eye on her, make sure she doesn't piss her time away?"

"Sure can do, boss," Adrian says, sending me a smile I quickly turn from.

I place Orange Marmalade's dog food under the electric can opener, taking off the top and bottom lids. Then I push the wet, pink can-shape into Orange Marmalade's bowl. The phone rings.

"Hello?" Daddy answers. "Who's this? Yolanda?" Daddy looks at me. "No, Yolanda, Willow can't come to the phone. She's grounded." Daddy hangs up and grabs a bottle opener and opens his beer. I hear gulp, gulp, gulp.

"Hey, Harvey, who's that cat with the Cadillac?" Adrian asks.

"Frank, a self-made man. Got his own business. Got a lot a dough. And he's got a part-time, half-brained white chick that lives next door. He comes to these backwoods to get away from the old lady. Nobody'd think of lookin' for him 'round here."

"I guess pickins are easy in Hicksville," Adrian says.

Daddy laughs, "Kiki's really easy, she's practically a child."

"No kidding," Adrian says.

CARL WOOTON

Ramblers and Spinners

—⟋m⟍—

IT SNOWED all day the Monday after Thanksgiving. After supper and home-work, my brother Will and I sat in the narrowly opened window of the sec-ond-floor apartment where we lived and watched the older kids run their bicycles down Sweet's Hill and hit their brakes at the corner beneath us and do four or five spins until they ended up in the next block in front of the Hoosier Cafe. Bradshaw Morgan got more spins than anyone else. He never got less than four, sometimes six, and once, although I didn't see it, he got nine complete spins. That was the winter before we moved to Nadirville, In-diana, and Bradshaw was already sixteen.

Jerry McCloskey, a fat kid, came off the bottom of the hill, hit the corner, spun, and went down, sprawling, the bike one way, him another. The others helped him up, but not without a couple of them slipping and falling on the packed snow.

I laughed and said, "I can do better than that."

Will said, "Me too."

I said, "I bet I could get six spins, at least."

From behind us, our older sister, Angie, said, "Bet you can't."

Will and I didn't know she was there, watching us, hearing us. If we'd known, we sure wouldn't have said anything out loud. She came closer so she could watch Bradshaw Morgan and the others. She was fifteen.

Will said, "I can."

She said, "You can't get six spins. You can't get any spins." Will was get-ting up to hit her. "You don't even have a bicycle."

The truth was more than Will could take, and he jumped at her. Angie yelled, and I grabbed Will and held him back. I really didn't care whether or

not he clobbered Angie, but I knew if he did I'd probably get the same punishment he did just for being there.

I sat on Will and told Angie, "You better get out while you can." She believed me and ran out of the room, calling for Momma.

I heard her say, "Will was trying to hit me," and Momma said, "Why
don't you leave them alone when they're in there together?" and I knew our
father wasn't in the apartment. If he had been there, Momma would have
said something like, "Angie!" and our father would have been halfway down
the hall already, coming to set things straight. Will struggled, and I got off of
him. He was strong for ten.

We went back to the open window, but the bicycle riders were all gone.
The snow fell harder, and the freezing air that came through the open window made my eyes water and hurt my throat when I breathed it in. But I
didn't close the window. The streetlight catty-corner from our building shone
on the tracks made by the bicycles. The falling snow was filling in the tracks,
but I could see them as though they were still in the motions of being made
while Bradshaw Morgan went spinning down the street toward the cafe.

Momma came into the room and said, "Shut that window, you two.
You'll catch your death. I swear!" Will shut the window.

I said, "I need a bicycle."

She said, "You got a money tree?"

Will said, "They don't cost much."

I said, "You won't have to get us nothing else for Christmas."

She said, "Get to bed. We'll talk about it later." She said it in the tone of
voice she used when she meant the discussion was closed.

Will said, "I'm going to ask Daddy."

She said, "He's got enough trouble without you bothering him about
some bicycles we can't afford. Get to sleep. You've got school tomorrow."

After she shut the door, Will said, "Do you think we can get a bicycle for
Christmas?"

I said, "We don't have a prayer."

He said, "I'm going to ask Daddy."

I wrote off any hope of finding bicycles beside the Christmas tree that
year. I had heard enough talk about signs of coming hard times. Momma, in
fact, had already said something about there being nothing but foolishness in
wasting good money on a tree we'd just have to throw out. But Momma's
talking didn't touch Will. Only a couple of nights later Will was true to his
word about asking our father for the bicycles. If I'd paid a little more attention to him, I might have expected him to do it, but I never would have expected him to do it when he did.

He did it at grace. Whenever our parents had had a few days in a row without arguing about whether or not we were going to end up in the poor-house, our father offered grace before supper. He never said anything more than thanks for good food and good health, but he ended it by indicating each of us should offer some kind of petition. My mother prayed for comfort for those mothers who had lost their sons in the war and for President Truman. Angie prayed for A's on whatever tests she had to take that week. I asked for new tennis shoes and help in algebra. I wasn't worried about an A like Angie was. I just wanted help! Then Will, with his hands together, his fingers extended out straight, almost whispered, "Please let me and Mark get bicycles for Christmas."

He said it softly and with his hands up against his mouth. Our father reached over and lightly moved Will's fingers down.

He said, "I couldn't hear that, Will. Say it again, a little louder."

"Please let me and Mark get bicycles for Christmas."

Momma said, "Will! I told you we can't afford any bicycles."

Will didn't look at her. Neither me. We both watched our father, half expecting some kind of explosion that never came.

He looked at Momma a half-second when she'd had her say, then looked back at Will, who still had his hands folded like he was thinking he maybe had better offer another prayer.

Then our father said, "What about Angie? Don't you want a bicycle for your sister?"

Will bowed his head further into his clasped hands and muttered, "And for Angie, too."

Our father said, "Amen," and there was a sound like someone blowing out candles on a cake. That was the first time I knew I had been holding my breath.

Momma mumbled something about people thinking they could pick money like apples, but she didn't make any more fuss during supper about Will's prayer. Nor did she say anything when Will asked again for bicycles for Christmas at supper every day the rest of that week. But that Sunday afternoon I heard her talking to our father in the kitchen.

Momma said, "You hadn't ought to encourage him to go on about bicycles. He's just going to be disappointed."

Our father said, "We'll see."

"See what?"

"Maybe we can work something out."

"You're wearing two sweaters because we can't afford to keep the heat turned up and you think we can pay for bicycles? You got a special kind of garden where you grow your money trees? Where are you going?"

"Downstairs."

Our father's business was downstairs. He made venetian blinds and sold them wholesale. Momma kept the books. They talked all the time about the business, but always as though Angie and Will and I were not there. Our father kept saying he thought things would pick up in the new year. Momma said things about ostriches and fools with their heads in the sand. I didn't understand probably half of what I overheard, but I knew business wasn't good. That was why the heat was turned down and we had to wear long-sleeve shirts and sweaters in the apartment.

Momma didn't like our father to work on Sundays, but he almost always did, unless they didn't argue or talk about how much things cost. Even I figured out that nearly every Sunday afternoon she said something to him about money not growing on trees, he was almost halfway down the stairs before she finished. Sometimes I wanted to ask her why she hadn't figured that out, too. But I didn't ask her, partly because I was a little bit afraid she had.

There was no grace before and hardly any talk during supper for most of the next week. Each meal grew sterner and more silent. I admit that even though I had refused to share Will's hope, I shared his dreams of descending Sweet's Hill at rocket speed and spinning through the intersection, and it seemed as though even the dreams were slipping through a crack at the edge of the stillness of those suppertimes. The only good thing about those times was that the kitchen where we ate was still warm from Momma's cooking.

During that week our father came late to the table, ate his meal, thanked Momma for fixing it, and went downstairs. Sometimes I heard him come back after we had gone to bed. He and Momma talked low late at night, and I couldn't ever hear everything. But sometimes I heard him say things like, "I've got to believe we'll make it," and sometimes something like, "Christ, Goldie, I'm doing the fucking best I can."

Near the end of the week, our father came to the table first and sat with his hands in his lap while he waited for the rest of us to settle in our places. Will was the last one to the table. He came hurrying, and as he sat in his chair next to mine, he flashed some kind of paper at me and shoved it into his hip pocket.

Our father prayed his grace, and he surprised us at the end of it by adding a petition: "Please let the County Commissioners act fairly when they award the contract for the new blinds at the Old Folks' Home." His voice stumbled through it, as though he was embarrassed to be asking for anything more than good food and good health. He cleared his throat, and Momma followed with a prayer for all the poor people who wouldn't have a proper Christmas that year.

Then Angie said, "Please let us have bicycles for Christmas."

Momma made a noise sucking in her breath. Will and I grinned and squirmed in our chairs, and our father stared at Angie and looked puzzled. Angie sat with her hands folded like she was imitating a statue of an angel. I didn't know what had possessed her, but I thought real quick that I had better, in fact, be quick and follow her example.

I said, "Please, God, let us have bicycles for Christmas."

And Will: "Please let me and Mark and Angie have a bicycle for Christmas."

Momma said, "Do you know how much a bicycle costs?"

Angie said, "$29.95. Will and I found some in the Sears catalog."

Will pulled the paper he had showed me from his hip pocket and handed it to Momma.

Will said, "There, at the bottom. I want a red one."

Momma said, "You hadn't ought to tear pages out of my catalog without asking." She looked at the picture and said, "That's thirty dollars. Times three, that's ninety dollars. And that doesn't include carrying charges. We don't have that kind of tree." She ignored Will's open hand stretched toward her, folded the paper, and put it under her plate.

Our father said, "Goldie, let's wait and see."

Momma said, "We're wondering how we're going to pay for the next tank of butane and you want to wait and see about some bicycles that nobody can pay for. I swear, Ernest. Sometimes I wonder."

She said that a lot, but she never explained exactly what she wondered about. Will and I used to guess late at night when we were in bed and couldn't sleep, but we never did figure out just what she meant. That night I didn't think I would ever go to sleep. Almost as soon as the light was out, Will said, "I bet we get them."

I said, "What made Angie come around to our side?"

He said, "Bradshaw Morgan."

"How's that?"

"I heard Ruth Ann Parker saying Bradshaw Morgan made Patsy Jukeman his girlfriend last summer because she had a bicycle and would go riding with him in the country—all the way to Raccoon Creek and the hogback—anytime he wanted her to."

Angie made no secret about wanting to be Bradshaw Morgan's girlfriend, but I was amazed Will had figured it out, even hearing what he did. He thought girls should be treated like poisonous insects, and he didn't waste much of his time worrying about how they thought. But he had understood Angie this time, and he knew as well as I that our father was not going to dismiss such a prayer from her lightly.

Will and I stayed awake until long after our parents went to bed. We whispered in the light from the street lamp about all the places we would go if, when, we got our new bikes. Finally, Will stayed silent when I asked him a question, and all I could hear was the sound of a car crunching the snow in the street below and, after that, the soft murmur of our parents' voices circling in the dark, cold air. Then suddenly our father's voice rose.

"Goddamnit, Goldie, all I said was we'll wait and see."

Then it was quiet for a few minutes, until their voices and sounds of them moving around came down the hall again. Sometimes it was like the thinness of the cold air offered no resistance to the sounds they made, and I pulled my three blankets tighter around me. The cold air and the darkness moved together around my head, and I had a vision of Bradshaw Morgan waiting for me in front of the Hoosier Cafe as I came down Sweet's Hill, hit a new glazing of ice in the intersection, and went into a string of acrobatic spins that awed even Bradshaw. I was almost into the last spin right in front of the cafe when I heard Momma's voice get almost loud, and she said, "Ernest! No! It's too cold!"

Will had to make a Christmas list at school. He printed his name at the top of his paper and the words A RED BICYCLE in the middle of the page. He told Angie about it, and she helped him to make others, some with his name at the top, some with hers, and some with mine. They all had the single item, A BICYCLE, as the total Christmas shopping list for each of us. We taped copies on the doors to our rooms, on the wall beside the bathroom mirror, and even on the bulletin board downstairs in the office of the venetian blind business.

We got a tree, but we got it less than a week before Christmas, after they were marked down. It was small, barely as tall as Will, because Momma said, "A big tree wouldn't look good with only one string of lights." We made chains of colored construction paper and hung peppermint canes on the branches. Momma always saved the thin, metal ribbons that she peeled off the tops of coffee cans, and we twisted them and hung them to shine like shook foil when the lights were turned on. And in the last days before Christmas, we watched our parents' every expression and listened for hints in their inflections. At night Will and I speculated about the meaning of their smallest gestures. He believed a Christmas bicycle was a sure thing. I agreed that all in all, the signs were good. I did not share his faith, but since Angie's prayer, I had begun to hope.

On Christmas morning we woke to the sound of our father yodeling in the kitchen. Sharp, heavy odors of fresh coffee and biscuits and bacon filled the warm air. When I threw off the covers, I knew Momma had turned up the thermostat. She was waiting outside the door when Will looked to see if there was a clear way to the living room.

Momma said, "Breakfast first."

That was her father's rule when she was a little girl. She called it a family tradition, and there was no point in arguing against it. We ate as quickly as we could, and we believed our parents took a great deal more deliberate time than they ever did with any other meal. But finally breakfast was done, and our father and Momma went into the living room to prepare for us. We crept along the hall as far as we dared in order to be as close to the living room as we could be when they called for us. Then our father yelled, "Come on!" and Momma shouted, "Don't run!" and we nearly leaped the last short distance into the room.

Joy! Joy! The purest joy I have ever known. Three bicycles stood in front of the tree. Our parents stood to one side, and Momma tried to take a picture at the instant of our amazement. Amazement and joy! Hope fulfilled! Each bicycle had a large sign taped to the handlebars to show whose it was. Will's and Angie's were red, and mine was a bright, glisteny blue like a clear sky reflected in water.

Will flipped up the kickstand on his bike, jumped on the seat and started riding down the hall with Momma yelling and chasing after him. I followed, but Momma turned us both around and pushed us back into the living room. We had to open the rest of our presents, the ones that had come in the mail from relatives. Sweaters. Books. Socks. One at a time. Each had a turn. Cards with notes about how sorry they were we lived so far away from everybody. And the bicycles stood at the entrance to the hall, ready, their clean lines defining speed and flowing spins on the icy streets that waited for us outside. Then, after the last package of more clothes from Grandpa Rambler, we were ready to go outside. Momma forced us into extra shirts and heavy coats and gloves with warnings not to stay out too long, especially Angie, because it was bitter cold. Our father helped us carry the bikes downstairs.

I wanted to go straight to the top of Sweet's Hill and come down to the intersection, but Angie and Will wanted to ride around town and make sure everybody saw our new bikes. I fussed, but I went with them. It couldn't take more than ten or fifteen minutes to ride past every block in Nadirville. And it didn't take a genius to figure out what Angie really wanted was to ride past Bradshaw Morgan's house. In a little while we had a crowd that wanted to ride down the hill and do tricks in the street. There were three or four other new bikes besides ours, and every boy who had one believed he had the bike that would one day break Bradshaw's record of nine spins on one ride. We were halfway up the hill when someone said, "Look!"

Bradshaw Morgan stood at the base of the hill beside his old bike, talking with Angie. Then, in a minute, he started up the hill, and Angie rode off toward the intersection to wait for us. Patsy Jukeman, Ruth Ann Parker, and some other kids who didn't have bikes were there, too.

There was no way up iced-over Sweet's Hill on a bicycle except to walk and push, slip and fall, push and crawl. Fat Jerry McCloskey led the way, and it looked like he spent as much time falling as he did pushing and walking. The sky was dirty grey and looked like the snow ought to start again any time, except it was too cold to snow. The wind blew stronger at the top of the hill, and not even shirts and a mackinaw kept it from slicing all the way through me. Ruth Ann Parker's little brother, Timmy, went first. The rest of us followed, with Will and me somewhere in the middle of the order. One went, and the next one counted to ten before he went because nobody wanted a collision at the bottom. Will was in place, then suddenly he was hurtling down the hill in front of me and I was counting . . . "one thousand eight, one thousand nine" . . .

"Go!"

A hand pushed on my back, and the cold in the wind stung my eyes and took away my breath. I pedaled at first, then held the pedals in a coasting position because the wheels were turning too fast for me to keep up with them. The back wheels hit a rut, came out of it, and I thought I was going to fall, but somehow I kept up and headed for the bottom of the hill. I looked toward the intersection and saw a blur of people and bikes standing around, keeping the center clear, and then I was there. I locked the brakes, turned the handlebars and spun, two, three, and went down. My leg caught under the bike, and I skidded along the street until I crashed into the rear wheel of a parked car.

Someone lifted my bike off of me and someone else helped me up and another voice yelled, "Look out!" Another rider spun through the intersection. This one did better than I had, at least four and a half good spins and without falling down. I saw Will on the other side of the street, standing next to Jerry McCloskey.

"How'd you do?"

He said, "I was awful," and held up one gloved finger.

Jerry said, "He's too light. There's nothing to keep him going. You turned too tight and ran into yourself."

I turned the handlebars of my bike and looked at the front wheel coming around and thought I understood what he meant.

Someone yelled, "Bradshaw!"

And we looked up the street to see Bradshaw coming toward the intersection. Nobody understood how he seemed to come down the hill so much faster than everybody else. He turned his handlebars, locked his brakes, spun, spun again and again, and looked like he would have gone forever if he hadn't been too far to the side. He had to stop to keep from sliding into the steel posts that held up the metal awning in front of the cafe. Angie and all her friends jumped around him like he was some kind of war hero coming home, but they didn't impress Bradshaw. He right away started moving back toward the hill for another ride.

We tried again. Will didn't do any better, and I did worse, even though I didn't fall. We went again, and Will got two and I got a little more than three again. I didn't turn the handlebars so hard, but I leaned too far, trying to help the bike pull itself around, and went down even harder than I had the first time. But I got up and inspected my bike. Just two spokes on the front wheel were a little bent, not enough damage to keep me off the hill. Bradshaw got six really big, looping spins the third time. He looked as smooth and graceful as a figure skater.

We had started toward the hill for another run when Angie caught up with us and said, "Momma says you've got to come."

She said it loud in front of everybody, and they all laughed.

I said, "Tell her after this one."

Angie pointed toward the building, and I looked up. The angle was wrong to see anything, but I knew Momma was standing at the corner window, waiting for us to show we were coming home. Everyone else looked up too, and they all laughed harder.

Angie said, "You better come," and turned away. Will followed her.

Jerry McCloskey said, "You better go home, Mark."

He said it like he was talking to a real little kid. Bradshaw looked over Ruth Ann Parker's head at me and grinned.

I said, "I'll go when I'm ready."

We climbed the hill again, but this time I hung back so I'd be one of the last. Bradshaw was always last. The wind blew harder. It had gotten colder. My face had almost no feeling in it. I went down the hill and before I hit the bottom I knew I was going to do better then three and maybe better than . . . I turned the handlebars, saw the lamppost go by twice, then the breadbox in front of the grocery store, three, four, I was going into five, and I could hear everyone yelling and then I felt the bike go. I hit the iced pavement hard on my left arm, felt myself slide, and heard a scraping sound somewhere away from me. Everybody crowded into the street to see if I was hurt, and they kept Bradshaw Morgan, who never waited a full one-thousand-ten, from spinning at all.

My father came down and helped me home. Jerry McCloskey brought my bike. I kept trying to look at it while my father steered me toward the stairs at the back of the building. The handlebars were twisted out of line and ends of broken spokes stuck out of the rims of both wheels. When they got it and me to the top of the stairs and stood my bike next to Will's and Angie's, mine looked like I had tried to destroy it.

My father said, "It'll probably be a while before I can fix it."

I might have said something if it had been just him and me on the landing, but I didn't say anything because Momma already had hold of my good arm and was pulling me into the apartment. The warm air of the kitchen where she had been cooking picked at my face and made little needles run up and down in my hands and feet. As soon as she decided my left arm wasn't broken, she made me drink a cup of hot cocoa. I waited for her to say something about the bike and about my not coming in when she had said for me to, but she didn't say anything. She just told me to go on and be easy the rest of the day because I had had enough of being out in the cold. I didn't argue, and I really didn't mind that the rest of the day turned out to be sort of like a thousand other days I remembered staying inside because it was too cold. It still was Christmas. Momma cooked everything. My father said my bike could be fixed, and I had made almost five spins on just my fourth try down Sweet's Hill.

In bed that night, Will said, "You did great!"

Momma turned the thermostat down again, and the sound of the wind blowing down from the top of Sweet's Hill made the cold air in the apartment seem even thinner than usual. I heard our father say, "I can fix it, Goldie. I'll get some spokes when I go to Terre Haute for the County Commissioners' meeting."

Momma said, "I swear! A brand-new bike torn up the first day he rides it. And it's not even paid for!"

The wind brought an ice storm the day after Christmas. The temperature went below zero and stayed there for the rest of the school vacation days. The roads in and out of town were impassable, so my father could not go to Terre Haute and get the spokes he needed to fix my bike. It did not matter much, because Momma wouldn't have let us out to ride anyway. Neither, it seemed, would anyone else's Momma. Will and I spent a lot of time looking out the window, waiting to see who would dare the hill with all the new ice and snow on it, but no one came. Not many cars even tried the streets. There was nothing outside except the whiteness of the frozen snow that covered everything, and the cold, cold air we felt when we got too close to the glass of the windowpane.

We had been back in school a couple of weeks when Momma told us the snowplows had finally cleared the roads and she and our father were going the next day to Terre Haute to meet with the County Commissioners. She told us in the evening because she wanted us to pray the commissioners would make a right decision about the blinds for the Old Folks' Home. I left that up to Angie and Will and thought real hard all night and all the next day about our father buying the spokes for my wheels. I even tried to think of ways to get out of basketball practice after school in order to get home in time to help him repair the bike.

It was already dark when I left the gym. Running was nearly impossible on the icy streets and sidewalks, but I ran when I wasn't sliding. I stumbled up the stairs to the landing. My father knelt beside my bicycle, and he was fitting the last spoke into place. He had thick hands with short fingers that made him look clumsy when he worked with small things, but he inserted the spoke into place without any trouble. He stood and handed me the bike. The handlebars were straight.

It was almost like Christmas morning all over again. I wanted to take it right then and ride through the streets to show everyone my bike was fixed and I was ready for the next run down Sweet's Hill.

Momma had heard me on the stairs, and she opened the door to the kitchen and said, "Supper's ready. We're waiting for you." The others were already sitting at the table by the time my father and I got there.

Our father prayed thanks for guiding the County Commissioners, and I knew that meant he got the order for the blinds at the Old Folks' Home. Momma said something about hoping we would use our blessings right. I don't remember what Angie and Will prayed for, but I gave thanks for the fixing of my bicycle and asked for the weather to get better. Then I realized we were having a Sunday dinner in the middle of the week, with dessert. Two freshly baked pies rested on the counter next to the stove. Our parents laughed and talked through the whole meal. They told us about the meeting with the County Commissioners. Our father gave a detailed description of buying the spokes for my bicycle, and Momma made sure I understood how much trouble he had had putting them in my wheels so I could be surprised when I got home from basketball practice.

She said, "I hope you'll take better care of your bike now. It isn't made for doing acrobatics."

She stopped short of forbidding me to ride with the others down Sweet's Hill. She didn't warn me of dire consequences if I played what she considered the fool again. But I understood that if I wasn't what she thought was careful enough, I'd be walking the rest of my foreseeable life.

I said, "I'll be careful."

After Momma saw that our light was out and the door was closed that night, I got up, wrapped a blanket around me, and looked out the window at the intersection. It was dark. Someone had shot out the streetlight. The snow and ice were grey and looked colder than they did in the daylight. The chill came through the glass, and I hurried shivering back to bed and pulled up the extra quilt Momma had put at the foot. Will was snoring. Momma and my father were making the noises they always made getting ready to go to bed, except they were talking and laughing more than they had in a long time.

Momma said, "Oh, Ernest!" and everything was real quiet until I heard Momma making sounds, sounds like little moans, sounds I thought I didn't understand.

Then those sounds stopped, and my father said, "Goldie, everything's going to be fine, just fine."

2

That winter broke every record it could for being cold. No one went out who didn't have to. We even got unexpected holidays from school, but ten or fifteen minutes outside drove the bravest and the foolhardiest alike inside. The bicycles stayed on the landing. Momma stayed downstairs almost as much as our father. She even went with him after supper and on Sunday afternoons. We heard talk about trimming expenses and cutting back. The thermostat was turned even lower. Sometimes it seemed if one of us—Angie or Will or I—even looked like we might ask for something, Momma reminded us there were lots of different kinds of trees in the woods, but none of them grew money.

They brought paperwork and bookkeeping upstairs to the kitchen table at night to save on heating costs downstairs. They talked about business. I didn't understand most of what they said, but I did understand that the order for the blinds at the Old Folks' Home had not turned out the way they had hoped it would. And they argued about bills that had to be paid. They yelled at each other, apologized, and yelled some more. Our father became more and more silent, except when he worked on the books with Momma. He brought his silence even to the supper table, and if Momma sat like she was waiting to say grace, he didn't seem to notice and served food onto his plate. At times he left the kitchen and went into the living room and sat in his big chair and stared out a window like he was seeing something none of us could see.

One afternoon early in February there was no basketball practice, and I returned from school with Angie and Will. When we walked into the kitchen, Momma was wearing her heavy coat. Two suitcases stood by the door.

She said, "There's no heat. We're going to Terre Haute for a couple of days." And she named some people she and our father knew who had agreed to take us in until somebody came and refilled our butane tank. Our father came in, picked up the suitcases and walked out without saying a word. Momma pretended to look for something in a cabinet the time he was in the kitchen. Then she made sure we had all our schoolbooks, pushed us out the door, and we all went downstairs to the car.

Before we got out of town, she asked, "Is there enough gas in the car to get there?"

Our father said, "Yes, goddamnit, Goldie. I'm not going to leave you stranded to freeze on the road."

"I didn't say you were. I didn't even think it."

"It's not my fault the gauge on the butane tank froze. It looked like we had plenty to last till next week. I would've paid the bill by then, somehow."

She said, "I'm not blaming you."

He said, "For Christ's sake, Goldie!"

Every morning our father left the house where we stayed. When I asked Momma where he went, she said, "He's taking care of business." He returned in the evenings, and they kept to themselves and whispered. Their friends seemed not to notice them. Will and I had to sleep on a pallet made of blankets on the floor. We were glad when after nearly a week there, Momma told us we were going home the next day. The apartment was almost warm when we returned, and the first thing Momma did was to turn the thermostat down.

The best thing was the weather came round to something more like normal. It was still cold, but it wasn't that wind-blowing, below-zero cold that kept almost every moving thing huddled in the warmest corner it could find. The sun was out most days, with the air bright and clear, and a couple of weekends after we were back there was a real gathering at the intersection beneath our window. They were all looking toward the top of Sweet's Hill. Even some of the grown-ups who didn't have anything better to do had come out to watch. Our father had come upstairs to see if we were going out.

Before I got my coat on, Momma said, "Keep in mind we can't afford to fix broken bicycles."

My father said, "Be careful."

On the way to the top of the hill, I felt all the excitement I had felt Christmas day. Everybody was happy to be out again. At the top of the hill we heard the crowd at the bottom yelling at every rider. Halfway down the hill I looked ahead at the intersection and it was like I saw myself already there, making tight, rapid spins, not even needing to count them because the crowd was counting for me. The chill in the wind burned my face, and off the bottom of the hill, leveling out, I saw my father standing in front of his business. He was in shirtsleeves in the cold air, his hands pushed deep into his pockets, as though that was all he needed to be warm. I had a flash of him kneeling on the landing, his hands holding the thin spokes of my wheels, and I did three easy spins and slid straight on toward the breadbox in front of the grocery store to keep from falling. I heard a murmur of disappointment from the crowd, and when I looked back toward the corner, my father had gone back into the building.

Will said, "What happened?"

I said, "Nothing."

Jerry McCloskey said, "He chickened out."

"Fuck you, Fatso!"

McCloskey said, "You want to eat snow, dipshit?" and looked around for somebody to hold his bike.

It might have come to something, probably big, fat McCloskey sitting on me and grinding me through the ice and snow into the pavement, but it stopped because the next rider down the hill lost control of his bike and came crashing into both of us and a half dozen others as well. By the time we got ourselves up, Bradshaw was at the bottom of the hill, and we forgot about everything except watching him. It was almost miraculous. Six, seven, eight, and he would have done the mythical nine and more if a car had not turned toward us at the next corner.

McCloskey and I had completely forgotten what had almost started be-tween us, and nobody else even remembered we were there. We had eyes and thoughts only for Bradshaw. He had challenged us with something much more than just the number of spins we thought were possible. He had shown us a grace and ease that we did not know how to measure and thus did not know how to achieve. And he knew he had done something special. He would not ride again that day. He leaned his bike against the wall of the cafe and became the center of the crowd still willing to watch the rest of us. We went again up the hill to ride down and spin through the intersection. Hardly anyone fell. We all knew we were having fun, but we—all of us, even Jerry McCloskey—rode without heart.

The effect of Bradshaw Morgan's ride went beyond that day. It marked the end of a season. We still rode, but we climbed the hill less often and with-out Bradshaw. Without saying anything about it, we waited for spring. Our parents talked about closing the venetian blind business. March came.

One Saturday some men loaded the drills and saws and other tools belonging to our father's business onto a truck, and a deputy sheriff padlocked the doors. Our father spent the whole weekend sitting in his chair in the living room staring at something beyond the window. Monday morning he left before we were ready for school, and Momma told us he had a new job as a salesman in a furniture store in Terre Haute.

The snowfalls stopped, and the ice melted. On Saturdays we rode four miles to the covered bridge over Raccoon Creek, and we planned how later, when the dirt and gravel roads had dried out, we would go first to the bridge, then off the main road to the hogback. That was a ridge that ran for several miles parallel to the creek and formed steep bluffs along the bank that we climbed and sometimes jumped from into the water in the summer. But the water wouldn't be warm enough for that until June, and in April Momma told us our father had taken another job in a town called Sullivan and we were moving when school was out. Nights in the apartment were quieter, and Will and I talked in the dark about the place called Sullivan. We agreed it had to be better than Nadirville, although we didn't know why it had to be. Sometimes when I stayed awake long enough, I heard a soft, soft sound like Momma trying not to cry.

Will and I collected empty boxes from the grocery store and stacked them on the landing and in the hall and some in every room in the apartment. Momma packed our winter clothes and other things we knew we wouldn't need first. She made us help every evening after supper. We filled the empty boxes, stacked them in the hall and the kitchen, and went back to the grocery store for more. By the time our father came home a couple of days before the last day of school to help us finish packing, we were living around, in, and out of boxes. Momma looked tired, and there wasn't much finishing left to do when he got there. Then two days after school was out, two trucks drove up and parked on the street that ran beside the building.

They didn't come together. The first one there was a big stake-body job, with lettering on the cab that said APEX FURNITURE, SULLIVAN, IND. The driver was a little man with gaps between his teeth that showed a lot because he was always grinning. Our father called him Norman, and he called our father "Mr. Rambler" and "Sir."

Norman wanted to start loading right away, and Will and I were eager to help him, even though most of the boxes probably were too heavy for us to carry down the stairs and lift onto the back of the truck. But our father said we had to wait, and he told Norman to come upstairs and get some coffee. Will and I stayed down and climbed over the staked sides of the truck. We were figuring out how to walk all the way around the outside of the truck without getting on the ground when the second truck drove up. It was a van, all closed in with big double doors in the back. ESTES BROTHERS, AUCTIONEERS was painted in big black letters on the side of the van, and two men sat in the high cab.

The driver got out. He carried a clipboard with papers on it. He shouted, "Hey, kid. Is this where the Ramblers live?"

I said, "Yes," and he started walking toward the front of the building. I called to him and pointed toward the double-door-sized opening for the stairs at the rear corner just as my father and Norman came through it onto the sidewalk.

The driver said, "Is one of you Mr. Rambler?"

He didn't say "Mr." in the respectful way Norman did.

My father said, "I am."

The driver looked at the opening, then at the windows on the second floor, and said, "Nobody told me this was a damned upstairs job."

Our father looked at Will and me and said, "Come down from there." When we were on the ground, he said, "I want you two to go play."

I said, "I want to help."

"There'll be plenty for you to help with later. This morning I want you and Will to go play. Find some of your friends and get up a baseball game."

I started toward the stairs.

He said, "Where are you going?"

"To get my bike."

"No. Leave your bikes here."

I said, "What about Angie?"

"Go play!"

He looked like he wanted to say something else, but the two men with the second truck were already starting upstairs and he turned and followed them.

Will said, "Come on." I went, but I didn't hurry.

We walked to the baseball field. A half-dozen boys were already there hitting and chasing flies and grounders. Will and I didn't have gloves, so we went into the outfield and shagged the balls nobody could catch. After a while there were enough for us to pick six on a side, with one left over. That one was Will because he was the youngest. I felt bad about him not playing, but he didn't seem to mind much. My side was picked to go in the field first, and by the time we got to come in to bat, Will had gone.

I remember very little about the game except what happened the next time I saw Will. I was playing second base, which meant I faced the road. We had played at least three or four innings when I saw Will running toward the field. He was calling my name at the top of his voice. Everybody turned and watched him for a moment, until somebody got impatient and called us back to the game. The batter hit the ball on the ground toward me. I moved into position to field it, but a runner ran in front of me and I lost sight of the ball. It went past me into the outfield, and everybody started yelling and screaming. Then I realized it was not a base runner who had blocked my view but Will, who had come onto the field. He was standing in front of me, and he was crying.

He yelled, "They're taking everything!"

I said, "What are you talking about?"

"They're taking everything away. Even our bicycles. And that man and Daddy almost got in a fight because that man called our things a pile of junk!"

The others shouted at Will to get off the field. Somebody shouted at me to get Will out of the way and to get back into the game.

Will said, "Come on!" and I ran with him off the field.

Somebody yelled, "Don't come back!"

Once we hit the road, I ran ahead of Will. It was only four long blocks from the baseball field to the apartment. Nothing in Nadirville was more than seven or eight blocks from the apartment. Will called to me to wait for him, but I kept on running. When I got to where I could see the side of the building we lived in, my father, Norman, and the two men who came in the second truck were standing in the street behind the van with the rear, double doors wide open. Momma and Angie stood together on the sidewalk. I ran around the front of the truck and stood on the edge of the sidewalk between Momma and the men in the street.

Momma said, "Come here, Mark."

I ignored her.

"Mark!"

I stepped back beside her. Her eyes were red, and she kept wiping at her nose with a wadded-up handkerchief. Angie had big streaks of tears on her cheeks. Will came up. He wasn't crying anymore. He squeezed in between me and Momma. The two men with the truck lifted the bicycles into the back of the van, closed the double doors and pulled a heavy metal bar down across them. The driver handed his clipboard and a pencil to my father.

He said, "Sign there, at the bottom."

My father said, "Do you know when the auction will be?"

The driver said, "Have no idea."

My father signed, and the two men got into the truck. We all stood there and watched as the van turned the corner and disappeared. My father stood in the middle of the street, and I thought he looked almost as old as Grandpa Rambler.

Norman said, "I'll back up to the door, so's we can load the boxes."

Without going upstairs, I knew the men in the van had left the boxes we had packed. I knew that everything else was gone, that it was going somewhere to be auctioned. I knew that what was happening had something to do with my father's business failing, with him going bankrupt, with bills that didn't, couldn't get paid. I knew that was why he and Momma both looked old and tired, too tired even to argue. And I knew that all that was why Momma stood stiff and still when he came up and put his arm around her shoulder like he was trying to shield her from a bitter wind. There wasn't any wind that day.

The truck Norman was backing up to the stairway backfired, and our father said, "We better get to work. It's a long way to go if we're going to get there before dark."

Momma said, "Everybody carries something, but don't try to carry anything too heavy for you."

Norman kept Will in the back of the truck with him to help stack and arrange the boxes the rest of us carried down to them. We worked slowly at first. Momma and our father stopped every now and then and just looked at each other before one of them picked up another box and went down the stairs. But emptying one room seemed to make us eager to empty another, and we worked faster and faster.

We were nearly finished when a small crowd of kids, led by Jerry Mc-Closkey, showed up at the corner. Most of them were on bikes, and they rode around, doing figure eights in the intersection. Ruth Ann Parker and Patsy Jukeman came to our side of the corner and Angie went to meet them. They acted like girls and hugged each other and cried.

My father asked me, "Do you want to go tell anyone goodbye?"

I looked toward the corner. Jerry McCloskey was playing chicken with another kid Will's age and rammed his rear wheel.

I said, "No. Can Will and I ride in the back of the truck?"

He had planned for us to ride in the car with Momma and Angie.

Norman said, "I'll ride with 'em."

That was enough. Our father drove the truck. Momma and Angie went ahead in the car so our father would know if they had trouble. When our father started the motor, the kids at the corner moved in front of the cafe. We turned and drove past them, and Jerry McCloskey and the other bigger kids on bikes rode into the middle of the street and followed us. Will sat with Norman on some boxes in the middle, but I found a small space where I could stand against the back stake-panel to watch the blurring motion of the road underneath me smooth out into a fine, black line in the distance. The kids on their bikes spread across the road and pedaled hard. They had found a new game for the moment as they raced and maneuvered for position to lead the pack. The distance between them and the truck gradually increased, but the way my father drove the truck slowly through town kept them from falling very far behind.

I looked over their heads at the intersection and at Sweet's Hill rising beyond it. Both receded, getting smaller and smaller until the hill looked like a narrow strip of ribbon that hung straight down from the sky and stiffened when it met the pavement at the bottom. I thought for a moment that I could even see the figure of a lone rider at the top. I imagined it looked like Bradshaw, as though he were already waiting for the next winter's snow and ice. The truck went around a sharp curve, and Sweet's Hill vanished. At the edge of town, the riders who had followed us turned off and disappeared behind a fencerow overgrown with blackberry bushes. They were headed for the creek and the hogback. No one had waved or shouted.

Then there was nothing but the noise of dual tires on the blacktop and a broken white line in the center of the road, a line of diminishing dashes that pointed to some place we had lived in once. We were moving to a place called Sullivan. I had no idea where it was, except that by the sun I knew we were headed south. We were moving because my father had gone bankrupt and because my mother sometimes cried in the night. We were moving because two men in a truck took away the things my parents called theirs and the bicycle that was the only thing I had ever called mine. No grown-ups had come to say goodbye to my parents. We had lived in Nadirville less than two years, and that was not long enough for anyone to believe our coming or going was any great matter. We were moving on a warm, cloudless day with a sky the same color my bike had been on that Christmas morning. It had not been said, but we all knew we would soon move again. I told myself that that, too, would be no great matter.

I climbed carefully over the boxes to the front of the truck. I stood against the cab and let the warm wind strike me full in the face. The narrow stripe of road and the tiny dashes of white down the middle widened and passed blurred beneath the front of the truck. Momma and Angie were well ahead of us so that whenever there was any kind of curve in the road they were out of sight for a moment. The truck seemed to speed up when that happened. There was a small space where I could look through the back window of the cab and see my father. He hunched his shoulders like he was trying to push the truck toward whatever was ahead with his own weight. He drove with both hands on the wheel.

JULIE KEITH

Pneumonia

—ᵐᵐ—

IN LATE AFTERNOON our house grew dark. Shadows gathered in the corners of my room and in the upper hall, while outside my window the sky turned from winter silver to deep blue. I'd been playing tea party with my doll Lucy and a fuzzy, yellow-and-tan teddy bear named Boom. We three played together a good deal, not always tea party, but sometimes orphanage or store or train trip. Lucy had fat, feverish cheeks and platinum hair. Boom was just a teddy bear, a little worn around the ears, soft and agreeable to hold. In the growing gloom, Lucy's curls and Boom's blond tummy were becoming harder and harder to see. Finally I said to them, "Excuse me, please," and leaving them on the floor with the doll teacups and doll teapot, I got to my feet and went over to the light switch.

By reaching up and pushing hard with both forefingers, I was able to punch in the button. My room flashed into brightness. For a moment I stood blinking and squinting and glancing around. The fan of light from my doorway reached out into the hall as far as the stairs. Normally this light would be met by more light from the hall and stairwell and by rattles and clunks from the kitchen to tell me my mother had finished her nap and gone down to start supper. But this afternoon there was nothing beyond my own light— only silence and darkness.

Earlier, when I'd come in from school, I'd sat awhile on the stairs, overcome with lethargy. The house had been silent then too, as it often was. My mother rested most afternoons, stretched out on her bed, sometimes dozing. All mothers did this, I assumed. Their children made them tired.

Eventually I'd hauled off my boots and snowsuit and headed upstairs to report in. My mother had been an actress in plays before she married my father, and her voice, though often weary, had a carrying lilt. Today though, as I arrived in her doorway, her whispered, "Hello, darling," barely reached me. Flopped on her flowered bedspread, her blonde head sunk into the pillow, she'd waved me away with a flutter of her hand—none of her usual admonitions to change out of my school dress and to have a glass of milk. After a moment, when it seemed unlikely she would say or do anything more, I'd gone to my room. I did not mind this. In our quiet house I was used to spending my afternoons with Lucy and Boom.

The house was not really ours. We rented it from a gaunt, dingy man named Mr. Meese, and some of his furniture was stored, covered in dust sheets, on the large, unheated sleeping porch that stretched like an afterthought across the back of the house. The door to it from the upstairs hall was kept locked, but I had gone out there a few times when my father was changing storm windows or screens and wanted me to stand beside him and hold the screws and washers and sometimes his big screwdriver. Depending on the season, the place was either hotter or colder than the rest of the house, and either way my father usually got very angry at the ill-fitting windows and screens. Neither he nor my mother cared much for the house or for Mr. Meese, and their distaste seemed to culminate in this porch. Perhaps that was why being out there made me uneasy. Nonetheless, we were lucky, as my parents often said, to have a house to live in. There was a war on, after all. Places to live were hard to find.

When the windows of my room had turned into mirrors of the purest black, my father came home. Light burst up the stairs and then so did he, his footsteps smacking hard on the wooden steps. He appeared in my doorway, his dark hair slicked back from his pale face, the whole of him smelling of smoke and train and downtown. The other men in the laboratory at the university smoked a great deal, especially the scientists. He had told me this once when the smell of his coat had made me sneeze. Now he said, "What's going on here?"

"There's no supper, Daddy," I told him. "Mommy's still resting."

He looked down at me for another second; then he turned and left the room. I heard his voice, sharp and alarmed, "Helen? Helen?" and the sound of their bedroom door shutting.

After a moment I put Boom back on my bed where he usually sat and placed Lucy in her cradle, making sure her eyelids had closed as they were supposed to whenever she was laid flat. "Hush," I told her. "Be good, darling," and I covered her to her hard little chin with a shawl from my dress-up trunk.

When my father did not immediately reappear, I went downstairs and got myself graham crackers and jam. I was not allowed snacks near suppertime, but for now it seemed all bets were off. While I was eating, my father came downstairs too. Our phone was in the hall, and I could hear him telling the operator what number he wanted and, a moment later, saying something in a quick, angry voice about the doctor coming at once. He made another call to our next-door neighbor, whom I called Uncle Fitz though he wasn't an uncle, just my father's friend. They sometimes played badminton together on Saturday afternoons. I could tell from what my father was saying that Uncle Fitz wasn't in but only the old lady whose second floor he rented as a separate apartment. "No, never mind," my father was saying. "Thought he might be there. I needed a hand just now, but never mind."

I had finished my crackers and jam and gone back up to my room when I heard the ching of the doorbell and my father's voice and then another man's, though not Uncle Fitz's. A moment later, they came up the stairs and passed by my open door. The unknown man—who was, I supposed, the doctor—carried a small, black bag. Neither he nor my father glanced my way. It was an astonishing moment. In plain sight of them, I could have been smearing finger paint on the floor or jumping on my bed or even playing with matches.

They paid no attention to me either when they emerged from my parents' room and I followed them downstairs or a little later when the ambulance with its whirling light pulled up outside and two men wearing grey jackets and grey caps came into the house carrying a stretcher. They hustled past me, and, led by my father and the doctor, went straight upstairs. I did not have long to wait before they all reappeared, the ambulance men first, descending with slow steps, holding the stretcher level between them. On it lay my mother, dressed, as far as I could see, in her blue bathrobe, the rest of her wrapped quite tightly in a grey blanket. With each step her blonde head jounced slightly. Her eyes, as she passed by me, were half-closed. Her face was flushed. Only after they had borne her out the door and the doctor had shaken my father's hand and gone out after them, did my father seem to take notice that I was there in the hall with him.

"Your mother's going to the hospital, Susannah," he said. His voice still sounded angry. Stepping around me he picked up our long-necked telephone and, with his other hand, lifted the receiver off its cradle and placed it against his ear. "Information, please," he said into the mouthpiece and gave me another look. "You go to bed." I went.

I'd turned out the lights and gotten under the covers before I heard my father's quick steps on the stairs. I held my breath. My bedroom door opened, the rectangle of light widening behind his tall silhouette. He did not ask if I had eaten. He must have forgotten about supper altogether.

"Did you say your prayers?" was what he said.

"No, Daddy." I felt him hesitate, and again I held my breath. The blackness of his shape grew large against the light, shutting it out almost entirely. My mattress sank under his weight.

He was apt to sit down beside me like this if I had committed some sin that day. The gist of his lectures I knew by heart. "You exhaust your mother . . . you don't honor her. Your willfulness . . . your selfishness. . . . You must pray to Jesus to make you a better girl." He generally took a long time to say all this, in a taut voice that made me think of a stretched rubber band. At the end, an apology, including the promise to say my prayers, was usually extracted from me.

Saying the required words, I hated my own mouth and tongue. The truth was I did not want to admit my sins. Not to him. Not to Jesus. I wanted to hold on to my anger and my sullen feelings. I didn't always honor my mother. He was right. I was happy being with her when she wasn't too tired. She sang bits of songs and laughed a good deal and held my hand. But whenever I asked if I might do something, roller-skate around the block or play over at a friend's house, she got a distant, weary look. "Not right now. I'm too tired," was her favorite reply, and often I had to resort to whining and begging to get permission to do the most ordinary things. Sometimes I could wear her down in this way, but other times she told on me, and then I got lectured and punished by my father.

My real prayer just now, so strong that I could nearly hear it and was vaguely surprised he couldn't too, went as follows: "Please make him go away. Please don't let him make me say my prayers with him. Please. . . ."

I felt his hand heavy on my forehead. "Nice and cool," he said. He didn't sound angry anymore. "Good." I would have liked to ask how long my mother would be away in the hospital, but I was afraid that he might stay longer here on my bed and that the anger I'd heard earlier in his voice might return. Then the weight of the hand was gone. My mattress rocked back to level.

"Good night, Susannah. Be sure you say your prayers." He was standing in the doorway now.

I took a breath. "Yes, Daddy. Good night, Daddy." As the door shut behind him, a thick, insulating blackness enfolded me. Far away on the other side of it, I could hear his footsteps fading down the hall. My prayer had been answered.

The next morning, when I came down to the kitchen for breakfast, a thick-waisted lady in a hair net and glasses was standing at the stove flipping strips of bacon. I stood in the kitchen doorway staring at her. Most of the ladies who came in to do our ironing and wash the kitchen floor were colored. (I had been instructed always to say "colored" rather than "Negro.") This lady, however, was as light-skinned as I was. She was stout enough to be a grandmother, but the hair confined beneath her hair net was dark, and her quick, decisive hands did not seem grandmotherly.

She glanced up from the bacon. Her cheeks were round and flushed. "Well, you'd be Susannah then. Right, dear? I'm Mrs. Peckengill." She nodded toward the kitchen table in the corner. "And this here's Robert."

I turned and saw a boy with short dark hair and a wide, solemn face. "Bobby," said the boy. He seemed near to my own age.

"I'm to be here while your mother's in hospital," said Mrs. Peckengill. "Your dad said you should have a fried egg. He's gone to work a while back. You want one or two?" I hesitated, and she must have caught a look of distaste on my face, for she added amiably, "Or you like scrambled better? I can whip them up in a jiff."

"Oh, yes, please." Scrambled eggs were a weekend treat, carefully prepared in a bowl with measured amounts of milk and salt, then whirred by my mother's eggbeater into a pale yellow liquid as smooth and pretty as paint. Mrs. Peckengill was already breaking eggs right into the frying pan, the same pan that a moment ago had held the bacon. Next she began to whack the eggs into submission with a fork. Shocked, I went and sat down across from the boy named Bobby.

The scrambled eggs set in front of me moments later had flecks of white and bits of bacon in them, and they tasted wonderful, as did the bacon strip, which was not crisp the way my mother cooked it, but floppy and shiny. My table companion ate his with his fingers, and after some hesitation—either of my parents would have stopped me instantly—I copied him, getting my fingers greasy up to the knuckles. When he had a piece of toast with jam, I wanted one too, but Mrs. Peckengill wouldn't let me. "Tomorrow, you get yourself down for breakfast sooner," she told me, ". . . you can eat all the toast you want."

"You're in first grade," said Bobby around his jam-covered toast. I couldn't tell if the remark was a question or if he was just letting me know he was informed. It was, at any rate, the first thing he'd said to me.

"I'm six," I said, to quell any doubts.

"I'm six, too." He gazed at me solemnly over his toast. His eyes, like his hair, were dark. I was not at a stage in life where I noticed features, but something about Bobby's face pleased me. I liked the way he gazed at me now, with direct expectation. As though he knew he had something to offer and believed I might too.

"Rules for school're different in South Evanston," said Mrs. Peckengill. She had moved to the sink and was running water into the dishpan. "Now, you get on to school, Susannah. Don't want to be late."

She was right. I found it excruciatingly embarrassing to be late, though I often was, the demon lethargy sabotaging me while I was still in my room trying to find my socks or lacing my shoes, causing me not to heed my mother's calls. This same lethargy could overwhelm me on my way to school, the weight of it pressing my boots to the sidewalk. At such times my steps slowed to a drag, I grew entranced with a leaf on a bush or with an icicle hanging from a mailbox; I forgot where I was going, that I was in any sort of hurry. It was only as I reached the corner and our red-brick, four-classroom school came into view that panic struck and I began to run.

That afternoon the sidewalks were awash with slush and half-melted snow. I fell twice on the way home, soaking my mittens and the knees of my leggings. As I sloshed into the house, Bobby came bounding down the stairs. "You're home," he called. Slinging himself around the bannister, he jumped down the last two steps. "We'll play burglars." He said it burg-a-lurs. I stripped off my sodden socks and my snowsuit, already reeking of wet wool, and left them on the radiator. Barefoot, I followed him to the kitchen. Over milk and sugar cookies, produced from a package by Mrs. Peckengill, he explained his plan. "I'll be leader. You'll be number two in our gang." As he spoke, he looked at me with the same expression I'd seen on his face that morning. It was clear he expected my agreement, and he was right. I hadn't a thought of rebellion. Our gang! My mouth full of cookie, I nodded.

Each school afternoon that week, we played burglars or red Indians or pirates. I did not know what pirates were and had to have them explained to me. We crept about in the snow-crusted yard or, indoors, crawled through rooms and even closets, always in dire peril. We rescued one another from enemies conjured up by Bobby, were kidnapped and wounded, but never defeated. Bobby discovered that we could get out onto the forbidden sleeping porch by climbing through the small, high bathroom window that opened onto the porch. To do so we had to stand on the rim of the tub and hoist ourselves up over the sill. In Bobby's presence I forgot my fear of the place. Once we'd made it through and crashed down onto the floor of the chilly porch, we could worm our way over and under the chairs and tables and chests, most of them covered with the dust sheets. I got filthy, but afterwards, instead of scolding me, Mrs. Peckengill merely threw my clothes into the wash pile at the foot of the basement stairs.

At the far end of the porch it was possible to reenter the warm, livable part of the house through a back door into my mother's very large closet. What this door served for in adult life I could not imagine. A couple of years later during a complicated kidnap and rescue game with Lucy and Boom, I would arrive via this route in my parents' bedroom, confronting to my surprise my mother and Uncle Fitz. My mother would actually be in the bed, lying as she often did beneath the flowered bedspread; her hand pressing a folded washcloth to her forehead. Uncle Fitz, in his brown leather jacket, would be seated on the far side of the bed, the way my father sometimes sat beside me. Uncle Fitz, however, would not look as if he was delivering a scolding or a prayer. His head would be inclined toward my mother as though he was sorry she had got so tired, and he would be holding her free hand in both of his.

Afterwards I would be able to remember in detail my mother's bare arm, dimpled at the elbow. I would recall too the scuffed leather of Uncle Fitz's jacket, scratched pale in patches like the toes of my shoes, and the way his hands enclosed and obscured my mother's hand. But I would have no memory of whether I'd left the room by the door into the hall or whether I'd retreated the way I had come. My only other memory would be of how sometime later, possibly on that same day, Uncle Fitz walked with me to the drugstore where he bought us both ice cream cones. On the way home, while I licked through the ripples of chocolate and got my hand all sticky, he explained that I mustn't tell anyone about my mother's sadness, especially not my father, as he might become very angry. It would be better from time to time, when my mother had one of her sadnesses, if no one knew that Uncle Fitz came to comfort her. I had little idea what Uncle Fitz meant about my mother and her sadness, but my father flying into a fury over just about anything was easy to imagine.

All this, however, and the promise of silence I would make and keep lay in the unmet future.

On that first evening of Bobby and Mrs. Peckengill's residence in our house, the lights in the house and the sounds and smells coming from the kitchen made life seem, although not normal, entirely comfy. When I peered around the door into the kitchen, it was not my mother but Mrs. Peckengill who looked up from peeling carrots. She did not say, "Oh, there you are, darling," in a weary, musical voice the way my mother would have. But she smiled, and as she did so her cheeks bunched into round red balls. Behind her glasses, her eyes were dark and calm like Bobby's.

"Your father's not coming home to supper," she told me. "Going straight to the hospital to see your mother. He's called and said he'll get his supper there." I accepted this news with happiness. Bobby would not be leaving yet. It did not occur to me to ask about my mother's condition. Where she was and how she was were matters for grown-ups. She had been away before, visiting my grandmother and also friends in New York. She would be back, I assumed, when the grown-ups decided it would be so.

That night and the next, Mrs. Peckengill and Bobby slept in the guest room. He and I were put to bed before my father came home, and I must have fallen asleep quickly because I didn't hear my father come in at all. The third night, though, my father came home well in advance of my bedtime. We had eaten supper a while before, and Mrs. Peckengill was finishing the dishes, with me and Bobby wiping the glasses and the silverware, something I had not done before and felt quite important about.

My father appeared in the doorway, briefcase still in hand, the evening paper tucked under his arm. "Well," he said surveying us, "I'm glad to see you have the children doing useful work."

"Oh, yes indeed," said Mrs Peckengill, placing a dripping plate in the dish rack. "My Bobby here's real useful at home. Never too early to teach 'em good habits."

"True," said my father. "Very true."

"Your Susannah's a good girl too."

"Well," my father said again, glancing from me to Bobby. "Well, we do try, her mother and I. A child needs a firm hand, principles." Mrs. Peckengill said nothing, but she wiped her soapy hand and laid it on my shoulder. The hand felt warm, and I had the unusual sense of being protected, as if she'd noticed something I hadn't and was fending off trouble for me.

"I make sure Susannah understands her transgressions," my father added.

A wave of something like electricity passed through me, and I stared at the floor. What I wanted to do was lift my head and scream so powerfully and so long that it would drive my father out of the kitchen and even out of the house. At the same time I wanted to turn and throw my arms around Mrs. Peckengill's ample hips, as far around as I could throw them at any rate, and never let go. While I was still standing there, eyes fixed on the linoleum, willing myself not to move, I heard him head up the stairs. Only then did her hand leave my shoulder.

"Mine's kind of wet, Mom." It was Bobby's voice. He was holding out his limp towel.

"So it is," said Mrs. Peckengill. "Give it here." She took the towel from him, handed him another, and we went back to drying dishes.

As soon as we had finished, Mrs. Peckengill too went upstairs. Bobby and I walked out to the hall and stood together in silence until my father came back downstairs, followed shortly by Mrs. Peckengill. He had taken off his tie and suit jacket and was wearing a sweater instead. She was carrying a small suitcase and a purple carpetbag that I knew held her knitting. At the foot of the stairs, she turned to my father.

"Be back in time to get you up a good breakfast, sir," she said to him, and sticking out her sturdy, thick-fingered hand, she seized my father's long one and shook it as if they were both men. I saw the surprised look on his face before he nodded down at her and gave her hand a return shake. For another minute they discussed which train he planned to take in the morning and exactly what time she would return. Then he helped her on with her coat. All through this flurry of our parents' changing of the guard, Bobby and I did not chat or say goodbye. We knew how things stood. We were children. He had to go; I had to stay. That was all.

When he and his mother had gone out into the darkness, my father shut the front door and shot the big brass bolt. Around us the house loomed suddenly large and empty. My father dusted the palms of his hands together as if they'd gotten dirty from the bolt. "She seems an efficient woman," he remarked and headed for the kitchen.

I followed him. He was washing his hands at the kitchen sink. After Mrs. Peckengill's heft, his lean frame seemed out of place. As he bent to get the towel out from under the sink, I could see the white line of his part bisecting his dark head. In those days men like my father who took the train downtown and worked in offices and laboratories wore their hair slicked down against their skulls. After he had dried his hands, he took from the oven the plateful of supper Mrs. Peckengill had left for him and carried it out to the dining room. His voice called, "Susannah, come in here and sit with me."

I went. He had seated himself at our dark wood table where, earlier, Mrs. Peckengill had set out a crocheted place mat with fork and knife and napkin. I slipped into the chair opposite him. On the table sat a plate of the same sugar cookies Bobby and I had had in the afternoon. They were store-bought, the kind my mother would have scorned. But Mrs. Peckengill was in charge of our shopping these days, and she had bought sugar cookies, and they'd tasted fine. I was wondering if I would be allowed to take one now. My father was slicing meat from the bone of his chop, carefully, with his long, thin fingers holding the knife like a razor, then cutting off the gristle and most of the ridges of fat and setting them aside as though he were separating wrong from right. His plate held the same canned peas and mashed potatoes that we had eaten for supper, so very long ago, it now seemed. When he looked over at me, his face still had the concentrated expression he'd had just now when he'd been cutting the meat. I kept my hands in my lap, grateful that I had not had my elbows on the table. Still, I could feel something coming.

"You don't ask about your mother?" said my father. "Aren't you worried about her?"

"No, Daddy," I answered honestly. Worry had to do with being caught and beaten up by the bigger girls or boys in the schoolyard or with the possibility of being punished at school or my father himself flying into a rage. My mother would be back, I assumed, just as she had come back from her trips. I had to wait. That's what children generally had to do, in my experience.

I saw his lips go flat against his teeth. I stopped breathing. "Your mother is extremely sick," he said, enunciating each word as if he were slapping me with it. "She has pneumonia. It is possible we may lose her."

I did not know what to say to this. There had been the doctor and my father, the correct grown-ups to take charge. Had my sick mother nonetheless been somehow lost, left in a place that was not the hospital, put into the wrong bed where no one could find her? It didn't occur to me to ask what pneumonia was.

"Your mother was very sick after you were born," he said then. I had not known this. "Her lungs," he was still speaking in the taut voice, ". . . are not strong. Your mother is not strong." He paused, his eyes on my face, and I understood that her absence of strength was my fault. My birth, my existence, had weakened her. Something about me, my will to resist, my intrinsic failure to be what I should be, continued to exhaust her.

At this point the unthinkable happened. My father's face flushed. He began to blink, and all at once tears were running down his long flat cheeks. He put his hand over his eyes. "Pray for your mother," he said in a thick voice, quite unlike the one he had just used. Astonished, I stared at him. He was crying. My father. There was a long silence broken only by the sounds my father made. Finally, he took his hand from his eyes and wiped his face with his napkin; then he took his big white handkerchief from his pocket and blew his nose. His nose and lips remained pink, but no more tears spilled from his eyes. His gaze settled on me again. He still wanted something, but I had no notion of what to do or say. Finally, after what seemed like several minutes, he picked up his knife and fork. As he did so, I reached for a cookie.

The crash was like a hammer hitting the table. Peas leapt off his dinner plate and went rolling across the table. I could see the dent where his fist with the knife in it had struck the wood. "You coldhearted child," he shouted. I shrank back blinded by panic. The cookie broke apart in my hand, spilling crumbs and sugar onto the table. His voice was going on. "Your mother in the hospital . . . selfish . . . no thought for anyone but yourself. . . ." And the worst of all, "You exhaust your mother . . . you wear her out." The very thing she said to me so often that I could almost hear her voice now underneath his. By the time he ordered me to my room, I, like him, had stopped shedding tears. Instead, I was filled with rage. At him, and at myself. How had I failed to catch the fatal sign that he was testing me? It was clear I should have said I was worried about my mother. And the cookie had been a fatal mistake too, though I had no idea why.

That I was selfish, deep down, bone-selfish, I did not doubt. I had been told so many times. And it was true. I did care more about myself than about anyone else. I could imagine no way to change that. I hadn't worried about my mother being sick either. People got sick. I got sick. Sometimes the doctor came, and I had to swallow horrid syrups. Eventually I got well. People always got well except for when children got polio and died or got put in iron lungs, but that was only in summer.

The thought of my mother lost had shaken me—I had nearly gotten lost in the train station the previous year, and I had been frightened—but just now my father had said she was in the hospital, so he did know where she was. She would be back therefore, the way she'd come back after each of her trips to visit my grandmother and to visit her friends in New York City. I had missed her before, and I would certainly have missed her this time, except that fate had brought me Mrs. Peckengill and with her, Bobby, the perfect playmate.

I did not see my mother for another ten days. On Saturday I was sent to a neighbor's house so my father could go to work for the morning and again on Sunday so that he could drive downtown to the hospital. Come Monday, Mrs. Peckengill and Bobby returned. All that week I ate my eggs scrambled and, when we had enough rationing coupons, bacon as well, and every afternoon I rushed home from school to play with Bobby. He and I went to China that week and stole jewels from evil kings. Each evening when I saw my father, I was careful to ask how my mother was. He said that she was being given a new medicine called penicillin and that it was helping her get well.

On Sunday new snow lay on the ground and on the tree branches in our side yard. My father went out to shovel our walk and then came in to call the hospital. When he hung up, he told me that my mother was now well enough to see me.

The drive downtown took a long time and involved many roads and much traffic. Our car was quite old, a two-seater Ford that, like our rented house, we were lucky to have on account of the war and no cars being made anymore. In summer on nice days, I was allowed to ride in the car's rumble seat. My father would pull it out like a trap door from the back end of the car and then lift me in. In winter I sat on my mother's lap, though of late she had complained I was getting too heavy. Today, however, I had the inside passenger seat to myself. Before we reached the tall buildings of downtown, we drove through suburbs and for a while along the shore of our Great Lake where it ran parallel to the road. In summer my parents had sometimes taken me to the big public beach where they'd laid a blanket on the sand, weighting the corners with their shoes and a thermos of lemonade or orangeade. At the beginning my father had always headed into the water for a swim, returning after a few minutes to stretch out beside my mother on the blanket. His black hair, wet from the lake, generally stuck up in odd tufts, and my mother would then try to smooth it. I'd been allowed to build sand villages and to jump around in the cold slosh of the surf. The lake on those hot days had been a dark blue, sometimes whitecapped expanse of water that had no opposite shore but reached all the way to the sky. I had no recollection of seeing the lake the way it was now—a winter lake, grey and flat, with slabs of snow-covered ice piled like huge, broken-up pieces of sidewalk along its shore. I could imagine climbing over those slabs with Bobby while the grey water slapped at our feet.

The hospital, like most city buildings, was built smack against the sidewalk. Its huge lobby reverberated with voices and the clacking of heels on stone floors. The din and the high stone walls and the stone columns and the people hustling here and there made me think of the train station where I had been taken to greet my mother on her return from one of her trips and had temporarily lost sight of her and of my father. My father, when he'd found me, had yanked my arm and shouted at me and that night had given me one of his bedtime lectures and forced me to apologize for wandering away, though I hadn't thought I had.

Off to one side of the lobby now, I spied a bank of elevators. I was fond of elevators, especially of the magic moment when the wall slid open to reveal the small, hidden room, sometimes filled with people, sometimes empty. We did not head for the elevators, however, but toward a circular counter in the center of the lobby. There my father spoke to one of the clerks, giving him my mother's name and the floor she was on. The man repeated her name into a telephone.

"Are we going to get in one of those elevators?" I asked my father.

My father looked down at me and shook his head. "Children aren't allowed on the upper floors," he said. "People are very sick up there. Children carry more germs than adults do." I was mildly surprised by this. I knew about germs. Germs were why I was supposed to wash my hands before supper and why I had to stay away from crowds during the polio season. But surely I did not carry germs about with me. "We'll see your mother in the visitors' lounge," said my father. He sounded happy. "Someone will bring her down."

The visitors' lounge turned out to be a kind of living room, with a sofa and a rug and several armchairs. At the far end a pair of large windows let in the daylight. The room was empty of people and smelled of ammonia and of something else that reminded me of coat closets.

My father and I sat down on the sofa. After a moment he got up again and turned on a lamp, though, with the light from the windows, I could hardly tell it was lit. He began then to inspect a pile of magazines sitting on a table. While he was doing this, I scrambled off the sofa and started to explore the room. Under a magazine I found a Juicy Fruit gum wrapper and, smoothing out the crumpled yellow paper, rolled it up and made a tiny pipe like a cigarette. If my father had not been there, I would have pretended to smoke it, the way my mother smoked a cigarette once in a while in the afternoon if she didn't take her rest and instead one of her lady friends or Uncle Fitz came over and they drank tea or sometimes cocktails with cherries in them and chatted and laughed and blew out thin streams of smoke.

A few moments later, just as my father was pulling his watch from the little front pocket in his trousers, the door swung open, and a tall lady entered pushing a wheelchair. The lady had on a white dress and, riding on the top of her head, a tiny white cap like a Dixie Cup. Staring up at this cap, I did not register for a few seconds who was in the wheelchair. Then I saw the person was my mother. She was wearing the same blue bathrobe she had worn the night she left our house, and part of it was covered by a blanket that had been tucked around her legs. She had on lipstick, very bright the way it was if she had just applied it in our hall mirror, and her hair though still wavy was not so blonde as I remembered. She also seemed quite small to me. My father had already gone over to her. He leaned down, and she lifted her face for him to kiss. When he had straightened up again, I went over and put my arms around her neck and got hugged by her. In the wheelchair she was the same height I was, and I was looking straight into her face as if she were my friend instead of my mother. "Are you well now, Mommy?" I asked.

"Better, darling," she said. "I'm getting stronger. Getting there slowly." She closed her eyes then and leaned her head back against the wheelchair as though it was suddenly too much effort for her to hold her head up straight. When she reopened her eyes, she glanced up and held out a hand to my father, who reached down and took it.

We stayed in that room for what seemed quite a while. While my parents talked, I walked around the room some more. At one point I thought of telling my mother about Bobby, but in her presence his existence seemed unreal, as if he and she lived in separate worlds and, no matter how hard I explained, would understand nothing of one another.

"Be good, darling," my mother said to me at the end of our visit. She hugged me again, and again it felt as if someone else, not my mother, were hugging me.

The lady in white wheeled my mother out of the visitors' lounge and across the lobby, with my father and me following along behind. It was as though my mother belonged here in the hospital now and we would always be her visitors.

By the time she had disappeared into one of the elevators, my stomach had begun rumbling. My father must have heard it or else he was hungry too, because he took me to a little restaurant in the hospital and bought me an egg salad sandwich and a chocolate milk shake. The food was served to us by two ladies in pink dresses and white aprons. They both smiled at him a good deal, and one of them referred to me as "your dear little girl." He was nice to me while we ate, telling me to wipe my mouth in a distracted but not angry way, and nice on the way home in the car, too. Sitting beside him in the front seat, I felt, as I had on that night with him and the doctor, that I was safe inside another period of immunity. All the rest of the way home, while I looked out the window at the downtown buildings and the lake and then at the miles and miles of houses and snow-covered yards, I basked in the glow of that immunity.

The next morning when I came down to breakfast, Bobby and Mrs. Peckengill were back. Bobby was wearing new lace-up shoes and knickers with long, thick socks like most of the boys in my school. He seemed pleased to hear of the resemblance. I spent part of breakfast telling him what the hospital had been like, dwelling on my mother's wheelchair and the little restaurant. He listened carefully, and I felt I had raised myself a notch in his eyes. He told me that he had once been to a hospital too. The hospital had been a dog hospital rather than a people hospital. He and his mother and his uncle and his uncle's dog had driven there in his uncle's car.

The dog had gotten a piece of glass embedded in his leg. "He kept chewing it in the car, and my mom had to tie her sweater over his leg, and then he chewed that. And he was drooling a lot too." The uncle, Bobby said, had driven very fast.

At the hospital, the dog doctor had given the dog a shot and then removed the piece of glass. Afterwards he had sewn the dog's skin together over the wound with a needle and black thread. While all this was going on, Bobby's uncle had thrown up in the dog doctor's sink.

"Uncle Charlie wasn't used to it is all," said Mrs. Peckengill. She popped the toast out of the toaster. "That's how it takes some people. The sight of blood." Buttering the pieces of toast, she handed us each one.

I took my warm piece. Bobby's stunning story had so topped mine that I did not resent it, but I had nearly forgotten to eat. Bobby passed me the jam. "He's a pretty nice dog," he said thoughtfully.

A few mornings later, after my father had left for work, Bobby pulled a small, white cardboard box from his pocket and put it down on the kitchen table beside his milk glass. The box had a cover and was the kind I saved for doll-house tables. All through breakfast he wouldn't show me what was in the little box, but as I was finishing my milk, he took the top off so I could see that inside was a Kleenex folded into a tiny square. He unwrapped it fold by fold to reveal two small, curved pieces of what looked like very thin china. The pieces were a beautiful green-blue on their convex side and white on their concave side. Their edges were jagged.

"Guess," he said, but I couldn't. I shook my head. "Robin's egg," he said. "I found them last summer. Under the tree at our corner. There was a nest in it, way up high. The babies don't need the shells anymore when they're hatched out." He glanced toward his mother, who had her back to us but nonetheless nodded her head.

I fingered one piece. It was perfectly smooth, cool to touch, and exceedingly sharp on the edges. The color was the most beautiful I had ever beheld. Eggs were not in my experience either beautiful or interesting. Out of them came only egg yolk and egg white, firm and opaque or runny and transparent to be sure, but never any sort of baby bird. I knew that eggs came from hens, but baby birds, including the fluffy chicks that appeared in the pet store window at Easter, had not seemed connected.

"One of them's for you. The other's mine," said Bobby.

I picked up one of the pieces. "No," said Bobby. "The other one." I put down the first piece and picked up the second, the one that was mine. I turned it and turned it feeling the sharp edges against my fingertips. The blue-green color was so beautiful it made an ache inside my stomach, the way ice cream made an ache in my jaw.

"You can't tell," he said. "Not anyone. Do you swear?"

I nodded. "I swear."

"And you can't show it to any other kids." He sounded already dubious about his decision to give me the piece of shell.

"I won't," I said. "I promise." Setting down the piece of shell, I went back to finishing my toast. If someone had asked, I would not have said that I was touched or moved by the gift. Such feelings did not yet exist for me. I was not even precisely pleased by it in the way I would have been by, say, a new dress for my doll or a piece of furniture for my dollhouse. But I understood that I had been honored, and honored in a way that did not seem to have anything to do with either of us being a child.

Two days later on Saturday morning, my father and I drove through a wet, swirling snowstorm to the city and this time brought my mother home with us. I did not see Bobby or Mrs. Peckengill again. He and I had not said good-bye on the previous evening nor in any way considered the issue of our coming separation. The world with Bobby and his mother in it was simply gone, and my old world was back.

In our house, life would go on in the same way as it had before my mother's pneumonia. Without Bobby I would renew my relationship with Lucy and Boom. The demon lethargy would return from time to time to settle its weight on me. My father would continue to generate his inexplicable rages. Yet there were certain differences. Expanding on our tea-party repertoire, I would sometimes lead Lucy and Boom on expeditions through mountains and secret castles in all parts of our house and yard. In the schoolyard I would dare for the first time to climb onto the top rungs of the jungle gym and to join a pack of my classmates in an ongoing game of wild horses. This game involved galloping all over the schoolyard, and previously I had been afraid of the shouting and jostling. Back home there was another difference as well, and I discovered it almost immediately.

On the Sunday morning after my mother's return, the snow had stopped. The sun glared through our winter-streaked storm windows, casting a rectangle of light across the dining room table. I could feel the warmth of it as we sat there eating breakfast—fried eggs and crisp, dry bacon, milk for me and coffee for my parents.

I was having a hard time with the bacon. It tended to shatter under the pressure of the knife, and I had just managed to fork a few salty shards into my mouth when my father turned to me and said. "You must be happy to have Mommy back, Susannah. You must have missed her."

It was in my mind to shake my head candidly, to say, no, I had not missed her. But right then, a shadow of warning stopped the words in my throat. I looked at him across the window of light emblazoned on the table. "Yes," I said, my eyes widening with untruth. "Yes. I missed Mommy."

He nodded and glanced over at my mother, who was sipping her coffee. She had eaten only part of her fried egg and had a moment ago declared that she could stay with us only a few more minutes before she needed to go lie down. Her head had drooped a little to one side as she had said this, and I'd seen the look of worry come over my father's face. That had been just before he'd asked me about missing her. Now she set down her cup and smiled at him. He smiled back at her, and I saw that my forced admission had been his gift to her.

In the years to come, my father would remain deep in the thrall of my mother, always ready to protect and guard her against all possible harm, his anger part of his weaponry, his devotion unshakable. Uncle Fitz, too, would go on listening to her sadnesses and drinking cocktails with her and making her laugh. He and my father would continue their Saturday afternoon badminton games as well, and Uncle Fitz would remain our neighbor, even when, after the war and before the next one in Korea, we bought a house in a suburb further north of the city and moved out of Mr. Meese's house. Uncle Fitz's own new house, smaller and more modern than ours, suitable for a bachelor, would lie just down the street within sight of our new living room window.

But sitting in the dining room on that glittering Sunday morning at the end of my seventh winter, I knew nothing of the future. What I knew was that I had been happy with Bobby and Mrs. Peckengill and I had not missed my mother. Glancing from parent to parent, protected by my lie, I knew too that I must hold the truth of all this and much more inside me forever, the way I would keep my piece of robin's eggshell hidden forever. The possession made a dark, unholy place somewhere deep inside me, a place where I could keep all that I saw and divined and understood.

CATHERINE HARNETT

Her Gorgeous Grief

SINCE YOU ASKED, I will tell you this: my mother did seek out calamities, listening for the tragic noise that led her there, to those gatherings of grief I came to know when I was young.

The days would start with her waking me from my deepest part of sleep, telling me in her urgent way that we needed to go, emphatically, now. I would dress quickly in the dark, not in the school uniform I'd laid out the night before, but in whatever I could gather from my drawers that seemed to match: jeans, the pullover, my zippered jacket for the long, cold trip to where this time? I had learned the set routine: ask nothing, crumple my still warm pajamas into the shopping bag kept under my bed, three pairs of underwear, another top, one more pair of pants and go, quietly into the cold, starred night where my mother warmed the car, its headlights off, till we were long gone down the block.

When I'd return to school in a few days, I'd bring a note which claimed strep throat, or a cold, or a sudden family death. Exhausted, I would try to find my place again in mathematics, having missed the crucial steps that day we traveled hundreds of miles to the place that girl had disappeared, or the executed man shivered one last time.

I would sleep in the back seat until the morning light shone in as my mother smoked her cigarettes and listened to the news. Years later I would recall this repeated scene as I rode in the back of a taxicab while the driver sought news of traffic jams, bringing it all back, the certain sound of AM radio.

We would stop for breakfast in a diner or a pancake house, lingering for only a short time because of the urgency, she said, of getting there as soon as possible. Her vocabulary, full of words like *arraigned, adjudicate, abduct* amazed me, how my mother rattled off these terms like other mothers could recite ingredients for cakes. She navigated highways and strange rural roads while other mothers drove to baseball games and home.

My mother was always put together well on these occasions, her Coty lipstick neat and pink, her ample dress coat and kerchief. On our outings she would wear high heels and hose, despite the long drives we took, as if we were headed to a sorority reunion or a dinner date.

There were so many trips, it is hard to remember them all, their particulars. When I look back I count perhaps eighteen or so, but they are jumbled and some indistinct from one another. All of our ventures ended in towns or cities across New York or Jersey, and each involved some kind of tragedy: a missing wife, a kidnapped child, house fires, homicides, a hanged college kid. Each trip was a pilgrimage, of sorts, a haj to the scene of the crime, or the home of the disappeared.

She would learn of misfortune by thoroughly combing newspapers she read at the town library each day while I was in school. For several hours my mother would read the *Post*, the *Record*, the *Sun*, the *News*, the *Journal*, and every local weekly she could find in the periodicals section. What the regular librarians thought of her I do not know; if they found her conscientious or eccentric, their opinions never made it back to me. All I know is that she copied down the names at the center of these tragedies, the addresses of the funeral homes, the makeshift rescue centers, churches where vigils were being held, courtrooms where the victims' cases were heard.

With characteristic precision, my mother would gaze at maps and plot our routes, though I saw evidence of this only after the fact, during our journeys when I would sit up front with her as she drove. Each time she created a file with a label she bought at the stationer's across the street from St. Genevieve's. The file would be marked with the name of the deceased, the missing, the accused. She would have Xeroxed articles and photographs, marking particular paragraphs and details. Once I read while she drove, drawn to the highlighted yellow lines written about the young scout who disappeared while delivering papers on his rural route. "At night, Timothy's dog, a black-and-white spaniel, sits by the front door, waiting. Timothy's aunt, Adrienne, says quietly 'they are the best of friends,' a tear rolling down her tired cheek." In the folder was my mother's to-do list along with the directions to the search headquarters: bring flat walking shoes, flashlight, buy dog bones.

When I asked my mother how long it would take to get to Timothy's, she replied, "As long as it takes." She reached over and squeezed my knee, and smiled, asking me to quiz her on the contents of the file. "Okay," she said, "ask me how old he was—or is, I should have said. How tall. What he was wearing when he disappeared. His favorite TV show." The list went on and on until she had exhausted every published fact, recited every aspect of his photograph.

Timothy was two years younger than I, his blond crew cut and light eyes staring back at me as I studied his face. This morning we would drive an hour past Albany to the VFW Hall, where volunteers assembled, photocopying fly-ers, assigning routes for searches through the woods, waiting for leads. When we arrived, hours past my normal lunchtime, my mother parked the car and sighed. "We're here," she'd say, as she did at every destination, and she'd read-just the mirror. "God, I look beat," she'd sigh, applying fresh lipstick and run-ning a brush through her hair. I wondered what the kids at school were doing now, the girl who sat next to me, dangling her skinny legs and writing on her hand with her bright green Flair. They were winding down their day as mine was grinding on, beginning in earnest now.

My mother made me neaten up, made sure my hair was combed and tame, wiped the pancake syrup from my chin. "There," she said. "Let's go."

Every time she arrived at the scene, whether a candlelight vigil where posters of the gone would be illuminated in the evening chill, a line of griev-ing visitors leaving flowers at the blood-soaked corner where a struggle had taken place, or now, in this hall; when she arrived she seemed to be familiar with the others who had come, seemed a piece of each community, the vic-tim's intimate. As she arrived at the appointed place, my hand slipped from hers, no longer her accomplice. I sat quietly in the corner of the hall as she consulted with the search leader on the route to take, and with which crew. I had learned from many of these trips to bring homework, books, a deck of cards to amuse myself, sometimes for three days.

She disappeared into the cold November afternoon, her map in hand. She had never looked so beautiful to me.

On evenings after afternoons like these, after the volunteers were fed, she and I would return to the car. We had the whole parking lot to ourselves; we'd bundle tight our clothes, prepared for the cold night of semi-sleep. Put your head on my lap, sweetie, she would say, and stroke my hair until she fell asleep, bone tired from the drive, from hours in the spangled woods.

I was afraid to move, once she slept, and I listened for hours to the sound of cars passing, to the long freight trains that crossed the parallels of night, in-sistent on their routes, regardless of this town's most recent tragedy.

I never remember good news arriving while we inhabited those strange, tense villages, no relief. The next morning I overheard that hunters came across the small pale boy, his canvas newspaper pouch covering his stunned blond head, tucked among the leaves of oaks and maple trees. "Oh how sad," my mother said, as she sobbed. "That little boy, how lonely his dog will be." A local reporter comforted her as she wept, his photographer capturing her gorgeous grief. Weeks later she would show me the grainy photograph she'd come across as she scoured papers at the long wooden library table, the article describing an unidentified woman's reaction to the grim discovery of Timothy Blake's remains.

There were several incidents that occurred during our many excursions, most of them involving my mother, all requiring that we quickly leave the other searchers and mourners without so much as a goodbye. But I once created an inopportune disturbance in a forgettable upstate town when I developed a fever of 104 degrees and began vomiting at the scene of Carolee Malone's brutal murder. Her beautician friends created a shrine in front of her duplex, where hundreds of flowers and several handwritten goodbyes diminished in the days of unrelenting rain. My mother expressed her deep chagrin at having to leave before Carolee's aging father arrived to plead with his daughter's killer, most likely that man she had been seeing behind her husband's back. She hurried me into our car, felt my forehead and let out a sound like despair, handed me an empty potato chip bag and told me to try to hold it in as best I could. I don't remember much of the long drive home that night, except for the persistent chills and nausea that have revisited me several times in my life since, always recalling the utter loneliness I experienced in the back seat that night, my mother's cigarette smoke blue and obstinate in the winter air.

On those occasions when we had to leave suddenly or silently on her account, my mother would flush with excitement and speak cryptically to me, her sentences spare and hurried. I rarely knew the particulars but caught fragments as she muttered something about the victim's family demanding to know who she was, or the investigating cop asking her to recall details of the victim's life. People often supposed that she was on intimate terms with the victim, or the executed, or at least with grief, and on that point I believed it too. It was real and palpable, her grief, and she bathed herself in sadness publicly, in its shared, overwhelming waters.

We'd leave quickly, the two of us on the lam, the way I imagined jewel thieves felt after a heist. We sped through towns one by one with their closed factories and signs announcing we entered and then left places where secrets would often lie buried with the gone. We longed for the smell and sheets of our own beds, and as we made our way towards home, I imagined the skeptical look my teacher would give me in the morning when I tendered yet another note. My mother turned the headlights off as she rounded the corner of our street and crept quietly into the driveway and its protective dark.

But there was nothing like the circumstances surrounding our last trip, the one involving that young mother with the beautiful Italian name.

I did not want to go that morning, early, when my mother woke me before dawn. I had a test that day, one that counted for the biggest portion of my grade that year, and I had studied hard for it. "You can make it up," she said. "Get dressed." While I protested, she pulled me from bed and said again, more firmly now, "Get dressed."

She hurriedly grabbed her papers, gloves, keys, tucked a stray hair behind her ear, and looked sternly at me. Nothing inside me wanted to make another long drive, to miss school, to sit playing solitaire for hours in the corner of a room I would never see again, in a town I hoped I'd never sleep in one more time.

It seemed my mother smoked more during that drive than she did ordinarily, rapidly switching stations on the radio even before the songs were over, looked impatiently in the rearview and pursed her lips. I watched the empty roads pass quickly by, the farms, the just-beginning light. I prayed inside that this time would be quick.

For some reason, perhaps the suddenness of this trip, perhaps my mother's mood, she never asked me to read her articles, or quiz her. Instead, while she hurried into the service station to ask directions after half an hour's aimless drive, I glanced at the front page of yesterday's *Newsday* which arrived each day at four o'clock. There was no map in her file, and all I saw was a photograph of the dark-haired woman, smiling, with three young children on a couch. My mother strode back towards the car, her face expressionless and worn. "Let's go," she said.

During the remainder of the journey, as my mother focused on the exit signs and landmarks the attendant had described, she talked softly to herself, distracted and concerned. "Poor Angela," she said, "didn't anyone see the warning signs? No one gave her help, the poor girl, no one. My God, it could happen to any of us," and her voice trailed off. I didn't dare ask her what she said, since she had forgotten breakfast for me, and it seemed pointless to make myself known to her.

We arrived at the place she was called to, seemingly out of a dark sleep, the place she was meant to be. This small town—its A&P, its pizza parlor, the Catholic church looming on the avenue, the railroad station where fathers left each morning in the dark, returning in the evening dark, bringing back the city's soot and salaries—this small town bred Angela, and all that happened.

"You're on your own," my mother said, "but don't go far." In the parking lot she smoothed her coat and checked her lipstick one last time before she joined the crowd waiting to enter the church. This time was different in a way; you could tell that something else had happened, something people rarely talked about.

I watched my mother on the steps of St. Rita's, her cheeks flushed with the color that she had in her face when in the fall we walked to school, her blue eyes bright, expectant. Her distraction lifted; she seemed different from the woman in the car, the one who seemed to keep her own secrets, loving each of them as she opened and shut them tight during our long drive that morning.

I am not sure what possessed me this time, after all my obedience, after my practiced invisibility. I waited for the long line of mourners to fill the church and watched from the car for just the right moment. The closed church doors were heavy, and I opened one slowly, overwhelmed by the smell of benediction and burning candles, that sweet devout smell that is like no other. The church was quiet except for the mournful organ and the rustling sound adults made at times like this. I watched from the very back of the church, wondering where my mother was sitting, and with whom. From the back, hundreds of women looked like my mother, bent kneeling with bowed heads, kerchiefs or chapel veils covering their heads.

At the front of the church there were three small white coffins, each strewn with carnations and greens. Each perched on small gurneys, ready to be offered into the earth in just over an hour, the small holes taking them in for their long forever sleep. I was terribly confused: where was Angela, hadn't tragedy befallen her, hadn't someone come up from behind her, sliced her neck or suffocated her as she slept? Who were these small white ghosts contained in boxes, did the same man who harmed Angela take these three too? Perhaps we were at the wrong event, perhaps Angela's would follow.

I am not sure when it all came clear to me; it could have been days later, or two hours, but when I focused on the facts I could not comprehend how or why their mother took their breath away, how she had driven to the river and had locked the doors, had let the car roll down the pier and watched it disappear, the slow maroon of it. Angela who will never see this town again, until she becomes a part of its dirt, who will never be that young mother, hushing three small boys in the pizza parlor on a summer afternoon. Who will never put them to bed again, exhausted from her day, who will never sleep next to the man who gave them over to her keep. And my mother, who understood.

There are nights now when I do not sleep and listen for sounds, for any little thing, for portents. I sit and think, drinking tea and watching the clock. I check on my spouse who takes up half the bed and sometimes more; on my children, the boy and the girl, each in a decorated room, and I remember them all, the ones who are somewhere else now. When I cannot sleep, I watch TV and for hours and hours become steeped in the details of today's missing girls, the accused husband, the young woman who left her apartment and never returned, her bones found a year later, peaceful in the park. See the parents weeping, the best friends, neighbors who saw nothing strange, and we can visit with them at all hours over and again, footage flickering during our long insomniac nights. What my mother did was hard, seeking them out, not waiting for this grief to be delivered, virtual and cold. She traveled far and felt it close and beating, fear, uncertainty and loss, their photographs, their preferences, the pets they left behind, and knew them all. She seems always at my side, especially on these long nights, saying nothing but reminding me of the power of my own hands, the way things turn in an instant, what can be done and what can never be undone.

JOHN McCORMICK

In the Meantime

———m———

I believe that history, properly undertaken, is the
record not of what happened but of what mattered.
—*Douglas Jerrold,* An Introduction
to the History of England from
Earliest Times to 1204

LATE AUGUST 1932. My father and I stood facing each other on a street corner in St. Paul, Minnesota. I would turn fifteen in three weeks; although he
was no more than fifty-two, he looked much older, frowning and troubled.
"I've got ten dollars," he said, "and that's all I've got." He rummaged in his
wallet. "Here's five. I'm sorry it isn't more."

"That's all right. It's plenty. I won't need much."

We shook hands, and he wished me luck. "Don't forget to write," he
called after me as I walked away, lugging my things in an old suitcase of his.
I pretended not to hear; I wanted to get out of sight of his old once-fine suit
and eternal brown hat to cover his baldness. I felt simply glad to be on my
way, on my own, away from his gloom and silences and away from his attempt to "make a home" for me. I was on my way to the state fairgrounds and
a job that would pay me eight dollars a week and get me out of the depres-
sion-ridden, hateful State of Minnesota. I was free. But then I remembered
that I had no address to which to write, for the good reason that my father
had no address as of that morning. We had read the *Odyssey* in school, and
I thought of Telemachus trying to find his father, while I was trying to get
away from mine.

In his efforts to eke out a living by selling houses, my father had met a
German-born widow with a house to sell. No buyers appeared, but one day

348

my father announced to me after school that he was going to be married to the German woman and move into her house. It was time I had a real home in place of the series of hotels and rooming houses we had lived in. I didn't like the woman from day one; she smelled of nervous sweat and cologne water. It was obvious to me that she didn't care for me, either. In the new household I was required to run the vacuum cleaner, wash dishes, and go to the shops for food. In the center of her dining room table a hideous cut-glass bowl was mounted on a cut-glass pediment. While vacuuming one day, I tilted the table, unintentionally, causing the cut-glass bowl to totter and fall, shattering like a dropped light bulb. The German, as I thought of her, didn't just weep, she bawled, accusing me of maliciously breaking her bowl, a wedding present from her previous marriage.

A month or so later on my way to the grocery store, I fell on the ice, and when I looked for the five-dollar bill the German had given me to pay, it was gone. I went back to where I had fallen but found only snowbanks, the clanking snow chains of an occasional passing car, and a sharp wind. This time the German wept tears of rage as she accused me of stealing her money. Believing that he had resolved the dilemma my existence was to him, my father refused to see that a civil war was taking place under his nose. Occasionally there would be a truce. In one such period I asked the German to teach me to speak her language. She was uneducated, speaking English with an accent. She was embarrassed by my request; a typical immigrant, she wanted to forget her birthplace and her mother tongue and be a good citizen among the other German immigrants of St. Paul, Minnesota. "You should not sit reading books," she would say. "You should go out and see the city." A nervous woman, she would sit in her black or grey dress, wringing her hands and frequently adjusting her eyeglasses.

If this is having a mother, leave me out, I thought. Before the first year of their marriage was up, separation and divorce were in the wind. I cannot be certain, but I think that without actually lying, my father had conveyed to the German by talk of big deals in the offing, by his daily cigars and by his Californian tailored suits that he was a man of means. He in turn seemed to think that the German had been left a tidy sum by the deceased, which sum no longer existed, if it ever did have any reality. Nor can I be certain that the German actually turned my father and me out of the house, but I think she did. Toward the end she wept continually and refused to speak to either of us. To me leaving that house was salvation from suffocation.

From my limited and selfish point of view, my father's marital disaster had one positive result. The German had a married daughter, Laura, who let rooms in her house near the fairgrounds to fair people who turned up in early

September, just before the annual state fair. Laura was kind to me; she had tried to teach me to waltz and provided occasional respite from the German's household. Laura treated me like an equal, an adult, and introduced me to one of her annual tenants, a Texan who traveled the country with all the apparatus of a bingo game on a ton-and-a-half truck. I begged him for a job, and he took me on, mainly, I think, to oblige Laura, who probably was more to him than landlady. Whatever his motive, I was and remain grateful to him for opening layers of the world, the existence of which I had had no clue.

I had sat as a spectator in the theater of adult life from early childhood, and had read about it from the time I was old enough to have a library card, but now I was immersed in that longed-for state from the first hour of my new job. Hank Myers, who turned out to be the foreman of the gang of four, had arrived at the fairgrounds the night before with the truck. The great tent had to be unloaded and set up, the benches and plank counters put in place, and the prizes placed temptingly on a kind of dais, above which Mr. Gray, our boss, would sit before a microphone, calling numbers drawn from a box when the whole affair was up and running. At first I called him Mr. Gray, but later he said I was to call him Gray, like the others. Jim, Stan, and I would sell cards to the gamblers for five cents and distribute small piles of corn grains to be placed on the numbers Gray called. The really high rollers would play two or even three cards at a time. When someone finally had five numbers in a row, he would shout "Bingo," and Hank would then verify the card by calling the numbers back to Gray, and the lucky winner would select a blanket, a kewpie doll, or a plaster bulldog for his prize. It was all simpleminded, straightforward, and, as I was soon to learn, unlike many games at the fairs and carnivals we worked, it was honest.

The day ran from seven in the morning to midnight or 1:00 A.M. We slept under the tent on pallets made of packaged prize blankets, covering ourselves with ones already opened. Those sleazy blankets could not keep out the cold as the fall nights chilled away the summer heat. I would wash in the fairground toilets, eat some bread, and go to work dusting the benches and folding the blankets, which would go as prizes during the day. By nine o'clock the mechanical organs on the rides would begin blaring, the Ferris wheel would turn, and the farm hands would be feeding and currying the prize animals on display. At first it seemed like real, glamorous life to me, but in a few days the endless, repetitious noise became annoying and the early September heat made the day long. Often a farm family—man, wife, and half-grown children—would stop at our tent, debating whether to invest their nickels in the chance of winning a needed blanket. More often than not the man or his wife would nod no, and they would pass on to the next stall with its clicking wheel and prize ham hanging before them to be won.

"Don't let those people get away," Gray would tell us. "Call 'em in, sell 'em."

Hank was good at barking, the carnival term for calling 'em in. He had been working the fairs for five or six years and knew carny lingo. "Take the load off your feet," he would bawl. "Only a nickel for one of these gorgeous prizes," and he would gesture like a Renaissance courtier at the gilded dolls. Sometimes I would try to imitate him, but I was uneasy and self-conscious.

The Minnesota State Fair was easier to work than briefer fairs. It went on for two weeks, so that there were slack times when we could sit down and talk. I mostly listened to the others, who did not talk down to me but nonetheless helped me learn how to cope with life on the road. I had only one pair of pants. Jim, a thin, tanned man of forty or so, told me to get another pair. "Why?" I asked.

"You'll get lousy, that's why. Tell Gray you have to go into town and get another pair in the Salvation Army."

Jim had been in the war and on the road ever since. He was not a professional bum, but he was a professional drunk and would work for a few weeks or months, then go on a binge, riding the empty boxcars between jobs. Jim, Stan, and I were paid the same wage, eight dollars a week; Hank got ten. I resolved to live on half my pay, and asked Gray to hold back the other half until I asked him for it. It was Jim who convinced me that I could live on four a week: "You buy crackers and sardines when you get the chance. Don't eat fairground food; it costs too much and it'll give you a bellyache." Sardines were ten cents a can and would make two meals on crackers. Often we had to eat fairground hot dogs or hamburgers, and Jim was right about bellyaches. I smoked a pipe and spent fifteen cents a week on a tin of Sir Walter Raleigh tobacco. The others smoked cigarettes.

The final night of a fair would always be crowded. People would put off their visits, or plan to attend them only for the fireworks that signaled the end of the fair and also the beginning of fall. We three underlings would work the tables until midnight and after. Hank would spell Gray as caller when Gray began to get hoarse. Finally we'd drop the canvas curtains while we packed the prizes and dismantled the interior equipment. Then came the exacting job of dropping the tent, whacking loose the three-foot iron stakes with a twelve-pound maul, and loading tent, prizes, and all on the truck and securing the load with sisal lines. That work would often take until daybreak, when Gray would set off in his small car and the rest of us would board the truck for the drive to the next fairgrounds. With luck we might have a day to set up; but often we would have to set up and begin selling cards without a break.

My apprenticeship in observation as a detached child in other people's lives proved valuable now that I had become an actor. I had grown tall fast and was badly coordinated, but watching how the others, Hank in particular, used their bodies, how they stood when driving a stake, and how they went about heavy lifting helped me get by until my own coordination improved.

One evening Jim came upon me in a field near the tent where I was driving a stake, knocking it loose, then driving it again. "What in the hell are you doing that for?" He stamped his cigarette in the dust.

"I'm practicing. Trying to keep my eye on the stake when I swing."

"Well, you're as green as they come, but you sure ain't yellow." From Jim that was praise, and I felt happy about it.

I liked heavy work, it made the day pass, but I was bad at it. Hank was a forbearing foreman. When I drove a tent stake too close to the tent or broke a plate on its way to the prize rack, he would only sigh, then show me how I had gone wrong. We smoked too much as we worked and broke off only to relieve thirst and other parts of the anatomy. Nobody swore, or not much, and then for considerable provocation at what Santayana calls "the authority of things." You could not force things against their implacable, unchanging nature. Hank and Jim and Stan were unskilled, but they had common sense; I learned before I was much older that the sense called common is anything but. Gray had common sense and dignity to go with it. He was a neatly put-together, small man; I realized years later that with his moustache and soft Texas drawl he was the very image of William Faulkner.

At the Iowa State Fair I became aware of two women, or girls, hanging around our tent. Both were tall and stringy, with dirty-looking long hair. They chewed gum and smoked cigarettes at the same time, flaunting their bottoms by their way of walking. I was vaguely bothered that Hank and Jim kidded around with these girls in slack times, passing them cigarettes and carrying on in what seemed to me an unmanly way. At age fifteen and two weeks I had some notion, deriving from schoolyard smut and dictionary hunts, of what went on in private between married people—an idea made all too vivid by what I would later recognize as a combination of hormones, libido, and plain lust—but my puritanical Catholic education had scarcely prepared me for the raw sexual play taking place before my eyes in the dust, heat, and racket from the "great midway" at that fair.

"Them's nice knees you got," Jim said to Lucille, the dark-haired, rough-skinned one. "I wonder what's up there between them?" And he laughed.

"You jest keep right on wondering, Jimmy-boy." She pouted and smiled her come-on.

Like the Minnesota Fair, the Iowa Fair ran for two weeks, and the girls would show up during the empty times in the morning and sometimes in the evening as well. Occasionally in their aimlessness they would even talk to me. They taught me carny talk, a variation of pig Latin that carnival people used around laymen when they were setting up a con trick of one kind or another. Lucille's standard greeting was, "Heeazow's your leeaziver?" (How's your liver?) I hated it, but I was fascinated by this simpleminded and scurrilous secret language. The girls were not yet whores but were well on their way to the next station down that line.

When we finally packed up and set out in the truck for Kansas, I chided Hank, my favorite: "I can't understand what you see in those women. Chewing gum with their mouths open and smelling like dime-store perfume." Hank, a natural gentleman if a rough one, merely smiled at Jim, sitting next to me, who smiled back. Neither actually answered, and I knew I was rebuked for pushing priggishly in where I had no business to be.

As we moved south the summer seemed to move with us, a good thing too, because I had no cold-weather clothing beyond a sweater, and it had turned cool and rainy toward the end of the Iowa Fair. Oklahoma was the next big one, but we played a county fair in Missouri and a carnival somewhere in Kansas. Instead of my riding in the truck, on a long jump Gray would take me in his car to help with the driving. Eventually we would stop at a hotel, where he would stake me to a dollar room, pure luxury, for there would be a big old bathtub on lion claws down the hall, possibly hot water and a wonderful soak, after which I would sleep for twelve hours. I had never been south before. I had read history and fiction about the Civil War and thought of the South as an admirable land of happy, liberated slaves and white warriors, noble in defeat. The reality soon displaced my ideal images. I didn't believe that any place could be poorer than the North, but Southern poverty in the depression, rooted in post–Civil War ruin, was bitter beyond any sweetening. A minor disaster provided my first taste of that bitterness.

We had played a carnival in Missouri that the natives seemed to go out of their way to avoid. Gray said we would have to pull up and get out. He wasn't even "making the nut," fair jargon for meeting expenses. We had driven the truck a mile or two when it stuttered, lost power, and exuded a black cloud from its tailpipe. Hank, driving, said "Holy smoke," and I laughed. "Shut up. Dammit, John, this is trouble."

"Pistons?" Jim asked.

"You said it."

Hank walked back to town and was gone for half a day. He had finally got through to Gray at his house in East Texas, where he had gone to tend to business before meeting us in Oklahoma City. The truck would have to be repaired in the town, and Hank was to wait for it and drive it to the Oklahoma fairgrounds. Jim, Stan, and I would have to make our own way there; Gray couldn't come up with bus money.

"I guess we could hop a freight," Jim said. "But they mostly go west out of here."

"Not for me," Stan said. "These Southern railroad cops are bastards. They'd as soon blackjack you dead as look at you. They near killed an old buddy of mine."

"Here?" Jim asked.

"North Carolina."

"It might not be so bad here. John, you never rode the rails, did you?"

"No."

"Well, maybe this ain't the place for your first lesson. We better hitch-hike."

"We better get ourself cleaned up. Nobody gonna pick up a bum," Stan said.

Jim was seething, I could tell, because Gray hadn't so much as bought us bus fare, or promised to. He said he was going to take a little rest, and he might or might not go down to Oklahoma. Stan told me to set out on the road first; one had a better chance for a ride than two, and a kid had the best chance of all. He'd follow maybe by bus if he had enough change in his pocket.

In a way I was glad to set out on my own, and I was tempted to try the boxcars that rumbled through the little town from time to time, sometimes stopping to take on water or for some other mysterious reason. Plenty of people my age rode them, whole families rode them. You would see gaunt women with little barefoot kids, standing in the open doors of the empties as the freights rolled through crossings and towns. I wondered why so many had become so desperate, mainly farm people they appeared, but I had to put such thoughts out of mind to consider my own next move. Hitchhiking was probably a better idea.

Not much traffic moved on the roads in that mean time, especially not in the South. I was five days covering some four hundred miles, plenty of idle time between rides to see beaten-down people in wrecks of houses, dressed in near rags and thin with the scrawniness of hunger. A few farm trucks went from farms to towns, and sometimes traveling salesmen in passenger cars would zoom by my begging thumb. A Negro (a polite term then) in an old

Model A Ford stopped to ask where I was going. After a few miles he asked, "You got money wif you?" "I've got a dollar," I lied. I had almost three dollars. "We going to stop at this here gas station. You put a dollar of gas in the tank and we can go right on." I protested that I had to eat on that dollar.

"Okay, sonny, then you better take yoself off right here."

By contrast, I had walked five or six miles into a large town and suddenly felt nails being driven into my thigh, a cramp such as I had never had before. I had been passing the large plate-glass window of a hotel, in which a white-haired Negro bellhop had been standing. Bent over in pain out on the street, I felt myself being lifted, then supported, to hobble into the hotel, where my rescuer sat me in a large leather chair and massaged away my cramp. He refused the small change I tried to give him, saying, "That's all right, that's all right."

Hank Myers, Jim, and I were squatted down in the vast railway yards in Kansas City. Stan had gone to Montana, to dig potatoes, he said. I had been sick as a dog on the alkaline water at the Oklahoma Fair but had got through somehow. Jim turned up again at the Texas Fair in Dallas, still vaguely resentful, efficient, and sardonic. The Texas Fair marked the end of the season in that part of the country, and Gray had paid us off, saying he hoped to see us the next year. I collected my withholdings and felt rich, a feeling soon displaced when Gray handed me a letter from my father. He must have found Gray's home address through Laura; now he was in still one more rooming house in St. Paul, and he needed money. I put five singles in an envelope with a note saying I wasn't sure of my next move. I had some satisfaction in repaying the five dollars he had given me a lifetime ago, as it seemed; but my satisfaction was troubled by the fact that my capital was substantially reduced by my gesture.

We had ridden up from Dallas on a flatbed truck, but it was taking us a long time to find out where the freights were going and when. We had to dodge around two or three times a day to keep out of the way of the yard cops. It was turning cold now in November; Hank was going home to northern Iowa, and Jim hinted at female hospitality in Minneapolis. Instructed by Jim, I discarded my suitcase for a blanket roll. "You can't hop no freight with that thing in one hand," Jim said, pointing to the old case.

We weren't alone in the yard. Real bums and transients needing transport like us would meet, exchange information about freight train movements, then part and meet again. The professionals claimed to know what would move and when, but often their information was faulty or malicious. After three days of uncertainty we decided we would take the first empty that seemed to be going north, if only to get out of "this goddammed K.C." as Jim put it. The best bet was a train making up not far from where we were. We filled our water bottles at a standpipe, made up our rolls, and waited near the line for the train to begin to move. We had newspapers to wrap around our legs in the cold night.

I knew I was in for a trial. The line ran on a raised embankment of gravel, and the boxcar door would be well above that. Jim instructed me in technique: "I'll go first and open a door. Sometimes they stick. You come next, and Hank will be behind you. You have to run along that bank, throw your roll in, then heave yourself up, get it?"

At dusk, sure enough, the cars began to move, and so did we. You didn't get in when they were stopped because of the yard patrol. You knew a boxcar was empty if the door wasn't locked and sealed. Jim said, "Now," and began to trot. I ran after him, ready to pitch my roll as instructed. I saw Jim heave at a partially open door as the train began to gather speed, not much, but a lot to me running in the gravel. I was almost at the door, just beyond the turning rear wheels, when I stumbled and fell. Before I hit the ground, with visions of a gory death, Hank pulled me up and said, "Run, John. Get in quick." I did so, trembling, sweating, and relieved beyond the telling to be alive and moving, my friends with me.

"You saved me," was all I could gasp at Hank. I felt foolish and ashamed.

"Nothing I wouldn't do for a mangy dog," Hank smiled.

"You go on tripping over your own feet, you'll end up a statistic," Jim said. Many died riding the rails in those years, one reason for the zeal of the yard police. The train finally cleared the yards and picked up speed. Jim slid the door open a few feet and studied the cloudy sky. "I still don't know if this mother is headed north or west. Can't see no sun at all." For the first time in weeks I could sit down with nothing to do. It was luxury, even if splinters from the wooden floor worked up through my blanket. Three miserable days were behind us, and I think the others were as tired out as I was. I didn't care what direction the train was taking. As it turned out, we were heading west and had to leap out somewhere in Arkansas to beat our way back and eventually north. "No place to nowhere," Jim said.

There would be many trips in many boxcars over the next few years, but trips and trains fade one into another. That fading I account for not through treacheries of memory but through the similarities of the settings, which suggested the exits and entrances of characters in an excessively long play or opera. Sometimes the train would stop for no perceptible reason, and I would risk jumping down and raiding a stand of ripe field corn, then rushing back to the boxcar before it began to roll. At other stops the car would be invaded by other travelers, men looking for work or professional vagrants moving to good weather before the northern winter arrived. Some would talk, but most were glum after trying to hit me for cigarettes or makings. I was always vaguely anxious that I didn't really know where the train was going, or why. It would stop, start up again, or shunt around in the yards of some small town somewhere. When the sliding door was shut, day and night were just about the same: there were no windows in boxcars. Often it was too cold for sleep. Newspapers wrapped around the legs helped, but sometimes they seemed to absorb the cold, not keep it out. I would get up, stretch, light my pipe, and watch the dim bundles sleeping near me, snoring or groaning against the swaying motion when the train got up to speed. Sometimes the strangeness was exciting, and sometimes it was threatening, for no reason I could put words to.

On that first journey, late one night on a siding, someone pushed into our car, grunted, and went to sleep. In the morning he saw that I had water in my canteen and offered me what he called "weed" in return for a swig. I didn't know what "weed" was, but Hank defined it for me: "Mary Jane, marijuana. Keep away from that gink. He's a wolf." I didn't know what a "wolf" was either. Hank said a wolf picked up stray young kids and traveled with them. I wasn't much enlightened, and asked why.

"They cornhole them," Jim said with disgust.

That enlightened me only dimly, but I gathered its meaning by intuition. The word sounded vile and in some dark way contributed to my growing resolve to settle in somewhere and go back to school. The theater of the boxcar soon lost any attraction; I knew I would have to make some other kind of life for myself. I was hungry for books again, for study, the only activity in which I had some competence. I had fled from the German and from my father's futilities, not from school.

Southern Iowa, and I decided I'd had enough boxcar vagaries. I said so long to Hank and Jim, jumped into a deserted freight yard, and headed for the little town, for groceries, and the road north. I would hitchhike to St. Paul and go back to school, provided I could find a night job. Two mornings later I rode into the South St. Paul stockyards perched above an enormous, stinking hog, my companion for the last several hours, the cab of the truck full of driver and friends. I took a streetcar to Laura's, asked her to rent me a room until I could find a job, and so rejoined the more or less conventional world.

ANDREW HUDGINS

The Secret Sister

—⟋ℳ⟍—

WHEN I WAS between ten and fourteen, I was perturbed that my life wasn't like the lives of people in the books I read. From the Hardy Boys to Penrod to Hercule Poirot to, hell, Brighty of the Grand Canyon, they possessed more understanding of the world than I did, and more insight into the nuances of other people's words and gestures. Their lives were full of precisely resolved drama that vibrated with significance and meaning.

Though I dimly knew I didn't want a dump-truck load of drama rumbling into my life, I envied the characters a tumult that was rich with possibilities for heroism, adventure, and psychological acuity. Mostly it was the understanding I envied, the book-people's ability to perceive the motivations behind each other's words and actions. Reading books, I could pull the characters' understanding over my head like a sweater and wear it as my own. The people I read about were teaching me how to think and feel, but in my life outside books my parents' actions were still as inscrutable as Sanskrit and the intentions of my brothers, relatives, classmates as unfathomable as the Marianas Trench, which I had read about in *My Weekly Reader*.

At ten I remembered how, when I was just four, five, six years old, I'd sit under the kitchen table and listen intently while Mother and her friends, other service wives, drank coffee, smoked, gossiped. While I stacked my brightly colored wooden blocks into elaborate towers, raced Matchbox cars around and through them, then toppled the precarious skyscrapers, the women talked. They cooed, their voices husky with amazement: "No, you don't mean it!" And someone archly replied, "Yes, honey, I mean it. Mean it, I do."

They laughed, they hooted, and, because "little pitchers have big ears" — significant flick of wise eyes in my direction — they whispered. They droned earnestly about friends and relatives, promotions and transfers, annoyances and outrages. Though I loved the music of their talk, I was fascinated by the lyrics because I could not understand them. Sliding on my bottom, I scooted across the carpet to my mother's feet and, making myself as inconspicuous as possible, I strained to follow the women's conversation. When Mom looked down and saw the look of absorbed concentration on my face, she began to edit her comments: "You remember what we were talking about the other day? Betty and the . . . ? Yes, that's what I mean. Well, today Shelly told me he'd done it again, somewhere over by the commissary." Though her careful obscurity foxed me, the people in books would, I was sure, have penetrated it as easily as Sherlock Holmes interpreted partially dried mud stains on the brim of a delivery man's cap.

But in one crucial way my life was like the lives of the people in books. I simply didn't know it yet. Though I'd had clues.

All my life—and I'm forty-seven now—I've received *Woodmen* magazine. My subscription began before I was born, but only when I was ten or so and reading steadily did my mother feel obligated to give me the issues. I was lying on my bed, reading comic books, when Mom came to the bedroom door, the day's mail clutched in her hand. "Here, this is yours," she said, and tossed the magazine at me. Mail? Me? I never got mail. I was a kid.

Her voice was studiously neutral—a tone that set my nervous system on high alert.

She stood in the doorway, staring back and forth between the magazine and me, her body clenched so tight she trembled.

I picked up the magazine. "What is it?"

"Just take it. It's yours," she snapped, and left the room.

What had I done? Trying to figure it out, I read the *Woodmen* carefully. I studied it and puzzled over it.

Woodmen is published by The Woodmen of the World, a fraternal insurance company based in Omaha, that sells insurance primarily in rural communities. The magazine was filled with articles about local Woodmen of the World lodges, articles accompanied by many pictures of lodge members standing in front of American, state, and lodge flags, staring blankly into the lens of an unseen member's Brownie Automatic. Between vaguely inspirational and patriotic articles about the importance of Arbor Day, Flag Day, and the birthdays of George Washington and Abraham Lincoln, *Woodmen* sandwiched longer and more insistent—nearly impassioned—articles alerting me to my insurance needs. They luridly detailed the unhappy consequences sure to befall those who turned their backs on home, auto, term life, and disability insurance.

My careful study of *Woodmen*, my detective work, failed to answer my questions about why I received the magazine and why its arriving at the house made my mother act so peculiar. Uneasily, I wrote her anger off as yet another adult act that, for all its apparent irrationality, grew out of a reasonable adult calculus beyond a child's comprehension—like the acts of God, which I was told at church would in the fullness of time be revealed as just, wise, and loving. Only much later did I learn that my subscription to *Woodmen* began when my parents, before I was born, bought a burial insurance policy in my name. If I died, they wanted to have the money to bury me.

Around the same time—we were living then in North Carolina on Seymour Johnson Air Force Base—I had to take my birth certificate to school and show it to the Pee-Wee League officials before I could sign up to play baseball.

"What's your birthday, son?" asked one of the men. "April 6, 1951, sir." If there's one thing a kid can be counted on to recite confidently, it's his birthday.

The man looked puzzled. "No," he said. He turned the paper around where I could see it and pointed at the date. "It says on your birth certificate it's April 22."

When I ran through the carport and shouldered open the kitchen door, Mom stood at the sink, peeling potatoes and carrots for supper. Spring sunshine poured through the kitchen window, and her face glowed in the soft light. Without turning her head, she said, "Hey, Kiddo. How was school?"

"Hey, Mom—my birth certificate is wrong."

"Huh? What do you mean?"

"It says my birthday is April 22."

Mom turned and stared at me, her mouth gaping.

"It says April 22, not April 6 like it's supposed to."

Her mouth began to work wordlessly until a choking sob broke from her throat. She threw her wet hands over her face and ran from the room, water streaming down her elbows and onto her blouse.

I couldn't imagine what I'd done. The faucet was still running.

Maybe she meant to leave it on. Maybe she'd come right back. I stood still a long time, waiting and thinking, before I turned off the faucet. The potatoes and carrots, half peeled, huddled atop one another in the sink, glazed with cold water.

I tiptoed down the hall to my bedroom. As I passed the shut door of her bedroom, I heard Mom crying. I stopped and listened to her fighting for control. She gasped, trying to hold the sobs down, but they forced their way up her throat and burst out in long rhythmic wails. I crept on down to my room and closed the door.

What had I done? Should I ask? Should I go apologize even if I didn't know what I was apologizing for? That might make things worse.

Later, her face red and swollen, exhausted from sheer exertion, Mom tapped on my door, stood in the doorway, and apologized for getting so upset. My birth certificate, she said, was right. She had simply misremembered when my birthday was. She was sorry. Next April 22 she baked a Duncan Hines yellow cake and topped it with a cocoa-powder icing—my favorite. Inspired by a tip from the *Ladies' Home Journal*, she wrapped nickels, dimes, and one quarter in waxed paper and tucked them into the cake for me, my brothers, and our friends to find. And thus my birthday changed from April 6 to April 22 with my hardly noticing the shift. Sixteen days, what difference did that make to me? I was a kid and didn't pay attention.

If I had paid attention, maybe I wouldn't have given in to fits of boyish petulance, complaining that I wasn't loved enough, given enough toys, allowed enough freedom. I even hurled at my mother the great slogan of sullen children: "I never asked to be born." It's meant to absolve the speaker of all responsibility because it assumes that only those who did, in fact, request to be born can be held accountable for their actions, while implying that his birth was the result of some caprice, carnal whimsy, or solipsistic act of self-replication on the part of his parents, who merely wanted a worker to mow the lawn for them.

Mom would have none of it. If she was washing dishes, she'd stop and wipe her hands. If she was sewing, she'd push back from the machine, leaving the needle poised above the fabric like a threat. If she was vacuuming, she'd drop the hose, snap the vacuum off, and walk over to me. She'd stop right in front of me, grab me by the shoulders, stare into my eyes, and say with hushed ferocity, "Nobody ever wanted a child as much as I wanted you. Nobody." She shook my shoulders for emphasis.

"The doctors all wanted me to get rid of you, but I told them I'd have this baby even if it killed me. I didn't want to live if I couldn't have you."

Her face was intense and determined, her eyes fixed on the distant past, as if she were once again having to stare down idiot doctors who couldn't understand how much she wanted me, how much she would suffer to bear me.

"Why, Mom? Why'd they want you to get rid of me?" The idea of a therapeutic abortion was beyond me. I was remembering stories I'd read about Spartan women abandoning unwanted or malformed babies on the mountainside.

"Because I was in such bad shape. Because they thought having you might kill me." She went back to what she'd been doing—washing, sewing, vacuuming. But I followed her.

"Why were you in such bad shape?"

"I just was. But nothing was going to keep me from having you, so it doesn't matter what was wrong with me. Go do your homework."

"I've done it."

"Then go over it again and make sure you did it right."

I squirmed miserably, overwhelmed by the passion and suffering in her love for me. But I understood that it wasn't me, the essence of me, my personal identity, that she loved first and so ferociously, but the idea of a baby. The baby that became me. I was loved first because I was her child, not because I was Andrew or because of anything I'd done or could do to merit her love.

Until I was thirteen, I thought Mother's insistence on how much she wanted to have me was simply her way of telling me how much she loved me. And it was that, but not simply.

During the three years that my father was stationed at Norton Air Force Base outside San Bernardino, California, and I was in sixth, seventh, and eighth grades, my Grandmother Rodgers twice flew out from Georgia to stay with us for month-long visits. I must, therefore, have been about thirteen when, with my parents off shopping for groceries at the base commissary, Grandmomma summoned Roger and me into the back bedroom. Mike, the youngest, was sent outside to play.

She shut the door, eased her bulk down onto one bed, the mattress bowing underneath her weight, and gestured for Roger and me to sit on the other bed, facing her. She plucked at the bodice of her dress a moment or two.

"Do you know you have a sister?" she blurted. She stared into my face, then Roger's, to judge how we reacted.

I thought she was joking. Of course I didn't have a sister. I'd have noticed. We sat and stared, waiting for her to continue.

According to Grandmomma, Mom and Dad had driven with Andrea, who was about two and half years old, to Griffin, Georgia, for Christmas. (Andrea! While Grandmomma talked, I mulled that name over and over: my name, my father's name, transformed into a girl. And if she'd lived, I'd have been somebody else, named somebody else.) Going home, they'd tried to save money by pushing straight through from Georgia to Fort Hood, Texas, where my father was stationed. In the small hours of the morning, somewhere in east Texas, Mom, driving while Dad slept, hit a patch of ice. Sawing the wheel back and forth, she fought to control the fishtailing car, which shot off the road and into a field, catapulting Andrea through the windshield, killing her.

Dad said nobody in the world could have handled the sliding car better than Mom had, Grandmomma told us with a defensive edge to her voice.

Even at the time, as a seventh-grader and not an especially perceptive one, I recognized that my father had lied, lied to exculpate Mom and lied to himself so they both could think of Andrea's death as an act of God in which Mom had played only a secondary role and played it well. This lie has been one of the moral touchstones of my life.

For years, while I admired my father in secret for his brave dishonesty, I excoriated myself because I wouldn't have had the presence of mind to tell such a thoughtful lie. And even if I did find the decency and imagination to tell the good lie, I lacked, I knew, the self-discipline to stick to it in the turmoil of grief. In his place I could not have restrained myself from lashing out at the woman who drove the car. Or so I thought when I was thirteen and for many years afterwards.

My parents, Grandmomma told us, regarded Andrea's death as God's judgment on them. Because they had loved her so much, they had, in effect, worshipped her. They were guilty of the sin of idolatry, and God had struck her down to punish them.

Above her bedroom fireplace, Grandmomma kept, she said, a large, studio photograph of Andrea. When we came to visit, she took it down and hid it under the bed because Mom couldn't bear to see it. Hadn't we noticed how that large area of the wall was strangely bare?

No ma'am, we hadn't.

When Grandmomma finished talking, she let out a large huff of air and plucked at the front of her dress, as if she were hot. She looked at us, expecting us to say something. What could we say?

Grandmomma swore us to absolute secrecy. We must never let our parents know that we knew about Andrea. If they found out she'd told us, they might never let her come visit us again. But we had a sister. We had to be told.

Roger and I kept our vows so diligently that we didn't discuss Andrea even with each other until we were adults. But at the time I hardly paid any attention to my own promises. My brain was racing—remembering, sorting, reinterpreting. "Do I believe her? Do I believe this wild story of my ordinary, everyday parents having a secret life of grief, guilt and suffering?" "Yes," I answered. "I do."

But I also wanted to see the evidence. A year or two later when we were staying with Grandmomma on our way from California to a base outside Paris, I looked under her bed to see if she really did have a picture hidden there. I pulled the photograph out and studied it. I tried to find a family resemblance, a psychic link, between Andrew and Andrea. I yearned to get some sense of her as a person, a sister, a predecessor, a double, a spiritual intimate. From the photograph, a child in a frilly starched dress laughed past the camera—a child's open-mouthed laugh, quizzical and tentative. She was just a little girl. She could have been any little girl. Disappointed and embarrassed, I pushed the picture back under the bed, taking care to place it exactly where I had found it.

Once I knew about Andrea, incidents that had been inexplicable now began to assume meaning. The *Woodmen* magazine. Even my misplaced birthday. I understood instinctively that my mother had confused my birthday with Andrea's.

Andrea's death explained why, as soon as seat belts were made available as retrofit kits, my father had bought four sets of them and in a muttering, sweating rage spent an afternoon installing them. He cut slots into the green vinyl-covered seats of our Chevy Impala wagon. From a careful distance, we watched him wrestle the bench seats out of the car. After drilling holes in the floor pan, he bolted the seat belt anchors to the frame of the car. Whenever my brothers and I got in the car, he checked to see we were buckled in, tugging at the belts, cinching them so tight we could hardly breathe.

Learning about my sister also threw a sad and subtle new light on how Mom responded when acquaintances asked her how many children she had. "Three," she said, or later, after Timothy was born, "Four." "All boys," she invariably added, then laughed. She laughed with a peculiar quality I'd recognized as peculiar, though I couldn't penetrate it. A strange note played against the amused, rueful tone of a woman mocking herself in front of other women whom she could count on to understand her plight, trapped in a house full of crude and brutish men. In retrospect I could hear a touch of giddiness in her lie, a giddiness that might have soared into hysteria if she had let it. I knew she got frantic at funerals. On the rare occasions when she absolutely could not avoid them, she broke down sobbing the moment we entered the church and continued crying and gasping for air in the car, at the graveside, and for hours after we had driven home. Her weeping made me feel detached and uncaring—a cold fish—because I didn't grieve as strongly as she did, but it also frightened me to see her sag, collapse, and cling to my father, her wet face tucked against his shoulder as if she were trying to hide it. Despite how she must seem in these pages, where I'm writing about widely spaced incidents that radiate from the most traumatic event of her life, my mother considered herself a trooper, not in the theatrical but in the military sense. She was not one to put her emotions on public display, and she distrusted those who did—an attitude that made her breakdowns all the more frightening to me.

These memories and perceptions, in some inchoate form, surged through my mind as I sat on the bed, absorbing what Grandmomma had told us. Her revelations explained too much to be brushed aside. I believed her. My next thought was, "Wow, this is just like something in a book!" My parents' lives and, by extension, mine suddenly possessed drama, heartbreak, violent death, and deep-buried family secrets—and I, like a character in a book, was unexpectedly entertaining insights into why the people around me acted the way they did. I'd yearned to have insight, and now I could see with fascinating clarity the psychological maneuvering that wound around the decency of my father's good lie. And I could see how my grandmother's vehement insistence that her daughter was not to blame for the accident made me doubt that my father had told her the whole story and doubt that she was telling me the whole of what she had been told. I could comprehend the despair that drove my parents' spiritually perverted yet utterly natural attempt to create meaning for Andrea's meaningless death. I was amazed—thrilled!—to find myself living a scene of revelation and epiphany—and ashamed of myself for reducing my parents' lives and mine to literary tropes.

Though I knew I would devalue my mother and father by thinking of them as characters in a book, they have left me no choice. Until Grandmomma told me about Andrea, my parents had never breathed a word about her, and only much later did they speak of her at all. When I was in my early twenties, my mother two or three times mentioned Andrea in passing, quickly, tentatively—testing me to see if I knew what she was talking about. When I was in my middle twenties, my father began on rare occasions to mention Andrea when her life helped pinpoint time: "That was in Florida, right after Andrea was born." "Andrea was just about a year old when we moved to Texas, but she traveled really well for such a tiny baby." These comments, too, seem slightly contrived to me. I think he is trying to tell me I have a sister, trying to remind me of what he has never told me. Trying to help me remember what I don't truly know. That is the extent of what I have learned about Andrea from my parents' lips.

My parents' silence, augmented by Grandmomma's swearing Roger and me to silence, forced me to approach them as if they were literary characters because in a real way that's what they are. In life you don't have to speculate why people do things; you can take them aside and ask, and then adjust your understanding according to how they reply. But with literary characters you must interpret from the limited evidence given to you in the book. Since I could not ask my parents about Andrea, I've become their interpreter, an interpreter whose attention they would have resented if they had known I was studying them, though, again like characters in a book, they seemed unaware that I was their reader, analyzing them, interpreting them, speculating about them. And like a literary critic I have continued to adjust my understanding of my text—my parents and their daughter—as new facts come to light.

A couple of years ago when my wife and I were in Atlanta, visiting my brother for Christmas, I mentioned that the only picture I'd ever seen of Andrea was the one Grandmomma kept on her bedroom wall. Roger stood up, left the room, and came back holding a small framed photograph. All my brothers were familiar with this picture, but I'd never seen it before. As talk, insult, and laughter volleyed across the kitchen table, I stared at the photograph, transfixed and strangely reverent. In it Andrea, at what must have been her second Christmas, when she was twenty-one months old, sits on the floor in front of the Christmas tree. She is almost completely encircled by my parents. Their shoulders touch affectionately behind her, and their knees nearly complete the circle in front. Andrea's mouth is parted in laughter and her large dark eyes are focused hard to her own right, anticipating more silliness from some aunt or uncle who is trying to get her to look up and laugh for the camera. There's a slight wariness in her look, but it's the wariness that precedes pleasure. She knows she'll be delighted again soon, any second now. It might involve *tickling*, though, and she'll keep her eyes peeled for that.

But it isn't Andrea who commands my attention, my strange reverence; it's my parents. These aren't the people I know. These aren't the driven, fearful, angry, and often grim people who raised my brothers and me. The sleeve of my mother's mock turtleneck sweater is pushed to her elbow, revealing a powerful forearm. Her right hand clasps Andrea's thigh, holding her in place for the camera. Mother looks frankly into the lens, a large, easy smile lighting her face. Though the viewing angle and the large plaid of her wool skirt make her hips look huge—perhaps she is still heavy from bearing her first child—I can see the taut tomboy build that she was proud of.

While my mother looks forthrightly ahead, my father looks down at Andrea. All the camera captures of his eyes are the lids, which makes him look as though he's praying. His thin lips even seem to move slightly, the way they do when he is reading his Bible. Everything about his face looks reverent, radiant with pleasure in his daughter. I've only once seen that look directed at me, and that was when I was born again and stumbled down the aisle to join the Southern Baptist church. Looking at the photograph, I felt a stab of jealousy for Andrea, so clearly adored by her parents, and her parents so clearly relaxed, confident, and happy. Happy! I never saw my parents look happy. Oh, they laughed and made jokes occasionally, especially my mother. But not to be melodramatic about it, they were sad people, with some fundamental capacity for joy drained out of them. Looking at the photograph, I understood at a gut level something I had understood only on an intellectual level, ever since Grandmomma had told us about our secret sister: all my life my parents have been grieving.

I already knew that in looking at Andrea I was looking at the person who had determined much of my life and outlook. On a level far beyond words, I have absorbed my parents' belief that the world is out to get me. They hovered over me, watching, watching, watching. But was it me they were watching, or the predatory world that was forever waiting for another opportunity to spring out and take one of their children? "No, you can't cross the street; it's dangerous." "No, you can't eat a corndog at the fair. You don't know who touched it or where their hands have been." "Just who is going to chaperone this field trip? Well, if I let you go I want you to stay near the teacher and don't leave the group. A dairy farm is a dangerous place." I grew up a fearful child, and consequently an angry one. To this day, my first reactions to most new situations are fear, then anger—all filtered through a pervasive low-grade paranoia that is finally abating. It has required a lot of self-monitoring for me to comprehend this emotional pattern and make allowances for it.

At Roger's kitchen table, looking at the way my father looked at Andrea, I began to grasp how his love might have seemed so excessive as to have tempted God's hand. And I understood, too, the corollary to that belief: if his idolatrous love had caused God to strike down Andrea, then wasn't he, in a direct and undeniable way, the murderer of his own child? I began to understand why my parents, though they hovered over me, protecting me from a hostile world, weren't demonstrative in their affection. Much of their capacity for joyous love had died with Andrea, leaving only the fearful kind, but they also didn't want to show their love too openly because they had done that once before and reaped the consequences. They wanted to keep me alive.

Late last year, my cousin Julie Carmean, who was finishing her doctorate in theology, sent a copy of her dissertation to my wife. Erin read it and passed it on to me, saying, "There are some things about Andrea in this you'll want to read."

Julie takes on the pivotal religious question of theodicy—why does God allow evil in the world?—and in her introduction to the manuscript she writes about several events underlying her intellectual fascination with this question. One was being sexually assaulted when she was in high school. Another was the death of her father in a terrible, freak car accident.

But the story that Julie grew up with, the one that first brought the vexed theological issue of theodicy to her mind, was Andrea's death. In the story Julie heard, my mother, tired because she and my father had driven all night, fell asleep at the wheel, and the car veered off the road. In the wreck, Andrea was flung from the car unhurt. "There wasn't a mark on her," Julie was told, except for one: the accident had dashed Andrea from the car and into a barbed-wire fence, which cut her throat.

Learning these new facts from the pages Julie had written for her exam committee was a strange and eerily literary experience. I find it, though, natural to resort to literary criticism to grapple with my cousin's version of the story. Isn't it, in addition to everything else, a story that is moving from oral transmission onto the printed page? And in the oral tradition we're familiar with different tellings of the same basic plot, as in the many variants of folk songs, such as "Barbara Allen" and "Frankie and Johnny." Or the motives of different storytellers can be preserved side by side, like the original pagan voices and the later Christian voices in *Beowulf* that quarrel over how the poem should be told and what it should mean. In this case Julie's version sounds closer to right than Grandmomma's. While my mother certainly could have lost control of the car on a patch of ice, her falling asleep makes more sense of both stories' insistence that my parents had driven all night. But maybe I'm being too literary: the writer always prefers a story in which events rise from human action, not chance. We can tolerate a good deal of apparent meaninglessness in our lives because we have grown accustomed to it, but why bother reading novels, poems, stories, or plays if they are meaningless? If Mom fell asleep, she was responsible for Andrea's death. If the road was icy, no one was to blame and Mom stood innocent in her mother's eyes. My father lied to protect my mother and told, I suspect, a truer version of the story to his brother, whom he could depend on to understand his grief, sorrow, guilt, and despair.

I'm a little skeptical of the new and horrifying detail that Andrea's throat was slashed on barbed wire; it smacks of the storyteller's delight in the vivid and peculiar. But a barbed-wire gash on Andrea's throat might explain why my mother, when the subject of funerals came up, insisted that she wanted a closed-casket service and I was to make sure that under no circumstances was my father to display her body. Then, surprised at her own vehemence, she'd stop, laugh, and say that if I didn't do what she asked she'd come back and haunt me.

The romantic—or is it gothic?—detail that, except for the wound on her throat, Andrea didn't have a mark on her is the only part of Julie's story that I am actively dubious of. Though it's possible that a child could be pitched through the windshield and onto a barbed-wire fence without being bruised, cut, and scraped, it's unlikely. The fabrication that was meant to spare the sensibilities of the grieving relatives actually, in my imagining, makes the gash in the baby's unbroken flesh more vivid, more violative, more horrible.

It gives the imagination one detail to focus on and conjure with—and as I think on it the single slash across the throat makes Andrea's death seem less random and more purposeful, more like a murder or a ritual sacrifice than an accident—the way Isaac's corpse would have looked if God had not, at the last minute, stopped Abraham from doing what he had ordered him to do.

Almost every week of their working lives, ministers like Julie have to comfort people through personal tragedies like sexual assault, the death of a parent, or the death of a daughter, and in her discussion of theodicy my cousin is reduced, by what she has heard and experienced, to arguing that God possesses only partial control over human actions and the world. It is one of the few logical paths open to her. If you posit that God is all good and all powerful, there is only one way to reconcile those beliefs with the presence of evil. That is to deny evil exists by insisting it is only an illusion. If we understood enough, if we stood where God stands, we would see that what looks like evil to us is in fact an unbroken chain of goodness working itself out for our greater happiness. I'm sure that friends, preachers, family members told my grieving parents that now we see through a glass darkly. God moves in mysterious ways. God wanted another little angel in heaven. The hollowness of these assurances is as clear to the despairing friends who say them as it is to the grief-stricken souls who, hearing them, have to choke back the bitter retorts that rise naturally to their lips.

Though these sad, inadequate consolations invite the grief-stricken, practically prod them, to curse God and die, I have heard these consolations—not believing them, trying to believe them—pass from my own mouth at funerals. What else can you say? Friends, grandparents, ministers might be able to shrug helplessly and say, "Though it makes no sense to us, in time God's plan will become clear," but my parents could not. They had to make sense of Andrea's death *now*, even if it meant taking on themselves the harsh, Old Testament judgment of a god who loved them enough to correct them in their idolatry. The understanding they arrived at may have meant a lifetime of sorrow—and it did—but at least it wasn't nihilism.

The last time my wife and I visited Griffin, Georgia, my Aunt Bess asked if we wanted to go to the cemetery with her. Because I hadn't been back to my mother's grave since her funeral nearly twenty years earlier, Bess was a little hesitant in asking. I don't like visiting graves—partly out of laziness, I suppose, but mostly out of spiritual ineptitude. What do you *do* at the graveside? I don't believe my prayers, however strong to however powerful a god, will affect her soul now. But I do have a profound sense that my mother is not there beneath her headstone—not there, not there.

Bess is of another mind and another generation, and she's a florist, too, which gives her firm convictions about how the dead should be commemorated.

Bess wanted me to go to the cemetery with her because, well, because that's what you do. Because that's how you show love, respect, gratitude to the dead. Because it's a family obligation. Because Mom would have wanted me to go. I went because Bess wanted me to, and in her Oldsmobile Cutlass the three of us drove through downtown Griffin, past the huge Dundee textile mills, and out to the cemetery, which overlooks the parking lot of a Circle K discount store. During Mom's funeral I had stood at the grave, looked down the hill, and watched a little girl who insisted on riding her new red Big Wheel from the front door of the store to the car. There she had to be pulled off the toy, shaken, and yelled at before she'd agree to let it be locked away from her in the trunk for the ride home. The mind is a symbol-making machine. I watched with such eerie, dissociated intensity that I remember those shoppers and their now worn-out and discarded purchases more clearly than anything else that happened that day.

I carried Bess's flower arrangement to my Uncle Buddy's grave and pushed it snug against his headstone. Erin and I stepped back in awkward respect while Bess paused for a silent moment, staring at the stone; then we all walked over to Mom's grave. On one side of it, a green stretch of clipped grass waits to be broken for my father, and on the other side is a very small grave that I had only vaguely noticed during Mom's funeral. The stone read:

ANDREA RODGERS HUDGINS
APRIL 6, 1948 ———, 1950

I scrawled the inscription on the back of my left hand with a ballpoint pen. But because I was embarrassed and didn't want Bess to see what I was doing—taking notes like a reporter at my sister's grave—in my haste I blurred the second date. Still, I knew Andrea had to have died in the last week of the year, the week between Christmas and New Year's, so I could calculate what I wanted to know: how old Andrea was when she died. Two years, nine months.

Only while writing this essay—in fact, only when I was nearly finished with it—did I realize I was there at the accident that killed Andrea. I was born April 22, 1951, two months premature. My mother had to have been three months pregnant with me when Andrea died.

I look again at the photograph of Andrea and our happy parents, and suddenly I notice the bouncy ball her right hand is resting on possessively. Didn't it become my ball? Don't I dimly recognize it as one of the toys I played with?

My boyish wish for something in my life to be like something in the books I loved has been answered with a poignant and distressing richness that overwhelms me. I can't leap the gap between Andrea and me. I've tried, and failed, to imagine what her life would have been like if she had lived it. And even less can I imagine what my life would have been like if Andrea had not died and we had been raised together by those happy people in the photograph. My imagination simply isn't up to the work I'm asking it to do. For me, because my parents never talked about her, never made her a living word but left her a brooded-over silence, Andrea remains an imaginary playmate that I cannot imagine, a literary construct that I cannot construct.

If to them she was the secret daughter, to me she is the secret sister; and try as I might, I cannot entice her to crawl, toddle, step out of the shadows of their silence. I sometimes feel that my parents, in their desire to protect my brothers and me from the trauma of having a dead sister, have let Andrea die in a new and different way. By not talking about her, they have slowly deprived her—and me—of what little life she did live. And now that my mother is dead, Andrea's thirty-three months live only in my father's mind. This way of thinking is uncharitable, but it is, I'm sure, exactly the reason that Grandmomma took Roger and me aside and told us we had a sister. She wanted us to know about Andrea so we could, in memory, preserve something of her against forgetting. Unlike my parents, Grandmomma did not much care what the task might cost us. And rightly so, I think. Rightly so.

One of the trials of Job is that his children die. While his seven sons and three daughters are eating and drinking at the eldest son's house, a whirlwind sweeps in from the desert, strikes the house, and collapses it, killing all of Job's children at once. But because of Job's faith, the seven sons and three daughters are, at the end of the book, replaced with seven unnamed sons and three named daughters—Dove, Cinnamon, and Eyeshadow. There were no women in the world, the Bible tells us, more beautiful than Job's new daughters. Like Job, my parents got a family back. Within five months of her death, Andrea Rodgers Hudgins was replaced with Andrew, and twenty months after Andrew, Roger was born—followed by Michael and, much later, Timothy. But even if one of us had been a girl, there could not ever be, outside the world of books, another Andrea. No Dove, Cinnamon, Eyeshadow. No restoration that would remove the grief and sorrow as if it had never been.

For all my failure to bring her to life in my imagination, Andrea is at the core of Andrew's life. Late one night, in the moment I have come to think of, perhaps melodramatically, as the moment that killed my first marriage, my wife asked me if I was happy. Without thinking, I said, "Happy? I don't believe in happy. I believe in duty." She looked at me with something like horror on her face, and began, dispiritedly, to argue. Though I knew then and know now that life is more complex than that, I wouldn't budge from my fatuous assertion. What I had blurted out was a bone-deep understanding of my life that I had absorbed from my parents. Not from what they said so much as how they lived every breath they breathed and measured every step they took, putting one foot carefully in front of the other. Good soldiers, still marching. In the moment of saying it, I understood, to my shock, that I believed it, and at the same time I saw I could no longer believe it, which made me, for a while, cling to it that more closely. As my parents knew, in a world of unredeemable loss, it has its virtues.

WENDELL BERRY

The Hurt Man

—m—

WHEN HE was five, Mat Feltner, like every other five-year-old who had lived
in Port William until then, was still wearing dresses. In his own thoughts he
was not yet sure whether he would turn out to be a girl or a boy, though instinct by then had prompted him to take his place near the tail end of the procession of Port William boys. His nearest predecessors in that so far immortal
straggle had already taught him the small art of smoking cigars, along with
the corollary small art of chewing coffee beans to take the smoke smell off his
breath. And so in a rudimentary way he was an outlaw, though he did not
know it, for none of his grown-ups had yet thought to forbid him to smoke.

His outgrown dresses he saw worn daily by a pretty neighbor named Margaret Finley, who to him might as well have been another boy too little to be
of interest, or maybe even a girl, though it hardly mattered—and though, because of a different instinct, she would begin to matter to him a great deal in
a dozen years, and after that she would matter to him all his life.

The town of Port William consisted of two rows of casually maintained
dwellings and other buildings scattered along a thoroughfare that nobody
had ever dignified by calling it a street; in wet times it hardly deserved to be
called a road. Between the town's two ends the road was unevenly rocked but
otherwise had not much distinguished itself from the buffalo trace it once
had been. At one end of the town was the school, at the other the graveyard.
In the center there were several stores, two saloons, a church, a bank, a hotel, and a blacksmith shop. The town was the product of its own becoming
which, if not accidental exactly, had also been unplanned. It had no formal
government or formal history. It was without pretense or ambition, for it was
the sort of place that pretentious or ambitious people were inclined to leave.
It had never declared an aspiration to become anything it was not. It did not

thrive so much as it merely lived, doing the things it needed to do to stay alive. This tracked and rubbed little settlement had been built in a place of great natural abundance and beauty, which it had never valued highly enough or used well enough, had damaged, and yet had not destroyed. The town's several buildings, shaped less by art than by need and use, had suffered tellingly and even becomingly a hundred years of wear.

Though Port William sat on a ridge of the upland, still it was a river town; its economy and its thoughts turned toward the river. Distance impinged on it from the river, whose waters flowed from the eastward mountains ultimately, as the town always was more or less aware, to the sea, to the world. Its horizon, narrow enough though it reached across the valley to the ridgeland fields and farmsteads on the other side, was pierced by the river, which for the next forty years would still be its main thoroughfare. Commercial people, medicine showmen, evangelists, and other river travelers came up the hill from Dawes Landing to stay at the hotel in Port William, which in its way cherished these transients, learned all it could about them, and talked of what it learned.

Mat would remember the town's then-oldest man, Uncle Bishop Bower, who would confront any stranger, rap on the ground with his long staff, and demand, "Sir! What might your name be?"

And Herman Goslin, no genius, made his scant living by meeting the steamboats and transporting the disembarking passengers, if any, up to the hotel in a gimpy buckboard. One evening as he approached the hotel with a small trunk on his shoulder, followed by a large woman with a parasol, one of the boys playing marbles in the road said, "Here comes Herman Goslin with a fat lady's trunk."

"You boys can kiss that fat lady's ass," said Herman Goslin. "Ain't that tellin' 'em, fat lady?"

The town was not built nearer the river perhaps because there was no room for it at the foot of the hill, or perhaps because, as the town loved to reply to the inevitable question from travelers resting on the hotel porch, nobody knew where the river was going to run when they built Port William.

And Port William did look as though it had been itself forever. To Mat at the age of five, as he later would suppose, remembering himself, it must have seemed eternal, like the sky.

However eternal it might have been, the town was also as temporal, lively, and mortal as it possibly could be. It stirred and hummed from early to late with its own life and with the life it drew into itself from the countryside. It was a center, and especially on Saturdays and election days its stores and saloons and the road itself would be crowded with people standing, sitting, talking, whittling, trading, and milling about. This crowd was entirely familiar to itself; it remembered all its history of allegiances, offenses, and resentments, going back from the previous Saturday to the Civil War and long before that. Like every place, it had its angers, and its angers as always, as everywhere, found justifications. And in Port William, a dozen miles by river from the courthouse and the rule of law, anger had a license that it might not have had in another place. Sometimes violence would break out in one of the saloons or in the road. Then proof of mortality would be given in blood.

And the mortality lived and suffered daily in the town was attested with hopes of immortality by the headstones up in the graveyard, which was even then more populous than the town. Mat knew—at the age of five he had already forgotten when he had found out—that he had a brother and two sisters up there, with carved lambs resting on the tops of their small monuments, their brief lives dated beneath. In all the time he had known her, his mother had worn black.

But to him, when he was five, those deaths were stories told. Nothing in Port William seemed to him to be in passage from any beginning to any end. The living had always been alive, the dead always dead. The world, as he knew it then, simply existed, familiar even in its changes: the town, the farms, the slopes and ridges, the woods, the river, and the sky over it all. He had not yet gone farther from Port William than to Dawes Landing on the river and to his uncle Jack Beecham's place out on the Bird's Branch Road, the place his mother spoke of as "out home." He had seen the steamboats on the river and had looked out from the higher ridgetops, and so he understood that the world went on into the distance, but he did not know how much more of it there might be.

Mat had come late into the lives of Nancy and Ben Feltner, after the deaths of their other children, and he had come unexpectedly, "a blessing." They prized him accordingly. For the first four or so years of his life he was closely watched, by his parents and also by Cass and Smoke, Cass's husband, who had been slaves. But now he was five, and it was a household always busy with the work of the place, and often full of company. There had come to be times, because his grown-ups were occupied and he was curious and active, when he would be out of their sight. He would stray off to where something was happening, to the farm buildings behind the house, to the blacksmith shop, to one of the saloons, to wherever the other boys were. He was beginning his long study of the town and its place in the world, gathering up the stories that in years still far off he would hand on to his grandson Andy Catlett, who in his turn would be trying to master the thought of time:

that there were times before his time, and would be times after. At the age of five Mat was beginning to prepare himself to help in educating his grandson, though he did not know it.

His grown-ups, more or less willingly, were letting him go. The town had its dangers. There were always horses in the road, and sometimes droves of cattle or sheep or hogs or mules. There were in fact uncountable ways for a boy to get hurt, or worse. But in spite of her losses, Nancy Beechum Feltner was not a frightened woman, as her son would learn. He would learn also that, though she maintained her sorrows with a certain loyalty, wearing her black, she was a woman of practical good sense and strong cheerfulness. She knew that the world was risky and that she must risk her surviving child to it as she had risked the others, and when the time came she straightforwardly did so.

But she knew also that the town had its ways of looking after its own. Where its worst dangers were, grown-ups were apt to be. When Mat was out of the sight of her or his father or Cass or Smoke, he was most likely in the sight of somebody else who would watch him. He would thus be corrected, consciously ignored, snatched out of danger, cursed, teased, hugged, instructed, spanked, or sent home by any grown-up into whose sight he may have strayed. Within that watchfulness he was free—and almost totally free when, later, he had learned to escape it and thus had earned his freedom. "This was a *free* country when I was a boy," he would sometimes say to Andy, his grandson.

When he was five and for some while afterward, his mother drew the line unalterably only between him and the crowds that filled the town on Saturday afternoons and election days when there would be too much drinking, with consequences that were too probable. She would not leave him alone then. She would not let him go into the town, and she would not trust him to go anywhere else, for fear that he would escape into the town from wherever else she let him go. She kept him in sight.

That was why they were sitting together on the front porch for the sake of the breeze there on a hot Saturday afternoon in the late summer of 1888. Mat was sitting close to his mother on the wicker settee, watching her work. She had brought out her sewing basket and was darning socks, stretching the worn-through heels or toes over her darning egg and weaving them whole again with her needle and thread. At such work her fingers moved with a quickness and assurance that fascinated Mat, and he loved to watch her. She would have been telling him a story. She was full of stories. Aside from the small movements of her hands and the sound of her voice, they were quiet with a quietness that seemed to have increased as it had grown upon them.

Cass had gone home after the dinner dishes were done. The afternoon had half gone by.

From where they sat they could see down into the town where the Saturday crowd was, and they could hear it. Doors slammed, now and then a horse nickered, the talking of the people was a sustained murmur from which now and then a few intelligible words escaped: a greeting, some bit of raillery, a reprimand to a horse, an oath. It was a large crowd in a small place, a situation in which a small disagreement could become dangerous in a hurry. Such things had happened often enough. That was why Mat was under watch.

And so when a part of the crowd intensified into a knot, voices were raised, and there was a scuffle, Mat and his mother were not surprised. They were not surprised even when a bloodied man broke out of the crowd and began running fast up the street toward them, followed by other running men whose boot heels pounded on the road.

The hurt man ran toward them where they were sitting on the porch. He was hatless. His hair, face, and shirt were bloody, and his blood dripped on the road. Mat felt no intimation of threat or danger. He simply watched, transfixed. He did not see his mother stand and put down her work. When she caught him by the back of his dress and fairly poked him through the front door—"Here! Get inside!"—he still was only alert, unsurprised.

He expected her to come into the house with him. What finally surprised him was that she did not do so. Leaving him alone in the wide hall, she remained outside the door, holding it open for the hurt man. Mat ran halfway up the stairs then and turned and sat down on a step. He was surprised now but not afraid.

When the hurt man ran in through the door, instead of following him in, Nancy Feltner shut the door and stood in front of it. Mat could see her through the door glass, standing with her hand on the knob as the clutch of booted and hatted pursuers came up the porch steps. They bunched at the top of the steps, utterly stopped by the slender woman dressed in mourning, holding the door shut.

And then one of them, snatching off his hat, said, "It's all right, Mrs. Feltner. We're his friends."

She hesitated a moment, studying them, and then she opened the door to them also and turned and came in ahead of them.

The hurt man had run the length of the hall and through the door at the end of it and out onto the back porch. Nancy, with the bunch of men behind her, followed where he had gone, the men almost with delicacy, as it seemed to Mat, avoiding the line of blood drops along the hall floor. And Mat hurried back down the stairs and came along in his usual place at the tail end, trying to see, among the booted legs and carried hats, what had become of the hurt man.

Mat's memory of that day would always be partly incomplete. He never knew who the hurt man was. He knew some of the others. The hurt man had sat down or dropped onto a slatted green bench on the porch. He might have remained nameless to Mat because of the entire strangeness of the look of him. He had shed the look of a man and assumed somehow the look of all things badly hurt. Now that he had stopped running, he looked used up. He was pallid beneath the streaked bright blood, breathing in gasps, his eyes too widely open. He looked as though he had just come up from almost too deep a dive.

Nancy went straight to him, the men, the friends, clustered behind her, deferring, no longer to her authority as the woman of the house, as when she had stopped them at the front door, but now to her unhesitating, unthinking acceptance of that authority.

Looking at the hurt man, whose blood was dripping onto the bench and the porch floor, she said quietly, perhaps only to herself, "Oh my!" It was as though she knew him without ever having known him before.

She leaned and picked up one of his hands. "Listen!" she said, and the man brought his gaze it seemed from nowhere and looked up at her. "You're at Ben Feltner's house," she said. "Your friends are here. You're going to be all right."

She looked around at the rest of them who were standing back, watching her. "Jessie, you and Tom go see if you can find the doctor, if he's findable." She glanced at the water bucket on the shelf over the wash table by the kitchen door, remembering that it was nearly empty. "Les, go bring a fresh bucket of water." To the remaining two she said, "Get his shirt off. *Cut* it off. Don't try to drag it over his head. So we can see where he's hurt."

She stepped through the kitchen door, and they could hear her going about inside. Presently she came back with a kettle of water still warm from the noon fire and a bundle of clean rags.

"Look up here," she said to the hurt man, and he looked up.

She began gently to wash his face. Wherever he was bleeding, she washed away the blood: first his face, and then his arms, and then his chest and sides. As she washed, exposing the man's wounds, she said softly only to herself, "Oh!" or "Oh my!" She folded the white rags into pads and instructed the hurt man and his friends to press them onto his cuts to stop the bleeding. She said, "It's the Lord's own mercy we've got so many hands," for the man had many wounds. He had begun to tremble. She kept saying to him, as she would have spoken to a child, "You're going to be all right."

Mat had been surprised when she did not follow him into the house, when she waited on the porch and opened the door to the hurt man and then to his friends. But she had not surprised him after that. He saw her as he had known her: a woman who did what the world put before her to do.

At first he stayed well back, for he did not want to be told to get out of the way. But as his mother made order, he grew bolder and drew gradually closer until he was almost at her side. And then he was again surprised, for then he saw her face.

What he saw in her face would remain with him forever. It was pity, but it was more than that. It was a hurt love that seemed to include entirely the hurt man. It included him and disregarded everything else. It disregarded the aura of whiskey that ordinarily she would have resented; it disregarded the blood puddled on the porch floor and the trail of blood through the hall.

Mat was familiar with her tenderness and had thought nothing of it. But now he recognized it in her face and in her hands as they went out to the hurt man's wounds. To him, then, it was as though she leaned in the black of her mourning over the whole hurt world itself, touching its wounds with her tenderness, in her sorrow.

Loss came into his mind then, and he knew what he was years away from telling, even from thinking: that his mother's grief was real; that her children in their graves once had been alive; that everybody lying under the grass up in the graveyard once had been alive and had walked in daylight in Port William. And this was a part, and belonged to the deliverance, of the town's hard history of love.

The hurt man, Mat thought, was not going to die, but he knew from his mother's face that the man *could* die and someday would. She leaned over him, touching his bleeding wounds that she bathed and stanched and bound, and her touch had in it the promise of healing, some profound encouragement.

It was the knowledge of that encouragement, of what it had cost her, of what it would cost her and would cost him, that then finally came to Mat, and he fled away and wept.

What did he learn from his mother that day? He learned it all his life. There are few words for it, perhaps none. After that, her losses would be his. The losses would come. They would come to him and his mother. They would come to him and Margaret, his wife, who as a child had worn his castoff dresses. They would come, even as Mat watched, growing old, to his grandson, Andy, who would remember his stories and write them down.

But from that day, whatever happened, there was a knowledge in Mat that was unsurprised and at last comforted, until he was old, until he was gone.

Copyrights and Credits

Notes on the Contributors

Jocelyn Bartkevicius is completing a memoir, *The Emerald Room*, based on "Hat Check Noir." Her work has been awarded the Missouri Review Essay Award, the Iowa Woman Essay Award, and the Annie Dillard Award. She teaches in the MFA program at the University of Central Florida and serves as book review editor of the journal *Fourth Genre*.

Wendell Berry, the environmental essayist, poet, and novelist, lives in Port Royal, Kentucky. He is the author most recently of *Given*, a book of poems, and of *The Way of Ignorance: And Other Essays*. His novel *Andy Catlett: Early Travels* is set much later in the life of Mat Feltner, the character in his story here.

Born in Harlem Hospital in 1930, **Jacqueline W. Brown** has lived in New York City all her life. She attended Hunter High School, Hunter College, and Columbia University. A retired clinical social worker and psychotherapist, her first published memoirs appeared in the Spring 2000 issue of *The Hudson Review*.

Hayden Carruth lives in upstate New York with his wife, the poet Joe-Anne McLaughlin. He has served as editor of *Poetry* magazine, as poetry editor of *Harper's*, and has received numerous fellowships and awards, including the National Book Award in poetry for *Scrambled Eggs and Whiskey* (1996). His most recent book is *Toward the Distant Islands: New and Selected Poems*.

Jan Ellison is a 2007 O. Henry Prize–winner and holds an MFA from San Francisco State University. Her stories have appeared in the *New England Review* and *The Hudson Review*. Her story here was cited in the *Best American Short Stories 2007* as one of "100 Other Distinguished Stories." She lives in the San Francisco Bay Area with her husband and their four children.

Nicole Graev grew up in New York City and recently moved to Boston, where she teaches high school English and writes nonfiction and poetry. Her articles and reviews have appeared in the *Washington Post*, the *New York Sun*, and *Seventeen*.

William Hallberg lives in Asheville, North Carolina, with his fiancée Christy. He is completing a novel entitled *Van Gogh's Ear*. The short story "The Rub of the Green" evolved into a novel with the same title (1989).

Catherine Harnett recently retired from the federal government and is now a full-time fiction and poetry writer who lives with her daughter in Fairfax, Virginia. She is the author of two volumes of poetry, *Still Life* and *Evidence*. In addition to appearing in this anthology, "Her Gorgeous Grief" will also appear in *Electric Grace*, an anthology of Washington women writers.

Andrew Hudgins is Humanities Distinguished Professor of English at the Ohio State University. He has published six books of poetry, the most recent of which is *Ecstatic in the Poison* (2003), and he is completing a new collection of poems, *Shut Up, You're Fine: Troubling Poems for Troubled Children*. He is also at work on a memoir about being a compulsive joke teller. He is married to the novelist Erin McGraw and lives in Columbus, Ohio, and Sewanee, Tennessee.

Elise Juska's short stories have also appeared in the *Harvard Review, Salmagundi*, the *Carolina Quarterly*, and several other magazines. Her third novel, *One for Sorrow, Two for Joy*, was published in 2007. She lives in Maine and teaches fiction workshops at the University of New Hampshire and The New School.

Julie Keith has published two collections of stories and novellas: *The Jaguar Temple*, short-listed for the Governor-General's Fiction Award, and *The Devil Out There*, winner of the Hugh MacLennan Prize and short-listed for le Grand prix du livre de Montréal. She lives in Montreal.

Liza Kleinman is a freelance writer who lives in Portland, Maine. Her fiction has also appeared in *Portland Magazine*, the *Greensboro Review*, and *Redbook*.

Fred Licht retired in 2006 as chief curator of the Peggy Guggenheim Collection in Venice, a position he held from the time the collection opened to the public in 1980. Although he spent his professional life in museums, he has published a number of stories and novellas in American journals. His novel *Villa Ginestra* will shortly be published in German translation.

Mairi MacInnes lives in York, England, where she retired after nearly thirty years in the United States. Her seventh collection of poems, *The Girl I Left Behind Me*, was published in 2007 in England, together with a reprint of her memoir *Clearances* (2002). "Porrock" is a chapter of that memoir.

Peter Makuck's poems and stories, essays and reviews have appeared in *The Hudson Review*, *Poetry*, and the *Sewanee Review*. *Costly Habits* (2002), a collection of short stories, was nominated for a PEN/Faulkner Award. He lives with his wife Phyllis on Bogue Banks, one of North Carolina's barrier islands.

After five years at sea in the U.S. Navy, followed by advanced degrees at Harvard University, **John McCormick** taught and wrote in Austria, Germany, Mexico, Japan, and at Rutgers University. With his English wife of fifty-four years, the poet Mairi MacInnes, he retired to Yorkshire. He has just completed *Another Music*, essays and reviews of fifty years.

Steven Millhauser is the author of numerous works of fiction, including *Edwin Mullhouse* and *Martin Dressler*. His stories have been included in *Best American Short Stories*, *The O. Henry Prize Stories*, and other anthologies. His most recent collection of stories is *Dangerous Laughter*.

Kermit Moyer, an emeritus professor of literature and creative writing at American University in Washington, D.C., is the author of *Tumbling* (1988). "Learning to Smoke" is one of the linked stories in his recently completed collection *The Chester Stories: A Novel*.

Robert Schultz's books include two collections of poetry, *Vein Along the Fault* and *Winter in Eden*, and a novel, *The Madhouse Nudes*. He has received a National Endowment for the Arts Literature Award in Fiction, Cornell University's Corson Bishop Poetry Prize, and, from the *Virginia Quarterly Review*, the Emily Clark Balch Prize for Poetry. He is the John P. Fishwick Professor of English at Roanoke College in Salem, Virginia.

Dena Seidel is an award-winning documentary editor, producer, and writer, with credits on films for National Geographic, Discovery Channel, and PBS. She is also the recipient of a New York Festivals Award for Best Editing and a New York Emmy Award for Outstanding Editing. She is a full-time instructor in the English department of Rutgers University, where she teaches documentary filmmaking and digital storytelling.

Elizabeth Spencer has published nine novels and several collections of short stories, the latest being *The Southern Woman: New and Selected Fiction* (2001). She has received the PEN/Malamud Award for Short Fiction, 2008. She lives in Chapel Hill, North Carolina.

Robert Love Taylor received the Oklahoma Book Award for his novel *The Lost Sister*. His fiction has been published in *Best American Short Stories, The O. Henry Prize Stories, Pushcart Prize, New Stories from the South,* and other anthologies. His most recent novel is *Blind Singer Joe's Blues* (2006).

Randolph Thomas's short stories have also appeared in *The Glimmer Train Stories* and *Southwest Review.* His poetry has appeared in *Poetry, Witness,* and the *Texas Review.* He teaches at Louisiana State University in Baton Rouge.

William Trevor was born in Mitchelstown, Co. Cork, in 1928 and spent his childhood in provincial Ireland. In 1994 his book *Felicia's Journey* won the 1994 Whitbread Book of the Year Award in the United Kingdom, where he now lives. He has been awarded a knighthood in recognition of his services to literature.

"Newark Job" was **John Van Kirk**'s first published story. Fictionalized from experiences he had as a boy, he recounts, "it now seems to me to be primarily a portrait of my father in his prime; if anything is real in the story, it is the man, imperfect but strong and resourceful, who fixes what is broken." Rejected ten times before being accepted by *The Hudson Review,* the story, he says, launched his career as a writer and a teacher of writing and literature at Marshall University.

James Wallenstein has taught literature and creative writing at Pratt, Wesleyan, and Hunter College. His stories have also appeared in *GQ* and the *Antioch Review.* He has won a scholarship from the Sewanee Writers' Conference and fellowships from the Mid-Atlantic Arts Foundation and the Virginia Center for the Creative Arts.

Barbara Wasserman worked for many years as a researcher and writer in documentary films. In 1967 she edited *The Bold New Women,* a collection of writings by women. She is now primarily a grandmother and memoirist.

Paula Whyman is a recipient of the Washington Writing Prize in Short Fiction and the Myra Sklarew Thesis Award. Her work has appeared in the Virgin Fiction award anthology and is forthcoming in the anthology *Gravity Dancers: Fiction by Washington Area Women,* edited by Richard Peabody. She was recently awarded a fellowship to the Virginia Center for the Creative Arts, where she worked on her novel.

Tennessee Williams (1911–1983) is recognized as one of the world's greatest playwrights. He was the author of more than thirty full-length plays, including *The Glass Menagerie, A Streetcar Named Desire, Cat on a Hot Tin Roof, Camino Real, Not About Nightingales, The Rose Tattoo,* and *Night of the Iguana.*

Carl Wooton teaches part time at California Polytechnic State University in San Luis Obispo. He continues to write and engage with bright young people in the classroom and to explore the rites of passage of the ramblers and spinners who have shaped his world.

Steve Yarbrough is the author of three story collections and four novels, the most recent of which, *The End of California*, was published in 2006. A native of Indianola, Mississippi, Yarbrough is the James and Coke Hallowell Professor of Creative Writing at California State University, Fresno, and the director of the school's MFA program.